Keepers
Saving the World

Laurel Hughes

i

DEDICATION

To All Who Journey Through Disaster

PREFACE

The towns of Marshland and Willsey, their inhabitants, and their visitors are entirely fictional. The disaster issues and mental health dilemmas portrayed are very real.
See www.keeperconnections.com for real world topical discussions, help lines, exercise scenarios, and additional information about the *Keepers* series.

CHAPTER ONE

Saturday, October 26ᵗʰ

MARSHLAND—Fair weather is expected to bring a large turnout to the annual harvest parade, which will take place in Willsey this year due to the flood damage in Marshland.

Mayor Schwartz offered his latest round of apologies for lack of repair to roads ruined by Green River's epic flooding, while the city, county, and federal agencies continue to argue over financial responsibility.

Schwartz did praise the speedy recovery of Marshland's citizenry, as evidenced by other repairs set in motion since last spring's deluge...

Somebody plowed into him. If not for quick reflexes, both he and yesterday's news would have ended up in the gutter.

"Sorry," said the stranger. "Did you see which way that cotton candy guy went?"

He folded and tucked away the spread of *Willsey Tribune* that had interfered with detecting the incoming hazard.

"Beats me."

A quick pat to the sweats confirmed his wallet was still there. He shifted to one side, making the pocket harder to get at. The likely pickpocket scratched at his choppy beard growth as he, too, scanned the walkway. Cursing under his breath, he stepped off the curb and sprinted down the shoulder.

The corner was turning out to be a major thoroughfare, most likely because of the good view. Was it really worth it? There would probably be more breathing room near the staging area. The side road from which the parade was slated to emerge also looked swamped. Pedestrians had to jostle this way and that to let each other by. The glimpse of a small, unoccupied area momentarily encouraged him to move—but, no. There were sawhorse barricades around it, and workers at the site telling people to stay clear.

He sighed. Might as well stay put.

*****

Sarah strained for a sighting as she peered between the hats and coat hoods blocking the view of the parade route. Still no sign of Lil. In the distance, the marching band warm-ups shifted into a faltering rendition of "Stars and Stripes." The festivities were about to begin.

Standard Lil. Same as high school. She tightened her muffler against the crisp breeze cutting against her wool coat. Regardless of the chill, the season was welcome. It brought forth a farewell to the old, and a sense of completion—especially this year. It was hard not to smile at the irony. It had taken disaster to get her home again.

A thunderhead of cotton candy rose up before her, an arm coming around from behind. "For you, my sweet."

And Paulson. The disaster had brought Paulson. Who at the moment was trying way too hard.

"I don't know what happened to Lil." She pulled off a respectable mass of the pink fluff and continued to track the incoming.

"Sean will get her here." Paulson stared at her consumption strategy, still panting from his quest.

She packed away the whole tantalizing wad, closing her eyes and relishing the unadulterated sweetness. Some things needed to be appreciated to the fullest. "Mom always got this for us on parade day, so we wouldn't pick at each other while we waited."

"I imagine it was easier to track down cotton candy when the Marshland parade was actually in Marshland. This vendor must have been half a mile away."

"Count your blessings. We're lucky there's a parade at all."

"They should have moved it to the fairgrounds," said Paulson. "At

2

least then it would still be ours. Having it here just makes us some kind of lame hangers-on to Willsey's Veterans' Day parade. This is a city crowd. Marshland parades are much more personal."

"The fairgrounds aren't any better off than the streets." Sarah licked at stickiness collecting on her fingertips, but gave up. It was only making matters worse. "I thought it was very gracious of them to change the parade date to accommodate us. Now it's going to be folklore: the year the floods brought together the two fall parades."

"I know most of those jokers on the parade committee. Typical bureaucrats, completely out of touch with how their decisions affect everybody else. They only changed it from the real Veterans' Day because it made for a three-day weekend during hunting season."

"Still..."

"Chances are the story will also be that it got rolled into Halloween. And that our float was an ark we built to rescue everybody," Paulson grumbled.

What a whiner. But an endearing one. That tousled hair, those dark and deep-set eyes—so intent on finding ways to please her. Even if his commentary about "the man" did go over the top at times, he had been so kind and caring to help her find Dad after the spring floods.

Hopefully being friendly in return for his kindness wouldn't end up leading him on. There was neither the time nor interest, especially with someone as complex as Paulson. Besides, it would get in the way of the limited breaks available for these visits; ones better spent catching up with her childhood soul mate.

Lil's plump form finally appeared, in and out of view between spectators. Her pale brown bob bounced to the rhythm of the band as she waved and shouted out at acquaintances along the way. Three-month-old Jerrod was slung facing her back, his tiny head joggling.

"Look, it fits. That cap I made him. Isn't it adorable?"

Lil elbowed her way through marginal passage. She swung her infant around and out, thrusting him into Sarah's arms. "Here's your Auntie Sarah, Jerrod. Be good, now. Yeah, she's a scrawny little thing. Don't let that worry you none. Auntie Sarah can handle darn near anything."

Sarah winced at the sound of the dialect. Lil's butchering of the English language hadn't been such a big deal while they were growing up. Looking back, it had probably been part of the attraction. After several years of higher education and city dwelling, the missing refinement felt at odds with the intimate link she hoped to reestablish. Going away to school would have helped Lil. Too bad she hadn't followed through.

Sarah cradled the seemingly boneless creature foisted upon her. Jerrod blinked into the sunlight, tiny fingers entwined in her convenient panel of chestnut hair. "Jeez, he's getting heavy. What do you feed this guy?"

Paulson ran his finger along the downy orange fringe erupting from under the fuzzy white cap. "Sure looks like his old man. Where is Sean, anyway?"

"Still looking for a place to park."

The passing high school band drowned them out. The Marshland fire brigade soon followed, lights flashing and horns sounding, setting the stage for what had brought them there: the float dedicated to the spring disaster relief effort.

"There's Chet!" Sarah waved at her informally adopted brother.

The float looked suspiciously similar to the sledge from the annual tractor pull, towed by this year's dragster-looking champion. Chet's massive form dominated the float's front railing. He removed his cap and swung it overhead in wide swipes.

"Disaster relief certainly turned out to be his calling," Paulson said, raising a hand of acknowledgement at him. "Did he tell you about his trip south?"

"I've been hearing stories about 'the 'canes' for months. I take it that's Alison."

An exceedingly slim woman with a bleach-blonde ponytail stood next to Chet, looking miniscule in comparison. Sarah guessed close to middle-aged, as was Chet. But they certainly formed an odd couple. Alison stared straight ahead, as if glued to the forward rail. Clearly no sea legs there.

"It's surprising, isn't it? That those two hit it off." Paulson shot Sarah a dubious look. It matched her own misgivings.

"I know. I love Chet and wish him the best. But Alison seems way out of his league." She lowered her voice, looking at Paulson sideways. "Maybe Chet's a project. Some kind of 'bird with a broken wing' thing."

Silence followed. Paulson was not taking the hint. Or choosing not to, keeping his mouth shut. What more did he know about it? Like, what had Chet's trusting innocence gotten him into this time? Given how awkward he was around the very limited attention he typically received from the opposite sex.

A different tactic was in order. "How's Alison working out with your psychological first aid team?"

"Okay, mostly. She has a way of stepping outside her bounds."

"Outside her bounds—how?"

"Like when she comes across somebody who needs traditional mental health. Instead of referring, she...tries her own idea of counseling."

"I didn't know she had mental health credentials."

"She doesn't. Just the PFA seminars we gave everybody at the start. She's supposed to stick to handing out pamphlets, do a little recovery cheerleading—that sort of thing."

"So she's a loose cannon."

Paulson pressed his lips together.

"Is it worth it then, keeping her around?"

"The boss wanted me to get rid of her. But she's coming along." He looked off at a goose-shaped float hauled by a hay truck. Children dressed as goslings scampered alongside. "Out here we're stuck with potluck. Besides, Chet's so attached to her."

Sarah turned and coughed, camouflaging the spurt of laughter. Paulson's inability to be hardnosed had once again gotten the better of him. Either that, or this was his latest excuse to disregard "the suits."

"The grant for the position runs out in a couple weeks anyway," he continued.

"So you decided against the extension."

"Right. People here look after one another. They'll be fine. Just the same, I wish you had moved back and taken the oversight position." He explored her face as if it might somehow reveal a way of going back in time. "I bet you'd have worked wonders with Alison."

Lil nudged her, giving her a knowing glance. She was becoming almost as annoyingly persistent in her matchmaking fantasy as Paulson was in trying to get it to materialize.

"Give it up, you guys. I'm not staying on."

"Think about it," said Paulson, nonplussed. "No more smog, rush hour bottlenecks, uptight city types, or hospital bureaucracies. Instead, you get fresh air, nature, and friendly people. Not so many lame agency rules. You could catch up with old friends, like Lil here." He smiled. "And me."

Lil caught her gaze again, this time adding a cheesy grin.

"Enough, already." The passing World War II veterans were a welcome diversion. Sarah watched for her father, Sam. He had never done anything in these parades before. Probably wouldn't have this year, either, if not for a buddy needing a wheelchair caddy.

"Here come the 4-H kids." Lil pointed as she stood on tiptoes. "The equestrians. Remember when I did that? Someday you'll be out there, Jerrod."

Several children and teenagers were mounted, the younger ones led by chaperones. Ribbons and badges from the county fair dangled from the reins and saddles. How proud Lil had been about hers, how she'd pasted them...

A sudden blast almost knocked Sarah over.

She swayed with the abrupt surge in air pressure, and a stab of raw fear. For less than an instant, or perhaps it was forever, silence coated all.

Was it a dream? She floated in it, confined as if in a deep well, limbs stilled by an invisible sea of thick mud. The walls of the well closed in, holding her up.

The squalls of an indignant infant heaved her out of the sensory mirage. It was people, not spongy brick and mortar, pressing in from all sides. Faltering whispers in the periphery skirted a reality that none appeared ready to grasp.

Voices became more insistent, then shouted: "What was that?" "Are you okay?" "Oh my God, look down there."

Snap out of it. She took stock. Parade activity had screeched into freeze frame. Paulson had his arms wrapped over her, Lil, and the baby. In fact, he was practically holding them up, sealing them from an evolving press of confused spectators. Down the road, a large cloud billowed. Dust, or smoke? People called out, snatching up children and shying away from open exposure.

"What happened?" Sarah shouted, to be heard over Jerrod's crying.

"Don't know," Paulson yelled, his eyes narrowing into intense assessment. He let the four of them be carried along with the others, away from the street.

Horses reared and screamed. Some had broken free and run off. A child that had been riding now sat in the road, howling and grasping her leg.

"Here." Lil dropped the diaper bag and gave her son a quick once-over. "I've got to go help. Those poor kids. Their horses."

She forced her way through retreating spectators and ran toward the equestrians.

Up ahead, fire department vehicles jockeyed to reverse course. The encompassing hysteria hampered efforts. Several first responders jumped from trapped vehicles and rushed by, gear in hand.

"Dad..." Sarah shot a fragmented scan over the chaos. "Where's my Dad?"

The elderly veterans popped into view up the road. Parade security was herding them to the sidewalk. The veteran Dad had been assisting had abandoned his wheelchair and was directing the alarmed men further back, urging them toward cover under a storefront entry. Cover from what?

One veteran had yet to budge, his feet frozen to the centerline. He was ducking, yelling, and pointing at the sky. Out of nowhere Dad appeared and grabbed the frail octogenarian by the elbow. He practically dragged him out of the street.

An incoming assault? She attempted to crouch, pulling Jerrod close and studying the sky. Overhead there was nothing but innocuous blue. The man must be having a flashback, a remnant of a war long-ended. The true source of pandemonium was somewhere near the beginning of the parade route, still hidden by haziness.

"You two all right?" Paulson's unwillingness to release them was unsettling.

She was not sure she wanted him to. "I think we're okay."

Several disaster responders from Marshland's relief effort float sprinted by. Bringing up the rear were Chet and Alison. Alison had him by the hand, dragging him. Chet lumbered along beside her, looking confused and unsure.

"What's she think she's doing?" said Sarah. "That's no place for Chet. He won't know what to do. He'll just find a way to get hurt himself."

"They're going to need me. Especially with those two getting in the way." Paulson guided her to a secluded bench next to a barber pole, still rotating as if nothing had happened. "Stay here."

He sprinted off with the disaster responders and vanished into the chaos.

"Paulson, wait." The growing uproar muffled it. She dug out her phone and touched speed dial. An odd busy signal rankled back.

So here she was. Stuck. Able to do little more than bounce a baby and stare in frustration at people swirling by. In the distance were sporadic cries of confusion, pain, and despair. The road was strung out with emergency vehicles aiming to reach them, a somber and reversed version of the cheery procession that had passed only moments earlier.

Her gaze fell to the gutter, coming to rest on a half-eaten cone of cotton candy. Trampled.

CHAPTER 2

Good God. Paulson slowed. The stench of sulfur and gasoline was overpowering. He pulled his scarf over his nose and mouth and tucked back hair hanging in his eyes. Squinting through the smoke and dust, the origins of some of the screams and shouts could be made out. They sounded oddly muted, like being in some kind of waking dream. The ringing in his ears added to the surrealism.

The scattered pattern of suffering was hard to take in. Several victims lay silent in the street or on sidewalks, some perhaps permanently. Sirens blared in the distance.

He took a deep breath. *Compartmentalize. Tune out carnage. Tune into needs.*

The Willsey first responders had been quick to put the visiting Marshland personnel to use. A couple of them were trying to set a perimeter. Here and there were other familiar faces—off-duty paramedics, leaning over the injured. And there was blood, so much of it. Everywhere.

His own ability to focus still refused to get in gear. Thoughts outpaced sensibilities. How was he going to be of use? He was only a clinical social worker, with minimal disaster training. Sure, he'd comforted lots of victims at single-family fires, and helped out with mental health needs after the spring floods. This was something all together different. Yes, similar needs were present. But with all these injuries, and so many people in dire physical condition, it seemed like anything he thought to do would only get in the way.

Why hadn't he paid more attention when the flood operation got set up? Politeness had forced him to stay awake during Lacey's instruction. He had dismissed most of it as pedantic overkill. If only Lacey, the seasoned disaster mental health manager, were here now.

He looked at his phone. Scrolling down, her number appeared, still there from last spring. Didn't she fly out to incidents like this? Looking around, it was clear *somebody* needed to take charge. He shook his head in dismay. There wasn't much chance of him figuring it out.

"Paulson—over here." It was one of the volunteer firefighters.

"What do I do?" Paulson jogged in his direction. "Circulate, like at a fire?"

"We've got casualties." The firefighter looked about to twist himself in two, struggling to face him and state the obvious without disrupting yellow tape rollout. "Keeping folks alive comes first. There are people here triaging. See what they need."

"I'm a social worker, not medical."

"That doesn't matter." The firefighter interrupted himself with a spurt of insistent pointing, redirecting a passing group of bystanders. "They need assistance. People who can keep a clear head. Just go in and do what they tell you."

Okay. So long as main priorities didn't get lost. First, make sure Alison doesn't do something stupid. Second, keep Chet from getting dragged into something traumatizing, or even dangerous. He had to succeed at these two tasks, if nothing else.

"Come here, Paulson. Hold this." The voice behind the disposable mask belonged to Jenny, a colleague at the health center. She was sitting on the asphalt and caring for a casualty. After he knelt, she grabbed his hand and planted it over an improvised compress. The injured man turned his head and blinked, groaned.

He felt his face drain. The man wore sweats. A rolled up newspaper stuck out from under his hoodie. It was the guy he'd almost knocked over earlier, on the hunt for cotton candy.

Jenny grabbed the newspaper and added it to the compress, positioned as if an exclamation point to the end of a crimson swash. "Just press down." Jenny repositioned Paulson's hand.

"What happened?" His eyes felt glued to his efforts, the persistent bleeding. It was not this poor guy's day. First almost getting knocked into the gutter, and now...this.

"There was an explosion in front of that building over there." Jenny nodded at a side street while she pawed through a personal first aid kit. "A car blew up, along with the front of a large building."

The area marked the beginning of the parade route. The lifting haze revealed a wasteland of charred and smoldering car remains. The building straight ahead was a total loss. Several others surrounding it were in bad shape as well. Vehicles further out, including a tour bus on its side, had collapsed windshields or other obvious damage. Firefighters were making the rounds with retardant. An occasional flame erupted from the scattered wreckage.

He had passed right by there during the cotton candy hunt. So many spectators had been standing around, or passing through. Maybe even hundreds. Just how many got hurt? He adjusted his scarf with his free hand, seeking escape from where his thoughts kept trying to take him.

It was impossible. Anywhere he looked, he saw people hurting or crying out. *And he had just missed being one of them himself.*

Returning his gaze to Jenny, he noticed blood speckles above her mask. Hers, or her patient's? "Are you okay?"

"Just grazed by a little flying gravel." She wrapped wadding over the man's thigh. "Pieces of that building flew everywhere. I'll be fine. Except maybe my right ear. Probably blown out."

So that was why she kept raising her voice. Here she was anyway, doing her thing as if it were just another day at the grind. How did she do it?

Ambulances snaked onto the scene. Jenny waved at a group of incoming responders. A couple of EMTs ran up and took over.

"Come on." She wiped blood off her arm and looked around at other victims.

Paulson urged his feet to move. They refused to cooperate, strangely numb.

Jenny grabbed his wrist and pulled. "Come *on.* There are plenty more where that one came from."

He followed her into the spread of greater devastation. Most of those in dire straits already had someone attending their injuries, or getting them out of there. Jenny led him to a street corner where a police officer was barking out orders.

Paulson froze.

Several motionless figures lay along the sidewalk, lined up and blanketed with dark-colored sheeting. At first glance, they looked like rock show fans camping out before ticket sales. The shattering of the illusion was quick and unmerciful, driven home by the presence of those nearby who were hovering, sobbing, or comforting one another.

A fireman draped a tarp over yet another mangled body. He spared a quick bow, performing the sign of the cross over himself.

One. Two. Three...*Stop it.* The urge to count fatalities just wouldn't leave him alone. Summing up bodies was pointless.

Dizziness pressed in; his stomach lurched. He stumbled toward a nearby tree.

"Hey, you."

Paulson tripped on something, barely avoiding a face-plant by catching himself on whatever it was on the ground camouflaged by tree shade. As his eyes adjusted, another draped body leaped into view. A gust of wind gently fluttered the edges of the tarp. He jumped up and backed away.

"You! We need you to step outside the yellow tape." The police officer yelled at him, gesturing that he move elsewhere.

"I'm an RN." Jenny held up her wallet and displayed her credentials. "He's a social worker, disaster trained. Where do you need us?"

"Serious injuries that aren't life or death are over there." The officer nodded toward a loose gathering, people either seated or lying on the steps that fronted the courthouse. "They're ones who can't get to medical care on their own."

So far it looked like there was only a single responder among the mix of dazed victims. He didn't look to be doing so well himself.

Jenny introduced herself. "Where do you want us?"

"Just start in anywhere." The paramedic didn't look up from what he was doing. "I've only treated two so far. There's at least a dozen we need to get to, ASAP. It's a nightmare. Our worst possible nightmare."

"Are you okay?" Paulson frowned at the paramedic's agitated fumbling. Was he really in good enough shape to be treating people?

"It doesn't matter how I am." The paramedic shot him a brief glare.

"Just do something."

"Let it go." Jenny's voice commanded him, low and earnest. "Check on him later. We've got bigger fish to fry."

A woman in uniform was cradling her arm. Jenny sat next to her.

"I think my shoulder's broken," said the soldier. "I landed on it."

"Hang on." Jenny left them to sift through a dumped jumble of medical supplies.

Paulson ordered the fuzziness to clear. *You're a professional. Act like one.* He sat next to the injured soldier. "You were part of the parade?"

"We were just getting ready to go out."

"Which group are you with?"

"Middle East vets. The courtyard next to the building that blew up was our staging area. We'd all be goners now, if it had happened any sooner."

A brief glance at others sitting, standing around, or helping with the injured revealed that many wore uniforms. Heroes, making it home in one piece, only to get blown up at a parade. Where was the justice?

Focus, dude. He introduced himself to Jenny's new patient.

"Forgive me if I don't offer to shake hands," she said.

"Understood." It was disarming, how she could joke around in spite of her physical distress. Not to mention with the sea of trauma surrounding them. She was certainly handling the situation better than he was.

Start with basics. "How long have you been back from deployment?"

"About two months."

"You have family here? At the parade?"

"My husband, and my daughter. They were going to sit near the end so we could hook up afterwards. They've got to be worried sick. I tried to call them but phone lines are jammed. If they turn up here after I'm gone, can you let them know I'm okay?"

As if *this* constituted "okay."

"If someone comes asking, I'll let them know."

Jenny returned, arms loaded. She quickly stabilized the injured shoulder. Nurse Jenny, always first to take any situation in hand. He needed to get into his own professional comfort zone as well, if he was going to be of any use.

"I'll go check on these others," he told Jenny. He inched his way along, uncertain if his eyes could be trusted to guide him.

The nearer victims concerned themselves with physical injuries, not emotional trauma. Certainly understandable. And appropriate. Besides, resilience needed its chance to click in. There was that group of newly bereaved...

A flash of white caught his eye—an athletic shoe, peeking out from under a ravaged parked car, lying at an odd angle. He moved closer for a better look.

A foot. There was still a foot in the shoe.

He squatted, forced himself to touch the ankle—it was warm, but as stiff as death. He spun around and combed the courthouse steps for the paramedic.

"Hey, someone got thrown under this car!" Hopefully it was an entire person. He'd probably lose it completely if it were the alternative.

Crumbled asphalt jabbed at the side of his face as he tried to assess the victim's condition. He couldn't tell a thing. "You okay?"

The limp figure wedged against the muffler neither answered nor moved.

The paramedic finally abandoned whatever he was doing and darted over. Sizing up the situation, he squeezed underneath the car, coaxing himself along with strained expletives. "He's still breathing. Got a pulse. Can't do much for him here. Get hold of his leg and pull with me. Gently."

From out of nowhere a row of helpers formed. Superhuman force took charge as they lifted one side of the vehicle. As he and the paramedic pulled, a bloodied face emerged—all the more dramatic, given the man's pale complexion.

With freckles, and spiky red hair.

It couldn't be. "Sean?"

*****

Jerrod had finally simmered down, thanks to the bottle of formula in the diaper bag. He napped against Sarah's shoulder, oblivious to the commotion in the distance.

Were they safe? Without knowing what was going on, it was impossible to guess. Maybe it would have been better to leave with Dad.

Paulson had said to wait where they were. True, it seemed protected here, secluded. The car might be safer. Perhaps they should leave the scene altogether. Then how would Lil find them? Especially without phones. The absence of clear direction was as frustrating as the catastrophe itself.

Over the last few minutes, the rush of people had changed direction, paying no mind to the obvious precariousness of the situation they seemed drawn to. Some called out names. Others were just looky-loo's, near as she could tell. A few stopped to ask if she knew what happened, or how they might help. As if she weren't dying for more information herself.

Especially if another bomb was getting ready to go off. Like Boston.

"Hey, hello! What happened down there?" she called to a passing group.

A couple clinging to one another slowed.

"Something blew up in front of that boarded-up bank on Fourth Street," said the man. "Took out the entire front end of the building."

"Oh my God." Her heart began to race again, sensibilities on the verge of slipping away. She drew Jerrod closer. "Did anybody get hurt?"

"Lots. Could be hundreds. We wanted to help, but they're clearing people out to make way for emergency vehicles."

A stocky middle-aged woman in an athletic suit wheezed her way toward them. Trembling gave away her status before she caught enough breath to form words. "Have you seen a group of teenagers? My sons are here. Somewhere."

"We know who to ask. Come on." The couple led away the frantic mother.

The three of them disappeared into the maelstrom. The discipline to not follow after them stretched to its limits. What was going on with Chet? And Lil, and Paulson. Where did they get to? What was taking so long?

Then there were all the hurting people who must be down there. She'd made a point of becoming qualified for situations like this, beyond her Ph.D. training. Even got in a week's worth of practice at last spring's flood aftermath. All the expertise, everything she had learned, was going to waste. Right then and there, when it was needed most.

Though, it had been different with the floods. There had not been much in the way of physical injuries. Just how do you go about helping people during something like this, when it's so much more devastating? Reviewing and checking off potential strategies helped occupy the edgy void.

But so long as she was stuck tending to Jerrod, it was a moot point. He had absolutely no business hanging around for any of it. She, on the other hand, belonged there. There would be as much emotional impact as physical. Probably more.

To top it off, memories of September 11th kept butting in, an unnecessary distraction. It snarled up efforts to think straight.

How shocked, how overwhelmed everybody had been that day, back when news of it made its way through her high school. Even though that disaster had been a thousand miles away.

Just how bad had it been down there, in this otherwise low-key metropolis? And how much worse is it going to be for people to recover when it happens in their own backyard?

A new screaming jag ramped up in the distance. It kind of sounded like that mother who had just passed.

Blast it all, Lil. Where are you? There was nothing left to see of the horse-containment operation. Lil had darted off down a far alley some time ago. Missing in action ever since.

A sigh of relief escaped when two familiar figures emerged from the remaining haze—the unmistakable bulk of Chet, with Alison at his side. At least Chet was out of harm's way. Even from a distance, they both looked flustered. As they drew near, the thousand-mile stare greeted her.

"We got us a heap of work to do," said Chet.

"We're supposed to go set up a place for all these people to come to." Alison recited it as if delivering a speech to a group of second graders.

Sarah cringed at the whiny nasal tone, reminiscent of a past vice-presidential candidate. Hopefully she didn't always sound that annoying.

"We're using that old church around the corner." Chet's adrenaline surge launched his arms, which waved around like cornered snakes. "We're gonna need you, too, Sarah. People are hurt, or running around scared. Well, you'd expect 'em to, with a bomb going off and all. But you know what to do for it.

"You, and Alison." He stilled the aimless flailing by landing an arm over Alison, gripping her, and almost lifting her off the ground.

"I need to look after Jerrod until Lil gets back."

"Just bring him along," said Chet. "He'll be okay at the church."

"She'll figure out where to find us." Alison managed to rock and bob in place in spite of Chet's arm. "Word's going out already. Everyone will know. It's what? An assessment center?"

"Nah, a refreshment center," said Chet.

"A family reception center." Trickles from last spring's seminars dribbled into Sarah's awareness. "It's a huge mental health undertaking, as important as getting people the medical attention they need. It's not the usual food and shelter routine, like we did at the floods. Yes, a reception center."

CHAPTER 3

The latest fleet of emergency vehicles was already parceled out. The paramedic ran off, searching for some other option to transport Sean. Paulson remained crouched next to their seemingly lifeless patient, praying for some sign, any sign, of consciousness.

Thank God the hospital wasn't far. How could it be happening? To Sean, of all people. A good man. He deserved as much as anybody to make it through this outrageous quirk of fate. "Hang in there, buddy."

Who was he kidding? Look at him, barely breathing. Imagining that some feat of magic might accommodate such pleas at least provided some sense of usefulness. Sean seemed so still. Really still.

He positioned his ear over Sean's face, and placed a hand to his bloodied midsection. No sound. No movement. Had they lost him already?

He looked around at those nearby. Where was Jenny when he needed her?

It had been some time since his last CPR course. His begrudging attendance at the regular trainings was solely to quiet the nagging of his superiors. At the moment, the only knowledge coming to mind was something about greater emphasis on chest compressions. He straddled Sean's body and began rhythmic pushes, about where his heart ought to be.

A vehicle drove up; a car door slammed. "Move over."

A sudden shove from behind toppled him to one side. Paulson

picked himself up to find some EMT taking over with Sean. Next to them was a utility van.

"Get the junk out of the back," said the EMT as he worked. "That's his ride, if we can get him jump-started."

Paulson ran to the back doors and jerked them open. Tools and spare parts piled up on the sidewalk, anything not securely fastened.

"Give me a hand." The EMT reappeared, carrying Sean. "He's breathing again."

They loaded him into the back and crawled in with him. A driver climbed in front and they accelerated into town. During a bout of especially turbulent swerving, Paulson pawed at the remaining repair equipment, testing security.

Without explanation, the van slowed. It came to a halt. Horns sounded. People were shouting.

"What's going on?" The EMT strained over the seatbacks to talk to the driver.

"It's impossible." The driver slapped her John Deere cap against the dash. "Cars are backed up, people all over. Half of Willsey must be on its way to the hospital."

"Your friend won't make it if we don't get him a higher level of care." If the EMT's sober tone was any indication, Sean's chances were about finished.

Paulson squeezed through the modest gap and took a look out front for himself. Vehicles on the narrow road winding up to the hospital were log jammed. Sidewalks crawled with surging masses of those trying to get there on foot. "We're stuck. We'll have to get out and carry him."

Next to him was a trolley, strapped against the inner wall of the van. After endless fiddling, the stays agreed to come loose. He yanked it free.

The EMT nodded his approval. "Better than nothing. Three, two, one. Lift."

While they transferred Sean to the trolley, the driver ran around to open the back. She didn't reappear. Instead, she was yelling at somebody out there. Paulson scrabbled to the rear window and pressed his nose against the dust-coated glass. His heart leaped to his throat.

The pickup behind them was too close. There was no way they'd get the back door open. It was bumper to bumper everywhere.

The EMT finished strapping Sean into place and took an impressive dive, face first over the seatbacks. After freeing a knee caught in the shoulder belt, he disappeared out the passenger door. Paulson leaned over the seats again, and watched the EMT bang on the window of the sedan blocking their path.

The vehicle appeared abandoned. Locked.

They would never squeeze out a man Sean's size over those fixed seatbacks.

Sean was trapped. Maybe they could figure out how to tear out the seats.

The EMT climbed in behind the steering wheel. "Hang onto him a minute." He threw the van in gear and stomped on the gas. The vehicle jolted forward, ramming the sedan and shoving it forward a couple feet. "How's that?"

Paulson let go of Sean and checked behind them. It worked—the clearance added wasn't much, but doable. He gave the EMT a thumb's up.

The driver jerked open the rear door, clunking it against the pickup's grill. They lifted Sean up, out, over the pickup and rolled his trolley toward the sidewalk. His feet dragged.

"Easier to carry it." The EMT grabbed one side, Paulson the other, and they were off.

Twenty feet from the emergency entrance, hardly anybody was moving, penned in by sheer numbers. A bullhorn blasted out instructions. It didn't seem like anybody was listening.

"Get out of the way!" The EMT was ready to lose it. "This man is dying."

His official-looking uniform seemed to carry some weight. At least, enough so that those immediately in their path were willing to press together and make way for them.

"You sure he's all right?" The trolley's edge cut into Paulson's midsection as they squeezed through. "He's so pale. Should we be doing CPR or something?"

They paused for a hasty recheck. "He's still with us. Keep moving."

"Why so many people? They couldn't all be injured."

"There's also everyone helping them get here. People worried about friends or family—they'll be checking here. Can't get them by phone."

"I couldn't get Sean's wife, or my girlfriend, either." Perhaps they, too, were already somewhere in the crowd.

"Probably a lot of off-duty hospital staff, too. Plus anybody else wanting to help." The EMT made an abrupt change in course, barely avoiding a child standing in their path. A man picked her up and set the girl on his shoulders. The mob continued to try to create openings, as best they could. "Then there's the 'worried well.' "

"Worried well? Isn't that an oxymoron?"

"People worried about the fumes. That it was poison gas, or something. Or they think anxiety symptoms are heart attacks. Most don't need emergency care. But with the terrorism hype..."

"How do we know it wasn't an IED? What else would cause an explosion like that? And look at this mess. It's as bad as 9/11. Didn't we learn anything about controlling chaos?"

The scene directly in front of the emergency room entrance looked more like a campus riot than a healthcare setting. They stopped moving forward a few feet from their objective. Nobody budged. Perhaps couldn't.

The EMT ignored protests and stiff-armed remaining human obstacles, propelling them forward. Paulson held on tight and squeezed through with the stretcher.

The EMT waved at the first set of scrubs in sight. "I got a red tagger here."

Additional staff appeared and snapped into action. After a brief consult with the EMT, they took over the loaded trolley. A pair of doors swung open. Both Sean and hospital personnel disappeared, the doors shutting behind them. The transition of care had taken mere seconds.

"Come on." The EMT handed off some paperwork. "There's surely more to do out there. I could use a second set of hands."

"I can't leave yet. Not until I know what to tell Lil."

"Good luck." The EMT wedged himself back into the crowd, and was gone.

Paulson's head was spinning, still gasping for breath because of the uphill free-for-all with a heavy load.

He never even got that guy's name.

"If you're finished, you have to leave." A brawny type in a security uniform towered over him. "Others need to get in."

"What about Sean? How will I know what's going on?"

21

"An information station's going up out back. You can check there."

The guard led him to an alternate exit. Once outside, he made his way to the rear of the hospital. In a grassy area, a work crew was spreading out a mammoth canvas tent. A scrawled-out sign that said "Information" was posted above a table next to the building. Several hospital personnel milled around nearby. A queue of the dazed and frantic had already begun to form, stretching across the lawn. In a far parking lot, a couple of media vans were setting up camp.

It was going to take forever.

Leaving was out of the question. He had to know more about Sean first.

But his skills were surely needed elsewhere. Like getting the formal mental health response up and going. Nobody else would be doing it.

What ever happened with Chet and Alison?

He retried Sarah's number. This time there wasn't even a busy signal.

There it was again, Lacey's number. *What the hell.* He punched the setting. It immediately rang through.

"Lacey here."

"Lacey? I...God, it's good to hear you. You won't believe this. How am I reaching you, anyway? I can't get through to anyone else."

"Because I'm long distance. I've been apprised. I'm on my way to the airport as we speak."

"I've never seen..." Words failed him.

"Are you okay? Remember—safety first, self-care first."

"I...I don't know." Thoughts splayed onto competing paths: what to say to Lacey, versus what to ask—and how much to reveal about the struggle to stay sane. "I just jumped in. I was there at the parade already. If I'd known what it was like, I might not have. It's unreal."

"Where are you now?"

"At the hospital. I helped a friend get here. But I haven't been able to get hold of his wife, or Sarah. They don't even know about it."

"Give me Sarah's number. Calling from here might work. You stay there until his wife shows up."

*****

"I ain't never been in this church before." Chet stared open mouthed at the sanctuary's austere beauty. "Sure is fancy."

22

Compared to the hideous proceedings down the road, it was downright breathtaking. Colorful patterns reflecting through stained glass glittered against the softly carpeted aisle. Crossing the room, the floating sensation returned to Sarah. Only this time it was from feeling bathed in peaceful reassurance—a semblance of safety, and hope. She hadn't been to church in years.

A quick prayer of thankfulness flickered within, regardless. It did its work. Somehow the situation seemed more settled. Ready to go on, in spite of the uncertainty of whatever it was that would come next.

At the end of the sanctuary, an arched opening led into a spacious fellowship hall. Other disaster workers were already there. The director was overseeing the furniture rearrangements.

"Here we are." Chet announced their arrival as if they had traveled halfway cross-country. "Can you tell us 'uns what we're supposed to do? I never seen nothing like this. It's unbelievable."

"I'm only holding things together until Damien gets back," said the director. "Remember him? He was a shelter manager during the floods."

"Sure, I remember Damien. A good ol' boy." A pause followed as Chet's thoughts took their time catching up with him. "That's right. He's from Willsey. Don't that beat all. He helped out in our town, and now we're helping him in his town."

"While we're waiting, make yourself useful by unloading that trailer out back."

"Sure thing, boss." Chet continued on to the back of the building with Alison, reciting a hodgepodge review of past experiences with Damien. His reenergized enthusiasm seemed unmarred by the horror of recent events.

How nice to have such innocence, to so easily tune it all out, merely by having a task to perform. And how odd to feel envious of him, disability or no. "What about me? Right now I'm tied up with Jerrod here. But his mother should be back soon."

"You're mental health, right?" The director glanced at the time display on the oversized digital clock on the far wall. "How long can you hang around?"

She had yet to think that far ahead. Nothing coming up could be more important than this. "Count me in for now. I'll get it sorted out."

"Good. We've got customers."

A woman with two young children entered the fellowship hall. The youngest child clung to the mother's skirt as they gazed around at the undertaking. Probably trying to make sense of a scenario as topsy-turvy as the mess they had left down the road.

"We're looking for my sister and her kids," the mother told Sarah. "We got separated. The police said someone here might be able to tell us something."

"Someone should be here soon." At least that was what Sarah assumed. It was what they needed to hear, too, so she may as well fudge it. "How about we go sit in the pews? That way we won't be underfoot while they're setting up."

The unexpected sound of a cell phone broke the strained silence. In fact, it sounded like her own ring tone. She stared at her pocket.

"Lucky you," said the woman. "What's your secret?"

"I have no idea." She repositioned Jerrod and checked her caller ID. "I don't know who this is."

"Here, let me hold your baby."

Sarah handed him off. The woman held him close, snuggling his tiny shoulder against her cheek. Jerrod stirred then resettled into the new set of arms.

It felt strangely cold, and alone, standing there without him. As if somehow now more vulnerable, or an anchor had broken away. Had she been comforting Jerrod, or had he been comforting her?

"This is Dr. Turner."

"Lacey here. How are you holding up?"

Sarah grabbed the back of a pew and steadied herself, suddenly aware of the tension that had been pulsing through her veins. "You must have radar. A bomb just went off."

"I'm on my way. What's happening?"

"I'm at a church. They're setting up a reception center." She stepped outside and circled away from a ladder-full of men installing signage over the door. Privacy finally presented itself in a side yard.

"It's a shock, of course." She repeated herself, raising her voice so Lacey could hear her over pounding wind gusts. She burrowed her free hand into the warmth of her coat pocket. "But I'm ready to get to work."

"I have an assignment for you. I just spoke with Paulson. He's been getting a friend to the hospital. He needs you to tell the wife. Someone named Lil."

"Oh my God. Sean?" The solitude so diligently sought was no longer an asset. Merged vulnerabilities once again swelled: living through the explosion; the aftermath of chaos; uncertainties about her friends; and now standing around, battered by the weather. Without Jerrod, fully alone for the first time since the explosion—except for Lacey's voice, a narrative from afar describing the unthinkable. "How bad is it?"

"Serious, apparently. I don't have many details. Sounds like he's okay for now. His wife's probably needed to get past HIPAA. You up to it?"

"Yes, of course. I'll tell her as soon as she gets here."

"Paulson's waiting for her at the hospital. As for you, just circulate while you're there. Same as any other service delivery site. Use common sense. You know the drill."

So her first formal assignment would be to tell her longest-ever friend that her husband was seriously injured. She took in a deep and determined breath, daring the lightheadedness to try and get the better of her.

"Watch out for Paulson," Lacey added before signing off. "He's hanging in there, but it's starting to get to him. You know how he is."

The previously sagging banners were now fully in place. Cars were beginning to collect in the church parking lot. Pedestrians could be seen plodding uphill, intent yet uncertain. Further down, a police officer was directing them. It was going to be a long day.

Sarah heaved the wood-block door open. The sanctuary was empty.

She continued through the sanctuary and into the fellowship hall, which was beginning to look more like a service delivery site. Tables and chairs were set out in familiar arrangements. The sound and smell of coffee brewing beckoned. Other refreshments were laid out along the pass-through to the kitchen, the usual comfort food selections. At least, it felt comforting to her.

Jerrod, however, was missing.

Her heart skipped a beat. She had left him with a complete stranger.

How could I be such an airhead? She hurried to where Chet was laying out flyers. "Did you see a family come in here? They were watching Jerrod."

"They went out that door over there, where we brought stuff in. Guess what? It was all sitting right there at the chapter house. And it got here just like that." He snapped his fingers. "Is this the greatest bunch of guys ever, or what? Sure is great to be..."

Sarah dashed down the short hall to the rear entry. She stuck her head out. There sat the half-emptied shelter trailer. But not a soul in sight.

She contained labored breathing and listened over pounding temples: yes, a snippet of sound—children squabbling, somewhere inside the church. Halfway back down the hall a side door hung ajar. She strode up and swung it open.

The boy and girl were sitting on the floor, competing for Jerrod's attention with favored toys. He was wide-awake, lounging comfortably on a yellow blanket. His bright blue eyes were gazing up at the kids, as if asking "and who the heck are you?"

"He woke up when nature called." The mother was stuffing diapering supplies back into the bag. "The pastor said we could use the nursery."

Sarah let out her breath. "Thank you for tending to him."

"I don't mind at all. He's a real cutie. What's his name?"

"Jerrod." Sarah scooped him up off the floor.

"Can't I play with him some more?" The boy's shoulders sagged as he lowered the toy truck he'd been soaring over Jerrod. "There aren't any boys in my family. Just girls. Girl cousins, too. It's not fair."

"Jerrod has been a good distraction." The mother's eyes held Sarah's. It was brief, but long enough for understanding to pass.

How would it end—what might this family learn about the "girl cousins" they were looking for? Innocence to be lost, prematurely. It was heart wrenching.

"We need to get Jerrod back to his mother," Sarah told the boy. "She should be here any minute. You can ask her when she gets here."

Most likely he would have to say goodbye to little Jerrod. Lil would want to get to the hospital ASAP. What comforts one may not jibe with the needs of the other. It swirled into such a bizarre mix of competing human and situational variables. With more likely to materialize in days to come.

It was nothing like the flood operation.

CHAPTER 4

A steady stream of the curious, distressed, and overwhelmed trickled into the reception center. A gathering at the canteen was taking advantage of the metal folding chairs set up around a bunch of tables, while the new arrivals were lining up at the information stations.

Sarah shifted Jerrod in order to fish around in her shoulder bag for disaster ID. Best to get introductions with new staff out of the way, before a difficult situation crops up, rather than after.

"Here, I'll take him." Alison was at her side.

Sarah slid over the infant. She found the correct slab of stamped plastic and attached it to her sweater. At least she hadn't put something on that morning that would get permanent pinholes. Little blessings everywhere. "There. I guess this makes me official now."

"It's lucky so many emergency people were here already." Alison's agitation clipped her words. Making sense of them took concerted effort. "What would happen if we had to go around and find them instead?"

"Better not to think about it."

Alison seemed more out of it than most of the clients filling the room. How well would she hold up? What Paulson had said about Alison had left a sour taste in her mouth. Especially since the types of boundary issues he had described didn't usually travel alone. They flagged other headaches lurking in the shadows.

Boundary disturbance personalities. Discovering someone in her caseload with such traits always felt like fingernails across a chalkboard.

Even if recognized, there was no way to immediately predict how severely the problem played itself out. At one end were the quiet, fragile types, more a danger to themselves than to anyone else. At the other extreme was *Fatal Attraction.* Not to mention how they always seemed to become a poison to any interpersonal system they entered, regardless of severity.

It meant a need to stay on the alert, to always listen with that third ear. If only there were a way to detect it before the inevitable blowouts—like a cell phone screen, that flashed whenever one of them called. With the color of the flash ranging from soft pink to florescent scarlet, based on severity. Someone should develop an app.

"What a sweet baby you have. All that red hair." A woman at the back of one of the lines was ogling Jerrod. Alison moved closer, giving the woman a better look. "What a little doll."

While Sarah introduced herself to the incoming staff, Alison continued to show off Jerrod. The bright-eyed infant wonder achieved immediate rock star status. Tension in that corner of the room dwindled to a distracted calm. Including Alison.

So much for therapy dogs. What they really needed were therapy infants.

Another police officer entered, carrying a young child. A frazzled-looking woman corralling several more was right behind him. One child wore a gosling costume minus the head. The youngsters scampered into the canteen area. A cacophony of metal scraping against concrete followed.

The officer zeroed in on Sarah's disaster ID. He deposited the preschooler in his helper's lap and approached. "We need a temporary location for kids who got separated."

"You should probably discuss it with the director. Is Human Services coming?"

"That's who that is, over there." The police officer gestured toward the canteen.

Two of the caseworker's small charges began fighting over a chair. She set down the preschooler to intervene. The preschooler made a dash for the door; so did the caseworker. Fighting resumed, and the coveted folding chair buckled to the floor. One of the combatants let out a howl. An elderly mass care worker stepped in with grandmother mode.

"Only one caseworker," said Sarah. "For all these children? Our disaster staff will help out as they can. But we're in limited supply, as it is."

"This caseworker was already at the parade. Tracking down anybody else hasn't worked out yet, the phone situation being what it is."

How unforgivably pathetic, this meager level of preparedness, thought Sarah. "What about contingency plans? Isn't there something written down somewhere for what to do during things like this?"

"Apparently this type of incident isn't in their playbooks. Who'd think there'd be a mass casualty here? This is rural Iowa. It's not like we're New York City, or Boston, or something."

"What's she going to do then?"

"A troop of Eagle Scouts at the parade volunteered to physically track down a few people. Ones the caseworker knew where to find. There's something coming out on TV and radio, too. For those who know to listen. They'll figure it out eventually."

Amazing. So many first responders and skilled volunteers on site by chance alone, and all that was getting pulled together was a bungling fracas.

Raised voices sounded across the room. She turned in time to witness the last of an exchange between Alison and a man near the door. Whatever they were discussing had built up quite the head of steam. Alison continued to move in, while he kept moving back. Finally he turned on his heel and left.

Alison's look of righteous indignation was disconcerting. It wasn't just the show of arrogance, or that she had run off the poor guy. There was something else. Something dark, even malevolent in that look. Maybe even a disconnect from reality. *Please, don't let her be the* Fatal Attraction *type.*

Regardless, Jerrod did not need to be part of such encounters, ones that inevitably ended with anger, and Alison as the primary cause.

"Thanks for hanging onto him." Sarah pried Jerrod loose from Alison and draped him over her shoulder.

"He's a sweetheart."

"I couldn't help but notice that man who just left. What happened?"

Alison made a show of adjusting a bra strap that already looked fine. Finally she lifted her chin and explained. "He saw the explosion and the people that got hurt. I told him to talk about his feelings. He didn't want to. But I didn't give up on him. I was going to make him do it. Something like that is pretty traumatic. Too bad he left."

So much for having reined in the loose cannon. "In the midst of fresh trauma, not everybody is ready to talk about their feelings right away." She had no idea what kind of redirection Paulson had already tried with Alison. But that was certainly one of the basics. "It was probably too soon."

"I know what I'm doing." Alison gave her a dismissive glance, and turned her focus to the cavorting children.

"Isn't this covered in psychological first aid classes they give for your position? I've never looked into it." She'd never seen that particular curriculum. It had to be in there, somewhere.

"I've been doing psychological first aid for a couple of months now. I have a good feel for these people." Alison looked down her nose at Sarah, as if lecturing a child speaking out of turn.

God help us. "The flood victims from last spring you've been working with—they're dealing with relatively old trauma. It's had a chance to percolate, to work itself through. It's nothing like what we're seeing here. If somebody needs something outside protocol, they should be referred."

Alison snorted. "Just like Paulson. You so-called providers are all the same. All establishment, and no getting involved. Big government control. Just sitting back and watching, while the little people get squashed."

Though she successfully squelched the urge to laugh aloud, her eyes no doubt gave away her thoughts. Paulson, establishment and pro-government? How could anybody look at that scraggly hair and three days' worth of facial hair growth, and see "establishment." Then there was that halfway-refurbished motorcycle he got around on. The woman must be blind.

"Laugh if you will, but the rest of us will see to it that these poor people get what they need," said Alison. "Psychological first aid isn't as complicated as you try to make it."

"No, it's not complicated. But traumatized people can be fragile. Sometimes they need special care, and trained professionals to provide that care."

"Whatever." Alison wandered into the canteen. She planted herself amidst the unaccompanied children.

Great. Next she'd find a way to retraumatize the children.

Nobody with such a loose hold on social boundaries had any business working with disaster survivors. Little wonder Paulson's supervisor wanted Alison out of the picture.

Sarah took the disaster director aside. "We've got a staff issue already."

"Maybe I should be listening in on this." Damien appeared, a stack of notebooks thudding onto a nearby table before he removed his coat. The transformation had already taken place: eagerness to get on board fully engaged; his usual easy serenity powered up into management mode.

"Good to see you again." She grasped his extended hand.

"What's up?" Damien asked her. "Other than the obvious staff shortage."

"There's a worker here whose idea of psychological first aid is more likely to create problems than help people."

"Alison, right?" The director stiffened as he tracked developments at the canteen.

"Who's this Alison?" Damien's olive-tinted brow knitted above intelligent blue eyes.

"We've had run-ins with her before, while working with flood survivors." The director made a barely decipherable nod toward the canteen. "She's with that PFA team, the one that county mental health put together. They say she acts like she thinks she's some kind of 'shrink.' It makes people nervous."

"So, she's supposed to be working with the flood victims right now..." Damien's eyes followed Alison's movements as she gathered together an assortment of treats. "I do understand why she wants to be involved. Every responder in the country is going to try to get deployed here."

"It's one thing for her to come and help out this afternoon. But she can't do both this and her flood relief position at the same time."

"Good call." The director grimaced, watching Alison's balancing act—a plate of treats in one hand, a precarious tray of plastic cups filled with a nondescript red beverage in the other. "So we think up a way to get rid of her."

Sarah thought back to the screening that had gone on for the flood operation. Screening had happened automatically, as workers first registered. She hadn't seen registration for this one yet. They were still in the crisis phase.

Of course—formal sign up. That would bring out where Alison was supposed to be spending her time.

"Maybe now's when we should take around the in-processing forms," said Sarah. "It would be the most practical and straightforward way to bring it up with her."

"If you want to field this, it's all yours." Damien handed the director some paperwork.

"I'm right on it." He sauntered toward the canteen, the proverbial cat about to swallow the canary.

"There goes your first satisfied customer." Sarah shifted Jerrod again, trading shoulders. The bursitis she'd forgotten about was kicking in. But the terror of Jerrod's brief disappearance was still fresh. Then that screwy Alison had ended up with him. Letting someone else mind him was no longer an option. She needed to do it herself. If only Lil had left behind that baby sling. It wouldn't help her any with the horses.

Her godson catnapped against her as she was swept up into the evolving survivor/helper culture. Damien made regular announcements, his reports expanding as new information came in. The mother of the stranded gosling was found. Word came in that the parents of two of the other unaccompanied children had been injured, one of them critically, both currently at the hospital.

After counseling out a volunteer who'd had a panic attack, Sarah realized Alison was no longer on site. Hopefully it meant the director had sent her packing.

Eventually the "girl cousins" showed up, followed by a tearful family reunion. Sarah passed around Kleenex and shared in their relief. While seeing them out the door, Lil's figure appeared in the distance, trudging up the hill.

*****

"Lillian White? Is Lillian White out here?"

At last. Paulson waved his hand from halfway down the line.

"Don't tell me you're Lillian." The attendant chawed at his gum as if it would get away from him if he didn't stay on top of it.

"We haven't been able to find her yet. I'm a family friend. I brought Sean here."

The man rustled through a pile of forms held captive against a clipboard. "I need to speak to next of kin. That's not you."

"Can you tell me anything?"

"Only that he's stable."

"All that says is that he's still alive."

The aid looked up from his paperwork, acknowledging the frustration of it. "Yes, he's still with us. When his wife shows up, bring her up to this table."

Paulson left the queue and stepped under the tenting, now fully installed. Others waiting for news were filling time with low conversation, or staring into space. Some took out handhelds, fiddling with them, or cursing them. He took out his own and tried both Lil and Sarah. Useless.

He helped himself to the industrial-sized coffee dispenser. As he operated the spigot, the rising surface of the steaming beverage rippled. His hand was shaking.

A vacant table invited him to sit. It was a chance to relax, to pull himself together.

So much was going to come of this, especially for those from Marshland. His clinical hours were already scheduled to the hilt because of those left reeling by the spring floods. Who knew how many Marshlanders had been at that parade? Maybe even ones already traumatized by the last disaster. It was not a good time to be the only social worker in town.

Spirited exchanges among soldiers sitting at the next table kept cutting in. One of them had a radio broadcast going. Occasional editorializing sprinkled in over its content. Other conversation had to do with where they'd been during the explosion, or recitals of injuries brought for treatment. Eventually they moved on to stories about recent deployments.

"Who knows? Maybe the next deployment will be right here in Willsey."

"Did anything happen anywhere else? Anybody heard?"

"So far the reports are only about here."

"Something would've been said by now if there were other bombings."

"Do they know for sure it was a bomb?"

"You know how it goes. Nothing'll get said until it's really obvious."

"Yeah, they'll analyze every last speck of dust before they commit to anything."

"What else could it be? A car and building just blowing up like that."

"In the middle of our staging area, no less. It has 'terrorist' written all over it."

"Probably a suicide bomber."

"Maybe we shouldn't sit together like this. We're creating another target."

"And here's the bull's eye right here." The resident comedian moved his Styrofoam cup to the center of the table.

Light laughter followed, more anxious than entertained.

"Seriously, though. It would take out quite a few people if a suicide bomber showed up here. Somebody needs to be thinking about this."

Anxiety spiked through whatever calm had settled.

It was true. Their frenzied convergence at the medical facility could in fact bring more malice and tragedy.

*****

"How can I even get there?" Lil stabbed palms into the air as she paced. "I have no idea where Sean left the car."

"Mine's nearby." Sarah laid a hand to her shoulder. "I'll get you there."

"You can't. Look at all these people. What about your work?"

"There are others here now. This'll close down soon anyway. I'll help out tomorrow."

The Miata was only a few blocks away, not far from where they'd watched the parade. They hurried along the shoulders of side roads in silence, preoccupied with possibilities nobody wanted to mention aloud.

Lil tossed the diaper bag behind the passenger seat and buckled in.

"Sorry there's no car seat for Jerrod. Hang on." Sarah nosed into traffic and accelerated, doing what she could to not jerk around her already traumatized passengers.

"I can't lose Sean." Lil wept. "He's all I've got that really matters."

Another wave of déjà vu bubbled up. Snapshot memories, of when she and Lil first learned of the twin towers. Lil had acted this same way, while most others were still in a state of shock. The two of them eventually ended up in front of Mom and Dad's television, finding comfort in sharing ideas of what it might be about.

So much changed at once during that interlude—her worldview, her personal life, even her lifelong friendship with Lil. It was right around then they began to part ways, the start of senior year. Lil became distant, as if purposely trying to distance herself. So it seemed.

Lil stopped talking about dreams beyond Marshland, too. It hadn't made sense. Lil had chattered about becoming a counselor since middle school, always hungry to learn more about it. Dashing off to help the equestrians after the explosion was certainly evidence that her altruistic drive lived on. Yet here she was, staying at home and playing mommy instead. And so dismissive—even critical—about Sarah's pursuit of such interests, ones they had once both shared. The sudden change had been so confusing, so hurtful. So unexplained. Was all that because of 9/11?

The snag in the fabric of their friendship was in a state of gradual repair, thankfully. But could there have been a better way to tell her about Sean? Would it have made a difference, if she had remembered how sensitive Lil was with this sort of thing?

Of course not. It would be impossible to share such horrible news without upsetting her. Or reopening related baggage.

As they neared the hospital, they once again dodged droves of human obstructions. Orange cones blocked off the ascent to the emergency room. Beyond the barrier was a clutter of abandoned cars, tow trucks, and other obstacles. Pedestrians weaved through in every direction. Emergency vehicles were accessing the hospital up a steep runway, coned off through the landscaping. Guards had been positioned to grant or decline entrance. Or give needy vehicles a shove uphill, as they were doing now.

Large chunks of rhododendron and other sacrificed foliage formed a pile in the middle of the front lawn. The sight alone made an old back injury twinge, reawakened by more recent memory: the flood debris. Only the ghost of her childhood home remaining on shore, the rest of it mercilessly washed downriver.

Mindfulness, Sarah. The here and now. Getting Lil to the hospital.

She circled the perimeter of activity several times before spotting a place to squeeze in on a side street. Technically the car was double-parked. Chances were, nobody would want out any time soon. Horde activity seemed to represent comings, not goings. "I'll wait here with Jerrod. You go find Paulson. He'll help you."

Lil stayed put. "I can't do this." She continued clinging to her infant, staring straight ahead. "I can't believe this. It can't be real."

The predicament was so removed from expectations for this day, this visit. She had sought out Lil as a cornerstone of yesteryear. Rekindling her friendship with Lil was meant to reopen doors, spur on a reconnection with roots. Instead, the day's bizarreness had turned it upside down. It stirred up the same ambivalence and confusion that had preceded her exodus from Marshland.

Sarah leaned over and wrapped her arms around the two, cursing the restricted space. "You can do it, Lil. You're one of the strongest people I know. Why do you think I came to you when things got to me at the floods, when I had a whole fleet of mental health professionals at my disposal?"

"It's what friends are for," said Lil.

"Yes, for friends who can handle it. You'll handle your crisis, too, the same as you helped me through mine."

Lil pulled away and wiped a sleeve against her nose. She planted a lingering kiss on Jerrod's downy head, mechanical and absent.

"When Paulson gets here, could you take Jerrod to Mom's?" Hesitating, Lil handed over the drowsy infant. "She'll be at the diner."

"Go ahead. Do what you need to. We'll take him to Shelley's. And fill her in."

Lil got out and jogged into the morass.

Jerrod stirred and grumbled, losing patience with being passed around. He nuzzled at her chest.

"Sorry, guy." She repositioned him over her shoulder. "Nothing there but a dry well. You'll have to wait for Mom for that."

The feelings the tiny creature aroused were a welcome shift in focus. So pleasant, yet so unfamiliar. Startling, even—this vague desire to breastfeed him, or in some other way satisfy his need for sustenance and comfort. She'd never considered herself to be the maternal type.

Then, what was the maternal type?

Mom—how wonderful it would be to seek out her own mother just now. Had Mom had feelings like these toward her, when she had been an infant? Did it continue, a relic of early attunement, even after she moved on to adulthood?

A new realm of emptiness opened, underscoring the gap in the place of a connection that had once been, and now was gone forever. It would have been so refreshing, so soothing, at this moment, Mom's gentle comfort.

She dug through the diaper bag and gave Jerrod his pacifier.

CHAPTER 5

She identified his gait before his physical features could be made out. At a distance, Paulson looked as nonchalant as always, ambling down the hill as if he hadn't a care in the world. As he drew near, however, signs of wear stood out like a weathered billboard. By the time he got to the car, he looked as if he had aged several years.

Sarah left the driver's seat and held out the keys. "It's all yours. We need to take Jerrod to Shelley's."

Rather than take the keys, he put his arms around her and the sleeping infant. He drew them near, holding them in silence.

It was something new, being close to Paulson in this way. Especially with the rawness of his grasp: inner strength at the core, but such an intense current pulsing throughout. Seeking comfort in return.

She freed up and wrapped a tentative arm around him. His heart was racing. Trauma there, to be sure. "Are you okay?"

He turned them loose and backed away. "Yes. Rattled, maybe."

"How's Sean?"

"Hanging in there. He was in surgery when I left. Lil's pretty torn up. I didn't want to leave her. But she said she'd be fine. That you'd given her a pep talk."

"That's Lil."

"She's spending the night. She wants us to look after her cats." Paulson revved the engine with a periodic pedal to the metal, as car after car drove past. While waiting to join the stream of vehicles, he shared a terse description of his day.

She listened without interrupting as he gave her a sterile account of minimal information. Apparently he was still figuring out what to do with it. What he did share was horrifying. "I wish I could have helped you somehow," she said as he finished.

"The drive back to Marshland will do me good. A chance to sort it through...if we can ever get off this curb."

"It's not any better through town." She looked back at the long line of traffic jamming up the arterial. "Roads near the parade route were almost completely backed up. Or closed down altogether."

"There's a back way. It circles town and meets up with the main highway. The roads aren't the greatest. I've used it for dirt biking."

"I know the route. It's near Mom's cemetery."

"Your mother's out here?" His fingers tightened over the gearshift. "I always thought she was at the Marshland cemetery. I even checked with the D-Mort guys, to make sure her gravesite wasn't one that got disturbed by the floods."

"She wanted to be at the top of a hill. She liked the idea of being close to the stars."

Someone finally noticed their turn signal in time to let them in. Paulson detoured through the first convenient alley and they left the bottlenecks behind.

It had been some time since her last visit to Mom's grave. Just the thought that they would soon pass near was a comfort. It begged for more.

There was Paulson to consider, too. The trauma he practically radiated, and did not have anything similar to comfort him. He could certainly use more of a break than tootling down the highway. Chances were, after they dropped off Jerrod, he would jump into the thick of things again, the same as she. How much good could he be in his current state? Never in a million years would he acknowledge temporarily impaired competence, and bow out for a while. How to encourage more productive functioning...she needed time to think.

"Let's stop at Mom's cemetery. I could use a quiet moment."

"Yeah, okay." He looked distracted.

She shifted Jerrod aside to get a better look at him. Whatever he saw in the rearview mirror had captured his attention.

There was sudden braking. Sarah tightened her hold on Jerrod.

"What's wrong?" She shot another glance at Paulson.

He was frantically gaping about. "There's someone hurt back there." He barreled the Miata through a gear-grinding three-point turn and backtracked.

"What did you see?" She scanned both sides of the road. Nothing explained the panic.

"Somebody under that SUV we passed. A car or something must have hit him. Nobody'll find him there in time."

The car skidded to a halt at the shoulder. Paulson tumbled out. He charged around the abandoned vehicle and periodically kneeled, craning his neck at odd angles. After circling it twice, he slowed and straightened. Then continued to stare at it. He scratched his chin.

When he returned to the car, he was unreadable. "I was sure I saw a foot. A shoe."

"Not surprising. You've seen your share of injured people today."

"But it was so clear. I swear I saw it."

"You know how it is. We see what we're primed to see." Though it was impossible to ignore what her therapist self was telling her. Lacey had picked up on something, even while speaking with him long distance. Acute stress? Flashbacks, already?

"But, you're right." Paulson attempted to smile. "Nobody could remove a body that quickly."

The journey continued in uneasy silence, unacknowledged demons dancing along in the wake. Sarah tuned it out, focusing on the calm of the rural panorama.

Amidst stretches of cornstalk stubble, a field of pumpkins dotted dark sod with vibrant orange mischief. Trees lining the occasional creek bed produced a kaleidoscope of browns, yellows, and reds, colors cascading to the ground in unison with the gusts of autumn. For a delicious moment, the parade seemed as if it had only been a dream. Until she noticed dampness, and the chunky infant sweating against her. At least, she hoped it was sweat.

"That's the cemetery, up there." She pointed up the grassy knoll. Did a discreet check of Jerrod's diaper. False alarm.

They turned onto a gravel drive and up into a gated area. It was well tended, the lawn neatly trimmed and no sign of floral remembrances left past their prime. She pointed the way up the hill, toward an aging elm. They parked and climbed out.

The musky woodland scents were a welcome contrast to the citified trauma left behind. She quickened her pace, the sooner to reach that familiar plot of earth. Paulson followed, up the bank and between gravesites, until they reached the modest headstone.

"It does look like one of the higher points of the cemetery." Paulson looked around at the park-like landscaping. "Closest to the stars."

Next to the headstone, a plastic vase with fresh flowers was skewered into place.

"Daisies. Mom's favorite. Dad must have been here recently."

Paulson read aloud the dates on the headstone and did the math. "So, she was sixty-one when she died."

"Too young."

"It's a nice stone." He kneeled and studied the small print. "Does that really say 'Star Fleet Academy'?"

"My mother, the Trekkie." Her eyes stung. Such a bizarre chapter of her mother's life.

"It's hard to believe Sam would do that. Even if Jane asked him to."

"She must have figured that, too. She arranged for the headstone herself, the same time as the plot. By the time Dad found out what she was up to, it was a done deal."

"What did he say when he saw it?"

"He just shook his head and muttered to himself. Like he always did, when she took off on Trekkie tangents." She freed a hand to touch at moisture collecting in the corner of her eye. "God, I miss her."

There was no response. Paulson just stood there, staring at the headstone.

This was not the Paulson she knew. His usual MO was to go barreling in and jump onto any type of emotional distress in anybody.

"Look." He straightened, suddenly cautious. "What's that, over there? Is there a body out here? How did it get here already?"

He crept back toward the elm, testing the ground as if navigating a minefield, and began looking around in the shadows.

Sarah stayed put. *Let it run its course.*

After a few moments he returned, sheepish. "I'm seeing things again."

She paused, not sure how or even whether to probe for more. "What did you see?"

"A dark form. Like it was moving along the grass, off to one side. A swirling, almost spinning motion. Fluttering. Then it disappeared."

She tucked behind her ear the fistful of hair Jerrod had tugged loose. A second flashback, already?

"When I first saw it, I thought it was a body. They were...they were covering them up with these dark-colored tarps." He jammed his hands into his Goodwill-reject jacket and stared at the horizon. Pale, ill at ease. Shutting down.

It felt like everything she knew about trauma was trying to claw its way out to the forefront at once. Her gut said to get him to talk, to put it all out there and sort it out. Get through it, get it over with. The way she would do for herself. But professional common sense knew darn good and well that doing so could cause more harm than good. Maybe even crucify whatever his resilience was doing to keep him afloat. Shutting down might be a good thing. For now.

Discipline. So much more difficult with a friend, than with a client.

So. Keep what's working for him up and running. Find competing responses for anxiety. Protect and pump up social supports. Avoid retraumatizing thoughts. Stop it dead in its tracks. If you can.

And hold it together yourself. The clashing and sorting of fragmented ideas was likely every bit as intense as his bone-rattling trauma reaction. More reason to watch her step.

Breathe. "There's a nice bike path through the cemetery. Feel like a walk?" Actually, hauling around a well-fed infant had already more than done it for her. She had sponged up every last drop of adrenaline delivered by the day's madness. A good nap seemed more in order. However, walking was a benign way to level him out, if anything was going to. "It'll be a while before we get another chance like this."

"I'm up for it."

She stepped onto the meandering trail of asphalt and set off at a moderate pace. Paulson followed, steady and silent. As they moved along, he did seem to loosen up some.

There was something else she ought to be doing for him. *Think.* Like, reciprocal inhibition. What would counteract all that anxiety without making him face it head on? In the middle of a cemetery, no less.

She bounced Jerrod, more instinctual than intentional. He was wide-awake again, throwing himself this way and that to eye the colorful scenery. Her shoulder was killing her.

She looked down at the vital creature in her arms. *The therapy infant.* "Jerrod's getting heavy. You mind? You're the one with the testosterone-enhanced muscles."

"Sure, pass him over." He placed a hand under Jerrod's capped head with the deftness of an expert, the other hand supporting his body, and lifted him to his shoulder. Jerrod nestled in, shifting his head around for a better view.

How was it that Paulson held a baby so naturally? Another facet of the man she knew nothing about. It would have been less surprising to see him stick Jerrod under his arm and carry him like a football.

They continued along the paved trail, taking their time at scenic viewpoints. Below them, fingers of fog moved in among the hills, filling in grooves like make-believe glaciers, ghostly reminders of autumn sun restoring moisture to the atmosphere. Nature's way of settling. Turmoil and transition coming to rest.

Their wanderings eventually took them full circle.

"This was a good idea." Paulson handed Jerrod back, readjusting the baby blanket with more care than expected. "Getting back to nature. It's like pushing a reset button. When all else fails, just take a deep breath of the real world." Some color had returned to his face. His eyes looked more focused, more online.

"Anything I can do for you? Like drive? You don't seem to have any trouble managing the baby."

"I can drive. But there is something you could do."

"Anything."

"Would you, uh, care to listen while I unload my morning?"

Sarah let out her breath.

*****

"Sure do appreciate this." Shelley tucked tiny Jerrod into a heavily swathed port-a-crib. "Poor little feller. Tough times on his Ma and Pa."

Paulson cocked his head and considered the child. Jerrod's pint-sized appraisal of his surroundings seemed to judge it as passable—at last, everything looking as it ought to. Watching the infant settle in brought a welcome sense of completion: at least one piece of order restored for a disaster survivor. He soaked up the vision until forced to tear away.

"Don't know how I'll find out anything about Sean." Shelley led them to a booth. "Phones ain't worth a plugged nickel."

"It'll get better. By now, most people have hooked up with whoever they're looking for." Images of those souls he'd interacted with over the course of the day flitted by. Some perhaps never to reunite with loved ones. *Don't go there.*

"If we hear anything, we'll get word to you somehow," Sarah told Shelley.

"Thanks." Shelley glanced in the direction of pans clattering behind the grill. "You kids eaten yet?"

"Not since the cotton candy Paulson got at the parade."

A chill dropped, spread. A collage spun up in a whirlwind, swelling. Scraps of recent history clipped and pasted, random in order, obscuring all else: darting between spectators, chasing down a vendor. Bumping into that guy with the hoodie. Passing through the site of an explosion yet to come. An explosion. Alison dragging Chet into hell, both of them disappearing into it. That same guy with the hoodie, bleeding out.

Awareness jerked him into the present. Shelley's sturdy support was ushering him along. Sarah had somehow already become seated.

Never had he felt so poorly grounded. Not even after 9/11.

"Set yourself right down." Shelley moved out the chair for him. "I got the Saturday special going. Be right back."

He ransacked scattering thoughts for a topic of the here and now. Anything. "Shelley's pot roast. It's the best."

"Good luck getting her secret. Not even Lil knows what she does. Mom tried to bribe it out of her for years."

"An amazing person. Jane." Safe conversational territory. For him, anyway.

"I wish I'd had more time with her." Sarah's gaze became distant. "To say goodbye. It happened so quickly."

"The cancer?"

"She'd always been careless about checkups. By the time they found it, there wasn't much to do. Chemo might have prolonged things, but Mom didn't want to go that way. Or have us see her suffer. She wanted to treasure those last days, to keep chugging along in that impulse-driven mania as long as she could. We didn't find out what was really going on until a couple weeks before she passed."

"That had to be so hard for you and Sam. And your brother." It was working. His supportive self was coming on line. There was still grounding to be had.

"For everybody," Sarah continued. "You can imagine what Aunt Millie said when she found out. She and Mom shared every little secret, even back in high school. Until this one. After Mom let it out, Aunt Millie hardly left her side. It was nice having her around. But there was so much I would have liked to talk over with Mom—alone, just the two of us. I never made an issue out of it. Then...she was gone."

"Was it anything in particular?"

"No." Sarah leaned forward, chin in hand. "Yes, actually. Everything about life. But, in part, the betrayal. Feeling cheated. That she let me down by doing things the way she did."

"She was in fact thinking of you. She didn't want you to suffer."

"There is that. But I trusted her. I trusted her more than anyone I've ever known. She was the most important person in my life."

It hit a distant nerve, a zinger into the not-yet-understood Sarah. Maybe why she always sidestepped hints of wanting more than a casual relationship. It might have nothing to do with him. Intimacy in general had burned her. Especially with that ass of an ex-boyfriend.

He busied his eyes with the line of cars filing past the diner. Exactly what was this baggage stacked between them? Other than his own, of course. Should he note it aloud? His judgment seemed highly suspect, given the emotional rollercoaster of the last several hours. Time like this with Sarah—he craved it. Dreamed of it. Wanted it all the more, after what they'd just been through together.

Don't squander it. "I remember back in your old neighborhood, when we first met. It was like you had some kind of chip on your shoulder. Was that it? Where you left off with Jane when she passed?"

"I don't know. Maybe. I guess the wall that shot up would say so. Who knows what was going on behind it? I certainly didn't. It's different now. Though it took time and water under the bridge, if you'll excuse the expression."

"Yes. Literally and figuratively." Paulson smiled, glad for the piece of humor.

"It's funny how everything came about. I discovered an interest in disaster mental health only after so much personal loss and pain."

"And our friendship, too." It was so charming, her easy personal revelations, in spite of the staggering journey they had just slogged through. It only deepened his admiration. She was so delicate, yet so formidable. Her friendship felt all the more precious.

The words that had just gotten out were once again fishing for more.

Sarah's voice became evasively pleasant. "Yes, that, too."

Damn it. If he didn't switch gears, he'd start looking desperate. "I've wondered if maybe the timing had something to do with your choice of career specialty."

"Could be. It's what I want to do. I do wonder at times...am I actually comforting myself when I work with others' losses?"

"It's what we all do. We can't build up a strength for somebody else without revisiting it for ourselves."

"So, if we're that practiced, why do we mental health types keep finding ourselves so messed up?" She clicked her mug against his, her eyes smiling back at him.

CHAPTER 6

The explosion site was deserted. How eventful it had been the day before. Now it was deathly still.

Paulson angled himself over and under multiple lengths of perimeter tape. The early morning sun sparkled against remnants of haze, dust particles stirred by the blast. It toyed with visuals, making the surroundings seem surreal.

Anything left of the car had apparently been hauled off, along with other scattered remains. Nobody would ever guess there'd been a parade and major mass casualty incident less than twenty-four hours ago. A darkened pit marked where the blast must have centered. Telltale markings here and there gave away where they'd used fire retardant. They sure had been quick to wash away the blood.

He continued on to the damaged building. They hadn't bothered to try to close it up. The whole front end was missing. He stood where the door used to be and looked inside.

Ash had drifted up against walls still standing, remarkably similar to how it had looked after Sarah's father's business, Sam's Body Shop, burnt down. It was relatively neat and tidy, considering what had happened. It was a crime scene. They would want to analyze it for some time before disturbing evidence. Did this mean they already figured out who was behind this? And why? Sure was faster than in the movies.

47

Debris had been piled in one corner, a mishmash of parade remains. He picked up the large poster draped over the top and held it in front of him. Dirt and partial shoeprints smudged up the bright and colorful etching, wiping out the gay mood it had once portrayed.

He froze. Lying at his feet was a rumpled sheet of that tarp.

There was a noise. Something moved under that dark shroud, rustling it. He recoiled when a rat scurried out. It disappeared into a crevasse in the wall. Was the rest of the family under there, too? He nudged the covering with his shoe.

A hand shot out and threw back the tarp. Sean sat up and grabbed his arm, glaring. His face was bleeding from rat bites.

"What took you so long?" Sean yanked at him, dragging him downward.

"Paulson, wake up."

He was on Lil's couch. Soaking in sweat, his heart thudding. Sarah was kneeling next to him. Gently shaking his arm.

There were hints of daylight peeking through the blinds. Morning had arrived. He pulled his arm away and laid it across his middle, more to assuage his sorry ego than get the hyperventilating under control.

"Are you all right?" Concern pushed its way through her sleepy eyes. So endearing.

But this was so embarrassing.

He tried to reset his bearings. They were in Willsey, having returned late to feed the Whites' impressive collection of cats. Paulson heaved himself up and rubbed his hands over his eyes, patted his face, urging his brain to get with it.

"That must have been some dream."

"One for the record books." He shared the gist of it. By the time he got through it, his innards felt more under control. Sort of.

"It weighed heavily on you, then. Getting Sean to the hospital."

"I didn't think about it as it happened. It was just hurry up, hurry up. Find a way. Do what you need to. Step after step after step."

"You succeeded. He got there in time. They think he's going to make it."

"Me and that EMT. We just...did what we had to."

"You're a hero, Paulson. You saved his life. If you hadn't found

Sean when you did, Jerrod might well be fatherless right now."

"I wasn't thinking about that as it played out. I guess my dream life decided to take care of it for me." He couldn't resist reaching over to scratch a cat's fluffy ears. It blinked back at him, appreciative. "I have a whole new understanding for people with PTSD." He stretched next to the cat, closing his eyes, begging the reset button to be fully engaged when he reopened them.

The cat sniffed at his ear. Yawned in it.

"You don't have PTSD." Her firmness underscored what he already knew, even though it was hard not to consider it. "Your symptoms are normal after something like this. They'll go away. Especially with the systematic processing you've been doing."

"I can only imagine how hard it is for those who have it go on indefinitely."

"It's why we do what we do." She already sounded ready and willing to do it. As opposed to his own state of ambivalence.

It was Sunday. "I need to figure out how I'm going to accommodate helping with this new operation. I'm barely caught up from everything that fell behind while working the floods."

"While you sort it out, I'm first for the shower, if that's okay. I'll let you know if I figure out where Lil keeps clean towels."

Lil's concept of housekeeping didn't offer much hope. Between that observation and his cell phone's rendition of "*I don't get no...satisfaction*," the return to the present began to feel complete. Lacey's caller ID popped out at him.

"Paulson. You up and at 'em yet?"

"Getting there." Fantasy drifted in as steam from Sarah's shower seeped under the bathroom door. How that form might appear, *au naturel*.

"Paulson?" Lacey again. The disaster operation.

Get with the program, dude.

"We're setting up here in Willsey," Lacey continued. "The church is headquarters now. The FAC—family assistance center—it's going to be at that hotel on the south end of town. Relatives are already turning up."

"You sure don't let grass grow under your feet."

"So, deployment. Was I right about you two being keepers? What's Sarah planning?"

"You were right about her being able to bludgeon her way through anything. Cool as an English cucumber. She worked the reception center, then rounded up Lil and got her to the hospital. Picked me up. Got me...on task. Took care of an infant, too, all at the same time. What a day. Damn, what a woman."

Lacey laughed. "Not much has changed with you in that respect, I see."

"Unfortunately, not much has changed with her either. I'm working on it."

"Can you get to headquarters this morning? If you're coming on board, I need to decide how to assign you. We need to talk first. ASAP."

The splatter of water against tile stopped.

"I suppose we can get there within the hour."

"Good. I'll watch for you."

"Wait. Can Sarah and I work together? At the same site?"

"I'll accommodate it if I can. Don't get your hopes up."

"I mean it. If I'm ever going to talk her into...you know. I need opportunity."

"That's not the highest priority right now, Paulson. Do it on your own time."

Didn't take her long to get into pilot mode. Still a typical bureaucrat.

"Let me give it some thought," she said.

*****

Sarah toyed with car radio knobs, hoping to find food for thought. Something other than whatever the day had in store for them. Unfortunately, the explosion dominated the airwaves, both local and national. Authorities weren't saying anything about what had caused it, or who might be responsible.

No terrorist group or individual was coming forward to claim responsibility. Antiwar extremists said that the soldiers had brought the Middle East conflict home with them. Others thought it was about antiwar extremists taking out their political views on the home front. Emotions ran high in both camps.

Rumors that the blast might have spread poison or a deadly virus also got a lot of press. Thankfully, public health officials were quick to share that tests had come back negative for the usual suspects.

"That'll take care of some of the 'worried well.'" Paulson guided the car onto the main highway.

"There were people coming to the reception center wearing masks. Maybe they'll get over it after that smell goes away."

"Masks were on some of the people waiting around at the hospital, too."

"By the way, something happened at the reception center you should know about. It concerns a certain employee of yours...Alison."

"God help us." He took his eyes off the road for a quick glance. "What now?"

"She ran off a traumatized client with nosey questioning."

"I knew it." He slammed his palm against the steering wheel. "Wait'll the boss hears about this."

"You think she will?"

"Yes, because I'll be telling her. Alison's on a short leash. She said if something like this happened again, Alison would be history."

"I don't blame her. It's obvious Alison doesn't understand trauma. And she's clearly not open to input."

Perhaps Alison wasn't any higher functioning than Chet after all. Musings about whatever was going on between Chet and Alison rippled, spilling over the brim of her comfort level. Was Chet in over his head with someone like her? Maybe she wasn't out of his league, after all—could be he was out of hers.

"I feel bad about it sometimes," said Paulson. "She's so enthusiastic. A real energetic go-getter. She's only trying to help."

"Makes it tough. She won't understand. Will there be fireworks?"

"Yes. Damn it."

"At least with her out of the picture, you'll have one less ongoing problem." While she, on the other hand, would be left wondering at all times about what was going on with Chet. With Alison no longer involved with either operation, her hold on Chet would be harder to track. Paulson should count his blessings.

The chaos and drama of the previous day was now organized and energized efficiency, thanks to the arrival of more seasoned aid workers. The layout was a photocopy of how flood headquarters had looked. Beat-up slabs of signage hung overhead, identifying various leadership stations. Familiar faces sat at some of the tables beneath them. Disaster buddies, relationships she had come to treasure. She searched for one in particular.

"Lacey." She quickened her pace to territory taken over by her mentor, soon rewarded with a motherly embrace. "Welcome back."

"Thanks, Sarah."

"Are you going to run the disaster mental health operation again?"

"Yes, and no. It's complicated. Good to see you, too, Paulson."

The two of them also hugged. Lacey cut it short and held him at arm's length, eyeing him over. "That was quite an adventure yesterday. Sure you're up to this? I don't want to bring you on board if you're one of the walking wounded."

At first Paulson looked taken aback. Next came his predictable knee-jerk stance of defiant determination. "Yes, it was difficult. I had a nightmare about it. I'm feeling better this morning. It just seems weird. That it's happening in Willsey, of all places."

Lacey gave a slight smile but didn't look particularly reassured. She shifted scrutiny to Sarah. "How about you?"

"I'm okay, I guess. As much as anyone is after something like this. I need to tie up a few loose ends. But I can work this one for a while."

"Good. We've been asked to take the lead in setting up the FAC. I'd like you, Sarah, to provide support over there as needed. Things will be fluid."

"FAC?" Whatever that was. "Um, could you review a few things for me? That training was a long time ago."

"It's different from usual DMH set-up. You'll be on the learn-as-you-go plan. I'll dig up and print out some materials. Yes, Wi-Fi's back. And the FBI has stepped in. For now, they're officially in charge, rather than emergency services, Public Health, or the like. Victims advocates have been activated. We're working out coordination details."

"I thought for criminal affairs, DOJ and victims advocates took charge of mental health." It was one of the few things she still remembered from the Death by PowerPoint, mainly because it had been an excuse to give her information-overloaded brain a break.

"That's protocol. At least on paper. Apparently the only 'ready' capacity around here is the disaster infrastructure. Local victims advocates are pretty limited. That's why we ended up doing the reception center. They must have liked what they saw, because they convinced the

FBI we should set up the FAC, too."

"The victims advocates are okay with that?" Such strategizing could easily turn south. It conjured up images of the political posturing that always took the place of common sense back at the hospital, whenever competing bureaucracies ended up on the same playing field. Not pretty.

"Remains to be seen. Eventually there'll be changes in 'who's on first.' We still don't know if this is going to be called a criminal incident, a public health emergency, a transportation disaster, a military invasion, or what. It'll get sorted out when there are more specifics."

"What about me?" Paulson's fidgeting had him perched at the edge of his tilting and tapping chair. "Will I be at the reception center?"

"Where Sarah's going is very intense. You need time to let things settle."

He didn't bother to hide his contentiousness. It promptly earned him one of Lacey's stern mother looks. Kind of like the Obama glare, whenever he was stuck listening to something outrageous.

"You know this as well as anyone," said Lacey. "If you're interested, however, there is something low key you could do for us."

"Low key?" He looked incredulous. "How could any assignment having to do with this be low key?"

"Away from the heat. There's a short-term call center going up. That warehouse in Marshland, the one we used for flood supplies. It's been offered up again. It'll be easy for you to help man it, since you live there."

"That's all my job will be?" An exaggerated jaw drop followed. "Answering phones?"

"If need be, yes, help with the phones. But I'm sending other DMH staff for that duty. Your job is staff mental health. To monitor personnel assigned there, and put together a plan for avoiding burnout. Work closely with the call center manager."

"I've never done anything like that before. Are you sure you wouldn't rather have me out at the FAC? Look at my experience with disaster crisis."

"There's some standard guidance I can go over with you." Lacey retrieved a few documents and slid them across the table, unshaken by the obvious attempt to derail her. "I also have a few ideas of my own. Look at this as an opportunity. It's always good to stretch your wings every now and then."

Paulson looked skeptical. Before he could come up with more fodder for protest, a heavy-set woman barged through the main door, eyeing the headquarters' unorthodox appearance as if it were road kill. She homed in on the DMH sign and stormed their way.

"Disaster mental health?"

"Yes." Lacey slowly swiveled her chair to face her.

"I'm a licensed counselor. I live here. I've been told that, for some reason, I need to come here first if I want to help."

"There's going to be a presentation later today for local mental health volunteers who want to join the response. It's not usual practice. It's very intense."

"That I assumed. My background's trauma. I work for an abuse program." The counselor held out a business card.

"Sounds right up our alley." Lacey traded a photocopied informational flyer for the card. "We'll be using community volunteers whenever we can."

The newcomer relaxed and became more engaged as Lacey reviewed the information on the handout. "Thanks," she told Lacey. "I'll be there."

Even as she walked away, she looked like someone who belonged. Sarah couldn't say exactly why. Perhaps Lacey's ability to read people was rubbing off.

"This is a big part of what I'll be doing today." Lacey fanned herself with a stack of handouts. "Separating the wheat from the chaff."

"You mean her background in abuse issues?" said Sarah.

"Not just that. Strong, having realistic self-confidence. Flexibility. Thinking clearly, and making adjustments on the fly. Able to effectively confront and function in the middle of what may seem like the absurd. She'll make good use of those capacities."

"Absurd—you mean the explosion?"

"A little. Mainly how the disaster operation pulls together. Ineffective collaboration plans for mass casualty at the local level is one of the profession's better kept secrets."

"What do you mean? How can they not be prepared? Everybody's heard of emergency management. It's been around a long time. Why wouldn't they know what to do?"

Lacey sighed and looked up with a thin smile. "You'll see."

CHAPTER 7

Tantalizing smells drifted across the room: poultry seasoning, pumpkin pie spices. Hot bread. Over at the kitchen pass-through, the church parishioners were busily lining up homemade casseroles, desserts, and other select morsels. It was enough to make Sarah's mouth water.

"Yes, that's for us." Apparently Lacey could still read her mind. "Have you guys eaten? Be sure to get a good meal in, before you get caught up in things."

As they joined the line forming, Chet strutted in. "Hey! Fancy meeting y'all here."

"Signing on today?" Sarah motioned him and his hangdog-looking companion to join them.

"Did sign-up last night. What a great bunch of guys we got. This here's Freddie. We're partners. Got us our own truck, even."

He grabbed the small man's shoulder and gave it a shake as he introduced each of them. Freddie endured it with admirable stoicism, straightening his cap and flexing his abused shoulder afterward. They spooned up their meals and gathered together at a far corner table.

"Where's Alison today?" Hopefully Damien's mission to get rid of her had met with success. Chet would know.

"She's coming in later. She had things to do first."

That didn't sound promising. Sarah glanced at Paulson, who was struggling with a stubborn packet of hot sauce. Otherwise looking neutral. Momentarily stalled.

"What's your assignment?" he asked Chet.

"I take around things folks need at the disaster sites. Ones still getting set up. Everyplace we got something going. I'm their man. Me and Freddie, here. For today, anyways. There's even going to be folks out at that warehouse in Marshland again."

"Maybe your permanent assignment will be there," said Paulson. "Just like the floods. Old times, old friends."

"No way, no how." Chet's head snapped back and forth in emphasis.

"Why not?" Paulson looked up from his fumblings. "You've been telling us for months about what a great time you had there."

"None of them boys are here this time around. Besides, that old warehouse is full of ha'nts now."

"They wouldn't use the building if it had a major pest infestation," said Lacey.

"No, not ants," said Chet. "Ha'nts. You know, spirits."

"Like, ghosts?" Paulson finally came to life, looking perplexed. Perhaps it was the first time he'd come up against Chet's superstitious side.

Keeping giggles in check would be no small feat. Sarah glued her eyes to her food, and prayed to be able to continue eating without choking.

"Really?" Lacey's softened tone gave away a shift into clinical gear. "I didn't hear anything about it being haunted when I was here last time. Surely a juicy tidbit like that would have found its way to headquarters."

"It was after we closed up. Took them ha'nts a while to show themselves."

Paulson moved in with his usual approach: the sledgehammer. "How did you find out? Did you see them, yourself?"

"Disaster buddy told me. Last summer, while we was out doing the 'canes." Chet leaned forward and lowered his voice. "I'm gonna let y'all in on a big secret. Not a whole lot of folks know." He peered about the room with an air of secretive advantage. "Remember that closed-off part of the warehouse, with them sheets of canvas? How we weren't supposed to use that part of the warehouse, or go back there or nothing?"

"I remember that curtain," said Paulson. "I wondered why it was there."

"'Pay no attention to the man behind the curtain.'" Sarah quickly covered her mouth, unable to quell giggling, in spite of the dirty look Chet was giving her.

"Well, I can tell y'all." Chet puffed himself up. "Remember how the graveyard got flooded? Down by the river? Some of them caskets popped right up out of the ground. Mostly just floated around. When the water came down again, they got left sitting in the mud. Some of them way downriver."

Lacey looked aghast.

Paulson picked up the thread. "After they found them all, they needed to figure out whose remains they were. Then track down family members. Last I heard, some of them still hadn't been claimed."

"Anyways, I can tell y'all where they stored them." Chet sat back, beaming.

"They didn't take them to the mortuary? You're joking." Paulson eyed him. Then looked to Lacey, finally showing recognition that her look of horror had been anticipatory, rather than reactive. "At the warehouse? Behind that curtain?"

"You bet," said Chet.

"That's...too creepy for words." Sarah hadn't heard this story either. Could it be true? "Going on right next to where Dad's shop used to be."

"Back when we was working that shop, I got the heebie-geebies going back by that place, anyway—always so dark, and empty-like. All those strange noises when the wind got bad. Just how ha'nts would like it. If it hadn't burnt down, I bet you them ha'nts would have set up camp at the shop, too. You know, maybe they set fire to it, rather than that old wiring."

A pause followed while cogs slowly rotated. Another Chet epiphany rose from the void. "I know what happened. They're the ones that never had kinfolk come claim them. That'd leave them riled, for sure."

"I never heard of ghosts setting fires," said Paulson. "I've heard people say they go thump in the night, rattle chains, throw shadows, or whatever. Maybe move things around or give people goose bumps. Nothing so methodical as setting fire to a building."

Paulson was actually taking this seriously? Maybe he was just humoring Chet.

"I bet we could find out on the Internet whether ghosts set fires."

Chet pulled out his archaic cell phone. "You can find out anything on the Internet. Ain't that something? Things we can do with gadgets nowadays. It's unbelievable."

So now the existence of "ha'nts" was even more believable than the Internet. Sarah quickly covered her mouth, guarding against the possibility of food flying out.

Chet disappeared out a door adjacent to the dining area, seeking a better signal. Once he was out of earshot, holding back was no longer an option. She held her middle as it ached with laughter refusing to be contained. Lacey let out a few chuckles of her own. Freddie shook his head and muttered to himself.

Paulson just looked at them. "He's kidding, right?"

Tears welled over the likelihood of that suggestion. She pulled herself together. "So, since when does Chet kid?"

"Yeah, I know. What you see is what you get. But...he believes in ghosts now?"

"He's always believed in that stuff." Sarah dabbed at areas suspect for mascara trails. "You wouldn't believe some of the stories. They're a riot. Mom was into it, too. They used to have these long kitchen table discussions."

"I can imagine what Sam thought about it," said Paulson.

"He'd just finish eating as quickly as he could. Then go turn up the TV." Another spasm of laughter threatened to take her to the floor.

Other headquarters staff glanced their way, some looking critical. She couldn't really blame them. What could possibly be so funny in the middle of a mass casualty disaster? For a mental health worker, of all people.

Sarah did what she could to reel it in. It was tough.

But she did not feel apologetic about the brief flight into normalcy. Laughter truly was the best medicine. The timing could have been a little better, though.

"At any rate, we should prepare ourselves." Lacey sampled her corned beef hash. "Once this one gets out, it'll race through the rumor mill like wildfire."

"I wonder what really happened." Paulson's concerned brow was still aimed in the direction of Chet's retreat.

Fortunately, Lacey was tuned into a more productive wavelength.

"I'm not going looking for details. We've got strategizing to do for the disaster in our own spiritual realm. Also, Paulson, something else I wanted to touch bases on. Your PFA team in Marshland? That's another reason I placed you there. It'll be easier for you to monitor."

Paulson looked thrown off. "I hadn't thought about that."

"How've they worked out? With the flood victims? We'll have people who are survivors of both disasters."

"Okay, I guess. I do have one problem child. She's been mixing it up with new disaster survivors already. I have to dismiss her."

"Firing." Lacey sighed. "Worst part of my job, anyway."

"She truly doesn't get it. Once she even passed herself off as a licensed provider at Willsey CMH. Got into some sensitive material."

"Good grief. Bashing boundaries with your job, too?"

"I've been working with her on it. But the boss said the next *faux pas* meant curtains. That *faux pas* was yesterday."

Lacey lowered her voice. "What happened?"

"It was something I was there for." Sarah took over the telling so Paulson could get at his lunch, his food appearing untouched. She reviewed the encounter between Alison and the client, with emphasis on Alison's more colorful behaviors.

"Hmm," said Lacey. "One of those. Any chance of catching up with the client and repairing the damage?"

"It wasn't anybody I knew," said Sarah.

"Those staff types truly are a pain. Might even be questionable whether anything she told you about the incident was on the mark."

"Last I heard, Damien was looking for a way to get rid of her." Sarah handed up her tray to a passing kitchen volunteer.

"I've seen other volunteers like Alison," Lacey continued. "They come and go. They've got big hearts, willing to do anything to help. The sky's the limit. Unfortunately, this type also tends to be, well, inept. Or socially-challenged. Or both. The sky being the limit is half the problem. We look for placements where they're not a nuisance. For some, that's impossible."

"How awful. Why do you think there's so many?"

"They're so available. They have trouble hanging onto jobs in the paid workforce, too. So when disaster strikes, they're not encumbered by as many ongoing responsibilities. All volunteer agencies deal with this," one way or another."

"What can they do about it? I mean, how do you fire a volunteer?"

"Same as paid staff. Document, document. Redirect, and give them another chance. Just like Paulson's done with Alison. If it keeps happening, send them on their way."

"So, from what you're saying, the most we can do is hope to fix whatever damage they cause." Sarah brushed patterns into stray crumbs on the table. The ramifications were unsettling.

"Another tragedy is the good staff we lose over it, ones who give up and take their valuable volunteer time elsewhere. It affects staff mental health, too, for those who stay on." Lacey nodded to where Paulson sat.

"So now Paulson does staff mental health at a haunted call center. Be sure to check standard guidance for protocol." Sarah doubled over again, barely catching herself before it had her off her chair.

Lacey looked to Paulson for sympathy. "Let's get Chuckles here to in-processing, so we can get down to business."

Sarah ping-ponged through the room as she introduced herself or reestablished old connections. She stopped to pick up a health status form.

The staff health nurse swiveled from her monitor to welcome her. "Just arriving? Or were you here yesterday?"

"I was at the parade when it happened."

"That must have been intense."

"Yes. In fact, if you've got a moment...I'm a little concerned. Paulson, the man over there with the DMH manager..." Sarah checked for anyone possibly overhearing. "Can we keep this between you and me?"

The nurse nodded.

"He was at the parade, too. By the end of the day, he was pretty ragged out. He's already having flashbacks and nightmares."

"So soon?" The nurse frowned, glancing in Paulson's direction. "Doesn't bode well, does it. There are short-term medications that can keep it from ramping up."

"I know. But it'd take physical restraints and force-feeding to get him to take any form of psychotropic. He does seem more with it today. But I suspect there's more to come."

"Last night I had trouble sleeping myself. I wasn't even there when it happened."

"I suppose it's better than having stuff like this be so commonplace that our brains automatically deal with it. Anyway, he didn't tell the DMH manager the full story about himself. Not while I was there."

"Where's he assigned?"

"The call center." Sarah looked over at the DMH station, where Paulson and Lacey had their heads together over something. "So at least he won't be dealing with life in the trenches."

"Good." The nurse looked relieved. "He'll be more comfortable there anyway. The FAC will turn into the ultimate in high society sophistication, complete with politics and pretense. It's not the place for someone who resembles a burnt-out throwback to the sixties. He'd just end up even more traumatized."

"Maybe that was Lacey's thinking, too." The added perspective was reassuring. Lacey was looking out for him already, even without the full details of his trauma reaction. "I'd feel better knowing someone's keeping an eye on him. I can't do it from the FAC."

"Tell Lacey. She's bringing in someone to monitor staff. All staff. Everybody gets interviewed for fitness. It's a mass casualty disaster."

"I consider it Paulson's call. He chose not to tell her everything. Yet, at least. Knowing him, he will eventually. I figure I should honor that."

Sarah looked up from a health form she was filling out to see Alison swagger in, every bit the *doyenne* on a high-powered mission. The nurse saw her, too. She rolled her eyes and turned back to her computer monitor.

Was there anyone who hadn't had a run-in with Alison? She certainly did get around.

"Is Paulson here yet?" Alison looked down her nose as if the two women before her were so much dirt. Or worse. "He needs to talk with me."

"He's over there, with Lacey." *What a piece of work.* If Alison were a cat, her tail would be twitching. Why Paulson had put up with her for so long was as much a mystery as the cause of the parade explosion.

*****

"What do you mean, you're letting me go?" Alison rose from her chair.

"I'm really sorry." Paulson powered up the best show of sympathy he could. "But I was very clear last time. You can't step outside your role. The liability is huge."

"That's ridiculous." Clenched fists dug in at her bony hips. "I don't do anything that I haven't seen you do at least a dozen times."

Maybe he should just drop his head into his hands and wish it away. It was timeworn, over-traveled territory. She simply did not grasp the difference between a licensed mental health professional and a PFA cheerleader. Was there anything that could crack through that hard-headedness? He had tried in every way he knew how. Maybe it was time to stop trying. "I'm sorry you don't understand. Stop by the clinic. They'll fix you up with your final paycheck."

Alison remained motionless, glaring at him as if the very concept of firing her was too outlandish to consider. The staring contest ended when she yanked off her employee ID and threw it down. It clattered across the table; he snatched at it before it could land in his lap.

"Thanks for nothing." She stomped off, no more clued in than when she'd entered.

Sarah stepped up from the sidelines.

"That went over well, didn't it?" His forehead felt damp. Moisture was gathering along the crest of his brow.

"But it's over for you. One less problem to deal with."

"The whole program will be revamped, with this new disaster." He brushed at sweat trickle with his sleeve before it could sting his eyes. "At least the boss will be happy."

An image drifted into his periphery, followed by a sudden splash of color. Over by the DMH table. It hadn't been there before.

It looked like someone was on the floor. Was that blood?

"What the hell is going on over there?" He got up and took a few tentative steps, unsure what his senses were telling him. "Is that Lacey under there?"

"What? I don't see anything." Sarah followed.

He dropped to the floor and poked around in the cache of supplies.

There it was, what he had seen. A burgundy sweatshirt. Someone must have just now tossed it in there. At first glance, it had looked like a pool of blood.

He silently cursed the latest spasm of half-wittedness. It had to have looked really lame.

"Seeing things, I take it." Sarah's professional voice purred, calm and supportive. Even so, it was obvious she was bothered.

"It wasn't as bad." He wiped clammy palms against his Levi's. "My heart isn't racing the way it did before."

"This, too, shall pass."

"So said Eleanore Roosevelt." Though the pounding in his ears distinctly disagreed.

"I need to be on my way." She looked hesitant. Concerned. "The FAC awaits."

"I'll be okay. Here, I'll walk you out. Let me carry that." He took the plastic bag of stuffed animals from her arms and followed her to her car, forcing bounce to his step. He loaded the bag into her trunk.

"Thanks." She paused, looking up at him. Those spirited grey-blue eyes were making an effort to look encouraged, upbeat. But she was clearly worried.

Without warning she reached up and wrapped her arms around his shoulders. She briefly brushed her cheek against his. "You take care of yourself now." She pulled back and looked into his eyes.

The intensity of it was nothing short of startling. Stealing any capacity for words.

She left.

CHAPTER 8

The warehouse bay door was up. A good-sized truck backed toward it, lining up with the loading dock. Chet and Freddie motioned it in like an aircraft taxiing into a gate.

Paulson hadn't missed anything.

He parked the rental car on the plot of land upon which Sam's Body Shop had tended to Marshland's dings, dents, scrapes, and cracks for decades. Over the summer, its charred remains had been leveled, except for the shed-like addition saved by the firefighters. Sam and Chet had dismantled and reassembled the shed on his riverside lot, where it was being used to house equipment during Sam's home rebuilding. Afterwards, they planned to expand it into a shop. Sam would no doubt return to less purposeful tinkering. Perhaps a sign that one day things really could get back to normal.

Paulson dodged his way around the logistics team's undertaking and stuck his head into the empty warehouse. It was nearly windowless, other than a smattering of skylights well overhead. The semi-darkness went right along with the chill within. It was as if the two actively conspired to reach out and envelope anyone who thought about entering.

Chet's casket story—it was getting to him. He shuddered and began to button his jacket. He flinched to a halt as an abrupt flash illuminated the far end of the building. Lighting fixtures continued to burst into duty, row by row, in concert with echoing clicks of the switches that prompted them. Once the room was bathed in buzzing and sputtering halogens,

Damien emerged from behind the control panel.

"Here we go again." Damien's kind features were a balm. Finally, a friendly and familiar face to fill some of this black hole sucking the life out of him. A welcoming grasp. An oasis of companionship in the middle of insanity.

"Same song, second verse." The setting almost felt human. "How did you end up with this duty? I thought for sure they'd have you managing the FAC."

Damien took his time answering. "They told me it was for my own protection."

"Protection? From what? That spread of goodies they always lay out? I know I usually hear my smaller arteries slamming shut whenever I look at it."

Damien's disgruntled glance said that whatever was going on, it was not open to humor. "I guess I can tell you. We're supposed to keep it quiet. The chapter got a threatening phone call. They thought it best that I'm kept out of sight."

"Out of sight? From who? What were they threatening?"

"Essentially, anyone who looks like me."

Race? He'd never given it much thought in regard to Damien. Yes, he had darkish skin, thanks to his mother's heritage. His other features and ethnic leanings were pretty ambiguous.

"Somebody got it in their head that this thing is because of Middle Eastern terrorists." Damien turned his back to the logistics team's struggle with the back of the truck. He stared into the depths of the future call center, examining the lighting. "Then the rumor mill took over. Word's going around that the soldiers were the intended target. Since there aren't many people around here with my skin tone, the higher-ups worry I have a target on my back."

"I didn't know you had a Middle Eastern background."

"I don't. Mom's from Jamaica. But try telling that to Bubba and Skeeter when they come around with their AK-47s, out to save the world."

"You're the best manager we've got. You should be front and center, not hidden away in some remote call center."

"Dad was pretty upset about it. He said I should thumb my nose at the bunch of them. I couldn't, you know. I had to do something helpful."

"It's their loss. I, for one, am glad we get a real manager here."

"Thanks." Damien relaxed visibly, perhaps taking in the legitimately earned compliment. He still looked uneasy, vulnerable. Nothing like the competent confidence he'd displayed in past disaster assignments.

"By the way, I'm in the same boat as you. My supervisor thought I was stretched too thin. She sent me out here for lighter duty."

"So this here's the 'island of misfit toys' of the operation?"

Paulson laughed. "Not bad. I like it. Maybe we should check out everybody else's story to see how they got banished here. How do you get so much time away from your nine to five, anyway? First the floods, now this."

"One of the perks of a family business. I think Dad likes the way my absences are slowing his supposed transition into retirement."

A slap on the back almost knocked Paulson to the floor. He turned to find himself facing the one-size-fits-all disaster vest strapped across Chet's chest, appearing shrunken to postage stamp size.

"Hey, Paulson, Damien. Give us a hand here. We got us a whole call center to unload. It's all donated. Ain't that something? Who would've guessed? Everything's right in this truck. Most of it anyway. No phones, but with everything we got here, at least y'all will have someplace to sit while you're waiting."

Grueling physical labor took care of the chill of the cavernous surroundings. Jackets and sweatshirts came off; sleeves rolled up. Companionable male voices echoed along with the thuds and scrapes.

It would have been less taxing if he'd kept that promise to get into better shape before the next disaster assignment. Only an hour or so of lifting and dragging had him left with the strength of a ninety-pound weakling.

The joint physical labor felt good, regardless. Almost revitalizing.

After the truck was relieved of its load, bottled water appeared and was passed around. They stood back and assessed the mound of furnishings, cubby walls, and cartons of office ware that would become their place of business.

"Round one completed," said Damien. "Now we just have to set it up."

"Got it right here." Chet pulled out a crumpled drawing. "We got other folk coming in tonight to do it. These guys had it figured out before we even got here."

"I need a breather." Damien plopped himself onto a cardboard box with the drawing of a filing cabinet on one side. The other men apparently agreed with him, as they took seats on whatever suitable object presented itself. They sat in silence, each to their own thoughts, tanking up and studying the last of the late-afternoon sun.

Paulson's thoughts drifted back to headquarters. Specifically, the church parking lot: Sarah's casual goodbye hug. It had come out of nowhere, mother-like and supportive.

The softness, her cheek against his. How the gentle warmth of her form had radiated through incidental touch against his. More than welcome amidst whatever developments this tragic incident would bring, as they lent a hand of comfort to those who'd gone through it.

A pang of anxiety stabbed at his gut—the last twenty-four hours attempting to resurface. He swallowed back the stomach rumblings. Maybe there were some antacids in his pack. Where was Jenny's stockpile when he needed it.

In the corner, where they'd piled packs and outerwear, the shadows seemed darker, different. He narrowed his focus—for less than an instant, it was almost like they were moving.

Just like at the cemetery.

Who was messing around over there, anyway? He got up for a closer look.

"What you looking for, Paulson?" Chet followed after him.

"Thought I saw something. Everything's okay, though."

"I know what it was." Chet glanced around. "It's them *ha'nts*."

Not again. "I was just seeing things. The sun's getting low. Shadows are playing tricks."

"Don't you worry none. I came prepared."

"Prepared? How?"

"You wait here. I'll be right back. Logistics to the rescue!" Chet lumbered out, a man on a mission.

"What, he's going to come back with tinfoil covering his cap?" Damien joined him.

"No, that's for space aliens. So, you heard about the ghosts, too."

"Hard to keep that one under wraps. Where did they keep those caskets?"

"The curtain was about there." Paulson lead the way toward the back of the warehouse. They studied the austere environment.

"Looks harmless enough to me." Damien extended his inspection to the rafters. "Nothing that people would think was haunting."

"Yes sir, that's just the spot." Chet was back, a large cardboard box under one arm.

"What's that?" said Paulson.

"This here's my ha'nt-fixings." He set the beat-up container on the concrete floor. "I been saving up supplies for years. Y'all need to be ready for any kind of disaster, you know."

"This I've got to see." Freddie and some of the other men began to take an interest in Chet's operation. Eventually the entire workgroup encircled him.

First Chet pulled out a mirror. "Ha'nts are scared of their reflection." He carried the mirror to the nearest wall and secured it on a convenient nail. "If they see themselves in this, they'll run off."

Nobody said a thing. Skepticism dripped from those who dared to share glances.

Next he pulled out what looked like some kind of homemade soap. Block lettering on the cellophane wrapping said "GHOST BE GONE."

"Here, Paulson." Chet handed him a bar. "This here has special ingredients. If them ha'nts smell this, they'll leave you alone. Anybody else need some?"

It was heavily floral-scented, whatever it was. The other men stepped back, waving Chet off with various versions of "no, I'm good." Chet went back to rummaging.

"I saw this once in an off-beat supply catalog," Paulson whispered to Damien. "They've got it for monsters, too. It's for little kids who are afraid of ghosts in the closet, or monsters under the bed, or whatever."

"Apparently it works for certain logistics workers, too," said Damien.

"I wondered where that god-awful smell was coming from," said the supervisor.

"Maybe it works for mouthy supervisors, too." Freddie fixed a pointed glare at his crew boss. "I got me one that's a real monster. Sure would like him off our backs."

The supervisor flicked off Freddie's cap. It became an excuse for everyone to let out laughter being held back. Except Freddie, who smacked their leader's arm with the hat before sheltering his pattern baldness.

"Got me an idea," said another worker. "Maybe I could use some of that to get my mother-in-law to move out."

Chet was too busy tearing open a good-sized bag of white rice to note the thread of his coworkers' harassment. He dumped about half the rice in the area where the caskets had been.

"This fix-it came all the way from the Far East. My cousin Elna told me about it. If ha'nts see rice on the floor, they think they need to count it. It's real hard to count them tiny things, you know. Easy to lose track. Especially if it's a whole lot, and it's clear down there on the floor."

"I wouldn't know." Freddie was still scowling. "Ain't never tried it."

"So them ha'nts get busy counting, and leave folks alone."

"What if somebody sweeps it up?" said Damien.

"You be sure to tell folks not to sweep there." Chet added a serious nod to the directive.

Damien shot a silent groan up toward the industrial-grade ceiling.

"Now here's the most important thing." Chet fished out a poorly constructed wooden box. It was decorated with dials, lenses, and other unidentifiable bells and whistles.

"That there must be the deluxe model," said somebody in the back.

"You bet." Chet plugged whatever it was into an outlet. "You just turn it on with this button here." He flicked a toggle switch. The contraption started up a low humming sound. "This'll scare off them ha'nts. It's real high-class technology."

"Where'd you get that?" said Paulson.

"This here's a family heirloom. It was my Uncle Earl's. When he passed, they asked us kinfolk if there was anything of his we wanted. I snapped this right up, before anyone else could lay hands on it."

"How special." Freddie's sarcasm was lost on Chet. "Does it work?"

"My Uncle Earl always had this going, there at his singlewide. It sat next to his TV for years. He never had no problem with ha'nts. Never, not one."

"But..." Paulson began. "Never mind."

"Now that's over the top." Damien finally lost his composure. "Why do you believe that thing's for real, and not some kind of hoax?"

"It's bona fide, all right." Chet smiled, generous with patience for trainees in the supernatural. "My Uncle Earl wasn't no dummy. He got it from the World Wide Web."

Nobody seemed to know what to say to that.

"How about a power pack?" The supervisor reached around like he was outfitting himself with a backpack. "You know, you wear it on your back and shoot a laser beam out the nozzle, like on *Ghostbusters*. I wouldn't mind having me one of them."

"Yeah, me too," said Freddie.

Chet narrowed his eyes. "Y'all know that was just a movie show." He closed the half-emptied container and carried it back toward his truck.

"Thanks, Chet," Paulson called after him.

Everybody else was too busy trying to be socially appropriate to say more, snickers barely held in check. Finally Chet disappeared from view.

"Elvis has left the building," said the supervisor.

The crew burst out laughing.

"At least we don't need to worry about Elvis's ghost hanging around here."

"How much do you want to bet our ol' Chet here believes he's alive and kicking, anyway."

"What a bunch of bull. That Chet feller needs to get a grip."

"I wonder what else he had." Damien pawed at the quietly humming ghost box, giving it a dubious once-over.

"I'm afraid to ask." Though it was hard not to smile. Bonding, companionable healing. The interlude had produced it in spite of the craziness. "Chet might have something in there too high-powered for us neophytes to handle."

*****

The conference complex was already teeming. Attaching disaster ID to her collar, Sarah sized up the scene. Camouflage-painted vehicles were everywhere, managed by those with matching apparel. A few of the standard red and white feeding trucks were parked off to the rear. There were ambulances, police cars, church vans. A few generic delivery trucks. A number of the less conspicuous vehicles were tagged with government signage: Public Health. FEMA. Department of Human Services. FBI. Homeland Security. Department of Justice.

Across the street was the ubiquitous gathering of media vans.

Lacey's comment about "who's on first" had been spot on. She was wallowing in it already, and she hadn't even set foot inside yet.

Just check in with the casework supervisor, Lacey had said. Do a little mental health surveillance. Smooth things over where you can; grease the wheels. Do what you can to stay out of the politics. Because they will surely be there.

So she was supposed to do some kind of Lieutenant Troi imitation. Could it ever be as easy as she made it look? Probably not. Being on the bridge of the *Enterprise,* or even hurtling through outer space, sounded a lot easier than finding her way through this mess.

The confusion inside was comparable to the parking lot. People were practically tripping over one another, scrambling to get their service areas set up. Most seemed cordial and cooperative with one another. Or perhaps were too distracted by tasks at hand for politics to rise to priority level. Yet—there was that rare squabble in the background. Maybe just overtones of impatience.

Finding her workstation was the first challenge. She scanned the room for the distinctive vest the casework supervisor would be wearing. She finally spotted the woman in a far-off corner, unloading a disaster kit while doing battle with long dark hair that kept swinging down into her efforts.

Sarah dropped the bag of stuffed animals and helped hold open the box flaps as she introduced herself.

"They told me to expect you. I'm Delores."

"Lacey said you'd help me get oriented. That you've been through something like this before. Like 9/11."

"Almost everybody who did disaster back then worked that one. It was the disaster of all disasters. We lost good responders because of it. Good friends." Delores ran her gaze over the roomful of responders, looking pensive. "You can feel it already. The intensity, apprehension. Just knowing you're here, though." She smiled at Sarah. "It makes it better."

She looked as if she truly meant it. Sarah's presence, alone, created calm? *In this?* It certainly left her more exposed to the chance of error.

"How are things going so far?"

"We've taken care of the practical arrangements." Delores stuck writing utensils in an orange porcelain cup decorated with a grinning jack-o-lantern face. "Our logistics team has most of it set up already. Our disaster partners seem appreciative that somebody knew how to go about it. The humanitarian spirit, the drive to help—it's mind-blowing."

Delores gave her hair another toss and leaned toward her. "There's also this...I don't know...underlying competitiveness? No knockdown, drag-outs but a lot of posturing. Can't really blame anybody. We're all juiced up into rescue mode. I haven't seen anything that would get in the way of services yet. As long as that's okay, we can live with it." She gave up and secured her hair with a band from her pocket.

"Right now, it looks like I'd just be underfoot in here." In the middle of this hive of activity, a reasonable and expectable DMH plan of action did not readily identify itself. Offering any of these scurrying staff a well meaning "how's it going?" was not likely to end well. All they needed was to get done whatever it was they needed to get done. "What about survivors and family members? Are very many here yet?"

"Lots." Delores emptied a bag of trick-or-treat candies into a miniature witch's cauldron. "They've been gathering all day, mostly in that big lobby near the lounge. We put temporary information stations out there. Counselors from county mental health are hanging around, too. They can probably tell you more than me."

When she found the disaster victims, the change to somber pall was mind sputtering, especially since the new arena seemed almost as populated as the energetic one she'd left behind. The dimly lit lounge appeared to be a draw. People slumped in the booths and addressed one another in hushed tones, or stared off with unseeing eyes. A few tended to tears with the Kleenex someone had had the foresight to set out. A couple of cranky children were running around, annoying the few who noticed. Equally cranky parents tried to reel them in. There wasn't anyone helping anybody.

No time like the present. They were hers now, her new client base.

What a staggering caseload. There was no way to get to all of them. Not on her own. She would have to be extraordinarily selective.

The tension was similar to the waiting area outside psychiatric lock-up. Everybody looked stressed, or at least distracted. While she sat with some of the more distressed families, other staff began to wander in and out. Their ID looked like victims advocate insignia. Perhaps the explosion really was criminally caused, after all.

Once satisfied that the lounge's most obvious trauma candidates were taken care of, she continued into the brightly lit lobby. There a full wall was lined with coffee and refreshments. A man in a pale blue Homeland Security polo was walking a young couple through a plethora of takeaways stacked on a long counter. In a far corner, a man was comforting a distressed woman, most likely the one whose sobbing Sarah had heard on and off for as long as she'd been there. At a distance, his identification looked similar to Paulson's county mental health ID.

An argument at the opposite end of the lobby escalated.

"I can help these people." The woman snapping out her indignation was sitting at one of the many tables. The victims advocate nametag worn by the apparent recipient of her tirade identified him as "John."

"This is a restricted area." John's light brown mullet with a wisp of premature gray, his crisp attire, and conservative deportment screamed upper-echelon establishment. Little wonder the staff health nurse figured Paulson would have trouble fitting in.

"This is America. People have the right to any kind of services they want."

"I appreciate your sentiments and concern," said John. "But this is not the place."

"If you'd lost a loved one in that bombing, wouldn't you want to get in touch?" The woman practically bellowed. "You and your kind certainly can't do anything about it. My services are the only way they'll have a chance."

"All services here need to be approved by administration. Take it up with them."

"I'm not leaving." She stood, her bulbous nose inches from his face.

By now most eyes and ears in the room were tuned in to the exchange. A trio of teenagers trying to sneak a peek into her intriguing collection of wares backed away. A couple of uniformed types moved closer.

"Again, I'm going to have to ask you to leave." John stood his ground.

The woman went back to setting out paraphernalia: a crystal ball, tarot cards, a few other items for which there couldn't possibly be a practical purpose.

John pursed his lips. He caught the gaze of a burly security guard poised for action. He gave him a reluctant nod.

"Come along, ma'am." The guard moved in and reached toward her.

"Mind your own business." She jerked her arm away.

A second guard took up the other side. Amidst loud protest, they struggled in tandem to guide her along. A third guard joined them, pushing from the rear. As they gained momentum, a fourth guard came forward. After giving the occult gear an unceremonious shove into its cosmically-spangled carryall, he took up the rear of the procession. Finally, the automatic sliding doors swooshed behind them. Stillness returned, other than murmurings. A few laughs.

"That was a medium?" Sarah moved in next to John. "How did she get in?"

"She had some kind of passable-looking ID. It dated back to the OKC bombing." John's eyes scrutinized the ID on Sarah's collar as he spoke. "Got her past security, anyway."

"I can't believe she tried it, with uniforms everywhere you look. I'm Sarah, by the way. Disaster mental health."

"John, victims advocacy, FBI. I'm told I'm the lucky duck who oversees mental health support. For the moment anyway."

"Then I guess you're the one I should be talking to. FBI...this was a criminal incident, then? A terrorist?"

"There's going to be a briefing soon. They'll bring you up to date."

The county mental health counselor established in the corner helped up the distressed woman. He escorted her toward the exit.

They passed; Sarah gasped. The woman he'd been comforting also wore CMH signage. "What happened over there? With the woman from Willsey CMH?"

John shook his head in frustration as he picked up and replaced chairs knocked awry by the medium's theatrical departure. Sarah pitched in.

"I warned her this might not be her cup of tea. Public Health insisted they be here. The possibility of contaminants and the mass casualty issues do make it a public health incident. They figured that meant they would be doing it all. Eventually I noticed how few mental health workers were turning up. When I asked security about it, they said CMH had told them to turn away any other mental health professionals. That only CMH was qualified."

"How could they possibly believe that whatever resources an overtaxed CMH system might spare would be good enough? Look at all these people. Every single one of them is at risk, family and survivors alike. Down the road, you know as well as I do, a hefty portion will fall victim a second time—PTSD, major depression, you name it. Even debilitating or life ending, for some. There's no way we can get preventive measures to all of them. There aren't enough of us."

"I understand their dilemma. They're being diligent about 'do no harm.' Clearly they weren't aware of mental health roles other agencies play during these. A case of the infamous 'failure to communicate.' It happens. A lot, when circumstances are this confusing."

What John said made sense. It was probably at the bottom of that smug look Lacey had given her while hinting about collaboration shortcomings.

Her blood boiled all the same, knowing that some people wouldn't be spared from eons of misery and expensive therapies just because there wasn't enough staff to get to them before they disappeared. "What caused the woman's breakdown? Do you know?"

"One of the first people she sat down with was someone whose son got injured. Then they had trouble getting him to the hospital. It was a mess out there."

"I know. Trauma on top of trauma." It reminded her of Lil, and getting her to Sean. How were they doing? In the on-going excitement, she had actually forgotten about them.

"The boy died. Apparently the worker has children that age. And she recently had a loss in her own life. To make matters worse, she has almost no specialized trauma background. The locals got presentations on basics at one time—psychological first aid, debriefing and the like. She figured that made her good to go."

"Maybe for some mild-mannered flood response, but not something like this. I do feel for her, her wanting to help in spite of her personal situation." Sarah indulged in a quick shoulder roll, loosening neck and shoulder muscles that were beginning to string her up like a noose. She was even more alone in it than when she had first walked in.

"Anyway, she's in good hands. The other counselor is very experienced. He's done victims advocacy with me before. But if he doesn't make it back, that's the end of local mental health support for now. I'm sure glad you made it. I was at a talk you gave after the floods. It was very insightful."

"Thanks." Whatever talk that was. She had given several during that stint. Had she already met John and forgotten? Awkward. However, he did not seem offended by not being remembered.

"Feel free to ask if you have any questions about what's going on." He was actually being overly friendly, if anything. "Who knows, by tomorrow it could be your agency leading mental health, and I'll be asking you how we proceed."

"This is so confusing. I thought there were federal guidelines that say who's responsible." Those handouts from Lacey's original training last spring sure would have been nice to take a gander at just then. Maybe she had more. Or it was somewhere in the new stuff Lacey'd given her.

"Yes and no. Federal guidelines conflict regarding mental health responsibility. If it's an NTSB disaster, like if that tour bus had caused it, Red Cross is usually designated. If it's a health incident, the public health system is supposed to be in charge of it. If it's criminally involved, it's DOJ and victims assistance. So on and so on—it's based on type of disaster. If it's all of the above, each entity still has that charge of ensuring mental health services."

"That's crazy. They can't all be in charge of it at once."

"Exactly. It makes for redundancies, and conflict. Maybe even traumatizing victims with excessive visits. However, FBI trumps all, even state DOJ, when there's criminality. That's what's happening now. If they don't find any, it'll be fruit basket upset at the top of the food chain."

"So what happens next?" Besides more flakiness. If not even the federal government had clarity, expecting the boots on the ground to know which way to go was ludicrous. *Breathe.*

"Wait for word from above. We'll both hear about it when things change."

At least she was lucky someone as straightforward and knowledgeable as John was around. A team player. Dealing with a prima donna in his position would be a real pain in the butt. "How many other victims advocates are here?"

"I'm not really sure. Volunteers of all sorts have been turning up. The media attention complicates things. At least, it explains why we're dealing with mediums already."

"There's more legitimate staff coming, though, isn't there?" The lobby was continuing to fill. Out front, a shuttle was emptying out another load of distraught-looking visitors.

"National victims advocates are deploying." His confident voice swelled over the din of the incoming. "And we put out a call for local volunteers who've had the training. At least to get us through tomorrow. I see a couple of them right now."

He pointed out a man deep in discussion with a young family. It was someone she'd seen around a time or two during the floods. Good— someone else with experience.

"Now where did she get to." John scoured the four corners. "Ah. Over there."

The person of interest was turned away. The rear view was dishearteningly familiar.

God, no. The woman turned. It was Alison.

CHAPTER 9

"Currently there's only minimal expectation that the explosion was intentional." The FBI rep at the podium was stiff and formal. "But for now, we're investigating it as a criminally involved act. While that's ongoing, we won't be releasing many details."

Hushed commentary swelled among the FAC staff. Hands were raised and questions tossed around, many of them already well chewed over by the press.

"What about toxins?" somebody said. "Won't they say something about that?"

"As many of you have already heard, Public Health found no evidence of a toxin, infectious virus, or any other significant biohazard." The agent's attempt to put worries to rest missed its mark. Not surprising. His overly-formal presentation style didn't exactly emit a glow of confident reassurance.

The troubled twittering stepped up: "What about that smell? There's nothing dangerous about those fumes?" "I was there, I smelled it myself." "Yeah, it reeked. Like some kind of weird gasoline."

"It so happened there was a natural gas valve in the area of the explosion." This time his delivery went overboard in trying to sound reassuring. It only made him sound more suspect. "A repair crew had been working on it. It's not a health concern at this time."

Another burst of call-outs followed: "That's what they said after 9/11." "Look at all the lung problems, and cancer, and other things they've connected to that." "Yeah, what about all the asbestos in that old building?"

"Not my domain. Take it up with Public Health."

"Was it a suicide bomb? That tour bus?" said a guy in the back.

That morning there had been a dramatic photo of a bus lying on its side prominently featured on the *Tribune's* front page. Little wonder the transportation accident angle was getting into the mix.

"No. The tour bus was cleared. The bus was just a parked vehicle."

"People are worried it will happen again." This time it was John questioning him. "Is there anything we can tell them?"

"Nothing has come to light to suggest the possibility of more explosions."

Like that was going to do anything to put this bunch at ease. Especially since there was no way whatsoever to be certain there wasn't another explosion in the offing, given how little they seemed to know. Sarah glanced around, expecting a mental health colleague to step in and offer something more useful.

Wait a minute. The CMH staff had bitten the dust, and they had sent away any other mental health professionals. If John had to ask, that meant he didn't have a credentialed mental health background. The only one Lacey had sent so far...was her.

She was it, the only one on site who could address it, if anyone was going to. It was outrageous—only one mental health professional on hand for a major incident that very well may have been purposely intended to promote terror. Unless, of course, any of the other victims advocates had additional credentials. There was Alison...

Sarah's hand shot up. "I might be able to speak to that."

The speaker's eyes locked onto hers, projecting a beady "who are you?"

"Dr. Sarah Turner, disaster mental health." Normally she went along with the standard of omitting her title when working with the disaster organization. But her brief on-site education had already taught her that credentials were everything. Especially with that FBI rep's steely gaze studying her ID.

"Keep it brief, please."

She stepped up and faced the group, only to recoil. A gargantuan assortment of intense and official-looking faces stared back. Focused exclusively on her.

What did I get myself into? She swallowed.

"Something like this...disrupts our footing." She cleared her throat. *Simmer down.* It was no different than giving any other professional presentation. Something she'd done with aplomb on many occasions. No different.

Right.

"This disrupts our footing. Not just going through a frightening and tragic experience. There's the uncertainty over what caused it, and not knowing exactly what will happen next. We might not be able to answer questions like this yet. But we can take back some of our sense of personal control."

Getting settled into familiar territory eventually coaxed in her autopilot. By its conclusion, even remnants of confidence were finding their way in. And relief. "Even children can be part of putting together a family disaster plan. In fact, it helps them become more resilient themselves. If you want to know more, we have plenty of websites and printouts for both clients and staff."

Sarah pointed at their corner. Delores grabbed a fistful of materials and waved them over her head.

"Thank you, Dr. Turner." The speaker turned to the crowd. "Anything else?"

It was as if she hadn't said a thing to help. After a brief pause, yet another smattering of concerns started up. Eventually it deteriorated into the same tittle-tattle that was rattling around as grist for the rumor mill. So much for the psychoeducational approach.

Were the soldiers the real target, perhaps some specific battalion? Which terrorists might it be, domestic or foreign? Do they really know how many people got hurt? Could it somehow be connected to the crossfire over next month's elections? How long will it take to find out anything? What is the FBI going to do next? What's everybody else in law enforcement doing?

Eventually everyone grew tired of hearing "no information to share at this time" and gave up. The briefing was over.

"Now what?" she asked John. "I don't know much more than I did to start with."

"We keep providing support, as best we can."

Away from the post-briefing lull, a distant wail gained momentum, a soul in grief. It came from the direction of the lobby.

"Time to mount the runaway sleigh again." John flipped shut his spiral mini-notepad and tucked it into his shirt pocket. "And hold on for dear life."

"Not for you, Sarah." Delores appeared at her elbow. "Replacement staff is coming. You're wanted back at headquarters."

"I wanted you here for the presentation." Lacey didn't look up from the handouts and training materials she was collating. "Right now you're the one with firsthand knowledge. People coming on board need an idea of what it's like out there, through the eyes of mental health."

"I was just getting warmed up. I thought I'd be at the FAC until closing."

"Too long for a mass casualty disaster. Delores said it was time to restaff."

So it was Delores' idea. Was that about being proactive, or trying to get rid of her?

Stop being so defensive. Delores was fine. Enough animosity was floating around as it was. There was nothing to be gained by adding in imagined slights.

"Hey, Sarah." Chet lumbered up to their pen, Freddie not far behind. "How's it going at the FAC? Paulson said to say howdy if I seen you. And here we are. Right here back at headquarters again. Don't that beat all."

"As long as you're here, how about moving some of these?" Lacey pointed at indiscriminately dumped piles of response supplies, swelled to the point where getting around them was becoming annoying.

"Glad to. Hey, Freddie. Give us a hand here."

Chet and Freddie pitched boxes as if they were empty. Hopefully there was nothing breakable in there.

Lacey gave her one of the handouts. "In addition to limiting time with clients, we make sure you get regular opportunities to unload. A safety valve, so to speak."

"With you?" Sarah scanned the handout content. It was about stress and disaster responders—specifically, disaster mental health workers. So they even expected professionals to crash and burn?

Like Willsey CMH. Yes, it could happen. It was within the realm of possibilities.

"You're with me today, anyway," said Lacey. "I've requested somebody in particular to come in for this duty. He gets here tonight."

"Do you always handpick your administrative staff?"

"Only if I'm lucky. Horace is especially good at this. I worked with him after a school shooting. I should warn you, though. He's a little different." A glimpse of tenderness sneaked into her all-business veneer. "Other workers call him the cowboy psychologist."

"A cowboy psychologist?" Chet hoisted another load of boxes. "There are psychologists like Sarah here, that just fix cowboys?"

"That's not what I mean."

"Don't make no sense to have psychologists just for cowboys."

"I meant that the psychologist is a cowboy."

"He's a rancher then," said Sarah.

"I don't really know. He dresses like he's just off the ranch. His speaking style sounds like not much more than an eighth grade education, let alone a Ph.D."

"And workers trust the expertise of someone who presents that way?"

"It's actually probably why he works out so well. He connects easily. I save requesting him for special duty like this. Of all the staff working one of these, we've got to make sure the mental health responders stay emotionally fit."

"Don't got many cowboys working this operation anyway." Chet wiped his hands on the front of his vest, his supply relocation task completed. He punctuated his leave-taking with the strut of "my work is done here."

"How's mental health response going at the FAC?" Lacey pushed around remaining supply containers to better fit within the cleared space.

Sarah described some of the missteps and confusion. "They even sent away some local chaplains trying to volunteer."

"That's a shame." Lacey took a fresh disaster vest from one of the boxes, shook it out and handed it to her. "Spiritual needs are huge. Someone just got here to lead spiritual care."

"So who will they lead if the chaplains have been sent away?" Sarah threw the vest over her head and tried to figure out the side fasteners.

"They'll get word soon enough through their own channels. They'll be back."

"Where are their heads at?" Sarah abandoned the struggle with ties, which at the moment seemed as ridiculous as the revelations of their conversation. "The CMH staff. They should have figured out what would be coming around the corner. Seems like a no-brainer."

Lacey reached over and adjusted the ties for her. "They're just handling it as best they know how. You're right, it doesn't sound like they understand how these things work. Why would they? When would people out here have opportunity to deal with anything even close to this? It would have been more surprising if it had come off without a hitch."

"One other caveat." Sarah paused, collecting herself. "Apparently Alison has taken the victim's advocacy training. She's assigned to the FAC."

"You have my sympathies."

"I can't believe this. Is there anything that woman hasn't gotten her tentacles into?" Especially regarding Chet, who was currently refueling with junk food at the canteen. There was no end to potential pitfalls her boundary issues might drag him into. His enthusiastic involvement with his response assignment was a godsend. But what about after the response was over with?

"It's not unusual. People often cross-train. It creates unfortunate illusions. Agencies get together and do the math, and figure they have big incidents covered. Then, when disaster strikes, they find out all they have is the same small group of people belonging to multiple agencies and organizations."

That would certainly explain why they were so shorthanded for this one. "But what do we do about Alison? You saw what she's like."

"We don't do anything about her. She's no longer our problem."

"She will be if she starts retraumatizing everybody at the FAC."

"If that happens, the victims advocacy folks will take care of it. All the same, keep your eyes peeled. In case you're the one who needs to blow the whistle again."

"How many of you have active, unencumbered licenses to practice in a mental health field?" Lacey's eyes scanned the group; almost everybody sitting in the pews raised their hands.

"Now, of you folks, who has trauma training and experience?"

About a third of them kept their hands up.

"You with hands still raised—you probably qualify, after a brief training and orientation. The rest of you are welcome to stay and listen if you like."

Attendees gathered up belongings and either filed out or moved forward in the pews.

Sarah moved near Lacey to whisper. "So many, even with the screening out you did."

"They come out of the woodwork, especially after professional organizations do call-downs. It's that tug of the gut, the need to help when things like this happen."

"I felt that myself. Right after the explosion. It was almost like being delusional. The drive to help, how I experienced my abilities. As if I believed I was superhuman. That I could save the entire world, if given the chance. If not for Jerrod, I probably would have darted off with Paulson and everybody else."

"Fortunately for Jerrod, common sense had you hold your ground. Not all resist the call when stepping back would be wiser. They're often the ones who nose-dive. It's why we're so careful to let people know the score. Otherwise they end up counted as casualties."

Anxiety. Excitement. Somber reserve. Eagerness to get started. Anybody could see it, hear it, feel it amidst the murmurings before her: a professional presentation about to begin, an atmosphere Sarah had been part of and at home with on so many other occasions.

She had successfully muddled through that impromptu speech at the FAC. For this one, there'd actually been a chance to prepare. It was for fellow professionals, ones who were about to tend psychological bumps and bruises in the community of her youth. It would be a piece of cake.

Lacey tapped her pen against a water glass. "First, I'd like to give you an idea of what's going on. Sarah here—Sarah Turner, a local psychologist with disaster experience—happened to be at the parade. She also helped with the reception center and FAC. Sarah?"

Sarah stepped up and took stock of her colleagues' steady attentiveness. Anticipatory silence overtook the sanctuary. They were ready. She was in her element. She could recite this material in her sleep.

"Everybody's dealing with it as best they know how. But obviously, this particular experience is both unique and extreme. There are the usual grief reactions for those who lost loved ones. Fresh, and raw. There are people worried about the injured, or about those still unaccounted for. There's fear of more explosions. You may even see people wearing masks because of fears about toxins—only a rumor, thankfully. Nonetheless, I've heard reports of some people refusing to leave home at all. And then..."

It ground to a halt, visions of Paulson's panicky flashbacks temporarily blinding her. It seemed like eons since she'd been in touch with him. Then there was Lil, the horror that had overtaken her as she learned about Sean. Dad, helping those elderly men get out of harm's way. She hadn't seen him since the parade. How was he doing?

Out in the pews participants were studying her with questioning looks. She had paused too long.

"And then." She cleared the rasp from her voice. "Then there are those with trauma symptoms because of injuries they received. Or witnessed. Or just missed being injured themselves."

She gave the point a moment to sink in. Maybe it was really to have a chance to reboot narrative footing. Somehow she wasn't getting this right.

Focus, Sarah.

"There are more anger issues after human-caused disasters, so there's a lot of blaming going on. So far I've heard blame placed on terrorists, in-fighting among soldiers or political camps, anti-war extremists, low-rider modifications by teenagers—and one person was positive it was a high school science project gone awry."

Light tense laughter echoed across the sanctuary.

"Such speculating adds conflict to the equation, fuel to the fire, especially relationship issues. People have difficulty keeping a clear head. For both disaster recovery planning and getting through everyday lives." *Myself included.*

She was speechless again, her thoughts bombarded with alternative realms. What was with these disruptive intrusions?

There was more she should be saying. But everything coming to mind was way too personal. Her tongue felt stiff, glued to the roof of her mouth. She realized her teeth were clenched.

"Thanks, Sarah." Lacey let her off the hook by stepping back to the microphone. She started in on her disaster mental health spiel. It was similar to what she'd done at the flood trainings, but with additional territory: the ins and outs of mass casualty.

Sarah listened from a folding chair behind Lacey, the pounding in her chest slowly becoming less pronounced. The struggle to stay on task was not like her. It didn't make sense.

She refocused on the new recruits. She could practically smell the sweaty absorption rate among them. Everyone was jotting down copious notes. Their learning curve was even steeper than hers had been, at her first disaster. Would they see her as a voice of experience? Somebody to count on, and guide them?

I'm not ready for this.

Lacey's presentation was referring to just that possibility. "Consider where you are in your life, and if this is the right time for you. If not, there will always be another disaster."

Lacey handed her a mammoth stack of materials. She passed them out amidst new murmurings. Halfway down the aisle Sarah staggered, a rush of exhaustion plowing through. She caught herself before she stumbled.

There could be no doubt. She'd reached the bottom of the well, sucked dry by events and emotions. Especially after talking about all those disaster stressors, ones she'd been effectively ignoring, until she and Lacey purposely dredged them up *en masse*.

"Do you still need me?" She returned the leftover handouts to Lacey. "I'd like to have some down time before it gets so late I pass out."

"Go ahead. I've got this covered."

CHAPTER 10

The water rippled in silence against the gentle evening gusts distorting the river's glassy surface. Sarah took a deep breath, savoring its sweet scent. The spread of river was nearly the only feature of the neighborhood still recognizable. The spring floods had wiped out nearly everything else. The very contour of the shoreline had been redrawn. Yet the river still flowed—steady, cold and deep—as it probably would for eternity.

It stirred old memories. Like Dad's lifelong testimonials over how he had built that house. Technically, that was probably accurate. It had actually started out as a two-room shack, inhabited by two starry-eyed newlyweds, for whom it had been nothing less than a castle. As Sam's Body Shop became successful, and his family larger—not to mention the growing recognition of the rickety structure that housed them—he refurbished, added on, updated, rebuilt, or did whatever else necessary to accommodate their growing needs. After forty years of it, the house turned into an indescribable hodgepodge. Regardless, it had been Dad's hodgepodge, and a source of great pride.

The ground she stepped out onto almost rose up to greet her. So familiar, so dear. Begging her to set aside any concerns about her good clothes and once again sit and amuse herself in the sun-warmed gravel. Off to the right was that bend in the road, the one where she'd chalk-drawn endless hopscotch courts, played the occasional game of jacks with Lil. Mom's multi-colored rock garden always kept the ball from being lost over the bank and into the river. Not so now, the rockery washed apart and scattered. A victim of flash flooding, the same as the home of her youth.

It had been well over a month since the last check on the rebuilding project. Dad appeared to have made considerable progress, well ahead of his riverfront neighbors. Others hadn't gotten much further than clearing away debris and toying with the foundation.

Dad had settled on a straightforward prefab structure, which gave him plenty of flexibility for whatever stamp of individuality he decided to add on. Off to one side was a stray pile of lumber bundled with Logan and Son's orangey-red strapping tape. Time would tell whether it would become an oddity or an asset.

"Get it closed up before everything turns to hell in a hand basket," Dad had told her. It looked like they were going to succeed. The roof was on and the windows in. Most of the main structure was swaddled in Tyvak, awaiting siding.

His tomato-red Ford was parked near the front door. She drifted toward the back, sounds of male voices and running construction equipment. As she rounded the corner, his buddy Stewy came into view, sitting on a rumbling Bobcat. He was making a study of the excavation pile that had been sitting near the shoreline for the last couple of months.

The Bobcat made an enthusiastic run at it. Victor, another Saturday night poker colleague, stood at the periphery, stooping over his cane and kibitzing. She knew full well Stewy would ignore everything he said. And if Victor ever noticed he was being ignored, it wouldn't make the least bit of difference in how either of them proceeded.

The whine of a table saw gave away Dad's workstation. He was sheathed in the same blue denim he had labored in forever, clear back to the body shop days. It triggered other early memories: Mom dropping them off at the shop while she chased after her latest whim, Sam delivering pint-sized lectures about bodywork to her marginally interested brother. Climbing around on the considerable collection of salvaged car seats. Curled up and napping by the time Mom got back.

Sam's tool belt hung tilted to the right, overloaded. As his slight, wiry body tended to business in a manner long-practiced, he seemed almost young again, in spite of thinning silvery hair and wisdom lining the creases of those gray-blue eyes. He was working on decking material.

As Sarah neared, she wondered why had he waited so long to start. It was a wonderful place for a deck.

The answer was already there. He had fully engrossed himself in the body shop, his second major source of pride—especially since he lost Mom. The flood got credit for introducing new possibilities. It had also introduced opportunities for rekindling lost relationships—especially theirs.

She hesitated to interrupt his work, entranced by the scene of transition. It would soon be dark. The autumn sun was already close to disappearing behind the feathery skyline that haloed Schwartz Marsh.

Was she really there to check on Dad and see the new house? Or was it to establish what still existed of life as it once was?

Home.

He finally noticed her. He finished what he was doing and secured the equipment, much as he would if there were children around.

"I saw the flowers you left Mom. They're nice."

He nodded at her, his stoic neutrality almost giving in to a smile. "She always was partial to daisies." He took off his tool belt and laid it on the table saw platform. "Come see the inside."

He walked her through the layout. She had little more than entered when she sneezed—sawdust, as usual. She held her scarf to her face while Sam described special touches he planned, where currently there were only studs and floorboard. Its Spartan status did not disguise how remarkably similar it was to the original. Main rooms were situated in about the same places, though fewer spare rooms had been tacked on.

"It'll be plenty enough for a small family someday. You could always add on."

She didn't react to the hint. No reason to get into that old debate. He wanted her to live in Marshland, but her profession required her to be elsewhere. Nothing out in the boondocks was going to support her career goals and interests. Just the same, it was heartening to know he was thinking of her and her future, even as he rebuilt a home for his retirement.

"You had time to visit your mother then. That disaster outfit running out of things for you to do?"

"We were on our way someplace else. Me and Paulson."

"A good sort, that Paulson. Once you get past the peculiar window dressing."

She forced simply smiling and nodding. It was so odd. How Dad approved of someone who oozed misplaced hippie. Especially on top of his utter disapproval of the traditional construction worker she used to date, a conflict that at one point had shattered her relationship with her father.

"You're right, it's been unbelievably busy. It makes the spring flood seem like no big deal."

He gave a questioning glance, bordering on offended.

"Not about what happened to people," she quickly added. "In terms of how wide the impact, the different types of damage. It just keeps getting bigger. It's so complicated, with all the extra agencies and organizations. Especially since we still don't know who did it. Or why. Terrorists? A suicide bomber? Who knows."

"Like the kamikazes, when I was a kid." Sam brushed stray sawdust from a window ledge, and bent over to scoop up a wayward nail. "They thought they were some kind of hero. Had big celebrations before they took off and crashed into whatever it was they aimed to crash into. If the TV reports mean anything, there isn't a vehicle, or body, or anything else lying around that explains what really went on in Willsey yesterday."

She wasn't there to talk shop. Nor was it clear exactly what she was looking for with this visit. But it definitely wasn't that. "I'm glad you decided to rebuild."

"Most of our neighbors are rebuilding, too. I got the better start on it." His eyes twinkled thoughts of competitive advantage.

"So Todd Goode's resort project will have to find some other place to land, then."

"That old fart has his hands full, with that building of his blown to bits."

"Mr. Goode owned that building?" Not really a surprise. Seemed like the man owned half of Willsey and Marshland both.

"It's been sitting there useless for years. When Chet told me which building blew up, my first inclination was that good old Todd took care of the problem with a little help from his no-account associates. And his insurance company."

"How horrible. Would he really risk hurting people that way? I know the real estate world thinks of him as a sleaze ball, but...this?"

He gave it consideration, then shrugged resignation. "Well, no. I suppose not even Todd Goode would go that far. Otherwise, it would be true to color."

"How is it going solo, without Chet?"

"A little better, truth is. Not much I can leave to him that doesn't have to be tended to again afterwards. Vic and Stewy come around when I need an extra set of hands."

"When I heard that Bobcat, I thought for sure it'd be Stewy on Green Gertie."

"No chance." This time he couldn't keep from smiling. "Green Gertie's just an uppity toy. Now don't get me wrong, she's one fine piece of machinery—that's a fact. But Stewy doesn't get the poor thing dirty unless he has to."

They paused at the newly installed kitchen window and watched Stewy and Vic play out their latest installment of male bonding ritual.

"All the same, Stewy couldn't pass on an offer to rearrange things a bit." He grabbed a nearby broom and swept at the sawdust that had fallen from the windowsill. It melded in with the sculpted pile in the corner.

"Miss Chet's company more than his help." The mumbled confession almost disappeared into his collar.

Had she heard it right? He would share something that personal, in a manner he never had before? Not with her.

"I could ask Chet to stop by after his shift, if you like." A filler. On short notice, it was the best she could come up with to build on the unexpected gesture of intimacy.

"He's been here already. Him and that Freddie. He showed Freddie around, the way he does. Freddie's keeping Chet on track, all right. He needs that, you know."

They stepped out the front door to face the roadway, where her vibrant Miata was nestled next to Dad's weather-beaten but well tended pickup.

"One of the things we do in disaster mental health is make sure everybody gets the support they need to succeed, including staff. There's something for everybody. A way to help somehow, even with someone like Chet."

Thus was she compelled to share a few basics about what had been going on over the last few days. Sam nodded at intervals. It was substantially foreign territory, as compared to his practical day-to-day world. But he was listening. Really listening.

"Jane always knew." He looked across the way. For an instant his gaze rested on Chet's dumpy homestead, still the two-room shack of the era of her parents' original residence. His gaze swept further, into the red and yellow hills beyond. "She knew you could do something like this."

Her throat tightened at what had just passed as a compliment. At least as good a one as her father was likely to come up with on the topic of her career.

"Thanks, Dad." She blinked back tears.

"Aw, honey." He gathered her up.

She relaxed against her Daddy. Tears flowed with neither resistance nor shame. The scents of builder and Old Spice smoothed out the edges.

He drew away. "I miss her too."

Dampness pooled in his eyes. Eyes so similar to her own. Almost like looking in a mirror.

*****

The ground jarring him was unmerciful. Paulson corrected and re-corrected, the bike flinging him from side to side on the uneven terrain.

It was well past dark. He'd stayed out too late. The eerie glow of a harvest moon brightening so many intriguing corners of landscape was too seductive to resist.

Especially after the conversation with the boss.

The distraction was a godsend—the pummeling winds, the dank scent of showers in the near future. Foregoing the helmet would have been even better, and letting the wind whip through his hair. The chill had delivered second thoughts.

Besides, it would violate a concession made during an argument with Sarah. She was a hard woman to please. It was best to take advantage of anything resembling common ground. Especially now that he was feeling a little more with it, fortified by a successful day of preparing to get at disaster needs.

On the other hand, conversations with the boss were becoming more and more like those *Peanuts* holiday specials Sarah liked, where adult voices consisted of a muted trumpet's wandering clamor. Her words had said to support the disaster relief effort. The undertones suggested otherwise, that clinic responsibilities were first priority. *Wah, wah, wa-*

wah.

He turned into the complex and left the mud-spackled bike nosed onto the bark dust. It wasn't an officially designated parking space, but nobody said anything about it. During the early days in Marshland it had been tucked away in the garage, a habit following along from life in a quasi-war zone district in Detroit. These days, security didn't get a second thought.

He creaked open the screen door then paused. Was that the downshift of Sarah's Miata in the distance? Or just wishful thinking? Less than thirty seconds later, her car was parked in front of him. Sarah climbed out. He stood looking at her, both of them wordless. She never turned up to see him, unless he arranged for it himself. Yet here she was.

"I was visiting Dad's house building project. I haven't had dinner."

"I'm pretty sure my cupboard is bare, unfortunately."

"I was thinking along the lines of Shelley's."

The diner seemed well attended for so late on a Sunday. Customers appeared to be sharing coffee and conversation more than taking advantage of Shelley's renowned home-cooked cuisine. The tension throughout felt like a rerun of what was supposed to have been left behind, back at the hospital.

Even here, in Marshland. Nobody wants to be home alone with their thoughts. At least people were connecting. This is good.

"Anything new about Sean?" Sarah asked Shelley, who was setting down two steaming plates of turkey and gravy.

"Unconscious. They told Lil he's probably out of the woods, though."

A recital of Sean's medical status proceeded while the aroma of the comfort food called up at him. Finally he stopped waiting on ceremony and dug in, before he started drooling into it.

"How are things at the FAC?" he got out between mouthfuls.

"Moving along. We were unbelievably shorthanded. I've never been so professionally overwhelmed. Not just the volume. The level of distress, too."

"I'm sure you handled it like a pro." He took care with the words, making sure his approval and support would not pass unnoticed.

"I had my doubts. My visit with Dad was...good."

The brightness of the dime store candelabra-ettes played up puffiness around her eyes. It had not been noticeable in the shadows of his front porch. Recent tears had been shed. "What resonated?"

"He's never said anything about being proud of me, about my career path. We were always at odds when I was a teenager. Around the time I finished school and was...well, more adult, Mom died. Another monkey wrench. Dad and I talked about it a little."

She hesitated, her lip quivering. "When I questioned whether I should stay with the operation, he really got his back up about it. He practically ordered me to 'get back in there and give 'em hell.'" She brushed away beginnings of the tears she'd failed to avoid. "It'll be a while before I have that kind of confidence. I was touched that...he was so sure I could do it."

"That's Sam." He nodded. "What I'd expect. Of him, and others of his generation, with something like this."

"How do you mean?"

"The John Wayne approach to conflict and adversity. Go in there and shoot 'em up. Save the world, then ride off into the sunset."

She stopped buttering her roll. "I'm not so sure I agree. There's more to it than that."

"I know. I've been following this ever since the twin towers."

"You were involved with disaster clear back then?"

"Indirectly. A colleague went to Ground Zero. I covered his VA group. Seeing how that incident affected those Vietnam vets, everything it dredged up—it piqued my interest. I've tried to stay up to date with 9/11 trauma ever since."

"So what's this got to do with my father?" She finished blowing at a forkful of mashed potatoes and took a tentative mouthful.

"Long story. That was a lost opportunity, what happened after 9/11. It was a chance for us to pull together. Like everybody did during World War II. Men going off as heroes, lying about their ages. The women back home, the 'Rosie the Riveters.' Victory gardens replaced front lawns. Rationing, and voluntary sacrifices. Everybody making do for the overall good."

"The Greatest Generation, they called themselves." Sarah smiled. "It's easy to see why they thought of themselves that way."

"Unfortunately, the Greatest Generation destroyed that mentality for the rest of us."

Her gaze finally rose to meet his, curiosity replacing her usual approach to making food disappear. "Destroyed it for us? How?"

It was all he could do to keep from rubbing his hands together. At last, a way to hold her interest, even if it was only an ivory tower spiel. She'd be absolutely dazzled by his knowledge and insight.

"Their cohort also promoted certain macho cultural lore." He urged himself further into academic stance. "It helped them deal with fears of the times, the traumas they endured. You see it all the time in the movies and TV shows from back then."

"In what way?"

"Like John Wayne, or Humphrey Bogart characters. These guys took over the screen. They became the most commonly valued standard for dealing with crisis. Later, it was Superman and other superheroes. Dirty Harry and Rambo types moved in, and a long list of others who burst in to save the day—usually all by themselves, and fully in charge. Along with lots of violence and other disregard for socialized norms."

"You think that made a big difference somehow?" She didn't look convinced.

"Rewriting what a hero is or does in our society gave World War II survivors a sense of vicarious control. Of course, upping sense of control helps with managing stress and fears. Later generations grew up in the middle of this. Self-sufficient macho-ism became an unavoidable icon of our cultural worldview."

"So what's this got to do with Dad?" She looked puzzled, even perturbed, rather than impressed.

He was screwing it up somehow. He raked around in the green beans for a different angle.

"The Greatest Generation pulled it off because they had a leader like FDR. There was 'nothing to fear but fear itself.' His fireside chats told people to focus on home, friends, and family during crisis. Critical survival wisdom we've only recently come full circle in appreciating. We didn't have that during 9/11. Those in charge had grown up in the shadow of that 'hunt 'em down and shoot 'em up' approach to adversity.

"So, instead, we scoured the globe for people to blame, or screwed-up situations to try to take control of. Like those lost cause wars in the Middle East. Our two main political parties ramped themselves up, one against the other, with their 'now listen, and listen tight' rhetoric. Neither side listening, of course. D.C. turned into a dysfunctional wasteland. Hate crimes entered a whole new realm—anybody who looks Muslim, or has ambiguous racial leanings. Did you know Damien got banished to the call center because of the color of his skin? That they were afraid he was a target?"

"Damien? Not Damien Logan."

"Even these crazy mass shootings, suicide bombings. Conspiracy theories about stuff in the past. They all take control of fears with the same misplaced coping—trying to be that one person against the world. A hero or martyr to some ideology. Playing the big man and acting out, instead of finding strength and solutions in community and family. Connectedness to fellow human beings. Assets that advanced the human race for thousands of years." He paused for a breath.

Sarah had a slightly expectant look about her, as if barely able to track the aimless monologue it was beginning to feel like. She slowly finished chewing a piece of turkey. "So you're saying the Greatest Generation, including my Dad, set us up to fail? That the 9/11 emotional aftermath, the incomplete healing, is their fault?"

"No, no. They weren't trying to hurt anybody. What I'm saying is that certain cultural ideals helped their generation cope with the fears of their times, as best they knew how. But ironically these very same strategies got in the way of our healing in the here and now."

Sarah set down her fork and stared at him. Unreadable.

Still not working. There had to be something, some kind of supportive data she might connect with.

"Look what went on in their childrearing beliefs. Parents back then were told that children were some kind of 'blank slate.' That they could control who or what their children became. It ignores nature plus nurture wisdom that guided pretty much every other generation before or since."

She looked frozen. Locked up, in an intense silence.

"Then...then look at what happens to relationships. That kind of macho mindset wrecks relationships that would otherwise help people cope or manage. They're so busy driving others away with ideologies, they don't see how their 'John Wayne-ism' destroys real opportunities to fix things. The end result is that America has not healed from 9/11. Not by a long shot."

Sarah wadded up her napkin and slapped it on top of what was left of her supper. Her eyes were hardened into dark, glistening marbles.

"You're way out of line. That doesn't describe Dad at all."

"I didn't mean it like that. I was just saying..."

"Maybe you should take a long hard look at your own mindset, Paulson. Isn't what you just described exactly what *you've* done here in Marshland? You putt-putted your way into town on that claptrap motorcycle. Practically dressing in costume, rather than a way anybody around here would ever relate to. You go all over town like some kind of *Kung Fu* wanderer, trying to turn everybody into whatever you think makes for better functioning."

"Now wait a minute. What I've been doing has been a big help. Until I came..."

"Exactly. I, I, me, me. The big man comes in and saves everybody. You sit there and do battle against anything 'establishment' that might help things along. All so you can stay wrapped up in your own private agenda."

Words failed to come to the rescue. Where was it all coming from? Did he really appear that self-serving?

"How do you explain why we've been so shorthanded for this operation? Lacey promised us that local DMH assets would likely double, even triple, after the floods. She said big disasters bring in lots of providers who stick with it. Instead, the new people disappeared over the summer, along with everybody else who was doing this before you got here.

"You, on the other hand, are always front and center during disaster. Paulson presenting at the community meeting. Paulson going door to door in the flood zone. Paulson giving interviews. Paulson in front of the camera. Paulson accepting a community service award. Paulson snapping up every possible hot shot call. Paulson, Paulson. I seriously doubt that's what your director had in mind when she made you responsible for the region's DMH issues."

"I...live...here." He emphasized each utterance. "The disaster staff knows I'll make myself available. Why wouldn't I?"

"Why wouldn't you give anybody else around here encouragement? Just say 'no' to the chapter, and mentor others into channeling their enthusiasm. Hook them up. Or tell organizations to give their awards to newbies, so they know they're appreciated. That's what they're really meant for. But, no. You didn't delegate a thing. You never lead any professional trainings. No plan building, no relationship building. Nothing that would pull together a team. Not even collaboration meetings with other agencies."

"I have a finger into most of them already. Why would I need meetings?"

"So the agencies and organizations can work together effectively. So we know what the others are doing. So people know what to do if phones are down when something big happens. So survivors actually get services. Need I say more?"

"Relax, Sarah. There's lots of experienced staff coming in. Besides, Lacey just oriented a whole new crew. By tomorrow we'll be crawling with..."

"If you'd thought more like FDR and less about being 'the big man' we wouldn't have been stretched so thin at the reception center, and the FAC. Not to mention at the explosion site, and the hospital, and everyplace else victims piled up afterwards. The mental health community could have moved in together as a unit, and made a huge difference."

There was no escape route from this escalating fury. He was trapped, groundless somehow. Other than the intense glare holding him captive.

"You know, the victims advocates didn't have any idea what we had or what we were doing. Until Lacey got here and sorted it out."

Realization stirred in his gut. Was she onto something?

"People went without." She paused, as if doing everything she could to contain herself. "Now they're scattering." The tirade went on, increasingly animated.

His ears began to buzz, like they had after the explosion. Only this time, the hum was fighting the sting of an assault that Sarah apparently thought he deserved.

"We no longer have a solid handle on who was or wasn't at that parade, with the beginning phases over," she went on. "From this point forward, finding them will be all uphill. Almost all we'll have is self-referral. You know as well as anybody how inadequate that is. We needed to strike while the iron was hot. Now it's too late. How many people will end up with PTSD? Major depression, or some other debilitating condition? All because Paulson Forbes has personal issues with things in society that he can't dictate or control."

Was she right? Was his hiatus into Marshland for the last few years—Paulson 'saving the world'—really nothing more than his way of saving himself? And now the community he held so dear was paying the price. At a time they could least afford it.

He dashed a sweaty hand through the tangle of hair in his eyes, grasping for clarity.

"By the way—about Dad. By the time he was your age, he'd created a successful business from scratch, built most of his house by himself and was raising a family. If you were anything like my Dad, maybe your own worldview wouldn't be so messed up."

"Sarah, I'm sorry. Really. I never thought that..."

She was already up, then gone. He stared down at lukewarm vegetables and congealing mud-brown gravy. His appetite had vanished.

Everything had turned inside out. A simple philosophical conversation, that's all it was. Wasn't it? But it had instead provoked Sarah into a rage.

She may well be right. Whatever this "agenda" was may have just destroyed a relationship. At a time when he needed her, leaned against the hope of having her, more than ever.

Other diners were still glancing his way, no doubt wondering about Sarah's abrupt exit. How much longer would there be anything left of him for their needs, the hurting in this community? How much longer before he ran dry?

Did he still even care?

CHAPTER 11

Monday, October 28th

"Who cares if he's 'stable'? What good is that? He's not even conscious. I want them to tell me he's awake. I want to hear his voice. I want my Sean back."

Lil looked so lost and alone. It was like their summer camp days. Sarah had always come prepared with a favorite book for down times. Lil, typically unprepared, would stew and fidget while they waited for whatever came next. Or fall into aimless verbosity while Sarah pretended to listen. Currently Lil seemed to be coping by means of both, vacillating between empty chatter and withdrawn silence.

But there was no camp schedule to move things forward. And the final outcome of Sean's injuries was an unknown.

"I don't know what I'd do if Jeri Lynn wasn't here." Lil told Sarah, as she pointed her thumb at an anxious woman hovering over another unconscious young man, Sean's roommate. "I'd just sit here and go crazy, listening to all these clicks and beeps by myself."

The small room was probably intended for one occupant. Both patients were hooked up to a forest of gadgetry. Sean was monitored by an assembly of mobile units, crowded around the head of a bed so narrow it looked more like a gurney. Perhaps it was. Both patients were pale, heavily bandaged, and motionless. At least as compared to his gray-complexioned roommate, Sean didn't look that bad.

It was disconcerting to see him so still, nothing like the lively character she knew him to be. Usually when hanging out with the Whites, it was difficult to get a word in edgewise. What to say or do with both of them silenced—one overwhelmed by her circumstances, the other having no choice in the matter—was a mystery.

"Your cats are doing fine."

No reaction.

"I saw Jerrod at his grandma's last night. He's the perfect infant."

Lil nodded, staring at the floor. She rubbed at her nose and sniffed.

"What's that?" Jeri Lynn stilled, scrutinizing both sets of monitors. "Something's off."

Sarah noticed it, too. The collective background murmur continued with its soft droning. But something was definitely different.

Light dinging started in—soft, but having the impact of tossing a lit firecracker into the room.

"Sean!" Lil fell across the bed and grabbed at his limp shoulders. "Are you all right?"

Sarah's eyes darted back and forth between the prattling sets of monitors. By moving away from Lil's cries, it was possible to make out that the alerts were coming from the roommate's hook-ups. He did look lifeless. But then, that was how he had looked when she'd first gotten there.

"Where is everybody?" Jeri Lynn flailed in place. "Somebody do something!"

Lil's paralyzed disbelief was as ineffectual as Jeri Lynn's agitated distress.

Whatever happened next was on her. Sarah stuck her head into the hall. In the distance there were visitors standing around. Not a staff member in sight. She clawed along the side of the bed, looking for a call button. Before she could get to it, an unannounced trio burst in, followed by a crash cart.

"I have to ask you all to step out." The nurse rattled the tacky mustard-colored curtain along the track between the beds.

Not being able to see the frantic activity behind the imposed barrier made it all the more alarming. Sarah and Lil moved into the hall.

Jeri Lynn was less cooperative. "I'm not going anywhere. Oh my God. Oh my God."

An aid appeared. "Come on. You'll just be underfoot. They need all the space they can get if they're going to help your husband."

They escorted the frantic young woman out of the room. From the waiting area, they heard occasional abrupt noises or excited voices of staff entering or leaving the far end of the hall.

Sarah took a deep breath. Situations like this happened all the time at work. It had never happened in a way that involved her personal life. It provided perspective, if nothing else.

Was it really so crowded in this facility that there was no place they could wait without being so exposed to the charged atmosphere of the rescue efforts? It was so inept. Unacceptable. The professionals who were supposed to be handling this were becoming as annoying as whatever perpetrator had caused the tragedy in the first place.

It was a distraction. It kept her off her game. Just like everything everywhere else, here was that same aggravating story—hospital staff overwhelmed by disaster, instead of being sufficiently prepared for the big emergencies.

She took another deep breath and refocused.

Yes, the scenario wasn't that different from her day job. She could do it here, too. Even it was with friends, rather than strangers. Perhaps especially so.

She draped a careful arm over each of the women. Joining them— the simple acts of touch and compassionate giving—did the trick, activating that magical transformation: her professional self, unbridling hard-wired inner fortitude that could take off by itself.

Eventually, activity at the end of the hall let up. An ominous silence set in. Minutes passed, seeming longer. When somebody finally opened the door, a sterile whine pierced the hush. After a couple of sharp voices, it ceased as well.

"No." Jeri Lynn backed away. "This can't be happening."

A nurse escorted her away.

Without Jeri Lynn to cling to, Lil's emotional rollercoaster derailed off the deep end. "What if that was Sean? What if it happens to Sean?"

Sarah wrapped both arms around her as Lil continued to shake. "Sean isn't anywhere near so bad off. We have lots of reason for hope."

"Mrs. White?" A balding, middle-aged man in standard office

casual held up some official-looking identification. "FBI" stood out in solid block letters. "I'd like to speak with your husband. That's him, down there?"

"He's unconscious. Is there something wrong?"

"I'd like a word with him when he wakes. You, too. In private."

"Who, me?" Confusion interrupted the attention Lil was giving to what was left of her makeup. She abandoned the half-baked effort and edged closer to Sarah.

"In private, if you don't mind," he repeated.

Her grasp on Sarah's arm tightened. "Not by myself. Sarah, too. She's a counselor. My counselor. I want her to come, too."

"Does this have to happen now? She's just had a horrible experience."

"Will she recover any faster if she's anticipating an interview with the authorities? Perhaps it would be best if we just get it over with." Give her something else to think about, his eyes added.

"I'm okay with it. As long as Sarah comes with."

They filed into a glorified closet lined with ancient file cabinets and overstuffed shelving. Lil and the agent sat in two lone chairs accompanying a small wooden table shoved up against the rear wall.

"Wait." Sarah squeezed in to stand behind Lil, her hands by necessity resting on Lil's shoulders. "This is about how Sean got hurt by the explosion, right?"

"Yes, ma'am. That's part of it."

"Shouldn't there be a victims' advocate here?" Lil could use that. To be honest, so could she. John had been so solid at the FAC, helping people understand their rights and protecting their best interests. Having him around would be reassuring.

"We'll get Mrs. White that kind of support as soon as someone frees up," said the agent. "I'll arrange the referral myself."

So John's colleagues were still stretched thin.

"Mrs. White, do you know where your car is right now?"

"Wherever Sean left it at the parade. What's wrong? Is it someplace illegal?"

"I can take care of it, if there's a problem," said Sarah.

"It's under control. I'm sorry to tell you that your car was damaged by the explosion."

KEEPERS SAVING THE WORLD

Lil's shoulders stiffened.

"In fact, it's in pieces," he continued. "It took a while to identify whose it was."

"Our ol' beat-up Accord? Why would anyone blow that up?"

Multiple ramifications caught up. "Someone was trying to hurt Sean?" She winced. Those poorly thought-out words were a mistake.

Lil's comprehending outrage spewed like a volcanic event. "Why would anybody do such a thing? Everybody loves Sean. Someone almost blew up my husband? And me? And my little Jerrod?"

"No, ma'am. The car was in the wrong place at the wrong time, apparently very near the epicenter of the blast. We can't give out many details right now. I'd appreciate anything you can tell me about that day."

Lil plopped her head into her palms, as if it had become too unwieldy to stay up on its own. "So he went ahead and parked there anyway."

"Where, ma'am?"

"In front of that old bank. The one that got blown to smithereens."

"What happened, Mrs. White?"

"Some of the parking spots were blocked off. Sean wanted to park right next to them. There wasn't quite enough room, so he got out and scooted a couple barricades over. Just a little ways, no big deal. Some do-gooders came along and shooed him off. Sean argued with one of them for a while. Finally, he let me and Jerrod out and went looking for a place by himself."

The agent jotted a few quick notes. "Who were these people? Did you get a good look? Were they parade staff?"

"I don't have a clue. They were on his side of the car. I hardly saw them. I just heard them arguing. Especially this one guy. Wasn't anybody I knew. They were pretty darned snarky, if you ask me."

Lil continued to share details of what little she'd heard of the argument between Sean and the mystery people. Recounting the episode did seem to be bringing her back to life.

Likewise, puzzle pieces fell into place—how it had come to pass that Paulson found Sean, injured, so near the site of the blast. It may well have been just as Lil figured. Sean must have parked there after the people left. Barely missed being "blown to smithereens" himself.

Had Paulson seen anything? He had passed right through that area during his search for cotton candy, no more than fifteen minutes before the explosion. If it had happened any sooner...

Why hadn't that occurred to her before now? Experiencing that kind of close call was a trauma exposure in and of itself, on top of everything else Paulson had been through.

Sarah winced again. She, too, had blown up at him, figuratively. How could she? At a man recovering from multiple blows. If only he hadn't said those things about her dad.

If...that was what he really was trying to say.

*****

Chet waddled up to Lacey's table, fiddling with some kind of stuffed toy.

"Look at what we just got." He handed it to Lacey. "Boxes and boxes of them."

"I don't remember ordering these." She turned the toy from side to side, misgivings chipping away at her usual administrative blandness.

"They're donated. Got us enough for every kid in Willsey and Marshland both."

Paulson stood next to Lacey. Interest in the toys fell somewhere between minimal and nonexistent. He had awoken dangling at the edge of the gaping crevasse Sarah had carved into his soul. Morning at headquarters seemed like a sideshow, some kind of halfway choreographed street performance, rather than a tactical powerhouse.

Nor did it feel like he was a relevant player.

Freddie also stood nearby, muttering to himself. "Dang mental health. Ain't a lick of sense in the bunch. Ordering stuff that takes up half the warehouse. Where are we supposed to put everything else?"

Lacey momentarily glanced at the responder who held such obvious disdain for members of their profession. Her lack of any other reaction spoke volumes. Especially since Paulson was barely holding in check a few choice comments.

"This one's not on me." Lacey returned the toy to Chet. "I've never seen these things before. I certainly didn't order them."

Paulson moved in for a better look.

It had to be the scariest toy clown in creation. The body of the doll was okay: ruffles, white polka dots on light blue, oversized shoes, ruffled collar, buttons in the right places. However, the light-bulb shaped head could be called nothing other than grotesque. The lips peeled back into an unnatural grin, the space between them painted black, giving the impression of toothlessness. The pale eyes were large and wide, green-tinted ivory, dotted with tiny pupils. The bizarre skull was covered with fuzzy green and orange hair that had an Einstein shape to it. However, its overall expression passed more for mentally vacant, startled or comatose. Kind of like something from *Invasion of the Body Snatchers.*

"I'd never give this to a child." Lacey sounded equally flabbergasted. "Especially one who's traumatized. I'm going to have nightmares myself already, let alone what it would be like to catch sight of it in my bedroom in the middle of the night."

Paulson agreed.

"It's just a toy, Lacey." Chet tossed it in the air and caught it. "Kids could have lots of fun with this. They're from Taiwan, says this here label."

"How on God's green earth did they end up here?"

"I bet they came on a container ship." Chet nodded to himself, engaged to the hilt. "It would take one of them giant container boxes, we got so many."

"If you didn't order them, I don't know where they came from," said Freddie. "What do we tell the boss?"

"Tell him...forget it. I'll handle it myself. I need to make sure these things never see the light of day." She turned to Paulson. "Good. You're here. Sit on the phone while I go take care of this."

He dropped into her chair and stared at the hard line, feeling as vacant as the toy clown.

Freddie continued to grumble. "Ought to send them to the D.C. office. Bet you anything they've got something to do with it."

"What're you doing here, Paulson?" said Chet. "You're supposed to be at the call center."

"Picking up staff. The phone lines are getting..."

Chet had stopped listening, his eyes riveted to the main entry. "Well, I'll be. If that ain't Sam Elliott, I'll eat this here clown."

"I hope you got a fork and knife and plenty of salsa," said Freddie. "I brought that feller in from the airport. His name's not Sam Elliott."

The new arrival did resemble an escapee from a Hollywood Western set. He set down a leather valise, an older style of baggage that looked like it had been through considerable action. As he straightened, Paulson saw a buckskin jacket, complete with fringe, blue denim shirt and shoestring tie. Cowboy boots. Topped off with a Stetson, which at the moment he was tipping at a worker attempting to steal a closer look. She backed off, startled, only to stumble over his luggage.

As the cowboy turned to help her up, Chet's confusion with the man from the big screen explained itself. He could win any look-alike contest, hands down. Trademark Western facial hair, the right coloring. Even at a distance, it was possible to detect a sparkle to those warm brown eyes—a hint of mischief.

Chet had on his *Willy Wonka* look of fascination. "You know, I think I know who that really is."

The new arrival finished reassuring the increasingly flustered worker then glanced up at the sign over the DMH table. Easy confident strides brought him to their group. A man who always knew what he was doing, but would take care not to flaunt it. A man's man.

"You must be the cowboy psychologist." Chet elbowed Freddie and beamed, enamored with the brilliance of his deductions.

Freddie slapped a palm at his forehead. "It could only be mental health."

"Pleased to make your acquaintance." The newcomer brought Chet's enthusiastic handshake under control. "Horace Blake."

"Chet Slater. This here's Paulson Forbes. He does counseling over in Marshland. That's where we're from."

Paulson stood. A warm presence passed through the touch of his new colleague's grasp, a comfortable grip. But as solid as the Rock of Gibraltar.

Chet continued to make the most of his roll. "That's mighty nice of you to think about helping out cowboys. I never heard of such a thing."

"We all got our own private firestorms," said Horace. "Don't make no difference who we are or what we do for a living."

"Back home, when them cowboys got all het up, we'd just hose them down."

"Whatever quenches the fire, I suppose."

Horace fell right in step with Chet's uncensored meanderings. Such detours usually left Paulson wanting to check the time and come up with an excuse to exit, stage right. But this guy was unflappable.

"Horace." Lacey was back—and delightedly lost in the vision of this imitation Marlboro Man. A bright crimson flush crept its way up from beneath her paisley-patterned turtleneck.

Horace snatched her off her feet and spun her around, hugging her firmly, and planting an aggrandized kiss on her cheek. Lacey's cultivation vanished as she held on tight and laughed like a schoolgirl. Curious looks drifted their way.

"Real nice to see you again, Boss Lady." He gently set her down.

"You too, Horace." She smoothed her rumpled vest and patted her middle-aged salt and pepper back into place. "Thanks for coming so quickly. Now, let's pretend we're professionals. I can hear the rumor mill cranking up as we speak. Have you and Paulson met?"

"Yes, we met." Though it was more entertaining to toy with the notion that Horace might have a horse tied up in the church parking lot, instead of a rental car. With a saddle for two, to accommodate Lacey.

"Paulson's running staff mental health at the call center." Lacey pointed at a flow chart blue-taped to the wall next to them. She had filled in names under some of the service delivery sites and position labels.

A yellow sticky with Sarah's name on it jumped out at him. *Don't go there.*

"Horace and I worked an airline disaster together," said Lacey. "When it comes to supporting fellow professionals, he's top drawer. I'm giving him oversight of staff mental health. You'll work together closely."

"I appreciate the help." Though he really didn't. There was no way around being diplomatic about it, even if the additional supervisory layer could only be a nuisance. But he could swear Horace had seen right through his careful delivery.

"The honor's all mine. I welcome the opportunity." Horace entered his name and contact information into Lacey's registry, every motion steady and confident.

"Paulson's a local. Probably the most experienced DMH professional in this region."

Paulson cringed. The commendation only served to stir up another replay of Sarah's tongue-lashing. *Get a grip.*

"You know these folks then," said Horace. "That gives us outsiders a leg up."

"Not to change the subject, but what did you find out about these?" Paulson picked up the clown toy sitting on Lacey's desk, then released it as if it had stung him. "These things are just plain creepy. We aren't really going to have to give them out, are we?"

"No. Turns out a supervisor new to logistics accepted them sight unseen. Sometimes companies use disasters to unload unsalable stock. They get it out of their warehouses, and get a tax break for donating it to charity."

"Really." How lame.

"Sometimes it works out. We can use what they send and everybody wins. As far as these things go..." Her musings appeared to have pained her into a loss for words.

"What will happen with them then?"

"It's the logistics manager's problem. B ut get ready to catch some flack. Especially if any of them find their way into circulation."

"Won't hurt anyone to play along with this." Horace's eyes lit up, as if a private joke were already afoot. "Might even be a little fun to be had."

CHAPTER 12

The main lot was packed. The overflow area on a nearby field seemed the less treacherous option for stashing the Miata.

Even from here, the line of disaster clients spilling out onto the sidewalk was easily visible. After picking through wheat stubble and a dash across the highway, the security personnel, metal detectors, and x-ray stations came into view; so did the tenseness, impatience, and general confusion among those who had gathered. Sarah merged in with the masses and settled in for a long wait. Until a hand touched her arm.

"There's a side door." It was one of the guards who had been milling around. "For staff only."

A shabbily dressed man near the end of the line dropped his cigarette and ground it out with his heel. His pocked jowls betrayed what must have been an excruciatingly painful adolescence of cystic acne. He glared at her disaster vest, and the security guard.

"Figures." Steely gray eyes bored into hers. Whatever thoughts lay behind those orbs were chilling.

Before she could consider the angry man further, the guard hurried her to an alternate entry. There security staff were messing around with handheld detectors, sniffing dogs and who knows what else as they assessed incoming crates of ripe-smelling bananas. After enduring one round of having her person scanned, she waited yet again for a matronly type to free up, who proceeded to test her shoulder bag's contents for gunpowder residue. Then her shoes.

It was unnerving. Everybody looked so serious. She would have liked to ask questions. But what if protocol for excessive inquisitiveness was a spontaneous strip search? The level of scrutiny so far felt like she'd already been through one.

"*Give 'em hell, Sarah.*" Dad's confident words.

You bet, Dad. Cleared at last, she edged into the converted banquet hall, more cautious than confident.

FAC functioning had clicked into solvency. The opposite end of the room contained several rows of nicely padded folding chairs and a well-stocked canteen, including several lounge-height tables and barstools. The area appeared to be standing room only.

Clients finished with security were directed to queues leading up to registration tables. At the head of these lines, they received instruction and were escorted elsewhere. Ultimately they appeared to be dealt out to wherever the various agencies had partitioned off private territory—by means of curtains, portable cubby walls, or basic furnishings.

Organized chaos.

Much of the room was commandeered by the military, disproportionately more than the number of visitors in uniform. She worked her way toward Delores. Their table was shoved even further back than it had been the day before.

"I feel like I've walked into boot camp registration." Sarah threw her coat over a chair. "What's with all the military? Don't they usually handle things in their own system?"

"The mix of veterans, active military, civilians, and family members got confusing. Even for administration. Who qualifies, and for what services, and who from? Military or civilian? Personal EAP's or disaster-related resources? Who should facilitate it—FEMA, Public Health, NTSB, DOJ, DOD—what? We still don't know for sure what caused that explosion. Until that gets sorted out, everybody starts by signing up here."

The supposed explanation was just so much alphabet soup. "I never dreamed there would be this many people affected."

"On the news they said fifty-seven deaths." Delores hesitated, apparently still absorbing it herself. "Probably to rise with all the criticals. Hundreds of known injuries. A kazillion friends and family members affected one way or another. Not just by the blast. People also got pushed down or trampled. Probably lots of minor injuries we never find out about. Who knows how many psychological injuries."

"Body counts." Images from the first part of the morning stirred; she shook them off. The insensitivity of media tracking certainly was alive and well. "Virtual rubbernecking. Or a page out of the Vietnam story. Did they decide the veterans were the intended target?"

"Nobody's saying. Everybody's guessing. Here, sign in." Delores opened the staff registry and slid it over.

Sarah added her entry beneath an impressive listing of fellow mental health workers. "Good grief. All these people are in here right now?"

"We're using every last one. Some are in the lobby. There are a few outside, too, working the lines. Patience is getting thin out there."

"I noticed." That complete stranger's reaction to her disaster vest had materialized without a hint of warning. Perhaps only a taste of things to come.

Delores appeared to pick up on her ambivalence. "We're in luck, though. There are newcomers here who worked The Pier the same time I did." She pointed out specific individuals dotting the crowd. "They're seasoned veterans of mass casualty. They'll be more useful to you than me."

That at least was a relief. Her own paltry level of expertise was not going to be so critical as conjectured while counting forget-me-nots on the motel curtain during the wee hours. Strange, but it was also a bit of a letdown. Something to analyze when she got a chance.

"Welcome back." John squeezed through the cramped accommodations. "Nice to see a familiar face. Sarah, right?"

"Yes. Good to see you again." Knowing John was still reliably available was a comfort. He seemed to know his way around, and was always generous in sharing what he knew. Not wrapped up in his own agenda. As it so often seemed with Paulson.

"Looks like the place has been taken over, doesn't it."

"You mean all the national staff." Delores stood and flipped her hair behind her. "We won't be strangers for long. Trust me."

"A lot has changed here since yesterday." Sarah tried to dredge up what Lacey's presentation had said about how she was supposed to fit in. Between the level of activity going on around them and its lack of familiarity, tying it all together was no easy task. Especially while actively avoiding return visits to reminders of her nosedive the previous evening.

"Are you still in charge?" she asked John.

"FBI, yes. Me, personally, no. Somebody from back East is here for that."

"So, what are you doing?" Besides hanging around in someone else's station. Again.

"I'm supporting one of the registration desks. We lost the mental health worker I was paired with. A crisis of some sort. I hit up Public Health for a replacement, but they're tapped out. They suggested I go begging here."

"Looks like you're on, Sarah." Delores printed her name onto a sticky yellow and added it to the cascade of post-its flowing from the wall chart.

*****

It was the biggest blunder of his life. So far, anyway. Would Sarah ever even speak to him again?

Paulson's newly delivered carload of personnel was clustered around their supervisor and receiving instruction. Earlier arrivals already manned the phones that had turned up in his absence, passing out advice or solace. Others were spending their downtime familiarizing themselves with resource listings.

The appalling stories they would hear; the nightmares they would be exposed to, re-exposed to. He was supposed to help them stay sane. Did he really understand how it would affect them? How they would feel? What they would need?

And would he be any better at this than at preparing their community for catastrophe? Especially now, with imagined shadows still floating around. Though not as often, thankfully.

"Seems like most of the incoming calls are the media." Damien appeared at his side, thumbing through a collection of faxes. "Everybody wants to be first to get out the news."

"Good morning." He gave Damien a second look, prompted by a preliminary impression of glazed exhaustion. "You look like you've been through the wringer already, dude."

Damien said nothing.

Radar clicked into gear—rising, turning, beeping. "Where's my station? For staff mental health." Mundane territory would be the quickest route to whatever was eating at Damien.

He led him across the warehouse to a back corner, well away from the phone bank operations. A curtain arrangement blocked off a secluded area. A collapsed card table leaned against a stack of grungy white patio chairs. Rolled up nearby was a tattered area rug. They worked together in silence, spreading out the carpet and arranging the meager furnishings.

So this was where he would be spending his days. Banished from the main activity, even within the confines of the call center. It was just as well. The thought of hiding out in a far corner had some appeal to it. "I suppose this will work. Privacy."

"Sorry about the chintzy table and chairs. I gave any nice stuff to phone bank workers. They'll be earning it. These things here are leftovers from last spring's warehouse operation. I'm making do with whatever myself. Get a load of this."

The warehouse's lone closed-off room was a small windowed office to the rear, in the corner opposite Paulson's station. Inside, emptied crates had been stacked to mimic a wrap-around desk configuration. Somebody had stuck a ragged sign over the door. Scrawled across it in black felt marker was "The Buck Stops Here."

"Got to give the set-up crew an 'A' for effort," Paulson muttered, as he circled the crate arrangement and checked out the creativity.

"The classy donated furniture ended up at the FAC."

"You know how it is. The FAC is visible. Cameras will be rolling. Everybody's worried about looking like they're doing good. Getting it right."

"You know as well as I do that it won't be long before they find plenty to criticize, no matter how well everybody does."

"That's a bit pessimistic so early in the game, isn't it?" He gave Damien's shoulder a playful shove, and braced himself for the return punch.

Damien's hands didn't even leave his pockets. "I got a phone call today. One of the first ones after they came on line." He paused. "I need to decide whether I'm going to stay with this."

Radar blipped louder. Damien the Diehard Disaster Junkie? It would take something extraordinary to pry him loose from a local mass casualty operation. "What happened?"

"Some guy asked for me by name. When I picked up, all he said was something like, 'you're not gonna get away with this.' Then hung up."

Anger gurgled up in a slow simmer—the gall of it, that anyone would think to threaten this kind and gentle soul. "Did you recognize the voice?"

"No. Neither did the girl who took the call."

"Does anyone else know about this?"

"The authorities are on top of it. I can't help but wonder if it has something to do with that threat at the chapter. The police aren't that worried. They think it's a crank call. Or they're just being tight-lipped. But it sounds like they're covering their bases."

Paulson scanned the warehouse, considering vulnerabilities. Both for Damien and the potential of collateral damage, should there be some kind of assault.

It was pointless. How do you protect people without having the slightest idea of what they needed to be protected from? Another explosion, maybe? When not even the authorities seemed to know yet who caused the first one. Or why.

"I feel stuck in place," said Damien. "There's no guarantee going home would make any difference. Would that put my family at risk, too? As far as that goes, how do I go about my job if I do stay on? Who knows? Now some overzealous fruitcake might misinterpret whatever I do. It could even be someone on this operation. Someone right here at the call center."

A troubling possibility indeed; one that hadn't occurred to Paulson. He began to feel damp, his forehead beading up again. How well he did he really know this set of responders? Most were from out of town. The ones he'd brought in from headquarters seemed like the usual legitimate disaster devotees—quick to bond, full of eager questions. But you never know.

A vague motion snatched his attention—that damned shadow again, passing over the pile of discarded packing materials near Damien's office. It disappeared with equal suddenness. A chill shot up his spine, the accompanying surge of anxiety almost as bad as that dream on Lil's couch.

What the hell is that? In the same area as before. Maybe I should be asking, who.

"What's over there?" Paulson spat it out, his mouth dry.

Damien jumped. He marched up to the junk pile, reclaiming composure along the way.

"You saw it, too?" Paulson followed alongside.

"No. I'm taking a look all the same. What did you see?"

"I thought I saw something move. Something dark."

They visually scoured the repository of cardboard boxes, Styrofoam, wooden crates, and other packing debris. When superficial examination revealed nothing, they began pulling things aside, anything large enough to possibly conceal something. Then shoving and tossing items. Eventually, most of the accumulation encircled its original resting place.

As they reached the bottom of the pile they slowed, and stepped into the space they had cleared. Paulson continued to toe aside this or that, not sure what he was looking for.

That creeped-out feeling hit again. Was he being watched?

This time instinct proved reliable. Their actions were being followed by the curious stares of the majority of the phone bank personnel. The phone lines were enjoying an intermission. The scattered ringing was replaced with low twittering.

An unoccupied worker left his station and came their way. "Uh, need some help?"

He and Damien just stared back at the would-be volunteer. They had to look like lunatics. A similar conclusion was readable in Damien's sheepishness. Then a bit of sparkle glimmered.

They both burst out laughing. The worker seemed even more confused.

"Help us out here, would you." Paulson began straightening some of the tossed debris. "This is going to be...our Magic Circle. We need to move things out a bit more. More space."

Damien played along. The phone bank worker, still having no sense of the ultimate goal, pitched in anyway. The end result was a good-sized empty area surrounded by the scrap heap.

"We'll get in and out here." Paulson shoved aside some collapsed cardboard.

"Hey, be careful." Damien put on a pretense of indignation. "We'll need that."

He re-flattened and stroked the abused slab. After blowing away dirt and picking off dust bunnies he propped it up against a stack of wooden crates. "This is going to be our official storyboard."

The worker stood blinking at him. "Our what?"

"Hey, y'all listen up," Damien called to the other end of the building. "We're having our first official meeting. Right now, before the phones start in again."

Staff looked at one another, not sure what to make of their administrative support.

"Come on, everybody. Now."

Rising in reluctant waves, they filed into the center of the ring-shaped pile of trash until they, too, formed a circle. The group faced Damien and waited.

"Um, there's no chairs," a woman standing next to Paulson whispered.

"Of course not," Paulson whispered back. "This is how we keep meetings short."

"I'd like to welcome y'all to the Marshland Call Center. I'm your manager, Damien Logan. We meet here in this circle twice a day. First thing before opening, then again after we transfer lines to the answering service."

He guided self-introductions. "Now. Is there anyone here who doesn't know who their direct supervisor is? Raise your hand."

Nobody moved.

"Is there anyone who doesn't know what they're supposed to be doing?"

Nobody spoke.

"Good. If that changes, talk to your supervisor. If that doesn't work, let me know. That guy in the back there is Paulson, if you haven't met him already."

Paulson obliged Damien's introduction by raising his hand.

"He's mental health. If I drive you crazy, he's the person you go talk to."

There were a couple of polite laughs.

You're dying out there, Damien.

"Any questions?"

"Yeah." It was the worker who had helped them set up. "That thing you called the storyboard. What's that for?"

"Oh, yeah. Right. The storyboard." Damien shuffled in place and glanced at Paulson. "I'm glad you asked."

Paulson stepped up next to Damien. "I'll tell them about it."

Just then a second shadow intruded. Fortunately, this one was explainable—someone entering the main door. The silhouette encompassed by morning sunlight left no question of who it was: the Marlboro Man.

And here Sarah accuses me of dressing in costume.

"This is how we're going to keep track of agenda items around here." Paulson held up the blank cardboard. "If a question comes up that you want to address in meeting, tack on a note, whenever it comes to you. You don't need to sign it. If you like, just draw a picture of the problem. But when it comes time for meeting, be ready to do some explaining."

Horace's progress through the warehouse slowed into a holding pattern.

"We'll just line them up, as long as there's space," said Damien. "Then when things wind down, we'll..."

Baffled expressions passed among the meeting participants. Damien noticed it, too. He cleared his throat and looked to Paulson.

"...we'll have a show." Paulson dredged up a marginal Pee Wee Herman impersonation. It needed work. "Right here in our Magic Circle. We'll tell our story. Act out high points as we say our goodbyes. However we want. Sing a song, if you like. Write your own, even. Draw a picture to share. Let loose balloons with notes attached. Raffle off your office chair. And whatever happens in the Magic Circle, stays in the Magic Circle."

"Paulson here does some other really cool imitations," said Damien. "He's going to match up celebrity impersonations with some of our more colorful headquarters staff."

What? He shot a glance at Damien, who radiated a mischievous grin. More like the Damien of old. *That's my boy.*

"Got any imitations of folks at national headquarters?" came from the periphery. It was Horace. "I'd hang my hat a little longer just to see that."

"Who knows," said Damien. "Maybe we'll even invite them to attend."

This roused some genuine laughter.

"I'll bet mass care could come up with some pizza," said Paulson. The suggestion appeared to produce an even greater rise in spirit. "So give it some thought during the down times, what you'll say or do for our closing festivities. What you will take away from this experience. Or leave behind. Any questions?"

"Here's the first contribution right here." Horace eased his way forward and attached something to the corner of the makeshift bulletin board.

"What in the world?" somebody whispered.

Paulson looked around at the bonding troupe of workers, hypothesizing potential outcome of this oddball development. A stereotypical representation of a cowboy jangles into their midst, wearing disaster ID, no less, inserts himself into the middle of a call center meeting, then does something intrusive. And outrageous.

Into *their* call center meeting, for heaven's sake. Indignation rippled here and there.

The outcome: ownership. Paulson smiled. They were on their way.

"This here's your first day," said Horace. "I know what y'all went through to get here. So this thing represents your pre-assignment adventure, whatever it might have been. Know that we appreciate everything you've sacrificed to be here. We're proud of y'all."

He tipped his hat and moved away from the storyboard.

A bark of laughter broke the hush. Dangling from the cardboard's upper left-hand corner was a grotesquely smiling clown.

CHAPTER 13

"I don't want no part of your type." He eyed her as he flicked away his toothpick. "I seen who you're in cahoots with. At that church. So back off."

Thus concluded the attempt to engage the man with the angry glower—as a spectacular belly flop. John took a few protective steps forward while Sarah complied with the heavy-handed directive.

Cajoling would be pointless. The signs were impossible to miss. This particular soul had arrived at a place where he could not be pleased, no matter what she or anybody else did. His frustrations were too great. The best his coping could manage was to look for someone to take it out on. Today, at the moment, she—or more specifically her disaster vest— was his official target.

Displaced anger. What sort of horrid burden did the poor guy shoulder?

"Is there something I can do for you?" John asked him.

He squinted at John's nametag. "Victims assistance. Now that's someone that could do something if they cared to."

After a hasty appraisal of their surroundings, he drew John away from the registration area. Sarah followed, far enough behind to be inconspicuous, yet close enough to hear if John managed to smooth things over. Or if there were trouble.

"I seen him," said the man. Even at a distance the trembling in his voice stood out. It was nothing like his earlier belligerence.

"Who?" said John.

"Down by that bomb. I was there. That towel head. He's the one who done it."

"You saw who set off the bomb?" John's animation mushroomed, at odds with the composure suggested by his physical appearance. "I'm a victims advocate, not an agent. But I can get one. They'd be very interested."

The man took a step back. "I ain't talking to no FBI. No, sir."

The tirade continued. John shot an occasional glance toward his agency cohorts, and toward Sarah. With all the people positioned between him and his station, catching anyone's attention would be a tall order. Perhaps it was up to her to go get someone.

Should she? They were supposed to stay together. She tried to remember what John had said before they started. Nothing came to mind that matched up with this particular circumstance.

"They're in it together, the government and them Arabs." The man's furtive glance threw daggers at the cluster of administrators at the far end of the hall. "Like the one I saw at the parade. Then big surprise. There he is at that church afterwards, strutting his stuff like he owned the place. Just waiting for the money to come pouring in."

"What money?"

"From these folks here." The man made an impatient wave at the spread of agencies behind them. "Who do you think?"

John really did have himself a live one.

"She's in on it, too." The man jerked his head in her direction. "The one sniggering back there. Same bunch. I saw her buddying up with him at that church."

"Surely you saw that their organization was helping people."

"I didn't hang around to find out what they were doing. I know better than that."

It had to be Damien he was talking about. Damien's presence at the parade was no secret. But this was the first she'd heard about him being near the explosion site. He'd been mum about his own experiences that morning. Exactly what did this man see?

"Y'all must be blind. They're here, too. Like...like...that one over there." He pointed at a guard standing near an emergency exit.

"He's Native American, not Arab," said John.

The man responded in careful measured tones. "So...he...says."

The guard appeared to figure out that he had become part of the discussion. And that it involved someone who bordered on spinning out of control. He maneuvered nearer.

The malcontent noticed. His defiance twisted into fear. "I'm outta here. I done my civic duty."

"Wait." John began to follow after him. "We really do want to hear about what you saw."

The man bolted for the front entrance. Confronted by a glut of people and security measures, he changed course, making a beeline for the newly unattended emergency exit. Before anyone could stop him, he slammed into the crash bar and disappeared. John and the guard followed, along with a few soldiers. A caustic emergency alarm pierced the scene.

It was as if a second bomb had gone off. Several people shouted at once. The organized lines melted into globs of stirred humanity. Clients and agency personnel alike looked around in chaos for explanation. A number of those hanging around in the lounge area leaped from their seats and hurried to the main entrance, squeezing out through space freed up by those who'd had second thoughts about trying to get inside.

Guards checked doors and tried to tell people what to do. The military personnel seemed to be functioning under some kind of contingency plan as well. Thank God.

But how vulnerable she would be, standing there in the middle of the conference hall, if it turned into a mass mob of everybody trying to get out at once.

Safety first, Lacey always said.

Sarah shuffled through the confusion, trying to avoid outright collisions but occasionally shoved off balance by those who'd gone into escape mode. When she reached a solid wall, she planted herself against it.

*****

Paulson returned to the staff mental health station to find Horace reclining in one of the plastic lawn chairs, a booted foot resting on the rickety table. His leather satchel, which looked more like an old saddlebag, sat open beside him. He was wearing reading glasses. His raised knee supported a dog-eared copy of *Siddhartha.*

"I like what you've done with the place." He didn't look up, finishing a passage that was apparently a more important thing at the moment. Finally he chuckled to himself, marked the page with a faded scrap of red kerchief, and returned the book and spectacles to his satchel.

"We gave the good stuff to the trenches."

"You misunderstand. Most times we're lucky to get any designated space at all for staff mental health. This here's well enough away from goings on that people might take to the idea of spilling it all, if they've a mind to."

"Location, location. Look. Why are you following me around already? What else have I managed to get wrong?"

"Sounds to me like I made it here just in time." His eyes twinkled. The corny yet relaxed drawl did have a way of downplaying the defensiveness that always seemed to be breaking loose at ill-advised moments.

This was his supervisor. He needed to find a way to get used to it.

"You done a debrief yet?" Horace made a casual gesture for him to sit.

He went along with it and shrugged. It wasn't clear exactly what those conversations he'd had with Sarah would be called. Their most recent tête-à-tête certainly hadn't left him feeling freshly renewed.

"From what Lacey says, you've been through almost everything there is to go through in this disaster. You were there when the bomb went off. You helped the injured. A buddy of yours almost died. A real war zone at the hospital, from what I've heard. Then this assignment here isn't what you'd call the sought-after plum position. Not for someone who sets store in being in the middle of things. I hear you're still overseeing those PFA teams for the floods, to boot."

It did sound like a bit much when systematically itemized. "I have a colleague I talk with. At least, I think she's still a friend. We got into an argument last night. It ended poorly."

"I imagine you're all a bit on the edgy side. You've been through a world-class nightmare. I'd be concerned if I didn't see a few flare-ups here and there. It's why it's a good idea to have somebody neutral to unload with."

In spite of the prickliness climbing his spine, what Horace said rang true. Sarah was the wrong person to debrief with.

Being reminded he'd been an idiot didn't help. Especially since it pointed out just one more way he'd made himself look like an idiot in front of Sarah.

"She said some things I hadn't thought of about preparedness. I missed the foresight. Sometimes I try so hard to..." He shifted focus to the junk pile, checking for dark or moving forms. Nothing. "Then when all hell broke loose, everything fell flat."

Horace got up and stretched. "How about we go for a stroll?"

They took the side exit and stepped into the retreating sunbeams of autumn, continuing on through the overgrowth blanketing Sam's razed lot. It had originally turned up as a cheery scattering of summer green, hiding much of the grimy ash. Now it was mostly stiff and brown. It rustled in its resistance as they waded through it. They stopped at the flagpole, the one structure on the lot left unscathed by the shop fire. A vigorous assortment of weeds girdled it.

Paulson blinked up at the crisp red, white, and blue fluttering above them. Sam had been there already. Paulson leaned against the flagpole and toed at the dead foliage clustered at its base. A large sprig immediately fell away. He picked it up.

"Another cycle meets its end." Horace plucked a long blade of grass. He chewed at the base of the stem as he gazed at him.

It was difficult to remember the last time he'd consulted with a peer in this way. Certainly not since Marshland. He practiced in isolation precisely because of his disillusionment with the system. He had no idea how or where to begin, even if he wanted to. However, Lacey would jerk his ass right out of there if he didn't go along with the program.

He fingered the handful of withered debris. "This is what I feel like. This, right here."

Going over events made them seem like they covered weeks, rather than days. During occasional pauses, he scoped Horace, hopefully subtle enough so that he wouldn't notice he was being monitored in return. Without exception, there was only caring attentiveness at the other end, steadily focused eyes that didn't miss a thing. Including that he was on the receiving end of Paulson's scrutiny. And that it didn't matter.

The more he shared about the last few days, the less his lower back ached. When current affairs ran dry, he moved into older territory: the fire of the previous spring, and everything that went on during the flood aftermath.

Out of nowhere, Horace threw back his head and laughed. "Is there a disaster anywhere in these parts that you haven't gotten yourself in the middle of, son?"

"Probably not. For the last few years, anyway."

"I reckon you truly are the local expert, then."

"I suppose."

"You know, I've done a lot of disaster, too. Real whoppers, like this one here. Where it seems like the whole world's come tumbling down on too many good people."

"Yet you keep doing it."

"What keeps you going is how you look at it." Horace flicked a lazy finger at the dead vegetation in Paulson's hands, which had somehow become mangled during their conversation. "It's like this thing you have here. May I?"

Paulson handed it to him.

"When there's a prairie fire, you can see those flames coming or going. The best you can do is keep from getting burnt up yourself. Can't do much else about it alone. In fact, we'd best not try to stop it. It's part of nature's plan, making way for the next generation. So you wait for rain or for the wind to turn it back. Or let it burn itself out.

"But if a tumbleweed comes along—why, that's a different story." Horace tossed the wadded up foliage. A whisper of air caught hold and swooshed it away. It landed a few feet in front of them. "When a tumbleweed passes through, it can snatch up those flames and take that fire right along with it. Stir up a heap of mischief all its own."

A boot halted the debris' attempted escape. He picked it up and handed it back to Paulson. "Now that's halfway manageable. You can stomp it out or take control, however you see fit."

"I get where you're coming from." Paulson tossed aside the dead weed. "It's just that there are so many tumbleweeds."

"You can't take charge of all of them. No one person can. No plan, no matter how thorough, can tend to every hurt that comes up in the throes of the main event. After things are over and done with, we'll take a look at what could be improved upon. It doesn't need to stop us from doing our best while things are rolling along. Or from taking care of that one smoldering tumbleweed that's sitting right there in front of you."

Horace picked up the debris wad and placed it firmly in Paulson's hands. "You watch over that, now. It'll remind you."

As they found their way back to his station, something seemed changed. The jingling of the phones seemed somehow more real. The calm lacing the soothing reassurances rendered by those who answered them stood out. Comforting.

They passed Damien, caged by his crate arrangement and poring over God knows what. The mass care workers were in the process of moving the canteen closer to the Magic Circle. The environment seemed orderly, peaceful. An organized whole. Things were pulling together. Needs were being met.

"You're good at this, you know," said Horace.

"Thanks." *If you say so.* The lack of conviction had to be obvious.

"That was a stroke of genius back there, that Magic Circle."

Paulson waited for clarification. By now there was no doubt that anything coming out of Horace's mouth had some far-fetched purpose or deeper significance. Probably usefully so, for those who could figure out what that significance was.

"An outstanding distraction technique," Horace continued. "I'd put it right up there with that new-fangled EMDR hocus pocus."

"I don't know that I'd go that far."

"There's nothing you and I can do that will make what these folks are dealing with taste good. But we sure can give them something else to think about while they cope."

"You don't think it's irreverent? Doing things this off the wall in the middle of a mass casualty disaster?"

"Nope. It's just what they need. You've given them something for the downtime, too. Sitting and doing nothing? All those juices flowing, and no place to go? Downright destructive, matter of fact."

"Damien and I just made it up as we went along. It seemed right at the time."

"There isn't any one right answer for these things. It's about what's fitting for the occasion. Sometimes you go with your gut. You're good at that, kid. Good instincts."

Yes, instincts—what about them? While with Sarah, they'd failed him completely. Or he had failed them. He had ignored what he normally did best. In retrospect, the crossover between her ability to cope and the bonding episode she'd had with her father was painfully obvious. At that particular juncture, there was no way she could be open to a discussion topic that criticized his generation. All he had succeeded in doing was to chop away at the line to her anchor. He'd been too damned focused on what he himself wanted. His own needs.

He couldn't shake the impression that the clown hanging on the bulletin board was laughing at him. "By the way. Why the hell did you bring that god-awful thing?"

"As a word to the wise. Better get used to them critters. They'll be joining you in your overflow space until we figure out what else to do with them."

"You're kidding, right?"

"You know, all those boxes could be used to build a coop for your barnyard fowl."

"Barnyard fowl?"

"Whatever is supposed to be eating this grain." Horace pointed toward the concrete surrounding the area rug.

The staff mental health station was sitting squarely on Chet's rice sprinklings.

CHAPTER 14

After the alarm stopped braying, it was obvious how anxious everyone had become. A number of clients had left, perhaps for good. Many others remained, apparently more concerned about not losing headway into the aid-seeking process than the possibility of being vaporized by a second bomb. The different ways people handled crises never ceased to amaze. "Did you catch up with him?"

"They're still looking." John finished a long drag from his water bottle. "What happened after I left?"

"Your basic mayhem." Sarah straightened stacks of handouts knocked awry during the exodus. "But everybody simmered down after several rounds of loudspeaker announcements."

"How are you doing?" He sounded genuine, not conciliatory. "You look a little off."

She did feel off. It had been a long morning, and the day was not even half over. There was also that nagging issue of all that had come to light about Damien, especially with Paulson saying he was being kept out of sight. Could the malcontent they'd chased after be the same one who had made the threats?

Probably not. He wouldn't advertise himself that way if his plan was to take matters into his own hands. He did have a few questionable beliefs, but he didn't seem stupid. Ignorant, yes. Dangerous, perhaps not.

"I'm all right. This pales in comparison to what else I've been through today." She described what had happened to Sean's roommate.

"Sorry to hear about it. Is there anything I can do?"

"That reminds me." She took a moment to sort through what was appropriate to disclose to John. As well as how much of her emotional involvement would be wise to share. "Lil needs support through this. She's been leaning on me. But how things go during catastrophic crime incidents is not my area of expertise."

"Someone will be assigned to advocate for her."

"You're the only victims advocate I've ever worked with." She laid a subtle hand at his forearm. "Lil is special. I'd really appreciate it if you could be the one who helps her."

"I'll see what's cooking." He smiled and patted her hand. "But I can't make promises."

Asking favors of someone she'd known so briefly felt awkward. Especially when he was always so accommodating. Maybe he had a crush on her, or was misreading her friendliness. Or it was just another episode of instantaneous disaster bonding, like with Paulson during the floods. She felt so joined with John already, reliant on his unwavering aura of confidence, even though he'd only been a part of her life for a couple of days. In other circumstances, she might well be dating him.

Was she okay with any of this? It seemed like she was always the last one to figure it out when she was being hit on.

Alison's sudden appearance at the staff entry helped change tracks. "Alison's back."

"Is that a wee bit of disdain I hear in there?"

"She got fired from a position recently. She blames me. In part."

Delores returned to their station, also tracking Alison. "I'm positive I know that woman. I wonder if we've worked together."

This annoying tradition, one that frequently cropped up among "lifers," was beginning to feel routine. Workers realized they looked familiar to each other, and then tried to figure out which relief operations they had in common. Sometimes it meant putting immediate business on hold for several minutes while they played twenty questions.

Most of the time it was best to let it run its course without interruption. Even though it was a nuisance, it also seemed to serve as some kind of sustenance, a thread of bonding that strengthened the cultural fabric. They got back on track eventually.

However, this particular installment brought on realization that she did not know where Alison had come from, period, before Paulson hired her. Her accent was not local.

"Looks like you'll get a chance to ask her," said John.

Alison was slinking toward their station.

Sarah squinted in spite of herself, blurring the reality of Alison's approach. *Where are ruby slippers when you need them?* Enough of Alison's mannerisms made their way through the avoidance strategy to be able to see scorn taking center stage.

"I'm taking some of these." Alison addressed Delores, ignoring Sarah. She snatched up an arbitrary assortment of the handouts that had just been straightened.

"Okay. So, where have we worked together before?" Delores gripped her pencil like a *Jeopardy* contestant preparing to signal a response.

"I've never seen you before in my life." Alison didn't bother to look up. She continued what appeared to be a concerted effort to return the table to shambles.

"I never forget a face," said Delores. "It's been a while, whenever it was. Could it have been a school shooting? Or an airline disaster?"

"I have no idea."

"What was your last mass casualty assignment? Have you been out to the East Coast?"

"I fail to see the relevance."

"No need to be snippy, Alison." John added a light laugh. "We're still colleagues. We're all on the same side here."

"Speak for yourself." Alison ignored the cluster of flyers her frenzy had knocked to the floor and continued about her business, whatever it was.

"If you need a lot of those, I can order some from the warehouse for you." Delores pulled out a requisition form. "That way you'll have a ready supply at your own station."

Impressive. Delores deserved some kind of award for patience.

"I'll get on fine, thank you very much." She turned on her heel and stomped off.

John looked after her. "Hmm. We'll need to keep an eye on that one."

"Alison McAllister." Delores drifted off, tapping her pencil to the tempo of the name. "Alison McAllister. The name has such a familiar ring to it."

The tapping abruptly stopped. A startled focus redelivered Delores to the here and now.

"What is it?" Sarah scoured the room for the next crisis.

"I know who that is." Delores placed a hand over her mouth and dropped back in her chair. "How in the world did I forget? It was after 9/11. She was there, at The Pier. She wasn't a coworker. Alison was a client. A survivor. Or claimed to be."

"Claimed to be?" At this point nothing about Alison would be surprising.

"It was a case that went on forever. *Forever.* When she applied for services, she said her boyfriend got killed in the twin towers. She was never able to prove he'd been there, or that they cohab'ed, or anything. Not even that they knew each other. I was beginning to wonder if the man ever really existed."

"What finally happened with it?" said John.

"I don't know. It was taken out of our hands. Homeland Security or FEMA or somebody stepped in. All I know is that we were through dealing with her."

John's gaze continued to follow Alison. She had swooped into his station and was holding his supervisor prisoner with a diatribe. "Something about this really smells."

*****

"He moved! His hand. He moved his hand! And if you watch his eyes, every now and then they do this little flutter." Lil demonstrated the effect with panache. She followed it up with a gleeful rendition of a touchdown dance, practically bouncing off the walls of the cramped hospital room.

"That's great news," said Paulson.

Whether to stop by or not had been a toss-up. The last thing he needed was yet one more downer to pile onto his existential gloom. But he hadn't seen either Sean or Lil since the day of the explosion. He wanted—needed—the connection. Their openness, and transparency; their unconditional acceptance of anybody considered to be a friend.

Finding Lil in good spirits and Sean's prognosis on the upswing was a welcome relief.

"It's all thanks to you." She wrapped him up and bounced again in her plumpness. "Thank you, Paulson. Thank you, thank you, thank you."

Pungent scents of oily hair, perspiration, and other unattended evidence of her emotions over the last couple of days met his return embrace.

When he had last seen Sean, his face had been a sickly gray, mottled with the crimson of blood he was losing, as they labored their way through catastrophe and uncertainty. He now looked almost angelic, in spite of the telltale bandaging. Peaceful and clean, bundled in a preponderance of white linens. His usual carrot-colored spikes were combed flat and parted down the middle, similar to how Lil styled Jerrod's hair. The steady sounds of the monitoring equipment felt reassuring: Sean was at least alive, if not yet completely well.

Several children's drawings were taped to the wall next to his bed. "We love you Mr. White" monopolized the top half of one. The rest of it contained a marginal stick figure drawn entirely in black, with the exception of a red Statue of Liberty-style crown on its head. Much more care had gone into the yellow and gold trumpet the figure held.

"Sean plays the trumpet?"

"That one's from Joey." Lil laughed. "Sean told me this story. It was when he saved the day at the spring concert. Joey dropped his horn and jammed up that little mouthpiece thingy all crooked. Sean was the only one who could get it pulled off."

Such a weird range of tasks a school custodian could get drawn into. It was heartwarming, the layer the story added to his understanding of Sean's role. It took some of the bite out, knowing he had done something to help return this man to the children who loved him.

"It could be any minute now he'll open his eyes and ask when supper's ready. I'm fixing baby back ribs first chance I get. His all-time favorite." Deviousness crept into her grin. "In fact, I'll sneak some in after he wakes up. This hospital food would put anybody in a coma."

A collection of familiar flyers was scattered over the Stryker table next to the bed.

"Sarah's been here?" The words came tumbling out, untempered. His acute interest had to sound obvious.

"Of course, silly."

"How's she doing?" He picked up one of the disaster handouts and stroked a thumb against the stapled binding. Did Sarah feel as adrift as he?

"After Sean's roommate passed, she said I could use something to read and take my mind off it. That, and having our car blown to bits. Those pamphlets were all she had on her."

The recovery printouts fluttered from his hand. "Your car blew up?"

"Don't you worry none." She lowered her voice. "We got the FBI looking into it. It's all hush-hush, of course. They say it happened because of where it was parked. They don't think the bomb was in the car or nothing. It was closest of the cars that got wrecked."

The celebrity status attained by her former means of transportation had her glowing. A fortuitous distraction, with everything else.

"I'm sorry, Lil. About your car." He relaxed against the wall and mulled over this development. "But we have plenty to be grateful for." That Sean survived it at all.

*****

Hurry up and wait.

Sarah sat on a frigid pan-flat chair. There was no telling how long she'd be left sitting here. She checked her handheld for the umpteenth time.

Fragments of the day swirled, mainly intrusive ruminations: The excitement percolating at the FAC. The episode at the hospital. The false alarm. Client needs yet unmet. Soap operas unfolding amidst certain agency personnel.

The failure to keep that toxic man from drumming up yet another fiasco.

She closed her eyes and forced herself to reground. Eventually it settled into a background blur, quiet and gray. The dull pulsing of an overtaxed metabolism became less noticeable. Slower...

Then there was Paulson.

Blast it all. She got up and checked the view out a near window, avoiding the view of high-powered single-mindedness behind her. The maples and other trees that so recently flaunted their red and orange glory were now almost bare, thanks to the overnight freezes. A bundled-up work party was on the church lawn, raking and bagging decaying leaves. Clouds were moving in; could be the frost would be back tomorrow. The last of the Indian summer had gone its way.

"I hear you're next."

Sarah turned to find a lanky cowboy towering over her. Even with having been warned, his just-stepped-off-the-screen impression was mesmerizing. Sure enough, his nametag identified him as Horace. "I hear you're an old friend of Lacey's."

"Heard nothing but good about you, too."

She immediately felt at ease. He seemed almost ethereal, so easy-going and connected. As if it seeped from every pore.

What, a Zen cowboy? Should probably keep that one to herself.

"Head on back this way. The pastor's letting us use his digs. Real nice guy. I like him."

The office was surprisingly large. Its sparse furnishings made it seem more so. It smelled of dusty books and an aging oil furnace, just short of making her sneeze.

As they settled into a pair of worn but well-padded wingbacks, his essence seemed to deepen. Such a powerful presence sat before her, in spite of the cheesy get-up. Now that they were alone, the idea of revealing samples of her innermost self no longer felt inconsequential. The gist of whatever got dredged up would most certainly be controlled by him.

"So, Sarah. What do you have to say about your first full day at an FAC? I hear you were right smack in the middle of that piece of excitement y'all had out there."

Thoughts about the day were now securely buried under a mishmash of stockpiled emotions—and tightly capped, thank you very much. Except for that one particular personal failure that refused to stay tucked away.

He read right through it. "It's all up to you, you know. Even us helper-types need to keep a lid on until it's done fermenting. Any part of your brew ready yet?"

"It's...I did something wrong." She paused, studied her shoes. They needed cleaning.

He said nothing—attentive, and eerily present. Not to be distracted.

There was no escape. "I blew up at someone yesterday."

"Not surprising. You've been waltzing through perdition itself the last few days."

"It was someone who's been through even more than me. He didn't need that."

"You made amends?"

"There hasn't been opportunity."

"You'll get to it, I imagine."

"I can't get it off my mind. I'm afraid that..." Leaving the chair, she circled the pastor's desk, slowing to reposition the contents of a pencil cup. "I lost control. I'm afraid it will happen again."

"You reached a breaking point. Understandable. It happens."

She dared a sliver of eye contact. "What if it happens with a client? Someone who's hurting. Looking to me for help? That's unacceptable."

"You've never dealt with breaking points before? When things got so tough you said 'whoa' and arranged for a breather?"

"Well, yes."

He waited.

"When my Mom died." She returned to the wingback and sat at the edge of the seat. "I was just finishing school, and preparing for licensure. I ended up putting it off for several months. I knew I wouldn't be able to concentrate on those exams. I wasn't so sure I should be practicing anyway while...off my game. So I completed my credentials later."

"Then you do have a handle on yourself. You know when you need to step back."

"I suppose." She scooted back into the chair, hoping it didn't come off as dismissive, even though it was. After all, the current circumstance was a different situation entirely. She toyed with the pearl button on her cuff.

Horace broke the silence. "See that cow on the wall? Looks a lot like that pasture coming in from the airport."

She noticed for the first time the painting facing the pastor's desk, a fawn-colored jersey grazing under a leafed-out tree. Green rolling hills made up most of the background. It wasn't very professional looking. Probably painted by a parishioner. "What about it?"

"Now that critter has it right. Have you ever seen a cow fretting over what might happen in the future?"

"I don't know how I could tell."

He laughed. "Well, you might see her stirring around or standing at alert if a predator was coming her way. Otherwise, if all's clear, she's perfectly happy to immerse herself in a nice sweet meal on a warm summer day."

"Yeah, but if she had a more advanced cerebral cortex she wouldn't be so calm."

"That's what gets us in trouble, all right. The illusion of the future."

"But the future isn't an illusion. It eventually gets here."

"Is that right, Sarah?" Even with an accepting and supportive smile, his attunement had a way of drilling through to the core. "You've found a way to live in the future?"

"Well, no." As if she really needed to respond to that. "I know what you're saying. But we do need to plan, so we don't create unnecessary problems. For ourselves or others."

"Planning and fretting are two different things. You can plan without fretting. In fact, the fretting part just gets in the way when it comes to planning."

"I know all this." She shifted in her chair. The inner struggle was even more annoying than the unpredictability of the give and take—not to mention the dilemma of how much of her ruminations to reveal. Including to herself. "It's tough to keep in mind, after..." Given his seeming clairvoyance, there wasn't any reason to complete the thought.

"We've all had our blunders. No doubt there."

In spite of his peculiarities, the reassurances were soothing. It was somehow familiar, like being with a valued mentor back in graduate school. "Things are different now, off balance. Everything used to be in order, in its place. What felt so certain and secure about my life isn't that way anymore. Terrorists? Out here, in the middle of nowhere? So much...uncertainty."

"The apple cart's been upset, so to speak."

"I can find ways to deal with uncertainties of the world. I always have. What I'm not sure how to deal with is the uncertainty about myself."

"Nothing's really changed. Whatever possibilities you fear, they've always been there. You lived, breathed, and enjoyed life. Are a darn good disaster mental health worker, too, from what I hear."

"It's part of my past experiences now, these new memories. I'm aware of other possibilities."

"So, you've found a way to live in the past now, too?" There he went again, finding humor in whatever she said.

"But we're aware of it as humans. More so than some stupid cow. Our thoughts are more complex. We have...choice. We have the ability to direct our thoughts."

"Like dreaming." He laced his hands behind his head and leaned back, staring at the ceiling. "Now there's the way to go. If you've got yourself an itch to live in some other time frame, that's one that can be mighty nice to visit."

Was this guy on the same planet? Or did he need a good hearing aid? "Don't you understand? There's harm that could be done to people. Even with people I care about."

He abandoned his study of ceiling tile and turned to face her. The old chair creaked as he slowly shifted forward, his hands folding in his lap as if contemplating prayer. It took a concerted effort to resist backing away; such energy flowed through his locked-in gaze.

"If you can direct your thoughts." He paused, searching. "If you can set up camp in whatever time zone suits you—why, oh why, do you choose to live there?"

CHAPTER 15

Tuesday, October 29ᵗʰ

"I'm taking your advice," said Lil, looking up to face Sarah.
It took a fair amount of care to avoid stepping on the herd of cats jockeying to be near their mistress, apparently still reestablishing their pecking order. "In what way?"

"See that flyer? They were passing them out at the grocery. I'm going to that." Lil interrupted nursing adjustments long enough to point at the neon pink leaflet on her coffee table. Jerrod arched in protest, his attempt to throw himself contained by her practiced grasp. He did not appear ready to be appeased over the disruption of his morning nap.

It was enchanting—mother and infant, the two of them so openly and freely providing comfort to one another. Sarah realized she was staring.

She picked up the photocopied flyer. The event it described was not one of the FAC resources. It sounded like some kind of generic support group, aimed at those affected by the bombing. Anyone who wanted to participate was welcome, refreshments provided. Bring your friends. "Has this been vetted?"

"There you go again. Your fancy words."

"How do you know if whoever's running it knows what they're doing? I don't see credentials listed. Who will be leading it?"

"They're church people. What other credentials do they need?"

"So it's for spiritual support, then."

"The lady said it was so we could get together, so everybody could help each other out."

It sounded harmless enough. Certainly better than nothing. Lil needed more opportunities to get out. With Jerrod home again, she'd be more confined, especially without Sean to spell her. Lil would need much more than Sarah could give. The FAC was going to be a fast track to burnout on its own, without adding Lil into the mix.

"Why this group, instead of the ones the operation sponsors?"

"It's at that church around the corner." Lil gave her a look of exasperation. "I don't have a car. I can walk to this one with the stroller."

"Won't your insurance get you a rental?"

"I'll get to it. Maybe that victims advocate will help. But this meeting is here, in our neighborhood. There will be other people I know. There's a sitter, too, if Jerrod gets cranky."

There were other troubling issues, such as Lil's lifelong skepticism of organized religion. However, the neighborhood was part of Lil's natural support system. It could be exactly what she needed. "I hope it works out. You'll have to let me know, in case I run across someone else who could use it."

"Come on by when you get off your shift, then. After it's over, you can take me and Jerrod to say hi to his daddy."

"Tell me more about Sean. He actually opened his eyes?"

"He did! Not long, but long enough. He asked if I was okay, and Jerrod. Then he went back to sleep. That's my Sean." Lil wiped at sniffles. "Mom brought Jerrod back and took us home." She snuggled her nursing infant and kissed his forehead. Jerrod squirmed in protest then got back to business. "Soon your daddy will be home, too, Sweetie."

"Heard anything more from the authorities?"

"That victims guy called. That's about it. The news says more than anybody else."

So far most of that was either speculation or rumor.

"What everybody says now is that a smoke bomb did it." Lil laughed. "Just like those little round ones we used to set off for Fourth of July. Remember them?"

"Yeah. But I don't see how you could get a smoke bomb to explode that way."

"That's just what set it off." Lil tossed her head. "Pretty darned creative, if you ask me. I looked it up on the Internet. I found a website on it."

"This is ridiculous. What'll turn up as an IED next—soda pop?"

"Nobody's taking credit for it yet. No terrorist group, no squirrelly selfie posting from some suicide bomber. No nothing."

*****

For once, Lacey's call was welcome. Most of the morning had fallen victim to the monotony of phone bank clients. At first, he had limited himself to mental health related queries, which, as it turned out, didn't need much in the way of counseling skills. Mainly how's, what's, and where's of services. Eventually he gave in and helped with the growing backlog of generic calls. His reward for this piece of generosity was feeling over-challenged and misplaced.

Then there were the professional responsibilities built into the farce. Sometimes the broad smattering of caller needs meant deciding at any given moment whether he was a tele-referral resource, or if he should apply his counselor persona—the latter dragging in a cumbersome set of regulations. Was he creating a conflict of interest and not recognizing it? Murky boundaries were involved, regardless.

He wasn't married to the idea that rules should always be followed. But some rules existed for good reason. Near as he could tell, there weren't any hard and fast rules yet for what he was in the middle of. It amounted to trying to think outside the box, when there still wasn't a box.

Irritating intellectual exercises of this nature had run in the background all morning, draining energy better spent with helping callers find solutions. It also left him more vulnerable to screw-ups. He'd done enough screwing up as it was.

To top it off, workers were recirculating stories about the warehouse being haunted. Most did so in good fun, with Halloween only a couple of days off. In the spirit of recycling, some practical joker had thrown together a resident specter, crafted mainly from white sheets of Styrofoam wrapping and a Burger King mask. Every now and then a shriek broke the silence as "Charles" popped up—or more usually, down. In spite of the laughter that typically followed, it meant constantly dealing with his somebody-in-distress radar being set off.

His own issues complicated matters further. How was he supposed to reassure people about ghosts when he couldn't stop seeing things that weren't really there?

I have way too much time to think. "Good morning, Lacey. What can I do for you?"

"A couple of things. First, how is Damien doing?"

"Damien?" Right, that crank call. Nothing more seemed to have come of it. In fact, it had slipped his mind altogether. "He's fine, all things considered. Why?"

"There was an incident at the FAC yesterday. Someone accused him of being in the area where the bomb went off."

"So what? There must have been a hundred people standing around there. Plenty more who passed by. Myself included. It was a main thoroughfare."

"The complaint came from someone who's concerned about what country he's from."

Not this again. Damien did not need this. Definitely didn't deserve it. "They're not taking it seriously, are they?"

"Not unless they can track down the guy who complained, or get something more concrete."

"Does Damien know about it? He hasn't said a word."

"Somebody got hold of him last night. You might want to follow up. One other thing. I was at an inter-agency meeting this morning. That little chickadee you released from your PFA team apparently got herself hooked up with the victims advocacy operation."

"I wish them well."

"It took her less than twenty-four hours to have a meltdown."

"No surprise there. What happened?"

"Apparently she took issue with the military chaplains and threw a tizzy fit. Right there in front of clients, in front of everybody. DOD and DOJ were quick to step in. Long story, short—she got her walking orders."

"Story's over then?"

"Almost. As distasteful as it is, she really should be offered a mental health exit interview. None of the other agencies or organizations see it as their bailiwick."

What had to be coming next was just what he didn't need.

Laccy apparently heard his thoughts. "She may be a pain in the neck, but she's still a human being."

"Probably. Though at times I wonder whether it's an adult human being or a five year old I'm dealing with."

"Keep in mind that she was at the explosion site, herself. You know how people tend to regress when overstressed. Alison's behavior of late certainly supports such speculation. It begs intervention, or at least a look-see."

"Her behavior's nothing new. It didn't start up after the explosion. She's always been like this." Though he hadn't considered the regression angle. It would certainly explain why she had become even more annoying than usual.

"You must have had some kind of collegial relationship with her. Are you the right person to give her a jingle?"

"Considering where we left off, it wouldn't be a good idea."

"What do you know about her? Does she have family, or any other support system?"

"She's not from around here. Originally, I think New Jersey. If I remember right, she moved around a lot before she got here. She does have a boyfriend."

"Chet, you mean. Nice guy, but not particularly...interpersonally tuned in."

"Well put. He has a disaster assignment; he'll be focused on that. Or whatever's directly in front of him at the moment. At best, he probably provides minimal evening socializing." A fleeting image of possible bedroom activity produced a shudder.

"So, she's isolated, too. Not good—especially for someone who's already fragile."

Lacey's reasons for why somebody should take the time for it made good sense. It still frosted him. With everything else tormenting day-to-day life, coming up with patience for Alison's benefit would not be easy.

However, Lacey had given him this "low-key" assignment so he wouldn't overdo it. There was no way he was going to make it look like he couldn't even handle this Mickey Mouse position.

The sharp beep of a truck in reverse echoed through the chamber.

Staff grimaced, stuck fingers in their ears, and looked exasperated as they strained to hear their callers.

The disruption and inconvenience had begun at the break of dawn. With space for the incoming load mapped out and organized, the office configuration was considerably cramped. Now the morning chill invaded the operation. Most workers were dressed for the great outdoors, heeding Damien's warning that the bay would be open for an extended period.

In this manner, the call center was temporarily transformed into some sort of autumn open-air café. Paulson sat and watched leaves swirl in as organized eddies, snatching up and carrying along any administrative debris that escaped makeshift paperweights. One worker set down her phone and darted off after a sticky yellow she apparently couldn't get by without.

And here he was supposed to keep spirits up in the middle of something this insane. They had every right to complain. At least it wasn't raining.

The fresh batch of coffee that the astute canteen worker had started up began to give off its magic aroma, a nice distraction. He closed his eyes, visualizing the little umbrellas that go on top of fruity lounge drinks—they would work out just as well stuck in marshmallows and floating in hot cocoa. He could pass out "cocoa cocktails" as a staff distraction. Or as an inroad to listening to people vent. Maybe next time. God forbid.

It would have gone better with a forklift. Chet and Freddie were making do with a squeaking hand trolley, restacking pallet after pallet of clown toys, and clambering up and down the growing mound to do so. White cardboard boxes with Asian script slowly became a barrier between him and the action. On one hand, the additional privacy would be good for mental health consults. Increasing the isolation of the mental health consultant himself, however, was not. Especially if he was going to do something about his own BS.

He scooped up the weed debris serving as card table ornament. It was now even more dry and brittle. Pieces crumbled off and scattered as he returned it.

Focus on what's right in front of you. What little could still be seen, with that mountain going up between him and the rest of the world.

Across the back of the warehouse, Damien was leaning back in his new chair, his first acquisition of real office furniture. He had his arms folded, his disinterested gaze occasionally captured by fragments of call center goings on.

"Knock, knock." He stepped into Damien's space.

"Just how many of those things have they got?" Damien's eyes tracked Chet and Freddie as they passed by with another load.

"Time will tell. Want to go take a look?"

"I'll pass." Damien stretched his long legs out onto a semi-collapsed cardboard crate. "We'll be living with them soon enough."

"I heard you got a call last night about that threat business."

"Yeah. Nothing specific. Just somebody else spouting off the same thing. If I look slightly different, I must be guilty of something."

"I didn't know you were down there, too. Where the explosion happened."

"Probably saw me when I went back to the car. One of the kids left his gloves behind. That's the only time I was near that area."

"You guys didn't get hurt or anything, did you?"

"No. This was way before the parade started."

"I guess I would have seen you. I was there myself. Helping with some of the injured."

"Anybody I know?"

"How about Sean White?"

Damien sat up, finally looking online. "Mr. White? The school janitor?"

"He's hard to miss. Who else has orange spikes across the top of his head?" *That's the ticket.* Focus him on others, the people Damien was there to help. Works every time.

"The kids love that guy."

"Got him to the hospital in the nick of time. Apparently he left his car right where the bomb went off. He's lucky to be alive."

"How's he doing?"

"In and out of consciousness. They think he's out of the woods, though."

"I wonder if he saw anything." Damien rapped together his fingertips, poised in front of his chest, his dark brow wrinkled in thought. "I mean, about the bomb."

"The authorities are thinking along the same lines. To hear his wife talk, everybody's practically lining up for a chance to interview him."

They sifted through a rehash of the bombing hypotheses, including a few new ones. It got Damien talking, more engaged. After draining the mileage from this diversion, he still wasn't back to his usual self. If anything, he seemed even more lost in space.

"Are you sure you're okay with it? Being here in the middle of the intrigue, when you feel like you're some kind of ongoing target?"

"It's worth it to me. Besides, how many other people do you know who'd be willing to step into this?" Damien threw a hand at his crate arrangement.

"Good point. Especially with the high profile stuff going on at the FAC. Now there's the volunteer magnet. Answering phones in a drafty old warehouse will never compete. All the same, your courage is impressive. I know I'd have second thoughts."

"Too bad you can't walk in my shoes for a day." Damien stood and faced him, a flush blooming at his cheekbones. "If I let myself be run off every time I got treated different, I'd never leave home."

"I'm ashamed to admit it, but until now I never thought about that. I know you for who you are. Racist BS—it never even occurred to me. Maybe I've been naïve."

"You're not from around here." Damien poked his head out at the sound of raised voices, which were soon followed by raucous laughter. He moved out to investigate. Paulson followed.

"There's a reason I don't venture out of this area much, other than for disaster." Damien's hands were clasped at his lower back, white-knuckled, as they circled to the other side of the boxes of toys. "People around here know me. They don't see the color of my skin. Don't give me any grief. I forget about it myself. But if something brings in people from elsewhere, like this, it's a different story.

"Hold it down over there!" Damien shouted as the full work area came into view. "People are trying to talk on the phone."

The collegial banter hushed; workers refocused onto whatever was at their desks.

This side of Damien was something new. Angry and short with people?

"Take it easy, guy. They're just coping with...with this." Paulson waved his arm at the pile of boxes. "A little levity goes a long way.

Would you rather hear them upset, or getting into arguments?"

Damien rubbed exhausted-looking eyes with a thumb and forefinger. "It's beginning to be a bit much is all, this business of turning us into a dumping ground for rejects."

"Hey, that's right. This is perfect. Now we really are an island of misfit toys."

Damien laughed.

At last.

"Don't worry." Some of the old Damien smiled back. "I know this may be the only option they've got for storing these things. But I can't help but wonder. If anybody else was running this call center, would the powers that be have found someplace else to ditch them?"

CHAPTER 16

"Your governor believes that in this neck of the woods, people don't need recovery services. Or if they do, they've got the means to get them on their own. You folks know better. You help family after family, barely scraping by as it is. Now they're in the worst circumstances of their lives. Rest assured, if I'm elected, recovery needs will receive highest priority."

"My opponent has forgotten we've been through this before. Look at Marshland. People are rebuilding. They're moving on. We're a strong community. We have our friends and families, houses of worship, helping organizations, community groups. And good old-fashioned self-reliance. We'll do it again, thanks to volunteers like you. I place my faith in the charity and spirit of the good people of Willsey, not more taxes for federal programs."

What were they thinking, bringing in both characters to address the volunteers at the same time. Maybe so they would only need to stand around listening to politicians once.

After another glance at the time, Sarah tried to look interested. And somehow get comfortable amidst the diverse assembly of responders packed into the lobby, forced to listen to what was supposed to be some kind of rah-rah thank-you speech. Media were by invitation only, but loitered in full force, regardless.

The mandate to temporarily shut down the FAC for the affair had given rise to volleys of protest, producing even firmer commands for patience and respect. They would be depending on whoever was elected to cooperate with long-term recovery efforts, whether the support came by way of a candidate who wanted to tap financially stretched federal programs, or the one who would squeeze dry what little was left of local resources.

It was small wonder the rumor mill kept cranking out stories connecting politics with the explosion. Lately, the most popular notion tied it to the incumbent's veteran status. Given the primate displays of aggression seesawing between these two candidates, imagining some fringy type resorting to arbitrary mass destruction as an answer didn't take much.

Fringy. Paulson. She felt her face tighten. How would he react if subjected to this? Lacey had been wise to place him in Marshland.

Paulson.

Time and distance from him had let hindsight settle in. His rant about the Greatest Generation hadn't had anything to do with her father. It was just Paulson, wading around in another piece of ideological folderol. His willingness to share it with her showed he'd come to trust her enough to reveal some of his innermost beliefs.

What had she done with that trust? Blast him with both barrels, personally and professionally. Just as insensitive as elected officials, using a mass casualty aftermath to serve their political ends.

There had to be a way to squeeze a quick phone call into the day. A spontaneous opportunity wasn't going to come up any time soon. Especially since he also had those PFA teams to keep track of.

As she scribbled down a reminder, another potential disaster lingered in the near distance.

"He wouldn't really do that, would he?" she whispered to John. "The governor. Try to end federal funds? Those PFA teams were really effective. He can't derail that, can he?"

"Services are pretty much a done deal. DOJ's hooked in. As far as FEMA goes, the governor wasted no time declaring a disaster. D.C. agreed before they even heard from us. So it's up to locals to decide which paper train is worth mounting. No way would either of those two try to derail it. It would be political suicide."

"If that's true, then everything we're listening to right now is only, well, what my Dad would call a bunch of hooey?"

"I suppose that's one way of putting it."

"Then why is he saying it? Doesn't he realize what it will do to all those traumatized people, even if it is just hot air?"

"He's in a tough spot." He gave her a serious look. "He needs to be fiscally responsible, no matter what's going on."

"Of course." She'd hit a nerve. Tactical adjustments were in order. John had proven a strong and dependable ally. Alienating him in any manner would be a bad idea. "All I'm saying is, why didn't he save it for some other time? If he hadn't taken the bait...oh my god."

"What?"

"Alison. Is Alison here?" She scanned the rear view of those clustered between them and the speakers, dreading that dye-job ponytail. "Limits to services could become a rallying cry. What will she stir up with this?"

"She's not here. She was dismissed."

"What happened?"

"She got into it with military services." John paused, looking off in the distance. "There's more to it than that. I'm probably about to step over some lines. But someone should know."

With a hand to her elbow, he backed her into a less crowded corner. Never had he sounded so severe, shown such beady-eyed intent—like he was someone else entirely. Hair prickled on the back of her neck. *How well do I really know this man?*

He appeared to notice the alarm she'd failed at disguising. His approach abruptly softened. By the time he got to the main scoop, it once again felt like they were a couple of high school kids, frolicking beneath layers of authority and sneaking in a conversation behind teacher's back. He did have his charm that way.

"I did some checking. Delores isn't the only one who remembers her. Some advocates who'd been at 9/11 knew all about her."

"What did you find out?"

"The guy she said was her boyfriend really did exist. But he didn't die at the twin towers, nor was he her boyfriend."

"Are you serious?"

"After he disappeared, they interviewed friends and family.

Apparently, Alison lived in the same apartment complex as him, back in Brooklyn. Those who knew him told the authorities he'd never had any romantic interest in her. As far as he was concerned, she was stalking him. When the authorities caught up with Alison, she said the guy had business at the twin towers the morning of 9/11. This contradicted what his roommate said—that he'd gone on a hike upstate to get time away from the stalking business."

Chet. Just what kind of person had he gotten himself mixed up with? "Why didn't the criminal background check show anything about the stalking?"

"There were no charges filed, or restraining orders. Anyway, a few months later his body turned up. It was at the bottom of a ravine, in a place he often hiked. It was ruled as an accident, though there was no way to be sure one way or the other. They were suspicious of Alison, though, with her being so insistent he was at the twin towers. Nothing came of it."

"Her story does make for a convenient cover-up, if she did in fact play a role in the fall into the ravine. On the other hand, claiming he died in the twin towers would also be a way for her to get mental health services she couldn't afford. Or sympathy. Maybe it's wishful thinking, that he disappeared as a hero of sorts, rather than because of an effort to get away from her."

"She did get 9/11 volunteer mental health support for a while, with the obvious issues. It didn't take long to figure out most of it was going on long before 9/11. Then his body turned up. When they told her she didn't qualify for the long-term mental health program—let's just say she was not pleased."

"It explains the rampages. Why she presses so hard for services for disaster victims. In her mind, she's a bereaved survivor herself. One who thinks she got a raw deal."

*****

"Hey, Paulson. How's it...Holy Toledo!"

He'd never seen Chet move so quickly—full speed, for the side door. "Wait. What's wrong?"

The big man stopped, gripping the crash bar with saucers for eyes. His free hand pointed. Just outside the skylight illumination, a floating Charles lurked in the shadows, staking claim over the mother lode of clown toys.

How did that get there already? "It's just a Halloween decoration, Chet."

Chet homed in for a closer look. Appearing relieved, he returned.

"With Halloween two days off, you can't never tell." Chet hunched himself over and propped up his massive trunk, hands on knees, scrutinizing the floor beneath his belly. "Good. You left that rice. Any more ha'nts bothering you?"

"None worth mentioning."

"Shouldn't be none at all. Not with Uncle Earl's ghost box." Chet straightened and threw a hand at the contraption he'd installed on day one. "Now just a doggone minute."

Chet picked up the electrical cord trailing from the unit. He held up the end of it and stared. "Here's your problem. It ain't turned on."

"We moved it out of the way during set-up. I guess I forgot to plug it back in."

"No problem." He set the device a few feet away from the card table and took advantage of the last free electrical socket. "That should take care of things."

The gentle purr was more noticeable with the wall of boxes muting the hullabaloo on the other side. It was actually a rather pleasant sound, as compared to the sharp echoes beyond.

"You want it right here for sure. This is where them caskets were piled up."

"Won't somebody trip over it?"

"Just use it like a foot rest. That's what Uncle Earl did. While he was watching TV. Nobody'll run into it with your feet on it. They'll see it right there."

"Yes, but...never mind." Sometime during the day he'd fill out a request for an extension cord. If nothing else, it was a good source of white noise during consultations. Like the one he was supposed to be having with Chet. "As long as you're here, how about having a seat? I'd like to pick your brain about something."

"Sure thing." Chet settled into a plastic chair and leaned forward in eager anticipation. Could well be the first time he'd ever gotten this kind of request.

"It's about your friend, Alison. How is she doing?"

"Alison? She's fine. I've never seen a disaster worker like Alison. She's always doing something."

"How about lately?"

"Saw her just last night. She was working on her laptop. Said it was something really big."

"She didn't seem upset or anything?"

"Alison's never upset. Just gets a little excited sometimes. Then she's fine, off doing something else."

"Does she get excited about anything in particular?"

Chet looked thoughtful. "Nope." He smiled back, awaiting the next question.

Better to cut to the chase. "All that work wears on people. I'm wondering whether Alison gets the support she needs. Like time with friends. Seeing as she's been working so hard."

"She sees people all day long. And me and Alison, we see each other somewhere almost every day."

"I was thinking more about what you two do to recover from the tension. Do you have a chance to get away from everything?"

"Sure thing. She likes to go around and see what else is going on for the disaster. We go look at places like that all the time."

He felt his teeth clench. Additional heat was the last thing that half-lit barrel of gunpowder needed. "I mean away from disaster. A break from it, not looking for *more* of it."

"She gets excited if I talk about doing something else. Alison's whole world is disaster. It's okay by me to take her around. I don't mind."

"You done jawing yet?" Freddie appeared from around the corner of Mount Clown Toy. "We got another delivery before lunch."

"Hope that helps, Paulson." Chet got up, the chair groaning relief. "You see? You don't need to worry none. That old gal's got everything under control. Her and me both."

*****

"This is Sarah." The dead silence at the other end, along with the sudden spike in anxiety, left the rest of the rehearsed message unsaid. In fact, it had disappeared altogether, as if she were starting from scratch. She should have written it down.

"Sarah?" Paulson finally responded. "Sarah. Good to hear from you.

153

To what do I owe the honor of this call?"

His question could be interpreted as either carefully diplomatic or blatantly sarcastic. If it had been the other way around, her attitude would most likely be the latter.

"Look, I'm sorry about the other day. What I said was completely unfair."

"I don't know about that. Some of what you said had some truth to it."

"Please don't take it seriously. It was a long day. A long two days."

"I understand."

"No, you don't." She tried again to collect her thoughts. Where did that polished speech get to, anyway? "When I saw you, I'd just had a really good visit with Dad. It sounded like you were saying the grief we're going through is because of something he did."

"That isn't what I meant."

"I know. Now. At the time I was too burnt out. I lashed out. I'm sorry."

"Apology accepted. Don't beat yourself up over it."

"It's just that I know you've been through a lot, too. All those...memories. You don't need me trashing your whole approach to life."

"This sounds like it would work out better talking face to face."

"With these assignments, there's no way to know when we'll end up in the same place at the same time. That's exactly why I decided to call. Before the silence got too big."

"How about tonight? I can come down there. Me and my claptrap motorcycle."

Hearing his easy laughter was like finding spring bulbs popping up through crusty snow after a long hard winter.

"Yes. No. Wait. I promised to take Lil to see Sean tonight, after her support group."

"Would she mind if I tagged along?"

"Of course not. She'd love it. You rescued Sean. In her eyes, you're a hero."

CHAPTER 17

The remainder of the afternoon floated. Merely knowing she wanted to see him chased away the doldrums of hermitage behind the mountain.

But the minutes crawled. Lacey was painfully accurate in describing the job as low-key. The DMH responders working the phone bank got the really interesting stuff. During downtime, they were gracious enough to invite him to join their impromptu peer review sessions. They discussed the nitty-gritty of phone counseling, or commonalities among the callers.

Still, it put him on the outside looking in. "Front and center," as Sarah had so aptly put it, was his comfort zone—the crisis work. This staff mental health angle he'd been saddled with was mainly preventive. At least so far, with workers still fresh. At this stage of the game, it seemed like the position hid in the background.

At the opposite corner of the warehouse, Damien was glued to his cell phone. The few threads of conversation he picked up on suggested that the lumber business had caught up with him again; in particular, with Todd Goode projects.

How did Damien do it, make time for this? How he kept coming up with motivation to stay and go on, in spite of the hassles.

It gnawed at him. It was there even on day one, when workers at the center were still strangers to one another. Paulson had formed acceptable relations with them. But everybody else seemed to have something more than the sum of multiple one-on-one connections. A common mission got forged, set in motion. At times, they seemed to function as one.

Back at the floods, he'd put in an appearance at Lacey's group meetings. But, that had been mainly for letting everybody know what he was doing, not group planning. The course before him seemed less certain. Had he stumbled somewhere along the line? Fallen, through some previously unnoticed hole in his professional foundation?

Somebody needed to hang onto the reins. Especially out in Marshland, where he was all there was to be had for everyday mental health disasters in living. In that respect, he really was alone.

His eyes fell to the wad of weed debris decorating his table. It was looking even more dilapidated. Loose specks of silt were spread out over the memos, reports, and announcements that had been dropped then ignored over the last couple of days.

"Look at what's in front of you," Horace had said. What was he missing?

Was it something Sarah saw, too? It was obvious that she liked him, in spite of her not so subtle misgivings about how he did social work. There was also good reason to believe she was attracted to him. Though it was also clear she had no intention of doing anything with it.

This hole. Might it have something to do with why she so freely, so sweetly offers friendship, but nothing more?

The light on the hard line flashed. Duty called. "Disaster services. Paulson speaking."

"Give me the manager," said a curt, fuzzy voice.

Paulson glanced across the back of the warehouse. Damien was well entrenched.

"He's tied up. Can I take a message?"

"You guys think you're pretty slick, don't you."

Paulson froze. "What did you say?"

"Just you wait. You won't get off so easy next time."

"Wait a minute. Who is this?"

The other end went dead.

*****

As Sarah neared the church, lively interchange could be made out. She checked the time. The meeting was running over.

156

She picked her way across bark dust to look through a wall of windows. In spite of the steamy splotches coating the glass, a large gathering was obvious, perhaps thirty or forty. It was impossible to hear everything being said. People were talking over the top of each other. In fact, it seemed a little too spirited.

A calming presence took over. It sounded like he was offering reassurances. Probably the pastor. There was a woman crying; someone yelled something out. Another person interrupted the assumed pastor with angry words.

Standing near the glow of the entryway was beginning to feel conspicuous, like being spotlighted for action. Would offering assistance in there be seen as an intrusion? Probably.

One of the double doors flew open, almost hitting her. Sarah stepped back as participants filed out. They looked anything but reassured by whatever it was they had just participated in. Those talking among themselves did so in uneasy tones.

Lil appeared, turbocharged. Her fit of indignation propelled her well beyond where Sarah stood waiting. She darted up and touched the back of Lil's shoulder.

Lil spun around, Jerrod clutched against her. There it was, that old familiar fire lighting up her eyes—a blaze that almost always fueled something righteously indignant. Typically, poorly thought out. "Good, it's you. You won't believe what I just heard."

"What's going on? What happened in there?"

"I got an earful, that's for sure. It's a bunch of bull. Nobody's going to help us."

"There are other groups out there, if this one doesn't work."

"No, not the group. This group is fine. Maybe the one thing that is. I found out the truth about all those agencies. It's only lip service. They aren't really going to help." Several expletives let loose while Lil attempted a one-handed collapse of her umbrella-like stroller.

"Here, let me do that." Sarah finished the job.

On the way to the car, Lil's venting carried on over the clomp of her impractical shoes. "How do we pay those medical bills? Sean'll be hospitalized for weeks, maybe months. We don't have that kind of money. It's twenty percent co-pay. And what about me and Jerrod? What do we live off of, without his salary? Where's money going to come from? It's not just us, there's everybody else, too. This'll bankrupt half of Willsey."

"Victims assistance, and other sources. At the FAC, they're already signing people up. You should, too, if you haven't."

"Hogwash. Those people signing up—they'll never get a thing."

"Why? Is that what this group is about?" As Sarah loaded baby paraphernalia, a heated argument brought up the rear of those exiting. A whiny nasal voice stood out above the others, unnervingly familiar. She slammed shut the trunk, slow to turn and confirm the inevitable.

Alison was beet red. Smoke billowed out over the pastor's attempts to placate her.

Poor guy. Perhaps now would be the time to step in.

No. Given Alison's attitude, it would probably just make things worse.

"Don't you see how wrong this is?" Alison leered at the pastor as if he worked the alternate side of the cloth. "Don't you want people to get what they need?"

"We really do appreciate your offer," said the pastor. "Thank you for that. But it isn't going to work out with this group."

"I belong here. I can make a real difference."

"I know you want to help. We teach forgiveness and moving forward, helping one another as we can. A protest rally doesn't fit with our vision of fellowship and goodwill."

A sputtering approached in the distance—Paulson's bike.

Good. Maybe he knew how to get the tantrum under control.

"We'll be remembering your concerns in our prayers, Alison. Best wishes." The pastor stepped toward her with outspread arms.

"The hell with it. With all of you!" Alison rammed two open palms at the pastor. She looked poised to follow it up with a swing. Probably would have, if he hadn't lost his balance, now sitting on the church lawn.

Her display of physical acting out was unexpected. Sarah froze, processing it. Images of John's account swirled. Could Alison in fact be capable of the worst suspicions against her? Until now, she had only shown difficulty with controlling verbal outbursts. Physical violence— that was something entirely different.

Paulson swept up from behind and helped the cleric to his feet.

"You!" Alison glared at Paulson with the look of a woman scorned.

"I should have known you had something to do with this."

"What's going on?" Paulson caught Sarah's gaze.

"You told him to throw me out, didn't you?" Alison's pupils were so dilated her irises all but disappeared.

"I don't know what you're talking about." Paulson looked Sarah's way again, still seeking explanation. Sarah edged his way while the pastor started in on a version of turning the other cheek.

"I'm sorry, Alison." The pastor brushed away grass clippings stuck to his clothing. "I'll leave you to your friends. I hope things work out for you." He checked the rear a couple of times as he made his retreat.

Sarah whispered over Paulson's shoulder. "She was trying to turn the group into a protest rally against the relief effort." There was plenty more to say. Did Paulson need warning, that there was risk of physical harm, given the new information regarding Alison's questionable past? She could hardly say more with Alison standing right there.

Paulson groaned. "Alison, what is it with you? If only you'd stick to protocol. You'd be such an asset. Just stay within the guidelines. We support people, we advocate for them. But we don't rally as their activists. We help them become strong for themselves."

"Don't you dare lecture me about protocol." Alison was visibly shaking. "You're no one to talk. You bend rules all the time. Two different standards, huh? It's okay for you, but not me?"

"Bending rules is one thing. Obliterating them with an atomic blast is another."

Chet's pickup turned into the lot. He squeezed out of the cab and lumbered their way.

"It's not fair," Alison blurted out between sobs. "You're all against me. Everybody's always against me."

It was time for the kid gloves. "We're not against you, Alison. You just need to tweak your methods. Maybe Paulson and I could help you with that."

"Why doesn't anybody ever like me?" She openly bawled, nothing held back.

The toxic blob of self-absorption was unreachable. The skirmish was lost; it was time to let it go. Hopefully there would be other chances.

"Aw, that's not true." Chet was finally on board. "I like you, Alison. Come on. What's done is done. It'll all be fine and dandy."

He threw an arm across Alison's shoulders and led her away as she continued to sob. Her attempt to shake loose did little, the arm draped over her practically as wide as she.

"I'll take real good care of her," he called back at them, giving an easy thumb's up.

Whatever that might be. Chet was so gullible, so trusting. Alison's colorful past lurked in the near distance. Chet was too big for Alison to push over or injure, unless she used a weapon. Could that, too, be a piece of her behavioral repertoire, yet to reveal itself?

Probably not. She went off on people with so little provocation. If she were inclined toward weapons, she'd surely have a rap sheet and list of casualties a mile long by now.

Chet could probably take care of himself, physically. But...the trouble Alison could get him into.

"That poor gal," said Lil. "You wouldn't believe everything she's been through."

"She's a...troubled lady."

"Of course she is." Lil stiffened, as if about to fend off blows. "You'd be troubled, too, if you were her."

Alison had done her work. Her rhetoric had Lil reduced into a puddle of misguided goo. How long had it been since Lil had had some kind of cause to chase after? When they were teenagers, there had always been something, like that group for rescue horses. Their senior year in high school, Lil helped out with the elementary school's special education program, filling in when the teaching assistant position got axed during budget cuts. Her outrage was reminiscent of conversations they'd had back then about the school board's actions.

"I know she means well."

"That Alison knows what she's talking about. She lost her boyfriend at 9/11. Who would know better than her?"

So John's sources were right. She could no longer dismiss it as embellished rumor. "There are reasons why different people get different assistance. It's apples and oranges. Everybody's different."

"You've never been where we are. How would you know?"

Somewhere in her bag of tricks there had to be something to help reconnect. So far it seemed like whatever she tried only pushed Lil further into fanaticism, just as in years past whenever Sarah tried to introduce logic. "You and Alison have something in common with Sean being hurt, and with her...having been through something similar. It's easier for you to relate. But what she's suggesting, nothing good can come of it. Only more pain and frustration."

"If she has that demonstration, count me in. I can't sit and do nothing."

"Let the system work for you. Put your energy into that. What would Sean want you to do? Be patient."

"Patience, my patootie." She clung to her infant, as if the audacity of it all was about to pluck him away. "If that bunch knows what they're doing, why haven't they rounded up the guy who did this yet? I don't think they're even trying."

"Law enforcement's done a lot. We don't hear about everything going on."

"They don't tell us because nothing's happening. It's just a big show."

Paulson found his tongue. "They can't say much. It helps them catch the bad guys. If they give away details about the situation publicly, it messes things up."

Lil snorted. "Just an excuse. Mind you, Alison is the first person who's made any sense in this. The terrorists aren't the real enemy. Not any more."

*****

"Why do you think you missed it?" Sarah's dainty hands were wrapped around a bulky mug of the cafeteria coffee. "Surely it showed."

At the time of the church debacle, Paulson had not yet bounced back from the phone call aftermath. Damien's reaction to it had danced between open-mouthed disbelief and indignant blowout. It had taken some doing to get him simmered down before the authorities turned up. In spite of their sticking to official jargon, they, too, seemed troubled by it.

Was the threat meant against Damien? The call center? The operation itself? What exactly were they threatening? Maybe it was just some jerk trying to get on Damien's nerves, perhaps over something that had nothing to do with the operation. Like a dissatisfied lumber client. The other end of the spectrum held the most disturbing scenario: forewarning of another explosion. More carnage. More catastrophe.

Given his druthers, he'd ignore the detective's directive to keep a lid on it and hash it out with Sarah, before it burned a hole in his stomach. However, that would serve only his needs, not hers. There was no way he was going to make that mistake again. Besides, it would burden her with something that might well turn out to be nothing.

It was time to set it aside, and let admin and the authorities do what they could with it.

Like that would end well.

"I noticed Alison's vulnerabilities," he said. "But she has strengths, too. The IT manager who had her last spring said she was great. Dependable, willing to do anything. I figured her past would be an asset. She'd relate to disaster survivors. She's good at PFA. When she's in the mood, anyway."

"She was certainly good at stirring up those people at the church."

"When she had problems with the PFA program, I always stepped in and took care of it. Then some of it got back to the boss. She wanted her out. I didn't want to give up. The work was good for Alison. It built confidence. She thought I was wonderful to stick up for her. She called it 'you and me against the world.'"

Which should have tipped me off in the first place. Revelation of this side of Alison had thrown him off, as much as Sarah's choice of conversational topic. Their meeting certainly wasn't going as he'd fantasized. "Probably why she felt so betrayed. I should have seen it coming."

"You had no choice." Sarah's sweet smile and gentle support made it more unnerving. It was like back in his internship, being explained the basics by a superior.

"She's the wrong person for PFA," Sarah continued. "At some point it was a given that she would decompensate. What we're seeing now is what she turns into when overstressed. What an Alison does when pushed to the brink."

"But she shows so much resilience. Every time she's shown the door, she finds another and steps right in. She doesn't give up."

"Actually, that's what scares me."

The whole thing had him off balance. The chat he had so looked forward to—revisiting a few minor professional quirks, making things right again, enjoying an island of peace away from that call center threat business—it was nowhere on the horizon. Instead, here they were in the middle of yet another controversy over his professional decision-making.

That Alison. Why had he been so sure he could rescue her from herself, even with the boss getting on his case about it? The more Sarah handed out her kind reassurances, the louder his gut seemed to rumble. More so, in light of Alison's sharp comments about bending rules, thoughts that kept racing well ahead of Sarah's gentle probing.

Yes, he bent rules sometimes. It was for good, greasing the wheels so things move more smoothly. Wasn't it? Alison's act was more like bending the rules on steroids.

But that drive, this mission she cooked up. There was no way around the comparison. Was it really so different from what he was doing in Marshland? How much of Alison's fanaticism was just a misguided version of his own "agenda," as Sarah had put it? Was he to blame for Alison getting so out of hand?

It opened up another disturbing possibility. Did firing her feel too much like what he deserved himself?

Sarah's lips were still moving, but words stopped registering. There was only the image of a concerned friend, and the chilly gust of cold realities blasting through the window. Was this business with Alison just one more thing Sarah saw in him, something that made her keep him at arm's length? It could well be why "just friends" was good enough.

Sarah was hesitating, looking indecisive.

"What is it?"

"There's more to this. Some things you need to know." She shared a tale of stalking, 9/11, a suspicious death, evasive maneuverings, narcissistic entitlement, and the advent of a one-woman mission to save the world from mistreatment by disaster relief.

His sweaty palm bobbled the mug handle. He dropped a napkin over the resulting coffee splatters and left it there. He looked away.

Surrounding him was a busy cafeteria, overrun with sterile metal and plastic. Hospital staff sat at much of it, along with a scattering of anxious and fatigued-looking visitors. An active grill somewhere in the rear made its presence known through an occasional sizzle from flipped meat patties. Everything seemed normal, in place, in this piece of the outside world. Yet untamed anxiety continued to try to steamroll from within.

Please, no shadows. Not now.

"You're awfully quiet." She was studying his face.

"Sorry about that. A lot to digest." He took a couple quick gulps of coffee, his hands unsteady.

He had seen Alison's breaking point. How much more would he be able to stomach, before his own crash and burn?

CHAPTER 18

Wednesday, October 30th

"Hey, check this out." Damien was sitting at his makeshift desk, engrossed in a podcast. It was another report on the parade bombing.

"Thanks, but I'm OD'd." Paulson turned to leave.

"Wait. Mr. White's in this one."

Paulson backpedalled and studied the monitor. "I saw him yesterday. Man, does he look better."

The screen held a shot of Sean in his hospital bed, as he'd been the night before, except now fully awake. Lil was seated next to him, bouncing a stewing Jerrod.

"...didn't tell them anything they didn't already know." Sean was propped up with several pillows.

"Can you tell our viewers what you saw?"

"I'd just parked my car next to some metal plates on the asphalt. When I got out, I tripped over one that was sticking up a little, like someone had been messing with it. Then I saw smoke."

"You saw the bomb, already lit?"

"No, just smoke. Coming from under the metal plate."

"Were you frightened?"

"No. I figured someone's cigarette butt had rolled under there."

"Then what happened?"

"I couldn't see a cigarette. But with so many kids around, curiosity might have gotten little fingers burnt. So I moved the plate to look for it. That's when more smoke started up, too much to be a cigarette. I thought maybe some street debris caught fire. But the smoke, it was pinkish. It didn't smell like tobacco. So something screwy was going on."

"What did you do then?"

"I remembered a police officer directing traffic at a nearby intersection. I was almost to him when I heard some funny popping sounds back there. Then there was a boom. That's the last thing I remember before I woke up here, with my lovely bride watching over me." Sean reached over and grabbed Lil's free hand. Her exhilaration filled the screen. She was clearly lapping up her fifteen minutes of fame.

"I guess it really wasn't anything new." Damien clicked off the concluded interview. "They said all along they thought it was natural gas and a smoke bomb. But it was cool hearing Mr. White talk about it. The kids will get a kick out of this. If they recognize him, without the spikes."

"Go, Sean. That's one of the best eyewitness reports yet. He sure was lucky to get away when he did."

"Think of how much worse it would have been if those soldiers had still been around."

"Maybe that's really who it was intended for. It probably needed more air to get going—which it got, when Sean lifted the plate."

"A lot of very lucky people, military and otherwise." Damien left his seat and ran a slow gaze over the phone bank personnel. "Unfortunately everybody's beginning to forget that." Aimless wandering accompanied discussion, taking them out of seclusion and drawn toward the phone bank collective.

"How do you mean?"

"People aren't so thrown off, or confused any more. More empowered, I guess."

"How's that a problem?"

"There's more anger. Some callers are out and out enraged—that anybody would do this to our annual tradition. It's personal. They're also getting impatient with day-to-day inconveniences. Then there's the kid's nightmares, or not wanting to go to school. And since we still don't know a whole lot, people worry it'll happen again. But the biggest backlash is anger."

"Have you talked to the mental health team?"

"Not specifically about this. They're aware of it though."

That was where he should be, with them—working on critical issues, not closeted in no man's land. Especially after that disgruntled caller. Not to mention Alison's rant, and everything she'd so easily stirred up at the church. Anger wasn't just a client problem. It was a staff problem, too. Everybody was getting on edge.

They passed the Magic Circle. The toy clown was missing from the corner of the agenda board. A sheet of lined yellow paper was pinned in its place. Paulson held it out for a better look. It portrayed a primitive sketching of a ghost. A conversation cloud saying "Ooooh" floated above a pile of what was probably someone's idea of caskets.

"What's this about?" Paulson let the drawing drop back to the storyboard. "Planning Halloween festivities?"

"Between Charles, the casket story, and Halloween around the corner, imaginations are getting out of hand. While it was still dark this morning, some of the early birds heard spooky noises. They couldn't figure out where it came from, with the echoes."

"We know it can't be ghosts. Ask Chet. He's got it covered."

"Maybe that ghost-busting machine of his needs a tune-up. We should ask logistics where to send it for maintenance."

"Don't. Not even in jest. Next, we'd hear Chet bought some kind of extended warranty."

Damien's hard line rang. He returned to his office, and was quickly drawn into intense discussion.

While here sat Paulson Forbes, sorting out ghost stories. At least it had been almost twenty-four hours without any shadows.

A few minutes passed before Damien hung up—they could pick up where they'd left off, if he was quick about it. "There's anger issues for staff, too. Maybe...what's wrong?"

Damien had paled. He continued to stare at the phone. "There's been some irregularity in the casework."

"What casework? For this operation? Except for the health services teams, all we're doing is tallying needs and making referrals."

"Casework leftover from the floods. The ones still open for building and repairs. Someone's found anomalies in the files. Financial anomalies."

Of course. In the excitement, the flood response had gotten shoved so far onto the back burner it would have gone unnoticed even if it boiled over. But admin hadn't forgotten.

"Sometime today someone's coming from headquarters." Damien crumpled into a slump. He halfway folded his arms, unfolded them, and finally just stuck his hands in pockets. "They're going to have a look around. The job director didn't come out and say it. But I can read between the lines."

Paulson allowed silence, dreading the direction Damien's thoughts were taking him.

"They think..." Damien paused. "They think I might have something to do with the discrepancies. I guess now I really am a suspect."

*****

Yet another dramatic change in setting had overtaken the conference hall. About half of the booths and cubbies had disappeared. Of the armed forces resources, only a single long table managed by a couple of bored-looking soldiers remained. The other military personnel were gone.

There weren't many clients on site, either. Finding the staff entrance locked up had been a surprise. Staff and clients alike received a cursory scan at the main entry, and continued in with little further ado.

"What's going on?" Sarah unbuttoned her coat.

"The beginning of the end." Delores stood and took hold of one end of their table. "Will you give me a hand? We're going that-a-way."

Sarah picked up the other end and helped slide the table into newly freed-up space. At last, breathing room. She pushed aside that boxes of pamphlets she'd almost tripped over a couple of times. "What happened to the military?"

"They've accounted for the majority of veterans and active duty known to be at the parade. They've gone back to usual protocol. Other veterans who were spectators could still turn up here. It doesn't take the whole ensemble for that."

"It feels empty. I'd gotten used to having the uniforms around. What's the deal with door security? Why the let up?"

Delores snatched up a pencil about to roll off the table. "Apparently they have enough of an idea of what happened that they aren't as worried about a second incident."

"What do they think it was?"

"Smoke bombs set off natural gas from a leaky valve under the road."

"So, was it an accident?"

"Who knows. With nobody taking credit, and the drop in security, that'd be my guess."

"Aren't they going to tell everybody?"

"Eventually. But I haven't heard any promises made."

John would know, if anybody did. Sarah scanned the room for him, unsuccessful. The absence of his calm professionalism, his friendly smile—it produced more feeling of disconnect and emptiness than the missing military presence did. It was not the same place without him. But even without him, there were clearly more helpers on site than people looking for assistance.

"So far, most clients here today are returns." Delores absently bounced the pencil's eraser end against the table's Melmac surface. "I guess those who want to come in have done it. Missing family members is less of an issue, too. At least for those who said they were looking. I bet we go into outreach mode soon."

Other DMH responders on site were standing around talking among themselves. The calm felt like a major flip-flop after the out-of-control clash at the church the night before. So much hurt had emerged there, so much stress and trauma. Too bad the DMH workers currently twiddling their thumbs hadn't been around for that one. If only resources were better hooked up with those who actually needed them. Including for the growing collection of those she couldn't stop thinking about.

Paulson—his battle with acute stress, not to mention finally opening his eyes to the consequences of his sometimes oddball professional practices.

Alison—her fragile shell imploding from the pressure of her experiences.

Chet—steady as Green River in his blissful naiveté, but so vulnerable to being led astray by someone like Alison.

Sean—stuck in a hospital bed, on a long road to physical recovery.

And Lil—so messed up by her distress that it could get her into some real trouble. Especially in light of Alison's influence on her.

"Could you do without me? I have a friend between a rock and a hard place. I'd be of more use to her than here."

"No problem for me. You better check with Lacey, though."

"I thought the memorial service was another week out." Visions of a nice, quiet afternoon of sipping tea with Lil faded into oblivion.

"This one's a private service." Lacey glanced up from the wall chart sticky-note frenzy that seemed to have taken her prisoner. "It was someone who did a lot of local volunteer work. Some of our staff will be there as mourners."

"Why me? What you just described sounds like a staff mental health assignment."

"Number one, you're available; two, you're well-schooled in grief issues." Lacey moved the sticky-note with Sarah's name on it off to one side. "Number three, it's in Marshland. Locals know who you are. Staff will know what you're there for. But it's up to you."

It was hard to come up with excuses to turn down an assignment in her own hometown. But it had definitely not been on the list of the day's priorities.

"Someone from DMH is already hooked up with the family," Lacey continued. "It'll be good to know there's a spare to tap for anybody else. Especially for any staff meltdowns."

If she only knew. She didn't dare tell her about the latest installment of the Alison story. No telling what Lacey might assign her if she heard about that episode. "All right then. I'll go."

*****

"You must be here for the search and destroy mission." Damien trumpeted it out as a battle cry, squaring his shoulders.

The short stocky man with peculiar horn-rimmed glasses jumped. He stepped back and eyed Damien, similar to a barn owl startled from sleep. "Eh? I beg your pardon?"

An assistant director Paulson knew of only as "Don" came up next to the visitor and lasered Damien with a dirty look. "I would like you to meet Alan Lebesgue. He's liaisoning from Canada, Crime Victims Services. One of the hospitalized is Canadian."

Damien looked ready to climb into a box with the clown toys. Either that or dig a hole in Sam's empty lot and bury himself.

Paulson interrupted the awkwardness by grasping Alan's uncertain hand. "Nice to meet you. Paulson Forbes, disaster mental health."

"I'm taking Alan around to various operational sites so he can see what we do for people." Don had yet to liberate his critical gaze from the mortified call center manager.

The hard line in the office rang, excusing Damien from further torture. As he tended to it, Paulson led the others on a tour of the operation.

"I've heard a lot about your behavioral health approach," said Alan. "You're all volunteers?"

"Ninety-five percent."

"Back home, needs after disaster are taken care of by the usual public health services. It didn't get separated out and studied the way it is here."

Paulson continued to engage their rattled guest as best he could. Don eased up, too, without Damien's presence to remind him of the welcome they'd received. Between questions, Paulson thought up ways to clear his schedule and come up with a strategy to inspire Damien. He needed to get a grip before the real investigators turned up.

"How long have you been here, Alan?"

"Since the day of the explosion. I'm from due north. We had an incident not long ago ourselves. After I got here, I heard there was an injured Canuck. So I arranged to stay in official capacity."

"How's he doing?"

"Still unconscious. I'll be here for him. The agencies I've visited with so far have been...hospitable."

"You'll have to excuse Damien." Paulson gave a subtle nod in the direction of Damien's office. "He's been under a lot of strain."

"I understand. I do appreciate everything you're doing, all of you. I must say I'm amazed. I had no idea so much could happen for people after something like this."

Alan looked saddened yet anxious. An odd combination. Something heavy-duty was eating at him, beyond the tragedy of the bombing or Damien's questionable hospitality. He was sure of it. The victim advocates he'd met before were much tougher skinned than this. "I'm amazed myself. Are there specific concerns you have? What do you do up north? Maybe we can do something comparable for your client."

"Thanks, but I'm a bit worn out. With my client's condition being what it is, there's no rush." He turned to Don. "I have some errands. If it's all the same to you, let's call it a day."

"I know." A recalcitrant Damien emerged from his office. "I know."

"It's getting to you," Paulson said anyway.

Damien invited himself into the mental health hideaway and plunked himself into one of the lawn chairs.

I guess the doctor is in. Paulson seated himself across from him, after sparing a quick glance at the latest additions to the piles of memos.

"How could it not get to me? I work my butt off for this organization."

"You do burn the midnight oil. I've meant to ask you about that. Is it really necessary? Surely your family would rather have you at home at the end of the day."

"No choice. Dad calls several times a day. He does the best he can, but filling in gaps from long distance takes time. Afterhours are the only time to catch up on paperwork for this gig."

"Can you do your best job of it, though? When you're so fried already?"

"My record is spotless. Of course, as soon as something's off, everybody forgets that."

No, it wasn't fair. But life wasn't fair. It was what it was. "It's entirely possible there are people out there who are drawing unfair conclusions. Only you can turn it into paranoia."

"It was a logical deduction. They said there'd be a headquarters visitor. Then an assistant director turns up with some nerdy dude. Just the type you'd expect to get a charge out of going through somebody's electronic records. So I blew it."

At least Damien was okay with talking about it. Not falling into that over-used rationalization that "it's not paranoia if people really are out to get you." This was good. Especially after getting a second threatening phone call. That would ramp up anybody's paranoia.

"Funny thing about paranoia. When you let it take charge of how you interpret and react to people, you create the very thing you fear."

Damien's quiet simmer did not appear any less vigorous.

"Are you sure you're up to meeting with the real investigators?"

"I'll get through it."

"I've little doubt. Before I take off, how about something for my confidence? I hope your 'I'm getting through it' won't also mean you're gone when I get back."

"I'm not giving up."

"That doesn't mean they won't give up on you. Sure you don't want me to hang around? I know I'd feel ganged up on if I were here alone, defending myself to a herd of admin types. There will be others supporting the memorial service. I won't be missed."

"I'll be fine."

CHAPTER 19

Sarah got there early, hoping for opportunity to squeeze in a few precious moments to herself.

Funerals were puzzling. Their main purpose was to move along the grieving process—needs of the living left behind, not the deceased. Yet so many make a big deal out of not wanting memorial services held for them when they pass.

It was hard to find the common sense of it. Didn't they want their loved ones to heal? Why would they care, anyway? They would no longer be around to know about it.

Then there was the fellowship among those who attended. Some would cry, perhaps sob mightily. The verbose would tell stories about the lost loved one. A preponderance of handkerchiefs would appear. Many others would settle for chatting pleasantly, sharing the latest with fellow grievers as they might at a holiday gathering, perhaps never mentioning the deceased. They used it as an opportunity to connect in ways other than expressing sadness over the loss.

How had people come to understand this—that they needed these occasions, these group support rituals that so reliably promote healing and transition, such that they could be found in practically every culture worldwide?

And, could one iota of it actually happen with the invading media extravaganza?

The event was the first formal remembrance of an explosion-caused death. Every television station, both local and national, was ready to get into the act. Yellow tape warned journalists of how close their presence was going to be tolerated. Recording equipment was beginning to line up behind it. Gaggles of news crews squawked at one another, jockeying for premium viewing space.

It was obscene. So far, more media personalities were hanging around than actual grievers. Now would be the best time for a break—at the river's edge, the one location that wouldn't force a view of the spectacle.

Green River seeped various shades of gray, complementing the billowing achromatic sky. Its benign peace seemed to envelope her, the trickling sounds almost hypnotizing. Funny how moving water always worked that piece of magic. Such resilience to its invisible yet determined flow, a current that would eventually caress the border of the first niche she had ever called home.

It was hard to remember the last visit to this particular stretch of waterfront. It tended to be underappreciated. With the cemetery so near, picnickers and other merrymakers usually gathered further downriver. Not so, for her and Lil. They had often taken advantage of its privacy: lounging on the grassy bank, enjoying the gentle breeze and shade of the cottonwoods, and solving problems of the world. Boys, clothes, hairstyles, horses, grades, boys...

"That drop-off area over there is the new boundary." Paulson appeared from behind, in his usual windblown state. Regardless of whether there was any wind to justify it. "Gravesites beyond broke away with the second round of flooding."

"And their spiritual remains reside at the call center?" She turned and smiled at him.

"Apparently. People are hearing spooky noises now."

"Oh, please." She reconsidered. "What about you? Are you hearing them, too?"

He laughed. "No. I even slept well last night, in spite of our run-in with Alison. Exhaustion must have done it. First good night of sleep I've had since this began."

"I'm glad."

"There seem to be enough real issues going on to keep my mind occupied. Apparently that trumps harassment by trauma specters."

A wisp of burden lifted. Paulson was recovering, as she had been certain he would. In fact, at that moment, he almost seemed like the Paulson of the previous spring, strolling along the old neighborhood's winding road as he searched for flood victims. There was something else, too. Something different about him. It was hard to place a finger on exactly what.

"How did you manage to get away from the FAC?"

"Things are dying down." She cringed. "I mean, winding down. Sorry about that. Politically incorrect choice of words."

"You have death on your mind. We all do."

"It wouldn't be sensitive to someone in active throes of grieving." She looked around for anyone who might have overheard. "How about you? Is it quieter at the call center?"

"Not really. If anything, we're busier. Phoning in is easier for people than going to the FAC. The DMH workers really have their hands full. People are beginning to get over the shock, and are getting upset with the lack of answers."

Tell me about it. The angry man at the FAC had been completely unreasonable. He'd certainly succeeded in stirring up trouble in a way she never would have predicted.

"People might think up something retaliatory to do against whoever they've decided is responsible. Then there's the whole copycat issue."

"Bite your tongue."

"I wish I were assigned in a way that let me do something to put a dent in it. Instead, here I am with this 'low-key' role. So low-key, it's not even necessary for me to be there all the time."

"What do you do all day?"

"Lately, babysit Damien."

Damien's status as a trauma victim—it had slipped her mind, with everything else going on. "How's he doing?"

"He's not adjusting well to the scrutiny."

Mourners were beginning to file into the church. They watched them gather while Paulson described the discovery of some casework anomalies.

"So what do they think it is? Fraudulent applications?"

176

"Don't know yet."

"Speaking of the sleaze factor."

Todd Goode and family climbed out of the classic Lincoln Continental idling in front of the church. The absence of pageantry in the patriarch's gait held her usual condemnation in check. He looked reserved and respectful as he exchanged polite greetings with others. How might he know the grieving family; what was the connection? Maybe it was because one of his properties was involved.

"Dad said it was his building that blew up."

"Poor guy. He took a hit with that tornado last spring, too."

"I didn't know."

"Most of a townhouse development. It got leveled. Or needed to be afterwards, what was left of it."

Paulson followed along as she ambled to the end of the new fishing dock.

"Dad joked that the bomb might be a plot for Mr. Goode to collect insurance. At least, I think he was joking."

"Todd isn't such a bad guy. I don't know much about his business dealings. But he's done things for the community. Like helping repair this dock."

She looked down at the neatly arranged planking under their feet. "They have a history, Dad and Mr. Goode. I probably don't have a balanced picture of the man."

"I should say hello to him." Paulson's eyes were following the Goode family's progress toward the building. "Sam's not the only one who entertains those sorts of thoughts."

As usual, Lacey knew what she was talking about. Several attendees on site were people Sarah had run into as staff during the floods. In all likelihood, they were involved with the current operation as well. A couple of them raised a hand in greeting.

She situated herself out front. If anyone felt the need for a listening ear, she would be well placed. With the massive presence of natural support, any needed action probably would be after the service. If then. Besides, it was better not to take up space inside the church. It rightfully belonged to loved ones. It already looked to be approaching standing room only in there.

Organ music started up. Those chatting at the entryway took the soothing chords of "Amazing Grace" as a cue to join those inside. Paulson had disappeared, somewhere around the corner with the Goodes.

She relaxed against a chilled pillar and took stock. Latecomers continued to fill the parking lot. Passengers ditched their vehicles and hurried into the building—except this one man at the edge of the parking lot, who remained motionless. Short, fortyish, long beige raincoat. He mostly stared downward, looking up every now and then. Indecisive about something. Whatever it was, he found it distasteful. His gloom projected itself as severely as the overcast sky.

He appeared to come to a decision and moved on. He picked his way across the soggy patch of lawn that fronted the cemetery. He read a few headstones, wandering without apparent purpose, until reaching the shoreline. After traveling the length of the dock, he stopped.

Something about him was familiar. Where had she seen him before? It was recent, for sure. Maybe he was disaster staff.

While descending the bank, past episodes of the twenty questions game came to mind, that ritual practiced among those who seemed to organize their entire lives around disaster hopping. Perhaps this was an opportunity to try her hand at it.

"Good afternoon. You knew the deceased?"

The man adjusted his horn-rimmed glasses and turned to face her. "No." His eyes were red—recent tearfulness. "I'm here with the disaster."

His accent was Canadian. Or maybe North Dakotan. His voice didn't ring any bells. But now she was absolutely positive she'd seen him before. On a TV interview, perhaps?

"I'm here to help, too. I'm a psychologist with disaster mental health."

"I've met a number of your colleagues." He toyed with a small rock in his hand. "Fine work you do."

"If you don't mind my saying so, you look unwell. Are you all right?"

He pitched the rock into the river, propelling it with startling force.

The man was sitting on a powder keg.

She glanced up the hill, to wherever Paulson had gotten to. He was still over by the church with Mr. Goode. Paulson briefly returned fixed eye contact.

"Would you like to talk? You don't seem to be planning to go inside. I'm not either."

His eyes began to well. "You're all so kind. It makes it that much more difficult."

"Makes what difficult?"

"I know what these things are like. We had an incident of our own not long ago. I wanted to help with that one. But it didn't work out. It's the same here. Nothing—absolutely nothing—turned out the way it was supposed to. And now..." He gulped back at swarming turmoil. "And now someone I had wanted to help...has passed."

"I'm so sorry." She placed a maternal arm across his shoulders as he caved inward. "A friend?"

"I never had the chance to speak with him. He's been unconscious."

"You were going to help him? You're with one of the agencies?"

"It's no matter. Not now."

His condition went far beyond simple grief. Compassion fatigue consumed the man, escalated to the most spectacular level she'd ever seen. Apparently Lacey's articles about burnt-out responders who work nonstop weren't exaggerating.

He wasn't from around here, that she was certain. He needed intervention. There was much more below the surface of his tears. So much more.

"I'm concerned about you. This is clearly a major blow."

"There's no need to worry about me." His tone was anything but reassuring. "Thank you for your kindness." He stepped to the edge of the dock.

"Wait." She flinched, his intentions becoming clear. "You're not going to..."

She grabbed at his arm, snagging it and throwing her weight to one side, interrupting his progress. He turned and snapped his arm away. His eyes were as blank as if he had already joined the depths of Green River. She dropped onto the dock, ignoring the stab of pain that shot up her knee. She went into a fetal position around his legs.

His knees smacked against the planking as well, his upper body flailing as he hung out over the water. He pushed against the edge of the dock, determined to complete the plunge.

"Paulson!"

The man's heavy coat would pull him under if he made it to the water. Hers could do likewise, if he took her along with him. If that happened she would slip out of it and...

Her cry had been unnecessary. The vibration of sneakers thumping against wooden planks meant Paulson was already there. They each grabbed a leg and dragged the would-be jumper the length of the dock, well away from the heavy current. As they reached the shore, the man twisted, jerking his leg from her grasp and kicking out.

Paulson grabbed at his hand, caught in crossfire. "Damn it, Alan. Ease up already!"

Free from restraint, the man that Paulson apparently knew sprang to his feet and rabbited for the park. Paulson bolted after him, holding his wrist. They disappeared behind the curvature of the bank. Paulson probably wouldn't catch up. Alan seemed very fit. Paulson was not.

What had happened, to create so much despair? Lacey's presentation had mentioned crisis situations like this, turning up without warning. That you may never get a full understanding of what exactly was going on.

Paulson knew who he was. Perhaps she'd get the whole story later.

Meanwhile, here she was again, left behind. Standing around with the humiliation of torn stockings, an aching knee abrasion, and the frustration of having delivered an only minimally effective suicide intervention. She felt around her pockets for her cell phone.

"Are you all right?" John dashed up from out of nowhere, his usual tidiness mussed by his haste. In the distance, a couple other suit types were on their way.

"Thank heavens you're here. We need someone to do a twenty-four hour hold. That was a jumper."

"Who? That vagrant?"

"That's not a vagrant. He's a social worker." She studied the downriver terrain while urging someone to pick up her 911 call. Hopefully one or both runners would pop into view between trees along the shoreline. "I have no idea what Paulson plans to do if he catches up with him."

"That CVS rep is the jumper?" John looked incredulous.

The two other men caught up. She recognized them from the FAC.

They were with law enforcement.

"Paulson needs your help." *Be calm, systematic.* "This road weaves along the wind of the river. Take your car. They also might have turned up on one of several cross streets."

The pair looked at each other, then her. "We can't. We don't have jurisdiction."

"What do you mean? Not even a simple twenty-four hour hold? Last I heard, that worked the same statewide, regardless of county."

"Sorry, ma'am," said one of them. "We're not authorized to do that here."

"Aren't there exceptions during disaster?"

"There has to be a waiver. Or agreements in place."

This is ridiculous. "That man is going to kill himself if we don't do something. Can't you at least go help find him?"

"If we get involved and somebody gets hurt or sued or something, there's no coverage. For us or the suspect."

"He's not a suspect. He's a mental health casualty. Why wasn't this taken care of by disaster planning? What are you even doing here, if you don't have authority for anything?"

"You need to let local enforcement take care of this one."

She realized her hand was empty. John had her phone and was conversing with the dispatcher. After establishing that assistance was on its way, he returned it. The peace officers looked relieved.

How humiliating. "Thanks." Her level of effectiveness was continuing its pathetic roll. She jammed the phone back into her coat pocket and left her hand tucked away, comforted by the warmth. Actually, both hands were chilled. Shaking. She pocketed the other one, too, seeking equilibrium. The sting of the scraped knee was becoming more pronounced.

Should she be grateful for John's assertiveness? She wasn't sure what she felt, outside of the scraped knee and a bruised ego. At least John had kept his head long enough to get the job done.

"Sorry for taking over like that," he said. "I figured I could get things moving faster than someone who needed to explain who they are."

"Emergency personnel here work closely with Paulson. I'd just have to mention his name. It wouldn't have been a problem."

The disconcerting loopholes in law enforcement protocol added to the frustration. Here they were, in the middle of a major crisis, and crappy preparedness was having serious immediate consequences for someone in their community.

How many other Alans were out there, struggling, not getting desperately needed assistance? At the FAC, other DMH workers had been talking about an emerging downturn in community morale. Was this one of the reasons? It would certainly be consistent with Lil's new soapbox. Even the church people had seemed wired. There was also what Paulson had said about callers' frustration with not having answers.

What would she find out next?

She shouldn't have asked. Disagreeable implications gnawed away: Paulson, and local DMH preparedness. They were not the only ones thrashing about. Child protective services at the church hadn't had their act together, either. The blunders by the local CMH staff, while the FAC was setting up. The traffic Armageddon at the hospital. The victims advocates had been so shorthanded they even recruited Alison.

Little wonder the community seemed to be falling apart around her. What did they expect? What else was waiting around the corner in days to come?

She was not an innocent in it, either. A second apology to Paulson was in order, what she'd said about him professionally. It wasn't his personal idiosyncrasies that had thrown a monkey wrench into the works. It simply was what it was for this relatively uneventful rural community. Pitfalls had most likely yawned wide before every local player.

"So he's a friend of yours?" John was wearing his best professional smile. Cool-headed, patiently waiting. Asking about Paulson. Trying to help with her meltdown, or feeling out what role Paulson played in her life? As if she knew herself.

"We're both with DMH. He works at the call center here in Marshland."

"So it's part of his nine to five then. When he works with the homeless."

She picked up on genuine curiosity in time to hold back a caustic rejoinder. He wasn't being sarcastic; he was serious. She took a deep breath.

How do I explain Paulson?

CHAPTER 20

Damien had a phone jammed in the crook of his neck. He held up one side of a conversation while he sifted through paperwork. Administrative stance, in its truest form. He looked up and nodded as Paulson entered the warehouse.

Paulson continued along the minimally lit passage. With everyone gone, the echoing footfalls and lingering staleness of long-term storage were more noticeable. No wonder the early shift felt spooked.

He tightened the athletic wrap looped over his wrist. There was nothing like a little physical pain to take his mind off things. Had it been worth it? Neither he nor the police had found Alan, last seen darting into somebody's side yard. Perhaps he took a leap further downriver. A few big rocks in the pockets of that raincoat, and it would take dredging to find him.

I knew that guy was in trouble. If only he had recognized how badly. Getting Alan into protective custody certainly would have been easier if it had come to a head while he was still at the call center. If only Alan had come back, if only he had made enough of a connection with him, maybe he would have returned for help when he needed it.

A diversion was in order, something to shake off the second-guessing. The accumulation of paperwork burying the card table was as good as anything. A sigh filled the void as he rummaged for anything worth messing with. Most of it was the ubiquitous disaster junk mail, and immediately found its way to the circular file. He set aside anything personalized or halfway interesting. Then sat and stared at it. Finally he snatched up the stack and jammed it into his inner jacket pocket. Tonight he would have a cure for insomnia. Things were looking up.

"How was the memorial service?" Damien seated himself in the opposite chair.

"I don't know. I ended up in the middle of a client crisis. How did it go with the investigators?"

"It went."

At times prying information out of Damien felt like the annual tractor pull. This time his passive resistance seemed to reflect a state of resolution, as if everything was decided and over with. That talking about it no longer mattered. Not good.

"I heard some of those strange noises myself this evening," said Damien. "Just the creaking sounds, not the voices."

"I've heard that before, too, when everybody's gone. Probably the wind. Did the investigators figure it out? That casework, I mean, not the ghost stories."

"It was in fact a call center port that did the questionable casework."

"What triggered the investigation?"

"Some large amounts of assistance went out, supposedly to certain clients. They're all building and repair cases from the floods."

"Legitimate clients?"

"As far as I know."

"That's about the only major cases left this late in the game, isn't it? There weren't any hospitalizations with the floods, or other big ticket items."

"True." Damien went silent.

"So what's the big deal?"

"They were Todd Goode operations. I'm his lumber supplier."

"Of course." Paulson shifted in his chair. Yes, Damien's family and Goode did almost all the major building projects in the greater Marshland area.

"The amount of funds that went out was far more than what the clients were entitled to. When they traced it to the caseworker of record, a dummy name came up. It happened last night, here in this call center."

184

"No way. What did the clients say?"

"We don't know if the money was actually sent to the clients. It was handled in a way that was untraceable."

"Embezzlement? They think someone's embezzling?"

Damien stood and began to pace, his boots crunching on Chet's rice. "They didn't come out and say it. When I finally read between the lines, I told them I would not discuss it further without my attorney. That's when they said it would be better if I were released from my duties. For my own protection, supposedly. COB today. I didn't argue. I told them I'd get things ready for my replacement. Whatever I can, that is, with my access to the casework program denied. They even took my key."

"They suspect *you*?" It was unfathomable. "One of the most dedicated volunteers we've got?"

"Can't say I blame them. It does look suspicious. I'm the only one who's ever alone here at night. I tried blaming the ghost, but they were in no mood for humor. Actually, neither was I."

"What are you still doing here, if you've been laid off?"

"There were a few critical things left hanging, thanks to the interruptions. After supper, I let myself in through the double doors. The one with the broken latch."

"I didn't know there was a broken latch."

"Hopefully not many people do. I installed a hook that I fasten after everybody's gone. If you know it's there, all it takes from the outside is a slim jim."

They crossed the chamber. Sure enough, up at the top of the two antiquated doors was a large sturdy hook.

"That only makes you look more suspicious. Why didn't you let logistics take care of it?" Though the hypocrisy of it stung. It wasn't as if he wouldn't do the exact same thing: ignore protocol and come up with the easy quick fix. Save the world, singlehanded. Damien's pass at it had certainly created a major complication to his life. Especially since he had installed something easy to break into, instead of a bolt or lock.

"I know, I know. But that would mean waiting for all the red tape with the landlord. Then admin would need to track down approvals from higher ups, and find union repair guys who can come out on a weekend. It would be at least another day before we opened. Probably longer. Who knows, maybe the whole deal would have fallen through. We'd have to look for someplace else and start over."

The more Damien shared, the worse it looked. It was hard to believe Damien could be guilty of anything more than a case of bad judgment. But developments did introduce a disconcerting hypothesis for why he so doggedly hung in with this assignment, in spite of the screwiness that kept cropping up.

Thank God for client-therapist privilege. It was going to turn into a real mess. Paulson chose words carefully. "You know, that could be how someone else got in."

"With that mountain blocking my view, anybody who was quiet about it could settle in at that port while I was sitting here. I wouldn't hear a thing. Especially with the noise from Chet's ghost box. A lot of the time when I'm alone here, I have music going, too."

"You would have heard that door opening. It's in dire need of WD-40."

"Not if they came in while I was out having a smoke, or in the can, or something."

"So tell them. The authorities."

"If they do a halfway decent job, they'll figure it out themselves. My attorney will convince them to look beyond the obvious."

"Do you have any idea who it could have been?"

"Frankly, Paulson..." Damien's soulful blue eyes met his, burdened with dull resignation. "I think I've been set up."

*****

Sarah knocked again and peered through the blurred excuse for a peek-a-boo window. Inside a few lights flickered; movement wavered at the opposite side of the warehouse.

"Are you sure this is the right time?" John moved nearer, also trying to see in.

She was close enough to feel his warmth. Flustered, she stepped back, as if giving him more room.

She found her phone and punched a speed-dial number. Paulson's ring tone sounded from within, muted. Eventually the figures in the distance approached and the door opened. Damien was with Paulson.

"You even got the manager to stick around for the occasion?" She belatedly picked up on a somber air. Paulson's eyes said "later." She went into hostess mode and did the introductions.

"Have you heard anything more about Alan?" Paulson asked John.

"No sign of him. We'll let you know when he turns up. They're trying to get hold of his home office."

"Ready for a tour?" Damien flipped on a few more lights. "Right this way."

"I'll wait here." It was eating her alive. She wanted to speak with Paulson, to acknowledge her newly mined guilt about her unfair comments and once again feel like all was forgiven. It couldn't happen with an audience.

There was that other nagging voice, too. Reminding her that repeatedly bringing it up made her look like an insecure twit—or preoccupied with the past, as Horace would put it. Maybe she should settle for forgiving herself and be done with it.

But there was that whole issue of preparedness. The fact that Marshland, even Willsey for that matter, was so woefully disorganized during anything like this. What would be the best way to approach it? Paulson's bond with her hometown had a way of clouding his better judgment. Bringing it up meant another possible run-in with that knee-jerk defensiveness. Once that battle line was drawn, it would be a lost cause.

He was fiddling with a wrap on his hand and wrist.

"How's your hand? Is it serious?"

"Don't know yet. Looks like you picked up a red badge of courage yourself."

She lifted her skirt slightly to expose the injury, the torn stockings having already found their way into a trash receptacle. "A skinned knee. It's been a while since I've had one of these." She dropped her skirt, having won his full attention, though not the type she was looking for. "At least I didn't land in the gravel. I'll bandage it up or something after I get back to the motel. You, on the other hand, should get that looked at. Excuse the pun."

He laughed. "Maybe after the excitement dies down."

"What's going on here, anyway?" She moved to peer around the supply pile and check on the tour progress. "With Damien?"

"He thinks he's on their list of fraud suspects. He's been let go."

"Damien?" It didn't make sense. The Logan family was more than well to do. Damien was bright enough to know that checks and balances would make it nearly impossible to get away with much for long. Besides, he wasn't the type. Was there a gambling habit, or compulsive spending? Drugs? A catastrophic medical situation? Investments gone bad? There had to be more to the story. "What do you think? It sounds pretty farfetched to me."

"Me, too. He thinks he's been set up. But guilty people say that all the time."

"Who will be manager now? Nobody else around here has done it, that I know of. Or even had the admin training. Have you?"

"No. Someone will turn up in the morning. Probably someone from out of town." Paulson walked her toward a haphazard circle of packing debris. "I'm more concerned about the staff. We bonded out here on this free-floating operational life raft, with Damien as skipper. The dynamics will change. Some are going to be upset, especially if it gets out why he's gone."

"Will they? Find out, I mean."

"Only if he tells them. The new manager will probably say something vague, like a personal situation came up. That means people will ask me about it. I'll be walking a fine line—sharing enough for people to feel informed, without violating Damien's privacy."

"You know, I've been thinking about the status of our local preparedness again."

He shot her a quick side-angled once over.

That was ham-handed. "Don't worry. I'm not going to lose it. I already did that this afternoon, when you went chasing after Alan and the out of town officers wouldn't help."

His posture became more relaxed. Those deep-set eyes once again looked ready for more, never able to disguise curiosity or concern—or that they could practically see right through people. At least he always seemed able to see through her. Such a contrast to John—his polished professionalism, his socialized confidence. They were a comfort. But gave away little of his personal status. He was still somewhat of a mystery in that way.

"They couldn't help chase down Alan because nobody had done the right red tape. Though, honestly, it probably wouldn't have made much difference. Alan was pretty good at making himself scarce."

"Agreed. He was certainly quick to disappear off my radar."

"It's not just law enforcement having holes in its planning. It was the same story with CPS—one caseworker at the church for a dozen kids. And she was only there because she'd been at the parade. Like my situation at the reception center, before CMH started turning up."

"Should we expect otherwise? With the cutbacks, nobody has free time and energy for disaster planning. We're lucky to get everyday disasters covered."

"That's why I'm thinking volunteers may be needed."

"To do what? It's the agencies and other bureaucracies that need to organize among themselves. That happens on the inside. I've done everything I can from the CMH angle."

That was doubtful. Especially with his attitude toward administrators. In fact, it probably put people off before the conversation started. "These big mass casualty disasters are different. More of it seems to be about communication. Especially in regard to overlapping agenda. If collaboration got set up ahead of time, or at least a few understandings about who will do what during which circumstance, that would be most of the battle."

Paulson looked thoughtful. "I see where you're headed with this." He placed a few chicken scratches on a scrap of paper. "Communication. Developing relationships. Collaborating for joint goals. These go hand in hand with mental health, with social work goals—things we do every day. But with the system as the client..."

"I never see any one entity consistently responsible for making mental health support happen. 'Who's on first' is different depending on the type of disaster. It can even change as it goes along."

"You're right." Paulson clicked the ballpoint pen in and out several times. "At least in terms of oversight by any one agency. Elected officials, yes. Not subject matter experts. Of those who really know how everything works, nobody's officially in charge. Except everybody's in charge of something. You can find an incident commander of some sort lurking around every corner. They can't all be in charge of mental health at once. But that's what the feds have saddled us with, for when something this complex happens."

"Surely there's a way local mental health professionals can help bring to light this catch twenty-two."

"You interested in being part of it?"

"I don't live here. It would be an interesting project, though. I could at least help toss around a few ideas about it."

"Lacey would have ideas on what to do."

"Such conversations with her always leave my head spinning. But it'd be worth it."

"Maybe we can't save the entire world." He half-winked, again showing interest in her bare legs. "But we certainly could better organize our corner of it."

She blushed. Would the guy ever give up?

"...and here we are at Mount Clown Toy." Damien and John had circled back.

"What's Mount Clown Toy?" said John.

"Supply overrun," said Damien. "There was no place else to put it."

John scoped the awkward conglomeration, stopping at the top. "What's that hanging over it?"

"That's Charles," said Paulson. "Some practical joker's moving a Halloween decoration around the building."

"Really." John continued to study the ceiling.

"I thought Charles was over by the canteen." Damien tilted himself to see what John was looking at. He stepped away and clicked on a few more halogen bars.

As her eyes adjusted, Sarah picked out the hanging object. It was almost directly over Paulson's station, just off the summit of the pile of boxes.

"That's not a Halloween decoration." John's tone was all business. "That's a body."

The inconceivable left her eyes riveted. An unwelcome hunch dropped her gaze to the scruffy carpeting. She gasped and stepped back. A drippy spatter pattern darkened the area below what most certainly was a recently deceased body. The faint scent of urine she'd dismissed as she entered—it hadn't been her imagination.

Paulson scrambled up the makeshift staircase of shipping boxes; John followed. Damien remained frozen, looking as paralyzed by developments as she. Paulson got to the top first, grabbed at the man's coat. He pulled him near and put his hand to the man's neck. After several seconds, he looked at John and shook his head.

He let go of the coat. The body swung away and slowly turned. The gentle sway was deceiving, not a hint of the self-targeted violence that had brought it into its final state. A vacant bluish grimace stared down at them.

She should have known. "Alan," she whispered. "How could you."

CHAPTER 21

Thursday, October 31ˢᵗ, Halloween

By dawn the body was gone. A strip of yellow tape now separated the call center from the back of the warehouse. A couple of investigators roamed the restricted area, hoping the morning light might reveal something that hadn't been obvious the night before.

Chet and Freddie were in the process of installing massive canvas curtains down the middle of the chamber, much like the one that had been used to screen off the caskets. At least the business of whittling away time by staring at that mountain of boxes was over, Paulson thought.

Call center workers began to arrive. Damien's replacement was already on site. It was Don, the assistant director who had brought in Alan. He had situated himself in an area duct-taped off near the main door. His newly claimed rectangle was outfitted with standard office ware, probably cannibalized from the workers' furnishings. All in all, a stiff island gracing concrete mediocrity.

Paulson's offer to help develop a sensitive way of breaking the news to the staff had met with peeved rejection. Don's strategy consisted of reciting a terse script as people entered, making it clear his only priority was that everyone receive the same message. Unfortunately, most seemed to interpret the said message as part of a Halloween spoof, some hanging on to this assumption no matter how firmly Don repeated his precise script.

A pair of newly-arrived workers celebrating the day as pirates joined in with the perceived make believe by claiming responsibility for the "slayin'." Don began to sputter.

Others on site who had begun their day in relatively good spirits appeared to be working their way through horror or disbelief. Those who'd had time for it to sink in could be found sitting at their stations, disoriented and unsure.

What do you do, after somebody hangs himself in your place of work. Expecting everybody to go about business as usual was absurd, even if the site of the incident was going to be partitioned from view.

It would be an interesting day: the trauma of the suicide, the dubious manner in which staff had been informed, Damien's sudden absence, getting used to a new manager, and a lot of questions that he either couldn't or shouldn't answer.

Nothing had been said about whether he was getting his card table and lawn chairs back. Or his "tumbleweed." Might not be much, but it was all he had.

He yawned, the borrowed swivel chair squeaking in time to syncopated twisting. He glanced at his travel mug, long emptied of Shelley's French roast. The canteen had been slow to set up, thanks to the disturbing disruptions and Damien's status. At least he could be reasonably sure that by the time he'd left him, Damien had abandoned his certainty that somebody was trying to frame him for Alan's death. Besides, the authorities were treating it as a suicide. The fraud situation was certainly going to pique their interest.

Be careful what you wish for. Alan had in fact come back to him, seeking the lifeline he apparently figured out would be there for him. Though he must not have waited around very long before he gave up.

The detectives had been quick to note the obsolete security mechanism installed over the defective double doors. Nobody was finding sign of forced entry anywhere. So either Alan had used the door with the hook, or someone had let him in. The second option seemed highly unlikely. But then, how would he have known about the hook, or the broken latch?

He could have seen it during the tour. But he hadn't taken Alan anywhere near that door. He didn't let him wander unsupervised. And in all the time he'd spent sitting around in this place, not once had he noticed that hook, until Damien pointed it out. Alan must have been one quick study. Unless…

The swivel chair stilled. Foul play? Could this have something to do with whoever had been getting in after hours?

He wheeled around at a sudden motion—a dark form delivering a glancing blow to the far boundary of his field of vision.

Damn it. He left the chair and sprinted toward the Magic Circle.

The officer kneeling in the taped-off area looked up at him. "Something wrong?"

Paulson tried not to look rattled. "No. Thought I saw something."

In the background, familiar voices were making efforts to insert real conversation into Don's canned speech. He turned in time to see Lacey and the Marlboro Man excuse themselves from the entry ritual.

Right on cue. If only there was something he could do about this chip on his shoulder. "Happy Halloween," he said as they approached.

"Son, you sure do have a way of finding yourself in the middle of whatever there is to be in the middle of." Horace smiled through his offhand remark with seeking eyes. "You doing okay with this?"

"Just another day at the office."

Lacey's glare made it clear from the get-go he was about to meet up with the no-nonsense end of a supervisory Smith and Wesson.

"What do you already know?" The clipped monotone was something new.

"A victims advocate from out of town hanged himself. He used the noose meant for Charles...a Halloween decoration," Paulson added, picking up on Lacey's confused dismay. "The back end of the warehouse is going to be off limits until they're done looking around for foul play. Damien was set loose yesterday because of some casework irregularities that were traced to here. 'Pencil neck' over there has taken his place. How's this for low-key?" Paulson joked.

"How about we go out front?" Lacey was not amused. "Privacy."

The morning chill confirmed that predictions of an early winter were more than just local conjecture. The search for privacy, however, was immediately foiled. Sam was situated in the middle of his lot, leaning against his Ford and admiring his flag. His multi-pocketed coveralls indicated he was ready for another day of pounding nails. Leave it to Sam for ritual and routine, come what may.

"Too bad about that feller in there," he said to Paulson as they passed.

"You heard already?"

"Everybody knows. Just ask Shelley."

Finding a place where they wouldn't be overheard took them almost all the way out to Main Street.

"Here's what you haven't heard. And keep a lid on it, until it becomes common knowledge." Lacey raised her voice to be heard over the passing vehicles. "They didn't find any victims advocate credentials in Alan's personal effects. When they checked with the Canadian authorities, they knew nothing about him being here."

"So who was he?"

"They did know him. He volunteered a lot for another agency. CVS had turned him down during a train wreck incident. They didn't sign him on because of...issues."

"So he's a disaster junkie?"

"Maybe. If so, impersonating CVS certainly cranks it up a notch or two."

"Here I thought Damien's junkie-hood was bad. How could this happen? How did he get by without ever needing to show anybody his credentials?"

"Weren't no reason to doubt him," said Horace. "That accent was Canadian. He showed off plenty of disaster relief know-how. Spoke disaster speak just fine. When was the last time someone asked to see your mental health license?"

He gave it some thought. "Never. Other than when I sign onto a disaster operation, or start a new job or something like that, it never happens."

"Me neither. Here you and I—we don't rightly fit the mold now, do we? Alan had it all in place, right down to those spruced-up penny loafers."

"Don took Alan everywhere," said Lacey. "There's concern that private information might have gotten shared. Everybody's backtracking over it. The agencies he visited want to be sure something critical didn't get out into the mainstream."

Paulson mentally retraced the tour he'd given Alan. "I told him only generalities, what we do and how we do it. Described a few resources and referral processes. I didn't bring up specific case details. I certainly didn't give away any state secrets."

"Surely you must have noticed something about him," said Lacey.

"Well, yeah. He was pretty tightly wound. There was...an unfortunate misunderstanding when he first got here. He did say he'd had a long day. Even then I suspected there was more to it."

"Did it ever occur to you to discuss this with me?" Lacey's words pricked; it was the sting of a kill. "That I might be able to facilitate something at my end?"

In hindsight the error was glaring. Even a rookie PFA outreach worker knew enough to assess further or refer when there were signs like the ones he'd just described. "Actually...no."

He'd been an idiot again.

Continuing to look at her was impossible. He shifted his gaze upward, toward Sam's innocently fluttering flag.

"As far as that goes, why didn't you call me or Horace last night so admin would know what's going on? If I hadn't heard from Sarah, I'd still be in the dark. I can see it now. Starting the day with the director in my face and demanding to know what the authorities were doing on our doorstep. What about you? Didn't you want guidance on protocol?"

"What protocol? There's something in the standard guidelines for when somebody offs himself in a call center?"

Her face dropped to her hands. The pause lasted eons. "I wish I could say no harm done. From what Sarah said, even if we got him to lock-up, he might well have picked up where he left off. But we could have at least had a shot at it."

He'd blown it. Again. This time he'd missed out on a chance to save a life.

If only he'd given Alan his full attention during that visit. His downward spiral could have been halted right then and there. Or at least flagged, so someone else could step in and do something. Instead—

"I need to have a word with Don. I'll leave you two to...whatever." As Lacey crossed the lot, her gait missed its easy bounce. She was taking it personally.

"Don't mind her, she'll get over it." Horace studied her movements as well, more accurately exposing concern than did his words. "She'll squeeze every last iota of detail out of half the planet, glue herself to that laptop of hers for a piece, and turn in some humongous tome of a report. Then we'll see the Boss Lady back."

"It's not her fault. It's mine." Openness unfurled without resistance, to this man so much a kindred spirit. Even in the midst of absurdity. Perhaps especially because of it.

Paulson reviewed the full story of Alan.

"It's Alan's fault," said Horace. "Period. True enough, there's always a chance you or me or anyone else could have done something that might've changed the course of things. But from what I've heard, there wasn't anything cut and dry to suggest Alan was thinking to call it a season. Don't know that I'd have made more of it myself."

"If you really were in my shoes, you'd feel the same as me."

"More than likely." Horace paused, the sporadic rumble of rush hour in Marshland occasionally interrupting the delicate silence. "What would happen if we went racing in with the men in white coats for everybody who presented an inkling of distress? Here in a disaster aftermath, no less."

"The problem was that I didn't check out that 'inkling of distress.' Or arrange to have it looked at elsewhere. That was my job, what Lacey put me out here for. I was too distracted by what was going on with Damien. Whatever was at the bottom of that casework fraud. Then there's those collaboration issues Sarah's always talking about. I was trying to get my head wrapped around that, too."

"So, story is, you went back to being everything for everybody again, instead of taking care of what was right in front of you."

A sinking feeling descended. Nausea. Old baggage stirring. Trying to reopen and expose its nasty wares. A place he did not wish to go. If only it would leave him be. "Lacey wasn't so sure she wanted to sign me on at all. I ended up here because she thought this would be 'low-key.' Apparently, low-key wasn't in the cards."

"You lay down your money, you take your chances. That one's on Lacey, not you."

"There's more to it than that." As if it wasn't obvious. "Not now."

"Your call." He put a hand to his Stetson, guarding against the mounting breeze.

"Maybe we should go inside." Paulson thought of the jacket he'd left on the back of his chair. Wrapping arms around himself had ceased to be of any use some time ago.

"First there's something Lacey wanted to be sure you knew about. That fraudulent casework admin's been sniffing around—they know for sure now that Damien couldn't have done it. A whole slew of witnesses over at Shelley's saw him dining on some of that fine meatloaf about the same time the program input that data."

"Why haven't they said anything to him about it? Do they have any idea..."

"By now they probably have. They're revisiting the notion of somebody causing grief for Damien. That crank call a couple days ago."

So not even Horace had been told about the second call. "If that's true, someone sure is going to a lot of trouble."

The mixture of voices inside the building was dying down; only Don's prevailed.

"Sounds like they're coming to meeting in there," said Horace.

Workers were rolling their office chairs to Don's area, there at Duct Tape Central. Apparently the Magic Circle was no more. They joined the periphery.

"Thank you for all your good work." Don read from a clipboard without looking up. "You've done a fine job. However, with recent events, we are merging call center operations with the national phone bank. This site will close. Today's your last day."

"Talk about short-timing it," a nearby caseworker mumbled.

"If you want to continue on this operation, check with your lead," Don continued.

Like he should bother to ask Lacey for another assignment. He wasn't sure if he even wanted one. Riding off into the sunset with Horace was the more agreeable option. Maybe Horace had a spare horse on him.

"Headquarters requests that if you leave the operation, do your exit interview with staff mental health here, so they don't get bogged down with too many people at headquarters." Don punctuated his deadpan delivery with a mechanical gesture in Paulson's direction.

Thanks for the wellspring of enthusiasm. At least it would provide structure to his day. Keep his mind occupied.

"Everybody stay and help with teardown tonight, unless there's a good reason you can't," Don went on. "Other than that, we're business as usual. Have a nice day."

The meeting broke up, everybody dragging as if they'd been dunked in Schwartz Marsh. The canteen monitor and her assistant stopped at Don's desk with questions. After minimal discussion, Don waved them off.

"No mystery that poor soul keeps finding himself banished from the mainstream." Apparently Horace also witnessed the exchange. "He sure do have a bee in his bonnet, don't he?"

"Or elsewhere."

One of the canteen workers hesitated nearby then approached. "Do you guys have a minute?" Her face was flushed.

They followed her to the junk food layout. She wiped up a few stray coffee spills. Paulson helped himself to the brew while waiting for her gumption to catch up with her.

"I can't do this," she finally whispered.

"Can't do what?" Paulson stirred in the double whites.

"Stay tonight and help with breakdown."

"It's no big deal. Just tell Don you have to leave early."

"He says I don't have a good enough reason. It's...those ghosts."

That's right. She was one of those who'd heard funny noises.

"Tonight's Halloween." Her eyes were determined, her mind set. "I do not want to be here after dark. In fact, I refuse. Especially after somebody just died here. I'm leaving at dusk no matter what that guy says. Sooner, if anything strange happens."

It did feel creepy. One more reason for everybody to be on edge. Given all that had been going on, it was questionable whether it was a good idea for any of them to be there.

"How about if I have a word with ol' Don?" said Horace. "Gives me a chance to try out this here title of 'Staff Mental Health Manager' that Lacey so kindly bestowed upon me."

CHAPTER 22

Lil burrowed under the piles of junk mail, laundry, and baby paraphernalia scattered over every surface of her front room's furnishings. "Where did that thing get to?"

"I don't even know what a baby monitor looks like." Sarah went along with the implied request for assistance with a visual once-over.

"It's a yellow boxy thing, with a speaker on the front. No, wait a minute. Maybe it's light green. Somebody gave it to me at the baby shower."

Sarah had missed the baby shower Lil spoke of. A patient crisis the weekend of the party had interfered. Lil had seemed understanding at the time. However her recollection of Sarah's absence that day continued to earn her the occasional disparaging look.

"I know I had it during our planning meeting." Lil dropped to the floor and checked under the sofa. "Jerrod was squalling up a storm. Alison said he was probably having bad dreams about his daddy, or about the bomb going off. We didn't hear him at first, our planning got us so peppered up."

God, no. She was palling around with Alison?

"It's okay, Mrs. White." The teenage babysitter cradled the contented infant. "I'm sure I'll hear if he starts crying. I'll leave his door open just in case."

Lil continued to upend and toss any stray objects so unfortunate as to be positioned in the path of her search.

"Tell you what." Sarah glanced at the time. "On the way back from the hospital, I'll pick up a new one for you at the mall. You'll have a spare. It'll be my make-up for not being able to come to your shower. Then we'll go split a sandwich at the five and dime."

Old practiced routines would do Lil good. Get her away from obsessing about the explosion or Sean. Or whatever self-destructive path Alison was getting ready to steer her onto.

Lil ceased the frenzy, hands on hips, hair slipping from her headband. She dashed it out of her face. "All right. Let's go." She scooped up the coat and purse that had found their way to the floor. "Besides, I can hardly wait to tell Sean what happened at that warehouse."

"You already know about that?" Sarah climbed into the passenger side of the massive SUV Lil had chosen for a rental.

"Mom called this morning. From what I hear, Dr. Turner, you were there when that guy took a leap. No holding back now. I can hardly wait."

So much for getting away from that fiasco. Perhaps there was a way to derail it. "By the way, you don't really need to worry about Jerrod that way. With how he's affected by the bombing."

"What do you mean? Babies are aware of a lot more than you think."

"Yes, even tiny ones are affected. It's more a matter of how their parents are doing, not what they themselves remember or think about it."

Lil didn't look impressed. "Alison says I should read him stories with happy endings, every night before he goes to bed. Especially ones with fire trucks and other helpers. That'll get him over it."

"It won't hurt anything. But at his age what's more important is spending extra time with him, and being calm and nurturing. Keeping to routine. Meeting needs predictably."

"I always do that anyway." She sounded offended. "You know, you're not the only one who's gotten around in the world. Alison's been all over, too. Even out of the country."

The SUV jolted to a stop; Lil rolled down her window to engage a passing neighbor with aimless chatter.

Why didn't Lil see through it? What a sell job Alison had going for her. Was it a case of charisma, the seductiveness of Alison's enthusiasm? It had even kept her on board with Paulson way longer than any mental health professional should have tolerated.

Or was it Lil's vulnerability, with Sean so badly injured, making her easy to be lead astray? She'd always had a thing for lost causes. However, if Sarah tried to approach the subject right now, it would not turn out well. Not a chance. Lil would only get more defensive and insistent.

What if Lil knew what the victims advocates had found out about Alison? John had shared that in confidence, a professional courtesy. If it looked like Alison was about to put Lil at risk of harm, would spilling the beans be justified regardless?

By the time the SUV was again in motion, the questions still dangled, unanswered. "I understand Alison worked with Chet in Puerto Rico after a hurricane."

"She was even at 9/11." Lil's sparkle returned with the changed topic, her defensiveness vanished.

The quick transition was reassuring. A returning sense of empowerment? Perhaps there was a silver lining to Lil's getting involved with Alison's shenanigans. *Never underestimate the power of a sense of purpose.*

"I've found out lots about what happened there," said Lil. "She has all kinds of great stories. I know a few things that even you don't know."

"Really? Do tell. I don't think I've spoken with anyone who actually witnessed what happened right after the twin towers came down." It was a semi-falsehood, but sort of true. A few of the FAC workers were from the Big Apple and had been at 9/11, though she hadn't had detailed conversations with them about it. But there was probably no better window into what Alison might be up to than her perspective on 9/11.

Tales of Alison's woe filled the remainder of the drive to the hospital. Most of the drama centered on how horrible it had been for Alison, everything she'd run up against while trying to get assistance for her supposed loss. What Lil described made it sound like disaster relief agencies and organizations did little more than run around like headless chickens.

How much of what Alison told Lil might actually be true? She had certainly encountered her own share of shortcomings during this disaster aftermath.

"She has lots of good ideas," said Lil. "Everybody should pay more attention to her."

"What exactly did you decide at your meeting?"

"Alison keeps a lot of it to herself. But she's got plans. She'll make sure people get a clue, all right. She needs our support once it comes together. Even Jeri Lynn's coming."

That freshly grieving widow? Sarah turned to cough, forcing her tongue in check.

"You should come, too. It's a worthy cause."

"I'm not so sure that's a good idea. What if it conflicts with what my relief efforts are trying to do? It would put me in a difficult position."

"You're smart, Sarah. You got all that fancy education. You'll think of something."

*****

The apartment screen door screeched the way it always did when the weather turned cold. Paulson offered Junior a pinch of fish food, their habitual manner of greeting. The fish sloshed the surface of the water as the flakes quickly disappeared. "Mind if I put on some coffee? I only made it back here for a few hours last night."

"Please do." Horace made himself comfortable on the worn sofa, setting his equally well-used hat next to him. "Wouldn't mind some myself."

It was the first time Paulson had seen him without the Stetson. His hair was wavy silver, full and healthy. A bit long, though not as long or wayward as Paulson's. It suited his face well, giving him a kindly grandfather look. Perhaps that's how he'd look when he got to be Horace's age. If he made it that far.

"By the way, that really blew me away." Paulson called out over the banging and clanking coffeemaker parts. "All I thought was going to happen was those two workers getting let off. I didn't expect you to have the whole place closed down by noon."

"Wasn't much to it. Just talking the IT guys into calling in a few favors, and throwing a few switches. Bringing in a few staff at the other end to pick up the slack. It wasn't a problem. Though I'll miss seeing that Magic Circle show. Especially the imitations of the higher ups."

"You had that ability, that influence, to make something happen."

"It did take a little wrangling. Mostly it was the *esprit de corps* Lacey and I had already forged with admin folks, and DMH alliances already in the hopper, that got it rolling. If we'd gone in all fire and brimstone, we wouldn't have been heard. Those poor phone bank workers would still be trapped in vexation and providing fair-to-middling services."

Paulson dragged a wooden chair into the cramped entry that served as his living room. He turned the chair backward and straddled it, folding his arms over the seat back and resting his chin. "That's a facet of staff mental health I haven't invested much into. There's so much else that matters more."

"Sounds like a story to be told." Horace reclined, as if settling in for the long haul.

For Paulson the proposition had an opposite effect. Too much surged at once, stirring the uneasiness already tormenting him, jabbing from the inside out. Visions of past and present flitted by, picking up speed.

"It's given me a lot to think about." Being able to pull it together was a pipe dream. How nice it would be if he could join Junior's relative state of calm.

"I'm listening." Horace's easy warmth agreed with his words.

Whatever he decided to say to Horace, it would be heard.

"If I have to pick a starting point, why not 9/11." A solid, concrete event. Surely there was a way to connect that with wherever he was trying to go. "I was practicing in Detroit. I covered for a buddy who went to New York City. When he got back, we talked about it. It was grueling. The first month was really chaotic. Everything that fell through the cracks, or otherwise got screwed up. Nobody'd ever done anything like that before. Not on such a huge scale."

"I remember it well. I was part of it. One of my first operations."

"Afterwards, I followed the recovery effort. I read a lot of the research that came out of it. Just what do we do that helps people after one of these?"

"So this is about your professional development?"

"No." Horace surely knew better as well. "Let's start over." Paulson got up, drawn toward the big black fish contentedly wafting about in the spacious tank. Her nose bounced against the pane facing him.

"I grew up on the East Coast. When I was a kid, New York City was magical. It seemed almost superhuman. It generated the region's pulse, nourished us, provided us with direction. Vitality. Looking back, I guess I also saw it as part of my identity. A source of confidence, and personal pride.

"Then the twin towers came down. Everybody scrambled around like they were helpless. It pulled the rug out at every level. The sense of strength, of invincibility—that we could protect ourselves from harm, come what may. It got annihilated. I felt...skewered."

"Painful, indeed."

Paulson studied his reflection in the glass. He caught a glimpse of the blurred image of his confessor, and the interested eyes that rested on him. "I knew I couldn't go there myself. I take comfort that I covered for someone who did. Still, it's always grated on me. Such a mess, yet I did nothing more directly to help. I started getting impatient with powers that be. Of any sort. Especially those who are supposed to protect us, or lead us. Everybody was so unprepared."

"True enough. It took a while to get a handle on that one. But we did."

"I was nursing along a bad relationship at the time, too, which didn't help any. The last straw was a client suicide at the hospital. I blamed administrative policy. At least, that was how I viewed it at the time. Looking back, I also blamed myself."

"And Alan's untimely end dragged that one out of the dustbin. No surprise there."

"Even then, I guess I expected to be everything to everybody. That I could take control where others had blown it. But I didn't see it. I just wanted out."

"So yesterday you found yourself tending too many fishing lines in the barrel and one slipped through the cracks. Just as it happened for those poor hospital administrators."

Horace was right. The ultimate result of his prioritizing had proved to be no better than theirs.

"With one exception that seems to slip your mind. Alan came back, came looking for your help. After only one brief meeting."

"For all the good it did." But yes, there was that one glimmer. Perhaps all that could have been done, given the circumstances. He'd done it. *Thanks, Horace.* "Anyway, I ended up in Marshland. Here I practice as I see fit. I do what meets the objective, whatever gets people what they need in the way they need it."

"I imagine at times your director finds herself a tad challenged by your method."

"She doesn't have much choice. I was the only one to apply that qualified. It's a halftime position. I barely make a go of it by chasing down freelancing."

"As Lacey tells it, you've had a huge impact on this community. She hears nothing but good about you from the locals."

Paulson considered it, then slowly nodded. "Thanks. I was beginning to doubt it."

"Any special reason for that doubt?"

He turned to face Horace. "For all my efforts, nothing I've done over the last couple of years really prepared our area for something like this."

"You're just hoisting yourself along the learning curve, same as everyone. Rural areas aren't so keen on planning for a mass casualty. It's not something folks around here would think of as a likely event. As far as that goes, there are still major cities that haven't come up with viable collaboration plans. Nobody believes it'll happen to them, whether you're talking about one individual's way of thinking or an entire system of government.

"Remember Katrina? Truth be known, that level of disorganization could hit its mark elsewhere." The glint of an ice chard flickered from deep beneath Horace's otherwise kindly gaze.

So Horace carried it around as well, the outrage. Yet here he was, calm and supportive throughout the gut spilling. Doing the job in spite of the BS. Coping.

"Whether my thinking is realistic isn't the point. It's about standing toe to toe with this...crusade, why I'm doing it. To take control, to put an end to the systematic insanity. I made huge sweeping changes in my life. Yet no matter what I do, things like this keep happening."

The wave of it, so much there. *Stop doing this to yourself.*

"As the big fish in the small pond, you can make a difference, just the way you did in this community." Horace glanced toward the kitchen and the final gurgles of brew. "But a mass casualty—why, that pond's more like a ginormous ocean. Succeeding at anything means you accept that you're a small fish, and you're going to do what small fish can do to get things right."

Paulson tended to the coffee, using it as an opportunity to regain inner footing. The hidden meanings floating around in their endless fish tank analogies didn't help a bit.

"If I'm essentially still recovering from 9/11, and I wasn't even there, what's going to happen with everyone who's actually in the middle of something similar?" He brought out two generous cups of joe. "The people here in Marshland, for example."

"You've already got the right idea." Horace accepted a mug. "Put that spunk to good use. Get to setting up services people need, rather than trying to do them all yourself. First, get on the bandwagon. Like me and Lacey did to get that call center boarded up."

Paulson sat on the opposite end of the sofa. "It's not my MO." He stared into the coffee, the heat of it warm against his face. "I'd be like Junior over there if you drained her tank. A fish out of water."

"Son, you hook up with folks without half a whit of thought. Like you did with Alan. That's all collaboration is. Joining up and figuring out what works best."

"How do I justify joining up with such mediocrity? Especially when I've accomplished so much by keeping to myself."

Horace chuckled softly. "True enough, there are plenty of quandaries in the world of mental health that could use some cleaning up after. You've put a dent in that here in Marshland. Because you joined with your director, and she with you."

"You can't be serious. At least once a week I get a call from her, questioning what I'm doing. Half the time, she sounds afraid to ask."

"You wouldn't still be here if she didn't have confidence in you and your 'MO.' She's got that bottom line to think about, and other liabilities. Yes, sir, you joined up with her, all right."

Junior blew a plume of multicolored gravel off the floor of her habitat. It swirled, resettled. "It's hard to see, when the need is great and resources limited. My requests for anything involving funds or provider hours almost always get turned down. I usually err on the side of saying 'sorry' after the fact. Otherwise nothing would happen."

"Day to day misadventures do have their way of leaving us feeling adrift and abandoned every now and then. Truth of the matter is, we're all part of something much bigger than ourselves, whether or not we choose to take notice of it. It's a matter of figuring out how and where we've squirreled away that *esprit de corps*. How to put it to good use. You're nowhere near so isolated as you reckon."

It was mentally exhausting. Horace probably had a few valid points. The sense of it would likely settle in later, after a good nap. At the moment, how any of this consultation applied to what to do next was a mystery. Other than the realization that this lame drive to do it all on his own was probably pointless.

Horace broke the silence. "Sure you wouldn't rather back out for a piece?"

"Is that Lacey's take on it? She wants to dump me?"

"The Boss Lady will go with whatever I say. I'm just doing what I'm here for, for DMH folks. I do want to be sure you're up to it. I reckon you know better than anyone."

It was tempting. Just give up, leave it behind, like the hospital. Head for the hills.

No. Running had accomplished nothing. Here he was, right back where he'd started, second verse. Actually third or fourth, considering a few other choice episodes of years past. The geographic cure did not work. "I need to see this through."

"Fair enough."

"Especially with Damien. I heard from him this morning. They told him he's in the clear."

"That's good to know."

"He's coming back to help with teardown. He says it will let him come full circle. A sense of completion. Same as me, I guess."

"An old soul, that Damien," said Horace.

Whatever that means.

CHAPTER 23

Lil and Sean spilled data dumps over one another while a flat screen unit blared in the background. There probably wasn't a piece of disaster trivia in existence that the two of them considered too minor to hash over ad nauseam. Whether they actually heard what the other was saying was questionable. It was good to see them getting back to normal.

Sarah shifted her attention to the television program.

"...so proud of everything the agencies have done. But it's time to let the community organizations do what they do best."

"Volunteer organizations fill in gaps. Not take over government responsibilities."

Not those two again. "You mind if I change channels?"

"Go ahead. No, wait." Lil's call-to-arms erupted. "Listen—this is exactly what I'm talking about. That jackass is going to keep us from getting help."

"Don't worry. Disaster affects all socioeconomic classes, not just ones conservatives call 'entitlement' groups. Even conservatives see that disaster needs can't be ignored."

"Well, that loser isn't one of them. He doesn't have a clue."

"It's a matter of community pride." Sarah paused, weighing options for getting through. "There was a study about charitable giving. Conservatives donate more when it centers on showing community strength, or upholding tradition. As long as no hint of government being responsible for every citizen's critical needs is in it somehow. They can relate to disaster consequences. It could happen to them, too."

"Well, it's all a bunch of bull, because that's not how it worked for Alison at 9/11."

"One swallow doesn't make a spring."

"What's that got to do with it?" Lil frowned back at her, the old proverb no more to her than irrelevant hooey.

It was a waste of words. Lil didn't have enough orientation to interpreting empirical findings. She wasn't that kind of colleague. In all likelihood, bringing up such evidence only confused Lil, or made her feel stupid. A different tack was needed. "Are you sure Alison had the whole picture? How could she know what was going on behind the scenes? I thought you said at 9/11 she was a client, not a disaster worker."

"Does that mean I don't know what's going on either?" Lil became steely eyed.

"Of course not." It was a lost cause. Lil's newborn community fervor was fully entrenched. As exasperatingly intractable as the other all-or-nothing conclusions and "save the world" rat holes Lil had darted into for as long as she'd known her. "I just don't want to see you give up, and miss out on things that would help you."

"First, there has to be something to be had. There's a town hall meeting in Marshland tonight. That joker's going to be there. He's going to hear us. We'll make sure of it."

So that was what Alison had up her sleeve—a public scene. Which, all things considered, was what town halls were meant for. Certainly a safer outlet for Alison's frustrations than physical or criminal acting out. Unless it was going to turn into some kind of violent sit-in.

"Look," said Sean. "They're talking about that guy last night."

The screen held a wide-angle shot of the warehouse, the flag on Dad's lot fluttering off to one side. The reporter shared an account of events Sarah already knew firsthand. Lil and Sean hung on every word. Sarah felt only regret. A photo of Alan that looked like it had been scraped off a driver's license sprang onto the screen.

Sean began fighting the bedding holding him prisoner. "That's him!" He finally worked a hand free and pointed. "That's the one who raised such a stink over where I wanted to park. He tried to stop me."

They listened, riveted, processing what it might all mean.

"You think maybe he knew what was going to happen?" said Sarah.

"How would he know about the bomb?" said Lil. "Unless..."

The Whites stared at each other, wide-eyed and newly silent.

Had Alan put it there? That was hard to believe. He had been so mild-mannered, and empathic. Not at all what anyone would think of as a mass murderer. Then again, so often it turned out to be just that—some quiet type nobody suspected.

However, if it truly was a terrorist statement, why hadn't he left a note, or YouTube posting, a tweet, or anything else to explain what he was protesting? He'd certainly hung around long enough to do so. He'd even gone to the trouble of creating a semi-false identity. What had he known?

And what more might he have aimed to accomplish by staying?

*****

The dullness of the late afternoon sun suitably highlighted the demise of the Marshland call center. The handful of phone bank workers who'd hung around for teardown had already left. The crime scene investigators were also gone, apparently satisfied that Alan's final state was of his own doing. The communications staff had come through and dismantled the hardware. Chet and Freddie remained, hauling the last of their former work setting to their rental truck.

Where did any other group or organization set up and break down an entire business so quickly and efficiently? Screw-ups aside, it was hard not to admire it.

Damien was on site as promised, closing out final details. Don had not been seen since lunch. Rumor among those who stayed was that the eccentric staff mental health manager had worked some kind of bureaucratic magic.

Paulson halfway listened as Damien outlined how to fill out some COB form. Dull as dishwater, but as good a place as any to start putting together a picture of how service delivery sites are run. Dropped boxes and furniture scraping against concrete occasionally interrupted the drone of Damien's deep voice. It helped with staying awake.

Ironically the slow, systematic removal of the mountain of boxes penning them in contributed most to the sense of emptiness. He couldn't stand it. He had to know what was going to happen with those things.

"Hey, Chet. Where are you taking Mount Clown Toy?"

Chet lumbered over, cap awry and sweat dripping from protruding fangs of brown hair. "The boss worked real hard to find a home for them toys. Every day. Seemed like that's all he was ever doing when me and Freddie came around. But he got it done. They found this charity for kids who don't got nothing. They're gonna repaint the faces. Every one of them will be different. Sounds like fun, don't it?"

"Sounds like quite the project."

"All except a couple boxes. They're out in my pickup. The boss said to bring them back to headquarters."

"What for?"

"We're taking turns mailing them to Lenny. One by one. As long as they hold out."

"Lenny? Who's he?"

"The supply supervisor. The one who accepted them. Any time we talk about them clowns, he says how he liked them all right. So it'll be Christmas once a month for him. For a few years anyway."

Leave it to the logistics crew. "By the way, do you want your ghost box back?" It was most likely still humming away, back behind the canvas. The crime scene investigators had gone all a-twitter when they came across it. There was even mention of the bomb squad. That definitely woke him up for a bit.

"Just hang onto it. Get cleared out first. That way y'all can be sure them ha'nts don't bother you none. I'll come get it later. Got to protect trick-or-treaters at my door, you know."

"How thoughtful of you." Damien gave Paulson an exasperated glance.

Such an odd adventure, the time spent with these men. Their quirks, their dedication. All that he'd learned about them during this particular jaunt into disaster response.

Yet they knew so little about him. Including the demons tormenting him of late. The one-sidedness of it all killed him. In the grand scheme of things, they were more everyday friends and acquaintances than temporary recipients of DMH services—and they would return to being just friends, once this was over with.

"Join with folks." The snippet of advice replayed itself in Horace's easy drawl. *"Find the* esprit de corp. *Be part of it."*

What would be wise to share? Given the weirdness going on lately, how much could anybody in his position become one of the gang and still hang onto professional credibility?

Just go for it. "The ghosts here don't seem to be affected much by that device," he told Chet. "I still see shadows every now and then."

"Are you sure? Always works fine for me."

"It's probably just me, not ghosts. I've been jumpy since the explosion. It's getting better, though. No need to worry."

Paulson walked up to where the debris pile had been; Chet followed. "When it happens, it's usually somewhere around here."

"Must be in your head, all right." Chet plucked the mirror off the wall he'd placed there during set-up. "No way ghosts would keep coming back by this mirror. It'd scare the pants right off them. If ghosts wear pants. Don't worry none about that stuff goin' on in your head, Paulson. That's the nice thing about thoughts. Soon enough, a different one comes along."

A patch of darkness dashed across the two of them. Then vanished, as quickly as it had materialized.

"Did you see that?" Damien hurried toward them. "Is that what you saw before?"

"Well, I'll be." A stunned Freddie looked up at Chet with renewed interest.

They scoured the area, searching for explanation. Only Chet seemed to lack concern. While they were busy scurrying about he just stood there, his grin slowly widening. Finally, he burst out laughing.

"All right, Chet." Damien dropped the empty crate he was checking. "This was your doing, wasn't it? I knew you couldn't possibly believe that crap about 'ghost-fixin's'."

"There's nothing wrong with my ghost-fixin's. This ain't nothing I had a part in. Y'all are seeing Sam. When we go out this door we'll see Sam there, sure as shootin'."

Paulson looked at Damien; Damien shrugged. They traipsed through the open bay. As predicted, Sam's Ford was idling at the edge of the lot, getting ready to move out. Chet waved him down.

"Go back in the warehouse," Chet called at them. "I'll show you your ghost."

They reentered and positioned themselves with a front-row view of the area under suspicion. Moments later the same eerie shadow passed. Fluttered.

Paulson slapped a hand to his forehead. "I've been an idiot. I was so sure those shadows were part of a trauma reaction, I never thought it through."

"Thought what through?" said Damien.

Paulson led him out onto the lot and pointed. There was Chet, raising and lowering Sam's flag, flapping away as it repeatedly passed the roof.

"Going up or down, it throws a shadow over that skylight, depending on the position of the sun. Or maybe which way the wind's blowing."

"Darnest thing I ever heard of." Sam's stooped figure came up next to them, hands in his coverall pockets. "A haunted warehouse. What a pile of hooey."

"There's ha'nts in there, all right." Chet unfastened the flag and handed it to Sam. "I got it on top notch authority. Paulson ain't seen them, though. All he's seen is this here flag."

Paulson couldn't hold back; a belly laugh took charge.

Chet and Damien joined him.

*****

"So you're heading out of these parts." Reading Horace was impossible. He would look relaxed and tuned in during an EF-5 tornado. He'd clean up at Dad's Saturday night poker.

"I know the ongoing need is great, but there are other people helping right now," said Sarah. "I'm not needed. Instead of making Lacey find me another job, I'd like to spend time with some friends who are in a bad way."

The formality could not be over with soon enough. It was only by a stroke of luck that Horace was in Marshland for the day. It did feel out of place though—sitting through a disaster debriefing while enjoying pie at the same diner, perhaps in the same chair, where she had devoured countless servings of it as a teenager.

"I guess this means I'd never make it as a disaster junkie." She spread the whipped cream evenly over the generous slice of pumpkin custard and licked away the glob caught up on the fork. "Maybe I'm not a 'keeper' after all."

"On the contrary. It makes you the better volunteer. Folks who do this for an adrenaline fix aren't so likely to do a decent job of taking care of themselves. Makes them marginal when it comes to caring for others, too. I reckon I'm preaching to the choir. I hear you've met your fair share of such folks."

"Like Alan, you mean." She should have guessed. There'd be no way around getting herself eyeballed over that one.

Horace sat in silence, waiting. She took her time, doing justice to it. "Could it be he was so desperate for disaster work that he set off that bomb? Like when a troubled firefighter becomes an arsonist on the side. Is it something like that?"

"I know the FBI paid the Whites another visit, held a candle to it. But that's all."

That peculiar little man, Alan. She'd seen plenty of severe depression. The context of facing Alan's symptoms was a first, however. How helpless she had been, back on that dock. No ER or psych ward next door. No easy referral process or ready crisis assistance. It was probably why the uselessness of those out-of-town peace officers had been so annoying.

But Alan was not a bomber type. And, blast it all, she somehow knew that guy. Or at least had seen him before. That was the more bothersome of the two. It was as if there had been a lost opportunity, some other context where she had missed the boat.

"I did what I could for Alan, whatever could be done under the circumstances." She verbalized it more for self-assurance than explanation. She drew up her pant leg and exposed a purple knee in the early stages of healing. "Here's the result. Not much of what I did involved mental health skills. It was just a chance encounter. It's not like he's one of my regular clients." Though that was feeling less and less certain.

"You're not second guessing again? Those should of, could of, and would of's."

"No." That was not so certain, either. Which Horace probably already had figured out, with t's crossed and i's dotted.

"So, right now you're throwing in with being there for your friends. Lucky people."

"It's complicated." She scraped up last bits of piecrust, savoring it.

The rest had disappeared too quickly. "Shelley makes this. From scratch. Lil is her daughter. We were friends when we were kids. We recently reconnected."

"All the more reason you'd want to be there for them. Those bonds are priceless."

"She's why I came for the parade. We ran into each other last spring. Meeting up with her again—it was almost like being back in high school. I miss it, having that type of friendship. Not just with Lil, even though she truly is one of a kind. After I left Marshland, nothing moved in to take the place of that relationship. Or any other close relationship, now that I think about it. I was so wrapped up in training and setting up my practice, it got lost somehow. When I came back for the floods, I rediscovered it, and the importance of my roots. They're part of who I am. Lil is my inroad back to that. Lil is the key. Reconnecting with her— that's the make or break of it. Everything else about home still feels too tentative.

"But it's different now. Most of the time when I'm with her we're gossiping and giggling, the eternal soul mates we always thought we'd be. At other times, I state the obvious and she looks at me like I'm speaking a foreign language. Then there's our careers. I respect her choice to be a stay-at-home Mom. But it doesn't go both ways. One moment she's in awe of my profession. The next, she acts like she doesn't understand in the least what I'm doing, or why.

"Then there's confidentiality. She says it's okay that I have things I can't talk about. But she acts hurt. Especially with everything going on right now. Perhaps that old connection is forever gone. That the new context doesn't have a leg to stand on."

"So, once upon a time you chose different forks in the road, you and Lil, in spite of being soul mates."

"I know about transitions." Hopefully the quick insistence didn't look as insecure as it had just sounded. "I run a large bereavement program."

"True enough. If one of your clients spilled this, what advice might you ration out?"

"Positive thinking, probably. Pointing them toward the growth at the other end. Let grief have its say, but steer them away from negative or defeatist embellishments."

"You've done that for yourself, I reckon?"

"Of course."

"How's it working?" His eyes glistened back, no doubt already noticing that the effort had failed. "Truth is, positive thinking and negative thinking are just two sides of the very same coin. A mighty tempting piece of silver it is, at that."

"How do you mean?"

"Both serve up an answer you can count on." He pulled a quarter out of his pocket and showed both sides; then toyed with it, flipping it. "It's either heads or tails, something predictable. Expecting the best or the worst. Real good at helping us feel in control, or prepared. But when it comes to transition, flipping this here coin gets you no further down the road, no matter whether it's heads or tails."

Both the coin trick and the analogy were easy to wave off. "There are reams of data out there about the benefits of changing from negative to positive thinking. I know firsthand that it helps. I've seen it in my clients time and time again. And for myself."

"If you were talking about worries over making a speech, or passing a test, or getting that raise someday—yes, positive thinking is mighty nice. But transition is a different kettle of fish. It's about being okay with not having the answer, and setting a spell with the uncertainty. It's about letting positive and negative debris clear so you can hear whatever that answer turns out to be, once it decides to surface."

Her face began to burn. *The nerve of the man.* Her entire, though admittedly brief, career had been spent studying the impact of death and bereavement, and how people transition through it. She'd reorganized her entire life around it. *And he's lecturing* me *about it?*

"It's not so cozy-like as having an absolute answer." He gave the coin a last toss and hid it away. "Makes no difference whether it's positive or negative. An answer's an answer. Something you can hang your hat on. Truth is, that's one big fantasy we create for ourselves. We can't know the future—or what the answer is—until it shows itself. When you free your mind of the cheap and easy substitutes, and open up and listen, it'll turn up."

So I humor him. "What do you suggest I do?" And get this consultation over with.

"Close the floodgates every now and then. Let those positives, negatives, should of's, and ought to's flow to the wayside."

"You mean meditation? Relaxation exercises?"

"Whatever's left, when that analyzing's not taking off like a house afire. If all else fails, listen to your breathing."

"I have a regular meditation practice. Normally. Since I got here, I've been running from one thing to the next."

"Take a stab at it right now, if you've a notion. Whatever your usual practice is. See if that draws up a picture of what you and Lil are about these days."

She closed her eyes and took a deep breath. His floodgate analogy fit well. Kaleidoscopic thoughts and feelings passed, shifting and reshaping patterns of recent images. It did seem to have become an entity unto itself. Lil. Alan. Paulson. Alison. Dad. Mom.

Your breathing. Know your breathing.

I knew it. She had in fact seen him before. Sarah opened her eyes.

"Something you care to share?" Horace tried to capture the eye contact she was avoiding.

"I don't know." She slipped on her coat and dropped money on the table for the pie.

It was important to verify such a hunch before sharing it with anybody, even if Horace's suspiciousness of her did make her feel like a teenager trying to trick her father into letting her stay out past curfew. He saw she was keeping something from him. Somehow he knew.

CHAPTER 24

Town hall participation was by invitation only, thanks to Marshland City Hall's sorely limited seating. Those hopeful for last minute vacancies gathered in groups on the lawn and walkways. Good spirits ruled, thanks to the camaraderie of community disaster bonding.

There was also entertainment provided by several women circulating with signs: "Don't Forget About Us." "No Disaster Victim Left Behind." "Disaster Victims Vote."

Some blue-clad peace officers stood nearby, murmuring amongst themselves. A van plastered with TV station insignia crept past.

The demonstrators looked ridiculous. Most passersby were making an effort to be respectful of the motley crew. Some apparently couldn't resist pointing or laughing out loud. Others maintained composure, but with poorly-disguised opinions similar to Sarah's.

The microscopic level of participation in Alison's demonstration was no surprise. It had to be a first for Marshland. Not just the demonstration concept, but also this business of making open demands for assistance. People around here took care of themselves. They looked after their own, and were proud of it. During overwhelming circumstances, they threw in and helped each other, like they had at the floods. They wouldn't have it any other way. Nobody had to go around insisting that others come up with this or that.

The women began to chant in unison. "We matter too, we matter too!"

"If it isn't Dr. Turner." Todd Goode and his teenage son came up the walkway. "Nice to see you home again."

"Sorry to hear about your building."

"They say bad things come in three's. This year I've had losses to a flood, a tornado, and a smoke bomb. I expect it'll be smooth sailing from now 'til December."

"We can only hope you're right." Mixed feelings kept her from saying more. He was a survivor of multiple disasters. Even if insurance diminished the financial impact, the emotional losses were just as traumatic, if not more so. He was vulnerable as a human being, no matter what else the man might be about.

"There goes someone else who doesn't give a hoot about everyday folks." One of the protestors looked pointedly at Todd as she spoke out at the crowd.

"Those losers need to get a life." Todd's son was obnoxiously obvious in his sentiments, no doubt intending to be overheard.

"Tell that to this new widow." Alison grabbed Jeri Lynn by the arm and pulled her forward. "How will she get on now, with her husband gone? Stuck with all those hospital bills? And funeral expenses?"

Jeri Lynn stood by, stiff and wordless.

Her forced bravado crumbled. She dropped her sign, and collapsed onto a bench under a leafless sweet gum tree. Sarah excused herself from the Goodes and joined her. Alison refocused on stirring up the others.

An inner slow boil threatened to bubble over while she tended to the shattered Jeri Lynn. Alison's idea of therapeutic intervention couldn't be any more preposterous.

Once Jeri Lynn's stabilization seemed satisfactory, Sarah forced herself in front of the rhetoric Alison was spewing. "Can't you see how difficult this is for that poor woman?"

"It's nothing compared to what will happen if that bozo has his way." Alison stood her ground. "Without me, she'll have nothing. At least Lil and I are here to support her."

Alison stomped toward Lil and gave her a shove. "Go tell 'em, Lil."

Lil stumbled forward, then waved her sign at newly arriving town hall participants. She offered some unintelligible rallying cry. They stepped back, startled.

"Please stay clear of the walkway, ma'am." One of the officers moved in.

It had gone far enough. Sarah corralled Lil and led her away, not without resistance.

Lil's indignation drew out anxieties long buried. It weakened the conviction that had carried her this far.

What would make a difference? What would be useful to say? As an angry and expectant Lil stared back, all that came to mind were disconnected bits and pieces of Alison's absurdities—spinning at will. It was doing more to pump up anger than help map out an appropriate intervention.

Set it aside, Horace had said. Easier said than done. Especially since there was no guarantee Lil would listen. Had any of their childhood connection survived?

Lil's current state might not let anyone get through even if she did bother to listen. But what would happen next—how far would it go, what would Lil get into, if there wasn't a way to reach her.

"All right, Lil." At a vacant grassy area, Sarah ended the uneasy trek by spinning to face her. "You keep complaining that I don't tell you things. Well, listen up. I'm about to fill you in on what you don't know yet about 9/11."

"Go ahead. I'm listening." Lil at least looked curious, even if the little patience she spared looked more like an angry glare.

"You know Alison's story about her boyfriend? It's a sham. That wasn't her boyfriend. It was some poor guy she was stalking. He was set to file a restraining order before...an incident took care of things."

"That can't be true." Lil's eyes darted away, spiking uncertainty. "Alison and her boyfriend lived together. They were inseparable. They were going to get married."

Little doubt Alison had such a story on tap. Probably complete with attention-getting drama, and other polished exaggerations. "They lived in the same complex, not the same apartment. She did a lot of camping out on his doorstep. He even contacted the authorities about her."

"She wouldn't lie to me." Confusion ate away at her display of certainty. "She wouldn't stalk anybody."

"Really. How do you explain why she's always in somebody's face? How has she managed to get herself thrown out of just about every relief program in town?"

"She's hurt, is all. She didn't get the help she needed after 9/11."

"She didn't get what she wanted because she made the whole thing up. She was one cracked cookie to start with. It had nothing to do with 9/11."

"Bull. She cares. She wants to help everybody. Like me and Sean."

"Is that so? What kind of caring humanitarian attacks an elderly pastor?"

"We talked about that. She was just excited. Sometimes the end justifies the means."

A rationalization Alison could probably rattle off in her sleep. "Lil, think about it. Is that your first choice when you're upset? Physical violence? I've seen you upset any number of times. Your differences of opinion have never turned into shoving matches. Have they? As far as that goes, we've had our own share of disagreements. I don't remember either of us ever laying a hand on each other because of it."

Lil's sign began to lower, the clash of competing facts and beliefs finally taking toll.

Over by the sweet gum tree Alison was back to chatting up Jeri Lynn, who looked anything but enthused. Alison had her by the elbow and was trying to lead her back to the group.

The coercion came to an end when Jeri Lynn's arm dropped from Alison's grasp. "I'm sorry. I'm not ready."

"Of course you're ready. Keep up the chant and you'll feel better. You'll see." Alison tried to force a stack of pamphlets on her. Jeri Lynn backed away.

"Leave her alone." Sarah wedged between them, ignoring inner alarms warning of outrage taking charge. "How many casualties do you have to inflict before you're satisfied? You, and your ridiculous ideas about what helps people?"

"Take your Pee-Aych-Dee and shove it." Alison tried to get around her. "I know what I'm doing."

Sarah repositioned to block her path. "Is that so. Like you knew what you were doing with Alan?"

Alison froze. "What about him?" She pulled away and thrust leaflets at a couple of indifferent bystanders.

Lil was hovering nearby. Watching, listening. *Good.*

"It was Alan you were talking to at the reception center. That client you ran off."

Alison blanched. "You're out of your mind." She picked up a sign and waved it in front of an irritated pedestrian. "Little people vote too; little people vote too."

Sarah kept up while Alison hounded her latest victim. "If you'd referred Alan when he first came to us, or even just left him alone, he'd probably be fine right now. He would have gotten the help he so obviously needed."

"You don't know what you're talking about." She jerked away from Sarah and out onto the sidewalk, yelling slogans at other fresh arrivals.

"If you leave your designated area again, you're going to have to take your meeting elsewhere." The officer who apparently had the "bad cop" assignment came closer. "You won't be getting another warning."

"Everybody's against me!" Alison threw down the sign and armload of materials, leaflets immediately caught up and scattering over the walkway. "I don't need you. Any of you. You watch. Big things are coming. No thanks to you."

She stormed to her vehicle and punctuated her departure with a noisy screech. Those left behind stood around at first, directionless without a ringleader. Eventually they began gathering up protest paraphernalia and decamped.

"Were you serious?" said Lil, while the area cleared. "You really think it was Alison's fault? About that guy who strung himself up?"

"It's probably an overstatement. We'll never know for sure now, will we?"

"I'll be damned." Lil sparkled, her eyes dancing with intrigue. "Does that make Alison a perp? Just like on *Law and Order...*"

Sarah didn't respond, sinking into a new arena of guilt.

She'd done it. She'd blown up, again. *Blast it all, anyway.*

On top of it were those "big things" Alison had just bragged about. With somebody like Alison, that was the greater concern. Especially after a confrontation like this one. Given her drive and tenacity, and efforts thwarted, there was no telling what she might be up to.

*****

"Thank you for your hard work and willingness to help out..."

Writing was definitely not his thing. He got in more than his fair share with mandatory chart notes. He didn't even use email any more than he had to, and texted so rarely he practically had to re-teach himself any time he couldn't avoid it. If stuck with communicating by way of electronics, it was easier to simply call.

Shadowing the outgoing call center manager quickly revealed the outrageous amount of administration that involved writing. Damien had assigned him the thank-you note task, wanting to make sure it got taken care of while the staff roster was still available.

Damien was busy with other tasks at the solitary computer unit left behind for COB trivia. The set-up looked insignificant and out of place as the huge chamber's sole remaining furnishing.

Paulson laid down the pen and rubbed his eyes. "You do this at every disaster?"

"If I can. Given the circumstances, I especially want to do personal thank you's. I think..." Damien's clicking away at the keyboard came to a sudden halt. "You hear that?"

"Yeah, it's really whipping up out there."

"No, not the wind. It was...a voice. More like a whisper."

Paulson lowered his pen again and listened, hoping not to be drawn into an encore performance of Damien's paranoia. All that could be heard was the wind whistling along the back of the building, the same as it had sounded on multiple occasions. The lights flickered lightly.

"*...get you.*"

The back of his neck prickled. *What the hell was that?*

Damien grabbed his arm. "You heard it, too, didn't you? I'm not just imagining it."

It couldn't be flashbacks. There hadn't been auditory illusions. Besides, Damien heard it.

"Where's it coming from?" Paulson stood, his legs feeling like he was supporting himself on noodles.

"It was like it filled the entire warehouse." Damien's eyes widened, searching.

The raspy voice sounded again, this time hard to make out.

"Don't know about you, but I'm outta here." Damien signed himself off the computer. He gathered up notes and began stuffing them into his briefcase.

"Wait." *I ain't afraid a' no ghosts: Ghostbusters.* "This very well could have something to do with that asshole who's been trying to get on your case." At least such a hypothesis came off sounding convincing. Even if experiences over the last several days had succeeded in stirring up doubts over the most basic of convictions.

"If so, he wins. He wants me gone. Fine. I'm leaving."

Focus, Paulson. He closed his eyes, forced an image of Horace's kindly gaze.

A little of the angst settled. *What's in front of you.*

Damien. He couldn't be allowed to just run off like this. He had to get back on the horse, reconnect with his sense of control, his confidence. The way he himself should have, back in Detroit. It was a rare healing opportunity, right then and there. Sorting it through now certainly had a higher likelihood of success than hashing through it months later with a PTSD therapist.

"Do you really want to spend who knows how long looking over your shoulder?" He matched steps with Damien's flee to the exit. "Wondering what's going to go wrong, what you'll be accused of next? Do something. Like, get those crime scene investigators back."

Damien stopped to face him. "I'm not calling the police on Halloween night to say I'm hearing spooks. Forget it."

"We can at least look around." Paulson did a quick three-sixty. There wasn't anything or anybody in plain view that would explain what they'd heard. "This could be your big chance to get to the bottom of it, and be done with it."

"*...gonna get you.*"

Damien took a few more steps toward the door, his briefcase clutched against his chest. His resolve looked tentative.

"It sounds like it's coming from back there, somewhere on the other side of the curtain." Paulson moved toward it, ignoring the butterflies doing a tap dance on his stomach lining. Even if it wasn't supernatural, someone might be playing out ill will. The world could be dangerous.

"Swell." Damien slowly set down his briefcase. "I haven't been back there since I turned on the lights. It gives me the creeps."

"Let's have a look."

Damien finally nodded; Paulson nodded back, buoying up his own courage. He stretched back the edge of the tightly secured canvas, producing just enough space to pass between it and the warehouse wall. The minimal jostling let off the pungent stench of mildew.

Trying to ward them away, perhaps? *Get a grip.*

"You first," said Damien.

"Keep your voice down. They'll take off if they figure out we're onto them." Paulson stepped through. The low lighting on the other side turned everything to a pale orange glow. The staff furnishings had disappeared, even the rice sprinklings, adding to a sense of disorientation. Even Chet's ghost box was gone.

A glance up at where Alan had taken his final breaths revealed nothing. No body. No Charles. No spooks. Not even the noose.

"Looks empty back here. Come on."

Damien poked his head through the gap to judge for himself. Apparently reassured, he slid through and joined him. "Have you heard it in here yet?" he whispered.

"I think it stopped." Which hopefully didn't mean someone was now sitting back and watching them from somewhere.

They tiptoed to the room that had served as Damien's office. It seemed palatial without the clutter of the crate arrangement.

"It does feel creepy with everything gone." Paulson peered into an empty wastebasket left behind. "As if the call center itself met some kind of untimely end."

"It did. Could this be a visit from the spirit of call centers past?"

"Wrong holiday." Hopefully the flow of distractive levities wouldn't run dry. "I don't see how anybody could possibly be hiding in here."

"Someone on the roof maybe?" Damien crossed over and opened the defective double doors. They stepped partway out.

Wind stirred up dried leaves, sending them scurrying across their path like a herd of mice. On Main Street, a princess, Spiderman, and some form of reptile marched along, partially filled pillowcases swinging at their sides. They giggled and chattered. Flashlights shined in all directions.

After the children passed, Paulson continued further out and craned his neck at the roof. The cloudy starless night didn't reveal much. But there definitely weren't any people up there. Damien's standard-issue flashlight was too weak to be sure of much else.

"I'm going up," said Damien. "There's roof access around the corner."

"Sure about that? Going up there, with this wind?"

"I need to make sure for myself. Otherwise it'll be just like you said. I could spend years wondering when the other shoe's going to drop."

There was nothing to do but accept the inevitable. Especially since taking an assertive stance was exactly what Paulson had told him to do. "Okay. What do you want me to do?"

"Wait inside. I'll bang on the roof and yell something. You can let me know if that's where the voice was coming from."

Re-entering alone made his skin crawl. He stopped just inside the door, hid his hands in his jacket pockets. It didn't help. He began tapping his foot to the rhythm of the first ditty to come to mind—an old Band-Aid commercial. When he started whistling it, the chilling echo that bounced back defeated the purpose.

Man up, Paulson. Big boy pants.

He began whisper-singing instead. *"I am stuck on Band-Aid brand, 'cause..."* Careful footfalls sounded above, heavy soles against metal roofing. A repeated dull thud—Damien's fist, most likely. It stopped.

"...coming down." Damien's voice.

No, it was nothing like the murky origins of what they'd heard earlier. Damien's words were heavily muted, but easily recognized as coming from the roof, even with whistling wind gusts in the background. The mystery voice had echoed throughout. Its owner had to be somewhere inside.

"...gonna..."

There it was again. That raspy growl. Not loud enough to make out much. Obvious enough to be startling. Coming from someplace near that office.

Paulson crept back into the depths of the warehouse, thankful for the soundlessness of rubber-soled sneakers. He examined every nook and cranny of Damien's office. Nothing.

The panel formation to one side, the one that housed electrical hardware, was the only other internal structure in the warehouse. It appeared to be a later addition, a modernization of whatever had been used before the installation of halogens and a contemporary bay door. There was a gap behind it, forbiddingly narrow. Obviously somebody's do-it-yourself project.

"You'll be sorry."

It almost dropped him to his knees, the abruptness and malice. Now there could be no doubt. The source of the threats had to be nearby.

Yet there was nothing to be seen. Not even a shadow.

A blast of cold air brushed up against him, ruffling his hair against his face. Spinning his head from side to side revealed nothing. *The doors.* He looked back—yes, still open. Leaves swirled in, defiling Chet's freshly swept floor. Too bad those rice sprinklings were gone.

What was with this sudden superstition? It was high time to stop being so damned jumpy and think it through. Be scientific about it. *What's in front of you.*

The only interior possibility not yet visually cleared was that access gap behind the light switches. Someone Damien's size would never be able to get in and check it out. His own small frame could probably get away with it, by sliding in sideways. It would be a tight fit.

He switched on whatever additional illumination could be had and took another look into the limited opening. Light entered a little further, but the line of vision ended at an abrupt corner. The access gap continued on to the left. Darkness spilled from the unseen leg of the "L."

Damien had the warehouse flashlight. Paulson's was a couple upgrades in quality over standard issue—at home, in his knapsack. He hadn't figured on needing it for an evening of writing thank-you notes. Ghostbusting hadn't been on the agenda.

Maybe it would be best to squeeze into the gap anyway, and check out what could be seen without it. It was the only way they could be certain. Without at least partway entering, not even a flashlight was going to reveal whatever was around that corner.

But what if someone really was hiding back there? Somebody dangerous? Then again, in such tight quarters, how much damage could a violent person do? As the person most able to get out in a hurry, Paulson would have the logistical advantage.

Then there was the issue of how big the offender might be. The voice had not been distinct enough to reveal anything about size. It was not even clear enough to tell whether it was a man or woman.

Only one pint-sized individual would fit in there comfortably. A child, maybe?

"Is somebody back there?" No answer.

Here goes nothing. He scooted in sideways, barely able to advance, his nose passing mere millimeters from studs and wads of cording. Every movement produced a bumped knee or scraped cheekbone. Thoughts raced ahead of limited progress: what might be in there, what to do if he found it.

Slow down. Pay attention. *It would be just my luck to get myself electrocuted.*

It was cooler back there, and smelled of dirt and old dust. The cobwebs he had expected were confined to corners. The pounding in his chest seemed even more pronounced with wall studs pressing from behind. To complicate matters, the flooring was uneven. His feet kept hitting unknown obstructions, throwing off his sense of balance. If not for the tight surroundings, the stumbling would most likely have had him on the floor by now.

A gun. What if someone was waiting back there with a gun?

That would be a long shot. Actually a very close shot. *Ha, ha.*

Surely if someone were in there with him, he would have heard something by now. Or whoever it was would have purposely made himself known. Or there would have been detectable movement, or breathing. At least something.

When the turn was within reach he maneuvered his uninjured hand forward and groped at the blackness. Feeling the corner post, he grabbed it. After pulling himself forward the remaining distance, he poked his head around and peered into the remainder of the dark enclosure.

A pair of floating, glowing eyes stared back.

CHAPTER 25

"Good as gold." Shelley handed Lil the groggy infant. "Like always."

Lil lifted Jerrod to her shoulder. He let out an undignified belch.

"Just ate." Shelley adjusted the burp rag sitting on Lil's shoulder. "I can keep him if you and Sarah want to go have a night of it."

The diner had cleared since the "pow-wow" with Horace. Most regulars were probably home by now, supporting local trick-or-treat operations.

The normalcy would do them good. Take some of the sting out of the morale problem.

Shelley began polishing nearby tabletops that were already pristine, as she dropped hints and pled a case for more time with her first and only grandchild.

"Could we get some tea, Ma?" said Lil.

"Coming right up."

Lil leaned across the table. "Okay, let's hear it. What's the real deal with Alison?"

Sarah fidgeted. The turmoil over the Alison debacle had finally settled. Lil had seen the light, and was open to reason. The tension that had had her on pins and needles ever since her return to Marshland had vanished. It was an ideal opportunity to heal old wounds. Clear the confusion they'd both tiptoed around, ever since their reunion a few months ago.

She'd already said way too much about the Alison situation. Was there a legitimate way to be vague? If there were, it certainly was staying out of sight.

"There are people who could get hurt if certain information got out. I can't say anything more. I wish I could. I'm sorry."

"I know. Secrecy, secrecy." Lil's sarcastic tone bit at Sarah's resolve.

So disappointing. Over the last few hours it had been going so well. Here was yet another unwanted resurrection, one of Lil's longstanding recovery tactics after a perceived putdown.

Was this all worth it? Maybe she should just finish packing and head back to her one-bedroom walk-up. The thought of doing so felt empty. She had in fact succeeded in having a place of her own, and establishing a respected career. She had that to go back to.

But it wasn't enough any more. She could not return, leaving things here the way they were. It would not be the same. It would be limbo.

Lil hadn't always been this way. The first time she ever targeted her with a snide comeback, it was like it had come out of nowhere. It had her feeling stung for days, confused. Hurt.

It brought to mind a swell of happenings that final year in Marshland, all those preparations to leave for college. One day, as everything was falling into place, it became apparent that Lil was not on the same bandwagon. All Lil could talk about was finding that special guy. Caustic rejoinders so similar to the one Lil had just blurted out had followed, eventually driving them apart.

Ignore it. The bait. Sarah waited in silence.

In absence of a reaction, Lil looked away. She began rocking Jerrod. Though his limp state of collapse made it clear he was already down for the count.

"I'm sorry. I didn't mean that. I know you can't talk about everything. Nobody'd confide in you if they thought you'd blab it all over town."

"I wish it were different. I wish we could share everything the way we used to. You do have your own secrets, though."

Lil pshawed. "Nothing in my life is important enough to be secret."

"There's your life with Sean. What you have with each other. You don't tell me everything about that. Nor should you."

"Of course I don't tell you every little thing about my marriage. I don't tell Ma or anybody else, neither. Some things are private."

"I respect that. Marriage is important. Certainly more important than the limited relationships I have with therapy clients. Now you have Jerrod, too. I'm envious."

"You?" Lil looked baffled. "You're jealous of *me*? You're the one who's been all over, and got those fancy credentials. People even call you 'Doctor'."

"I'm glad I had such great opportunities. I was lucky. But when it's all said and done, it's your personal life that counts. That's what makes you happy. That's what makes everything else meaningful. Especially having someone...special, to travel alongside. Like you and Sean."

"You could have it too, you know." Lil adopted a coy smile, ever obvious in her insinuations.

Sarah leaned away, propping her chin in her hand. The water glass dinged quietly while her manicured fingernail flicked against it. "Please don't start in about Paulson again."

"When we were kids, hooking up with someone was a bigger deal to you than it was to me. I was the one who wanted to be a counselor. Remember? You always talked about working in a lab. 'The future mad scientist,' that loser boyfriend of yours called you."

Her early fascination with the sciences, that adrenaline rush upon first encounter with the joys of trifling with empiricism—where had those feelings gotten to? Buried somewhere, during the all-consuming focus on a degree and credentials. The feelings were still there. Psychology had turned out to be well suited for satisfying such an itch. But the training track also led to working with mental health patients— while Lil abandoned her similar dreams.

"I don't remember exactly what it was that got me started. I think my earliest interest in studying the human condition was back when you were talking about it. Things you'd read that pertained to counseling."

"Then I get some of the credit, don't I?" Lil struck an exaggerated pose of importance.

"I wish I could take credit for that little accomplishment you've got there. He's the real prize."

Lil plucked Jerrod from her shoulder and handed him across the table.

Sarah pulled him in. "That smell." She nuzzled him. "There's no way to describe it. The sweetness."

Shelley returned with a tray of tea makings and a plate of pumpkin-shaped sugar cookies. "You girls hardly ever get together any more. The Halloween party's at the Grange. They even got a band."

"I thought that got cancelled." A news story had gone on and on about it, how people were not sure how to celebrate anything after a tragedy like the one they'd all just been through.

"Those radio wags don't know what they're talking about." Shelley poured salt into a shaker. "The real story is what you hear people talk about around town, and here, in this diner."

It made sense that Shelley would know. The robust survival of Shelley's Diner was in part supported by its role as Marshland's primary informal meeting place. Everybody used it that way. As she had earlier, with Horace. "So, what are people saying?"

"We don't sit around and fret when something goes south." Shelley's head tossed in indignation. "Just like after the floods. We do what we need to and move on. Life goes on."

"It didn't sound like that at the FAC."

"Of course not. People in the worst shape go to places like that. Including radio folks looking for stories. The real world comes to this here diner. Sure as heck, no real Marshlander would do away with our annual Halloween tradition. Especially after we already had the parade moved all the way out to Willsey."

"I'm glad to hear it." Had she been over-pathologizing the situation? An occupational hazard. Maybe her hometown was better off than others had led her to believe. Shelley would have the most accurate read, there at gossip central. A glimmer of healing in sight?

"Get yourselves over there. You'll see for yourself how Marshland really is. All that dinking around in disaster got you jaded."

"Maybe Paulson would be interested in going," said Lil.

Sarah gave Lil's smirk a dirty look.

"Don't forget, Jerrod can stay here," Shelley called over her shoulder.

Jerrod seemed satisfied to make a night of it right there in the booth. Sarah was in no hurry to go anywhere, either. She rubbed his downy tuft of red hair against her cheek and drank in his sweet warmth. "Your Mom's right. It's too bad we drifted apart."

"Drift nothing. I heard from you maybe once after you went off looking for degrees."

"I was overwhelmed. Growing up here is so sheltered. You don't realize that if all you've ever known is something like this sleepy tight-knit community. I was in over my head."

"It was before then." Lil picked through the assortment of teabags. "By graduation we were already in different directions. You...pretty much abandoned me."

It caught her off guard, the possibility of such a perspective.

Lil had driven her away, right? For reasons known only to Lil.

"You were going out to have those adventures we dreamed about doing together. Later on, I was so proud when I heard you got into graduate school. But I was still here by myself. Alone."

"I didn't know. You never told me you felt that way. I never understood why you didn't come with. I thought it was because I no longer mattered, with high school over."

"Of course you still mattered. I..." Tears began to well. "I could have used you. You were supposed to be in my wedding, like we always said we'd do. Ma was too busy to help much. I had to figure out most of it myself. Then trying to have Jerrod. It took five years. *Five years* to get pregnant and have a family, the very thing I gave up everything else for. With Ma dropping hints all the time about grandbabies. I felt like such a failure."

"You could have called me anytime." Sarah stretched a free hand across the table and placed it on Lil's. "You know that."

"No, I didn't. We hadn't talked in ages. You were working hard on your schooling. Doing important things."

"How did we go wrong? We had been so close."

"A lot happened at once back then."

"Applying for schools, deciding where to go," Sarah listed. "Finishing off high school. Dumping boyfriends we'd outgrown. Leaving home. The crossroad of finding ourselves, choosing pathways. Everything was out of sync. Like when the needle on Mom's old record player screeched across a vinyl. All of the sudden, the old track no longer applied."

"And 9/11." Lil stopped messing with teabags and bit into a cookie; crumbs fell. "That's for sure. Look at what it did to Alison."

"She's the extreme case. However, I think so, too. It was around then that things changed for us. Yet think about it. The very same trauma did such different things to us. I went in search of answers, looking for a way to make a difference. I always thought it was what you wanted, too."

Lil opened the teabag that had been on top. She plunked it into her mug of hot water, along with a couple packets of sugar. "It was. But I didn't have a family like yours." She squeezed a lemon wedge into the concoction, wincing when it squirted back at her. "You had two parents and an older brother for backup. I had just me and Ma. She was almost always here, working the diner."

"I remember. I probably spent more afterschool time here with you and Shelley than I did at Dad's shop. Remember how things would get busy, and she'd get us to load the dishwasher? We thought we were being given some great privilege. I always felt at home here. And safe."

"Me, too." Lil scooped ice out of her water glass and dropped it into her tea, cubes knocking as she stirred. "For me, this was it. It was all I had to come to. When those planes started crashing into everything, all I could think of was getting my ass over here to the diner. I don't think I even felt my feet touch the ground again until we'd been here a while. It was as if I'd gone completely numb."

Lil's pristine detailing of those first hours after 9/11 brought it back. "I noticed something was wrong. Even while we were sitting in front of the TV, watching those buildings come down over and over again. In retrospect, I was shutting it out emotionally as it happened. I didn't work it through until much later. Mostly in graduate school, while learning about trauma reactions."

"When we were done at your house, we came here." Lil gazed at her beverage. "For tea."

"Is that when this tradition started?" Sarah looked down at her own turquoise mug, the aroma of chamomile rising with the steam. How weird would it be if they turned out to be the very same mugs they had comforted themselves with on that devastating day, long ago.

"I wanted what you wanted, to go off and see the world. I couldn't. I couldn't face leaving here. Not then. Later, after I got over it, I met Sean. That was the end of that."

"You can still have it. It's never too late to go back to school."

"No way. Sean wouldn't move to some college town. He loves his job. He likes being where the rest of his family lives. They're my family now, too. This is where I want Jerrod to grow up. If 9/11 did anything good, it made me appreciate what we've got here in this part of the country. Jerrod is safe here."

Reams of disconfirming data pushed back: what about Oklahoma City, or the movie theatre shooting? For that matter, what about what had just happened in Willsey?

She bit her lip, squelching the urge to drive home obvious realities. There was no way Lil would be safe merely by cocooning herself in Midwestern cultural norms. Surely she saw that, with all they'd been through. How could she not abandon every last sliver of doubt: catastrophic disaster can happen anywhere, even in their little town.

But, no. It was not the time for it. That thread of denial—Lil still used it, needed it, just as she had needed to pull back and lick her wounds those many years ago. She'd get there when she was ready.

"Deep down I knew there was something wacky about Alison. But joining in with that group of hers was like waking up again. A way to better the world, like you do. It's still in me. I felt so...alive."

"The community college has social service degrees. Vocational counseling, drug and alcohol intervention. Probably some others. You could go part-time while Jerrod's little."

"I don't know." Lil's gaze rose from her tea, a hesitant glance. "I haven't done a real class since...when you were here."

Of course—they'd always done their homework together. In fact, Lil used to joke about only making it through school because of being best friends with the girl with the four-point GPA. It wasn't true. Lil got decent grades on her own. It would be different for her to go it alone.

But those studies, the ones about how women advance in certain types of intelligence after giving birth...

"You could always call if you wanted. I'd help any way I could. We could Skype if you got stuck or something. Promise. Cross my heart."

She slid Jerrod aside and drew a reflexive "X" over her heart. Vision blurred as Lil did the same. Lil's eyes also moistened.

Another long-lost ritual, resurrected.

*****

Look at what's right in front of you, Horace had said.

Paulson could do nothing else. The two orbs had snared him, slowly draining him of both courage and purpose.

Sweat trickles traced a jagged pattern down the back of his neck. Tense muscles twinged, straining at the odd angle. He was paralyzed—trapped—by the press of tight quarters and that unvarying stare. So still, so centered on malevolent intent. Zeroing in, motionless in its otherworldly glare.

Motionless.

Motionless, Paulson. The eyes hadn't moved since they'd first come into view. Whatever they belonged to, it was stationary.

He forced himself to reach out. The softness of cloth met his hand; the eyes joggled. He took hold of the fabric, but it held fast. It was attached to the wall somehow. He gave it a good yank. As it came free, something plastic bounced against the walls and clattered to the floor. He moved the cloth object into the light.

A clown toy. With glow in the dark eyes. What were those designers thinking?

"Paulson?"

"Back here."

"Back where?"

"Behind the electric panel." Paulson banged his free hand against a stud then cursed. The forgotten wrist injury throbbed anew.

"What are you doing back there?"

"Hand me that broom. I'm trying to get at something."

A broom handle appeared. A confused Damien peeked around the corner. "Are you stuck?"

Paulson snatched the broom and shoved the toy at him. "Here, take this."

Damien pulled it out. "What the hell? I thought we were through with these things."

One-handed scooping and jabbing with the broom scooted along whatever the fallen object was. Once out and unencumbered, he picked up the small plastic box.

"Gonna get you."

They both jumped.

"What is it?" said Damien. "A player of some sort?"

The only distinguishing feature on the chintzy sulphur-colored unit was the speaker grill. "More like an intercom."

Damien moved in for a closer look. "Hey, we used to have one of those."

"What is it?"

"It's a baby monitor."

"So someone has the other unit?" Paulson slapped a hand over the speaker grill. "Can they hear us?"

"No, it's bare basic, one-way only. At least ours was. Besides, they would have heard us by now if it were two-way. But..." Damien glanced around. "These things don't reach very far. At least ours didn't."

Paulson met Damien's measured gaze.

"They've got to be somewhere right outside," Damien whispered.

CHAPTER 26

"Lighten up, Sarah. We're supposed to be having fun."

"I shouldn't have handled it that way. No matter how outrageous Alison's behavior was. I'm a professional. Losing it is the complete opposite. I was so public about it, too."

"You didn't get a choice." Lil turned them out onto a dark and nearly deserted Main Street. The SUV swerved around crumbling potholes and other hazards cluttering the main thoroughfare. "Just think. If those government hacks had stopped bickering long enough to fix this road, none of this would have happened. We'd have had our own parade. Right here, where it's supposed to be. My Sean wouldn't be in a hospital bed. He'd be coming to this party."

Sarah stared out at the passing structures lining the brief commute to the warehouse. Their familiarity was comforting, as if those sentinels of childhood somehow bolstered safe passage. Strings of colorful lights, glowing renditions of spooky characters, and tamer autumn décor adorned shop windows. Carved pumpkins flickered at almost every door. Rare clusters of older trick-or-treaters and teenagers were still on patrol, in spite of the late hour. A few adults in costume appeared bound for the Grange.

Marshland, on Halloween night. With Lil. She was back.

"What would have happened if you weren't there for Jeri Lynn?

What about me? Would I be part of Alison's next piece of tomfoolery? You did the right thing. As far as that goes, why didn't you talk me out of it sooner? Yeah, I know. Confidentiality."

"Alison's so fragile, and unpredictable. I worry about her next caper, if only for her own sake. Then there are innocent bystanders like Alan. I wonder if I need to report this. If so, to whom? For what purpose? It won't bring Alan back. There's nobody at critical risk because of it. That we know of, anyway. I should talk to Lacey."

"Nothing's going to happen between now and tomorrow. Let's kick back and have ourselves a bash. We deserve it. Girls' night out, if Paulson doesn't come."

"Park over there, on Dad's lot."

"What for?"

"Old time's sake."

They stopped on the spread of asphalt that once fronted Sam's Body Shop. Distant memory resurrected the weathered wood on cinderblock structure that stood no more. Visions of Halloweens past paraded by— Dad still there at dusk, tinkering away with that one last task. Stopping by to show off her costume, before hitting the streets with Lil. He'd tease her, pretending he didn't know who she was.

Dim lighting flickered at one end of the warehouse, a dreary call to reality returning her to the present. Paulson's Yamaha was up against the near wall. "Still there, all right. The professional volunteer. He's got to be exhausted."

"That poor overworked man deserves a little fun."

As they unbuckled their seatbelts, the door to the side entry slowly opened. Damien's head emerged. There was sudden movement off to the left.

"What's that, a deer?" Lil craned forward.

The shape became better defined as her eyes adjusted to the darkness. It wasn't an animal. It was a person, leaning over something in his or her hands. Now bolting around the far corner of the building. Lil clicked the headlights back on. The figure was already gone.

"Hey, you." Damien shot out the door. "Come back here."

Paulson immediately followed. They, too, disappeared.

"What's going on?" Lil started to get out of the car.

"Wait. Safety first." She pressed Paulson's speed dial number. He didn't pick up.

"Whoever it was is gone now." Lil peeled Sarah's hand off her coat sleeve and climbed out. "I'm going to have a look."

Standard Lil. Ready to chase after any piece of whimsy no matter how ill advised. "Hold it. I'll go with you." To ensure Lil's safety, of course. The preference not to be left alone ran a close second. Or perhaps it was that she, too, couldn't resist the tug of adventure, to once again be caught up in the excitement of the reckless fun and games of Halloween night with Lil.

She was falling behind. She picked up her pace and advanced to where she could get a full view of the other side of the building. There was nothing to see, other than Lil running up ahead. The echo of multiple shoes slapping against concrete could be heard in the far distance.

Off toward the forest was the sound of a car door slamming. Lil changed course and headed toward it, undeterred by the bitter cold blasting along the back of warehouse. She quickly vanished in the blackness.

"Wait up!" Sarah ran blindly; the wind fought her, blowing her coat hood from her head. She pulled out her flashlight and had it flicked it on in time to catch the tail end of Lil's departure. The beam of light exposed Lil's location—near a small dark-colored sedan, hidden in tree shadows bordering the far end of the lot. She was peeking in the windows as if trying to make something out. She tried the driver's side door.

"It's locked. This is Alison's," she called out as Sarah caught up.

"Just our luck. Is that who they're chasing? What did she do now?"

"See that there, in the front seat? It's just like my baby monitor. Not the new one you got me. The one that's gone missing."

Sarah aimed the flashlight at it.

"In fact...that one really is mine. See those teddy bear stickers? I put those there myself." Lil straightened, and placed a hand to her hip. "That bimbo took my baby monitor."

"Why on earth would she take that?"

Lil looked away from the car and wrinkled her nose. "What's that funny smell?"

Sarah noticed it, too. A sulphurous stench. Easily identified.

Smoke bombs.

*****

"Hey. Slow down." Panting handicapped capacity to yell across the growing gap between himself and Damien.

"She's getting away," Damien yelled back.

"Can you see her?"

Damien slowed to wait for him. "Not since she went around the back of the warehouse."

"Geez, dude." Paulson collapsed against a telephone pole, wrapping arms over the cramps pulverizing his midsection. "Then...what are we...running for?"

Damien adjusted his jacket and looked around, sheep-faced. "I don't know. But we made great time getting here, didn't we?"

"For all we know, she's gone the opposite direction."

Silently acknowledging the joint conclusion, they turned back. Along the way, they took a closer look down a few of the back alleys and side streets.

"Thanks, I needed this," said Damien. "Now I know. It was just someone's childish idea of a Halloween prank."

"Probably. Or maybe revenge for booting her out of the reception center."

"That's who that was?"

"I think so. I didn't get that good a look. But the waif-like physique was about right. So is the passive-aggressive MO."

"I don't know if I buy it. Any self-respecting disaster worker would have used duct tape to hold that speaker in place."

"Yet jamming it in with that clown toy as a makeshift shelf showed responder-level resourcefulness. Alison wouldn't have known where we kept our supply stash. If she needed something last minute, she'd make do with whatever was handy."

"That's a lot of trouble just to get back at someone. When would she have done it? We'd see her during the day. There's afterhours, but how would she get in?"

"Could she have known about the hook?"

Damien winced. "Please, don't. I've been dreading that one coming back to haunt me."

"Literally." The attempt at levity won an impatient glare.

"It would be easy enough for her to get in with the right tool."

Paulson retightened the wrap on his throbbing wrist, loosened during the chase. "How would she know it was there in the first place? You can't tell from outside. The only ones with keys are you and...logistics."

Damn it. He had been too dismissive about Sarah's concerns. Chet's association with Alison—perhaps she had something there. She might have been using Chet. How deep into it was he? "Let's give Chet a call, and feel him out."

$$*****$$

"Where's it coming from?" The smell was pervasive. Its origin could be in almost any direction, the way the wind was churning.

"Probably just kids making spooky atmosphere. Mist machines. It's Halloween."

Traces of apprehension lining Lil's shadowed face suggested speculations similar to her own. Neither of them was apparently brave enough to mention smoke bombs. Especially while so exposed—out in the open, and in darkness, no less. It had never bothered her as a child. Any place in town felt safe, night or day. Especially so close to Dad's shop.

Several years of city dwelling had done much to fine-tune precautionary instinct. Not to mention where events of late had taken them.

"Let's wait in the call center." Sarah began walking back to the warehouse. "Somebody there can probably fill us in."

They returned to the side entry, the door left gaping by Paulson and Damien's hasty exit. Sarah looked inside, and gasped.

It was gone. The call center was now just an empty warehouse. What had she missed?

"I thought you said the call center was in here." Lil declined to enter.

"I don't know what's going on." The vanished furnishings only added to the surrealism, of everything being not as it ought to be. Even that pile of white boxes was gone. She and Lil were the only live bodies on site.

The rumor of hauntings, dimwitted as it was, reared its spectral head. Wind picked up, battering against the metal roofing. As a moaning sound started in, the origination of the term "spine-tingling" ceased to be a mystery.

"This is just too weird." Lil took her arm and pulled her away. "Let's get hold of Paulson from the party."

*****

"If that don't beat all. They even got eyes that glow in the dark. Too bad them folks are going to paint them over."

Chet had listened to their tale, minus their suspicions about Alison, as if it were some kind of bedtime story. Hints of any preexisting awareness did not materialize. What interested him most was the paint coating the clown's eyes. He kept rubbing his thumbs over the luminous green, as if massaging fine silk for quality.

"Can you think of a way someone could have gotten in?" Paulson asked him. "We're pretty sure nobody did this while we were open."

"Me and Freddie have the key. We check things out every night. I never saw nothing. Freddie wouldn't do nothing like that."

Freddie did have his cranky litany of complaints over the peculiarities of life in disaster response. For Freddie it served as a release, a coping mechanism. It probably made him less likely to resort to destructive acting out.

"I'll ask him." Chet reached into his pocket.

Damien stopped him. "Let's think this through."

Chet pocketed his phone and stared back.

"Now, Chet, think hard. Is there anyone else who might have been in here afterhours? Like someone to come in and do floors or restrooms."

"Naw, Freddie and I always did that. Except the time Alison helped out."

Damien pounced in with a machine-gun volley of questions, overlapping Paulson's attempts to be heard. Chet sat there open mouthed.

"Me, first," Damien told Paulson. "This is my call center, what's left of it. I need to see this through."

He was absolutely right. It was time to step away and watch Manager Logan take charge. He was back.

"Let's start at the beginning. What exactly did she do? Don't leave out anything."

"Well, she didn't do nothing wrong. It was after she got laid off from the FAC. She always used her laptop out in my truck while me and Freddie did our jobs. But Paulson here says a little work is a good thing when folks get all het up. So I brought her inside. We're always doing set up and clean up and the like. She likes seeing things disaster workers do. So we put her to work with dusting."

"So you watched her the whole time."

"Mostly. But Alison wouldn't let nobody into the warehouse. I'd hear it, anyways."

As far as Chet was concerned, Alison was beyond suspicion. It was true he'd probably spent more time with her than any of them. With Chet being Chet, however, there was the question of how much factual accuracy was represented by his worldview. Not to mention that anyone's biases are bound to be skewed if criminal developments involve someone they trust enough to share their innermost selves with.

Damien had paused, seemingly for effect. "Now think carefully. Did she ever use any of the computers? Maybe she was curious, and wanted to see how they worked."

"No way. I would have seen that. Besides, it takes a while for that fancy system to warm up. It's not on afterhours. Except when you're still here with this one."

"Thank you, Chet. I appreciate your insights."

"Sure thing. Any time. You done here now? See, I'm supposed to clear out the rest of this here equipment."

"Go right ahead."

Chet dived into final unpluggings and repackings. On the way out, Damien stopped and picked up the briefcase he'd abandoned before the mad dash to the roof. Paulson caught up.

"You thinking what I'm thinking?" Paulson whispered to Damien.

"She cased the joint, and came back later for a Robin Hood number?"

"It fits. Except the hacking into the casework program. Unless I really missed something, her techie skills aren't that good. She's more like data entry level, not a hacker."

"Nor was the reasoning all there. Did she think it wouldn't get out at some point?"

"Actually, whoever's behind this could have it right. The organization may well let the clients keep the extra money. Giving it to disaster victims, then taking it back? It's not as if they amount to drastically huge sums. The people it went to certainly need it. Those who donated it would be okay with where it ended up."

"I don't know. That line of reasoning's pretty sophisticated."

"For Alison, you mean. You're probably right."

"There's more to this." Damien unlocked his car. "Someone else has to have a finger in it. It'll make for an interesting conversation with the higher ups."

"Glad it's you and not me."

CHAPTER 27

As a kindergartener she'd called the Grange the "pineapple house." The entry's fanciful brickwork looked more like tropical fruit to an imaginative five year old. It brought back memories of the many events the setting had hosted.

The Grange housed the collective markers of community transition and ritual: graduation ceremonies, memorial services, proms, association meetings; celebrations organized around virtually any holiday. The Who's Who of Marshland lined the walls, past and present. It was a repository of tradition for those who called Marshland home. It bonded them as family.

Lit strings of tangerine-sized pumpkins and pale green skulls bordered the yellow glow streaming from its crosshatch windows. Winners of the jack-o-lantern contest lined the porch; ribbons displayed their selected honors. Streamers decorated the underside of the "pineapple's" crown. Country western gaiety from within enticed passersby.

"Come on." Lil threw her hat and coat onto the already swelling pile of belongings in the back of the rented SUV. "They've started without us, those dogs."

As Lil ran ahead, familiar banter sounded out. Detouring to explore further, Sarah found Stewy, Victor, and several others huddled around a card game on the far side of the porch. Saturday night poker was apparently enjoying a bonus night.

And, lo and behold, there was Dad. He was studying a handful of cards with the same intense scrutiny as with a woodwork project. Attending two major community events in one week had to be a record for him. Mom had always needed to drag him away from the shop or his latest garage project to get him to join in. In fact, the previous spring, some family friends had confided about being worried over how much time he spent by himself, now that Mom was gone. Here he was, anyway, entrenched with his buddies and conspiratorially nodding for another card.

"Dad. I didn't know you were coming."

"Didn't expect to see you either, Sarah." He picked up the new card and added it to those in his hand.

"Just like old times, isn't it? I've missed this." Shelley had been right. Amidst the liveliness and laughter, there was not a trace of the tension she'd seen at the disaster service delivery sites. It was Marshland as remembered.

With a disgusted look, Sam threw down his cards and stood. "I'm out."

They escaped the noise of carefree revelry by moving to the opposite end of the porch, where a scarecrow was holding court.

"I think I was an undergraduate the last time I came to one of these." She fingered the straw sticking out from under the scarecrow's hat. "How about you?"

"Been a while. That's a fact."

They traded memories of noteworthy costumes of years past. Mom, of course, had always dressed as a *Star Trek* character. One year she made tribble costumes for Sarah and Nate, a big hit. Dad never wore a costume. He always got a kick out of seeing how the local dignitaries "made darn fools of themselves" in this manner.

Regardless, Halloween was Mom's big night. It was at her insistence that they always attended the party at the Grange. It didn't take long for memories of other family activities to catch up. She chattered away about them while they took turns pointing out costumes of newly arriving guests.

A lull arose; Dad had gone silent. When she looked at him his eyes were glistening, gone moist. But he was smiling.

"Good times, those were," he said.

When she finally made it into the Grange, it was a full house. Even in costume, almost everybody was identifiable. Fellow sojourners of childhood journeys—a little older, perhaps wiser, but still recognizable. There was also one familiar face she wouldn't have expected to see at her hometown's Halloween bash. Wearing a bright orange t-shirt no less, with "Halloween Costume" printed across it in big block letters.

"John. How nice of you to visit us."

"Hey, good to see you here. Much nicer circumstances, huh?"

Here he was again, turning up wherever she happened to be.

"Hello, Sarah," said the woman next to him.

At first glance, she couldn't place her. Her hair was stylishly pinned up. And—she was no longer wearing that tacky disaster vest. She had on a low-cut angel costume. "Delores?"

"We decided to accept the gracious invitation extended to visiting disaster responders." John took Delores' hand in his.

So, he had been loitering at their station because of Delores, not her. That was the end of that mystery. Though it left mixed feelings. The idea of having a secret admirer like John was flattering, even if it had felt a bit weird.

Oh, well. There was already plenty to contend with by way of Paulson's not-so-secret attentions. Speaking of which, had he done anything with her text message? A quick look found a fumbled return message splattered across the screen. She smiled.

"Come outside a minute," said Lil. "Cigarette break."

"I thought you gave that up because of Jerrod."

"I did. Jerrod's not here. This is my one and only chance. Believe you me, I need it."

A weathered picnic table sat outside for just such a purpose. Lil swung a leg over one of the benches. Sarah joined her, taking care to sit beyond the curling smoke trail. A muted country version of "Louie, Louie" drifted out.

Lil took a deep puff of her cigarette and let it out slowly, sighing in ecstasy.

"You should give it up altogether." An ancient and oft-repeated injunction. She had hounded Lil about it all through high school. The vintage music in the background seemed to underscore its staying power.

"I know," said Lil. "Someday."

"You ladies got room for one more?" Damien joined them. He accepted the offer of Lil's lighter and they began puffing in tandem.

I give up. "What happened to the call center?"

"Calls are being handled elsewhere. It was awkward after the casualty. We finally got that bull about ghosts figured out. It was a hoax."

"It was all a put-on? Chet will be disappointed."

"Somebody hid an intercom, and was transmitting spooky noises."

"Really. Did you figure out who was doing it?"

"We don't have definite proof. Alison tops the list of suspects."

"Alison?" This would be one for the memoirs. "Why?"

"Who knows? Paulson thinks it's because I threw her out of the reception center."

"Alison's issues are more purposeful than vindictive. If she really did go to that much trouble, it had to be something more than revenge. Her agenda to save disaster survivors—that would be my first guess."

"My baby monitor," Lil piped in. "We saw it in her car. I bet that's what she used. That's why she stole it." She sucked in and blew out a dose of nicotine. "I'd love to give that woman a piece of my mind."

"She actually stole somebody's baby monitor to do this?" The glimmer of Damien's cigarette lowered to the table. "That is one messed up lady."

"I can see her rationalizing it, if it served her purposes." Sarah rubbed her nose, allergies protesting. "The ends justify the means, or something like that. Good old one dimensional reasoning."

Her nostrils began to sting. It wasn't an allergic reaction. Something was wrong. "What's that smell?"

"Cigarette smoke, silly," said Lil.

"No. It's that other smell. The one by Alison's car, only stronger. Like...smoke bombs."

Excited shouts sounded out front. Concerned, not entertained.

Suspicion gave way to terror. *Smoke bombs. The explosion.*

Sarah whirled to look back at the Grange building, fully loaded with celebrating friends and family.

Please, no. Not here.

*****

Paulson scanned the crowd from the entry, picking out neither Sarah nor Lil. He broadened his search into circulating among the guests, in so doing exchanging pleasantries with a mummy, a witch, and a lame caricature of Mayor Schwartz. The atmosphere was buoyant, like his own mood. It was a chance to party, to spend time enjoying these remarkable people. With Sarah on site, as well. It didn't get any better.

Raised voices started up at the front of the building. Curiosity drew him to where others were already lining up at the windows. He peered out with the rest of them.

The lighting over the Grange parking lot illuminated an ominous ring of multicolored smoke. It surged from somewhere underground, rippling with the wind, a translucent curtain enveloping the small figure positioned within. The features of a costume—devil's horns, a sparkly red cape—became identifiable before he recognized the person.

Alison.

"You think you know hell?" Her gesticulating went wild as she cried out to her gathering audience. "I'll show you hell. You don't know hell until you've been in my shoes."

What in the world was she up to now.

John came up from behind and grabbed his arm. "It's that whack job, Alison. She's standing on one of those metal plates. Just like at the parade. See that pink smoke?" He bolted to the band set-up and grabbed a microphone.

"Wait." Paulson tried to catch up. "There's some situational awareness..." It was too late.

"We need to evacuate the building, folks." John gestured toward the back of the building. "Not out the front. Everybody out those emergency doors."

Merrymakers slowly quieted, questioning whether to take this visitor's directive seriously. The matter was decided after a local teenager burst in, breathless.

"It's a bomb!" He flew toward the back of the building. "Run for your lives!"

Realization took hold; screams followed. People pushed around, seeking and snatching up loved ones as they made their escapes. A few local volunteer firefighters attempted to put some order into it, with only minimal impact.

Thankfully there were plenty of exits to the rear. People were getting out, rather than trampled. The building quickly emptied, most escapees collecting as confused groups at the far end of the back lot. Some furthered their retreat by leaving behind a wake of squealing tires.

"Come on!" John pulled at Paulson's arm. "You've got to get further back."

Instead, Paulson returned to the window and assessed the progress of the spectacle. The smoke bombs had finished, fizzled out. Alison was ranting, apparently unaware of the status of her special effects. Perhaps she didn't care.

"There's no need for panic," he told John. "This can't end the way the parade did."

"What are you talking about? Of course it can."

"Those plates cover drainage repair from last spring's flooding. Not gas line access."

"You can't know that for sure. How do you tell which is which?"

"Because there aren't any natural gas lines through Marshland." He left the emptied hall and stepped out on the porch. He finally spotted Sarah, standing around with the group encircling the PFA worker from hell.

"What is it with you?" Damien was standing nose to nose with Alison, practically folding his tall frame in two to do so. "Those asinine ghost imitations had my staff incapacitated. Don't you realize what you did to service delivery? What the hell did you think you were doing?"

"Anyone else would have just left." She threw back her shoulders and jabbed at the sky with what was supposed to be a pitchfork. "Not you. You kept coming back. Every night. We made up for your stupidity. We did the real work in the wee hours. Real assistance. Look what you've done now. You closed it down completely."

"See what I mean?" she spat out at Lil, who looked dumbfounded. "They've shut down the call center when anybody with eyes can see the work left to be done. They're all the same."

"It's not closed." Damien kept his cool, but was but firm. "Because of you, it's been transferred to the national hotline. The same services are still available to everyone."

"Yeah, I'll bet."

"What about this here, Mother Teresa?" Damien threw a hand down at the metal plate they were standing on. "Imitating that parade tragedy caused a stampede in there. People could have been hurt, even trampled to death. Where does that fit into the needs of disaster survivors? If anything, all your little stunt would accomplish is more casualties."

"People aren't supposed to run off like that." Her lower lip quivered, the ironclad repartee showing signs of cracking. "They're supposed to pay attention. They were supposed to listen. Nobody listens. Why? Those damn gas lines wrecked everything."

No.

"Everybody was finally going to hear. Why doesn't it work out? Why doesn't anybody ever listen?" She began to wail, escalating as if competing with the moan of a gust of wind swooshing through them.

"It was a publicity stunt?" Paulson stepped up and joined the group surrounding Alison and Damien. The audacity was making word retrieval near impossible. "That destruction…all that carnage. Just to make some lame point?"

"You." She glared at him. "Only a bastard like you would cancel the whole project. That extension was a must. There's more to be done. We need to go on. Little people matter, too! Little people matter, too!"

It was too kooky to absorb, too far-fetched.

Like that other time and place, once again spearing and haunting him. *9/11.*

It was a rerun, the same groundswell of anxiety surging through his gut.

Paulson closed his eyes, lectured his innards to settle. *Think.* What's the connection?

A couple of hijacked planes, taking out the twin towers. The worldwide disbelief that followed, the despair. Interview snippets of a decade past, a movie producer noting that as fiction, the twin towers saga would never find its way to the screen. It was too unbelievable.

Yet the unbelievable had happened again. Right there, in their own parade. And left its mark on them, one way or another. Especially for the wailing and babbling disaster junkie falling apart in front of them. And, of course, Alan.

Now there was a whole new population of victims, those subjected to the results of Alison's misguidedness. A new episode of absurdity, staggering this small town and taking Willsey along with it. All because some zealot wanted a federal program extended. Truth really was stranger than fiction. You couldn't make this stuff up. Weird was the new normal.

Right up his alley, some would tell him. Oddly, there was a sense of peace about that.

He glanced over at Sarah, her chestnut hair fluttering in the breeze, her gorgeous eyes working their way through shock, the same as everyone else. They could work together at preparedness, make headway, even if nobody could ever be completely prepared for what might be around the next corner. There would be more misjudgments, more misplaced priorities. With everybody, himself included. He could be at peace with that. Because they'd do what they could. They'd mitigate what they could. Life was what it was.

Other spectators were putting together two and two about Alison's apparent role in the explosion. The outrageousness had temporarily neutralized them as it had for him; multiple brands of astonishment draped over uneasy silence. The audacity, the gall. The destruction and misery. There was no immediate game plan drawn up for addressing a situation as bizarre as the one playing itself out in front of the Grange.

Here it was anyway, suddenly in his lap: a possible first step. To implement, right now, unfolding insights. Ones already succeeding at slowing the churning in his gut.

But as far as what exactly to do—he would have to punt.

"Alison, we didn't need that long-term PFA program. We did our job. It was good work. And you were part of that. People are moving on."

"I was making a difference." She freely sobbed. "I was!"

What more could be done or said? What would Lacey recommend? Nothing in her standard guidelines could cover this one.

The opportunity for impact would soon be as fizzled as the smoke bombs. Sweat trickled down his back, in spite of the autumn chill. "Do you have any idea what you've done?" *Not good.* But he couldn't stand there and say nothing.

Off to one side a shadow closed in.

Not again. He closed his eyes, willing it to vanish. Mind over matter.

A pair of headlights blinked on. The shadow was the state patrol cruiser.

"It wasn't supposed to happen," wailed Alison. "That hole was supposed to be sewer repair, like this one."

"It was your doing." Lil had come to life. Even in darkness, there was the glitter of eyes dilating, full and black. "You did this to Sean."

She lunged at Alison, as might a mother tiger protecting her own.

He threw himself into her path. They tumbled to the ground in a tangle of flailing arms. His jacket lining ripped as his injured wrist banged against the ground. A paralyzing stab of pain shot up his arm.

When Lil scrambled to her feet, Sarah was right there, embracing her from behind.

"More violence is not the answer," she whispered over Lil's shoulder.

"I was duped by this bimbo." Lil struggled half-heartedly against Sarah while she shrieked at Alison. "How could you? How could you do this to my family? While pretending to help us?"

"I *was* helping. All you need to do is stick with me. Just stay the course."

Others realizing the original threat was gone wandered over. Traded glances of skepticism and dazed concern moved on to understanding. Then anger. Making whatever assumptions worked for them. Closing in.

Radar missiles burst from dry dock; inner alarms clanged. The situation was going to get really ugly, really fast. Paulson tried to push himself up off the ground. His wrist gave out, followed by a new surge of pain.

Two lawmen moved in, sandwiching Alison and cuffing her as a couple other squad cars pulled up. "Move back, folks."

Most went along with the officers' instructions, through mutterings and a few cheers.

"It was all a big mistake." Paulson told the police. "What's going to happen with her?"

"There's a whole lot of people who'd like to have a word with this gal," said the deputy. "Let's make sure they're ones who aren't going to cause undue harm."

"We've got to do more," Alison bellowed as the officers led her away. "We're not done yet. There has to be a way to end it..."

The slam of a car door swallowed the flapping, glittery cape and the remainder of Alison's rant. As well as his screwed-up attempt at intervention. Perhaps there wasn't anything more to be done within the current context. At least he'd given it a try.

He eased himself from sitting to standing, nursing his throbbing wrist. In so doing, a collection of papers fell from the torn jacket lining. They hit the asphalt with a momentous splat, a fitting exclamation point for the end of Alison's performance.

"Looks like you're finally going to have to replace that relic of a jacket." Damien squatted to inspect the scattering paperwork, snatching up pieces the wind threatened to carry away. "Looks like the call center isn't closed after all. You brought part of it along with you. Love it so much you just can't give it up, huh?"

"These are from last night." Paulson reordered the retrieved items, making sure they were all there. "I forgot. Hope this doesn't affect my performance evaluation."

"Depends on how many oversights are in there. You may do time."

It wasn't funny. Paulson stepped under the porch light and thumbed through the crumpled messages, squinting—less because of poor lighting than the dread of discovering his attitude toward red tape had bungled yet another critical piece of business.

"It all looks like old business." Damien's anxious breathing hit the top of Paulson's head as he tracked his progress. "Except that one for somebody called 'Dr. Forbes'. You got credentials you haven't told me about, buddy?"

"Must be confidential." Paulson moved away for privacy and put his back to the wind. Hair squiggles blew into his face. He brushed them out of his eyes and ripped a jagged opening across the top of the sealed envelope. Inside was a neatly handwritten note.

Dear Dr. Forbes:

Thank you for your assistance. But there is no hope for me. I believed what Alison told me. That here in the States, disaster assistance is nonexistent. I thought that with my technical know-how and Alison's creativity, we would find ways to help.

It went horribly wrong, worse than I ever imagined. All I did was help with smoke bombs. I deeply regret and am horrified by the role I played.

After I watched that magnificent reception center spring into action, I tried to talk her out of further action. I hope my helping her find a way to salt the computer program casework distracted her from doing anything else harmful to others.

Here at the call center, and other service sites, I saw just how good you are at what you do. You are to be commended.

You have all been so kind.

Alan

Paulson continued to stare at it. He slowly refolded the note and returned it to what remained of his inner pocket.

"Anything I need to know about?" said Damien.

"Nope. Private business."

*****

Sarah stayed until the band packed up. For her and Paulson, it was no longer a party. They were back in the grind of mental health surveillance. Interestingly, the trauma unloaded by many was not the false alarm. Instead, partiers talked about where they had been or what they had been doing on the day of the parade. A couple of them even revisited what they were doing on the morning of September 11th, 2001. Just as she had, immediately following the parade incident. Another expectable piece of normal to tuck into the data base.

She caught an occasional glimpse of Paulson as he circulated. It was reassuring to see him go about it in his easy professional stance, much as he had while rescuing Marshland from the spring floods.

Except something had changed. As usual, it seemed to come naturally for him, the *Kung Fu* wanderer in his element. But those eyes, ones that somehow always managed to penetrate her forehead and connect with whatever was hidden within. They said something more.

Between conversations, he briefly caught her gaze as he passed. He nodded at her.

It hit her. The clamshell had opened. She was welcomed, and there might actually be a chance that it was possible, to see back, inside him.

She heard only bits and pieces of the accounting shared by the Mayor Schwartz look-alike who had cornered her. She was too caught up in unexplainable sensations, in addition to tracking Paulson's progress around the room. Analysis was getting her nowhere. But the warm feelings that began to settle in—they suited her just fine.

Hours of talking left her parched. The flurry of activity near the beverage table meant the punch cauldron would soon be hauled off. "Wait. Can I have some of that?"

"Allow me." Paulson stepped up and ladled some of the pink brew.

"Did it get spiked this year?" She sampled it. *Just what the doctor ordered.*

"I think there's a touch of gin in it." His eyes sparkled a hint of secrecy. Like maybe he well knew who was responsible.

She laughed.

"I love hearing that laugh of yours. It's like a choir of little bells." He stood close, relaxed. At ease. His eyes asking to be invited for more.

She felt her face flush, and looked away. The development was far afield from the usual conclusion to an evening of applying professional skills. She was unprepared.

His hand came up and tugged at a wayward lock of hair lying against her face. She looked up to meet his gaze again, expecting to find his usual puppy-dog begging. It wasn't there. Only caring, and acceptance.

He gently twirled the bit of hair he'd caught between his fingers. "Whenever you're ready."

She smiled into those eyes that saw everything. She nodded.

CHAPTER 28

Sunday, November 3rd

Chet's management of business as usual would never lead anyone to suspect that his girlfriend had just been hauled off for perpetrating a mass casualty disaster. He went about day-to-day life with his usual enthusiastic optimism. At the moment, he was trading barbs with Freddie and the rest of the logistics crew, as they pieced together disaster headquarters' new home.

"It don't change nothing," he'd assured Sarah. "I bet I get to see her even more than I did before. She ain't going nowhere."

Freddie was the one who had begun to drag. Chet eventually asked Paulson to have a word with him. It was then that Freddie acknowledged he was the trickster who created Charles, to harass Chet about "ha'nts." He was also the one who had left Charles swinging at the summit of Mount Clown Toy. His malaise apparently stemmed from his belief that this had been where Alan got the idea to self-terminate.

It was good Paulson was the one to help Freddie work it through. Not just for Freddie's sake, but for his own. As Paulson reviewed the session with her, his crooked smile grew in increments, his eyes twinkling with the extraordinary pleasure he always seemed to get out of life in the trenches. This in spite of the fact that the most impactful part of his intervention came not from his professional skills, but from showing Freddie concrete evidence of Alan's earlier attempt: the cast covering his broken wrist.

"Doing the real work," he referred to the consultation. "Not paperwork."

Yet, what had changed in his appreciation for the behind-the-scene complexities that make such intervention opportunities possible? Rome wasn't built in a day.

He was still reporting the occasional disturbing dream. He and Sarah both acknowledged it as normal; it was early. The nightmares would end in time, as would his other symptoms. There were also things about him that had changed for the better. Not just whatever was evolving between the two of them, but also a qualitative difference in his give and take with everybody. Something about him was more genuine, more connected. Less wrapped up in Paulson.

"I see the Borg has once again landed," Sarah told Lacey. The warehouse was most of the way transformed back into a panorama of disaster signage and administrative activity. "Apparently resistance really is futile."

The scene presented such a peculiar collision of time frames. Here she was in this nondescript building, one that had served her childhood as little more than a backdrop to her father's work setting. Now here it was, once again turning into a hive of critical professional activity. Her own particular realm of professional activity, no less. It was as if it had situated itself purely for her benefit, like an open door, inviting her to enter.

"The church was a lot more comfortable." Lacey's practiced hands were again unpacking and arranging desk paraphernalia. She could probably do it blindfolded. "But they need their fellowship hall back. We won't be around much longer, anyway. A different site will be used for long-term. This will do us for now."

"Won't what happened in here bother people? About Alan?"

"Those of us still around are lifers. We've made do in significantly worse. Remind me sometime to tell you about 'The Cave'."

"Anything new about Alison?"

"Word through the grapevine is that she's about to be evaluated for fitness to deal with her legal predicament."

"Did she 'fess up about the man in the ravine?"

"She admitted to making those threatening phone calls, but so far I haven't heard anything about the stalking victim. My sources say she's still bemoaning her status as a bereaved 9/11 victim. Perhaps she's deteriorated to where she believes her own story. Very sad. We may never know what happened with that guy. But I know where I'd lay my money down."

It was a relief that Alison was in custody. From behind bars, it would be more difficult for her to lead Chet astray. With her safely tucked away, Chet's attention would eventually turn elsewhere anyway. "What happens next? For disaster survivors, and their mental health needs?"

Lacey started to speak, then hesitated. Her gaze had landed on a suited woman across the room, deep in discussion with Horace.

"It would take hours to explain," she finally said. "There will be more for clients. And more politics, more jockeying for power or publicity. In the end, people will get the services they need."

"You sound so certain."

"There's someone here you need to meet."

Horace and his conversational partner joined them.

"This here's Dr. Amy Proctor," said Horace. "She's been hanging her hat out at one of them Ivy League places."

"We still have a place for you, Horace." She gave his shoulder a playful shove. "The call of the wilds stole him from academia," she said to Sarah.

"Sarah is the psychologist I was telling y'all about."

"*The* Amy Proctor?" That name, one so frequently seen in print. The prominent trauma psychologist was standing right in front of her. In a dilapidated warehouse, next to Dad's burnt-out lot. When would the surrealism end?

She realized she was gawking. It couldn't look particularly professional. Yes, professional. That's right: She, Dr. Sarah Turner, was a professional in this field as well. "I've read some of your work. You do trauma research, right?"

"Ever since 9/11. I understand you also have an interest in research."

"Nothing like the work you've done." Sarah looked from her to

Lacey, to Horace—who had said what to whom? "I have a project going at a hospital. There's nothing hardcore in the way of outcome research yet."

"A program I'm part of has an interest in exploring PFA effectiveness," said Amy. "There's a grant in place for something like this."

Her toes began to tingle. Money already there, without having to beg for it? Unheard of.

"It's a unique circumstance here in Marshland," said Amy. "Resilience training and other interventions took place just before this incident because of last spring's storms. It's an ideal opportunity to see the preventive value for subsequent incidents. Not to mention everything else we'd learn by tracking intervention this time around."

"I knew about the PFA program. I heard it would be revamped for the new disaster. But I didn't know a grant was coming down the pike. How did you get onto it so fast?"

"Actually, a newspaper article brought it to my attention. There was this photo that just about jumped off the page at me. It was someone I'd hired once to help with data input. At least, that's what she was supposed to be doing. It didn't work out. You'd recognize the name."

God, no. "Not Alison?"

Amy pursed her lips. "The article mentioned the series of disasters here over the last few months. When I read further, I realized there was an opportunity."

"So, I reckon you finally figured it out, why things didn't work out so well with Alison." Horace's eyes were having a humor fest.

"Cut it out, Horace. I need Sarah to take me seriously."

She's worried about me—what I think of her? This prominent, well-published researcher? It was unfathomable. *My God.* What were her expectations? Were they ones she could actually meet?

"If this branch of the project pans out, the primary investigator will need someone local to track things," Amy went on. "It so happens you come highly recommended. There aren't any particulars yet. Most of it will get figured out after you say yes. You'd be able to define much of your role. Even become a primary investigator yourself, if you want."

It was too good to be true. A major research project right here, in Marshland. Spontaneously unveiled, when she hadn't even gone looking.

"Let's talk."

*****

Paulson helped himself to more coffee while he and Horace watched from a distance.

"Looks promising, don't it?" The glint sparkling over the rim of Styrofoam suggested Horace already had the outcome figured out. "Last I listened in, they were tossing around fancy words like independent variable and random selection. Got myself right out of there."

"Sounds serious. I wonder what will come of it."

"Now, don't get your hopes pumped so high you take a header if it falls through. Besides, from what I've seen of Sarah, she'll be barreling full speed into that project of hers when she comes to town, not what you have in mind."

"I mean the research findings. What will they find out? The learning curve for this keeps getting so unbelievably steep."

"Can't argue with that." Horace continued to sip at his coffee.

"Little of what I remember from the basic training covered what I did for this disaster. I had to figure out something new every step of the way. I know, think outside the box is the name of the game. This felt more like mining some far-off planet for answers."

"You did fine. Nice piece of work there, how you helped your buddy Damien get his confidence back."

"That's exactly what I mean. Nothing in those guidelines Lacey keeps waving around talks about ghostbusting crises. Or the specifics of what to do if you're *part* of the mass crisis, for that matter. Everything was off the cuff. Pure instinct."

"Don't know that it's possible to set up one grand design for saving the world, let alone one for helping those who think they're gonna save it."

"What do you mean, think they're saving the world?"

"Alison, Alan, those two-bit characters duking it out on political warpaths—or any of us disaster folks, truth is. Hearts are in the right place. We try to save the world in whichever way we reckon will lead everybody out of the firestorm. It's just that sometimes, if we're not on the lookout, we get ambushed by our limitations."

As it was for me. Horace would never point it out directly. But the lesson was there. "I did learn a lot. Especially...expectations. I mean, what constitutes real world expectations. The absurd is now acceptable. Planes used as bombs, hijacked and purposely flown into buildings. This week, major death and destruction because of disaster activists misplacing a smoke bomb. We can't be completely prepared for the absurd. But there's got to be a better grid for guiding us through the aftermath."

"Now you've got the picture. Glad you're rustling up a little expertise for next time. This won't be our last mass casualty disaster."

"Any suggestions? I mean, where do we take it from here?"

"Well, there's mitigation, minimizing the damage. Like that school shooting, back in Oregon. They didn't keep two casualties from turning into mass casualty because good guys with guns came riding in to take care of bad guys with guns, or because they'd beefed up relevant CMH services, or because of more background checks for gun owners. They won the battle because they'd put together a decent lock-down plan, and implemented it when things got dire."

Planning. Just like Sarah kept talking about. She would approve.

"Takes a piece of ingenuity here and there, but you don't strike me as one to shy away from dipping a toe into the unconventional." Horace's eyes twinkled. "I imagine y'all got schools around here somewhere."

Sean's hospital wall, now entirely plastered with children's drawings, certainly testified to their presence. Those kids deserved to be kept safe. Yes, helping schools review their plans could be a beginning point. Then move on to figuring out how those plans meshed with other local agencies, and with emergency services. Something to keep busy with, while Sarah was preoccupied with number crunching.

"How quickly it's changed." Paulson scratched at beard growth getting out of control. "Planning aside, there's so much new out there on trauma and the brain. What these experiences actually do to people."

"The wheels of progress will continue to turn," said Horace. "Just don't you forget—pull yourself together and zero in on that one firestorm, sitting there right in front of you. What you need to do will present itself."

If only it always worked that way. Especially in the one way that mattered most.

"Except...with Sarah." Now she was leaving again, with no way of knowing for certain when she would be back.

"Good luck with it, son."

Paulson turned to find a bright pair of blue eyes scrutinizing him.

"Look here, Jerrod. It's your Uncle Paulson." Lil tugged off the cap and let Jerrod's red hair go wild. "We just had a visit with Grandma. And look." She pointed outside. "Today Jerrod got to see his first snowstorm."

A snowstorm—already? He looked out the open side door. He made out a few stray flakes. Lil's usual expressive overkill was apparently ramped up to freeway speed.

"We're trying to catch up with Auntie Sarah for a last goodbye."

"You'll have to stand in line. She's talking to someone about a possible position here."

"Here?" Lil grabbed the front of Paulson's shirt. "You're teasing." She turned to Horace. "Is he serious?" She started in on him before Paulson could respond, which was just as well. It took everything he had to keep from getting thrown to the ground by Lil's enthusiasm.

"Yes, ma'am. It's true enough."

Lil released him to do a replay of the touchdown dance she had performed in Sean's hospital room—a more conservative version, weighed down with infant and diaper bag.

"Nothing for sure yet." Paulson straightened his jacket, checking to see if the safety pins still held together the lining. "It's a possibility."

"Here, I brought something for you and Sarah." She pulled out a small rectangular item wrapped in crumpled gift paper. Pastel teddy bears with umbrellas floated on it, tiny paws holding signs that said, "Congratulations on your new little one."

He questioned her with a confused look.

"Sorry about the wrapping paper. That's the only kind I had. It's really a thank you for everything you and Sarah did for us."

While he removed the gift wrap, Sarah joined them.

"This is for both of us." He handed it to her.

It was a polished wood-framed photograph, a shot Lil must have taken while they were waiting for the parade to begin. It showed Sarah holding Jerrod. His fingers were tangled in her hair. Paulson had cotton candy in his hand, and was smiling over the two of them.

"What a sweet picture," said Sarah. "Thanks, Lil."

They hugged their goodbyes and the Whites left.

Sarah continued to admire the photo. She placed it on Lacey's desk, where the skylight illuminated it nicely. It held such gaiety, anticipation. Innocence revisited.

"Interesting that she gave the two of you only one copy." Lacey smiled at them.

Sarah groaned. "Not you, too?"

"So who gets custody of our gift?" said Paulson.

"Let's leave it with Lacey for now, so she doesn't forget about her 'keepers'."

"Looks good there," said Lacey. "A nice homey contrast to this administrative clutter."

A shadow arose—fluttering, lingering first alongside Sarah and Paulson. It passed over the desk and swirled near the photo as if caressing it, then ascended, diminishing into nothingness as it retreated out the skylight.

www.keeperconnections.com

ABOUT THE AUTHOR

Laurel Hughes, Psy.D., is a licensed psychologist in Oregon. She has participated in over 50 disaster operations with the American Red Cross. Her experiences range from major catastrophes, such as the Events of September 11th, to minor local flooding. She also dabbles in disaster mental health program development and technical writing. Among such efforts are the Behavioral Health Emergency Response Plan and Field Guide for the Oregon Department of Human Services, and numerous materials for the American Red Cross—including joint efforts with the Substance Abuse and Mental Health Services Administration of the U.S. Department of Health and Human Services, and the U.S. Department of Defense.

Made in the USA
San Bernardino, CA
09 November 2015